Dark Tides

A Charity Horror Anthology

Gestalt Media

The following stories are reprinted here with the author's permission:

"Terror from the Briny Depths" by Elizabeth Massie

"Flange Turner" by Gene O'Neill

"Black Mill Cove" by Lisa Morton

"Devourer" by Andrew Lennon

"A Quickee" by John Skipp

"Eternal Valley" by John Palisano

"Widow's Point" by Richard Chizmar and Billy Chizmar

"Show Me Where the Waters Fill Your Grave" by Todd Keisling

"A Night at the Lake with the Weird Girl" by Ray Garton

"Night Dive" by F. Paul Wilson

"The Abalone Thief" by Matthew Brockmeyer

"In the Shadow of the Equine" by Kenneth W. Cain

"Thicker Than Water" by Paul Kane

Contents

PREFACE

DEAR Reader,

The book you hold in your hands is a special one. First, let me thank you for purchasing it – many people will benefit from the sale; even if its inception was due to a tragic event.

I'd like to give you a little background as to who I am, why I decided to put this anthology together, and a bit about the entire process – with the hope that it will hold a more special meaning after you read it.

To hear me speak, you would immediately guess that I am not from Virginia Beach. You'd pick either New York, or New Jersey. Well, you'd be right. I was born in New York and lived there for the first 24 years of my life. The how and why I moved isn't relevant, but I did; and have called Virginia Beach my home for the last 30 years.

While we've had our share of incidents like any major city, Virginia Beach has been a safe, and inviting, city; and still is. However, on May 31st, 2019, a disgruntled city employee entered his workplace, and shot 16 people – 12 fatally – adding Virginia Beach to the ever-growing list of cities with a senseless mass-shooting. While I don't personally know anyone involved, I do know people who do – and it's for them, and the families of those involved, that I decided to do something.

I am a voracious reader, with horror being my primary genre. Thanks to social media, I have become friends with many authors. Many of them are award winners, yet relatively unheard of outside the "horror community". When I heard of the shooting, I immediately decided I needed to do something; something to benefit both communities. My original idea was to approach twelve of my favorite authors and ask them each for a story – one for each victim. I ran the idea past a few people and the response was mind-blowing! I then presented the idea to my long-time friend Jason Stokes, who started his own independent publishing company, and his words were something to the effect of, "Hell yes, I'm in! But, why limit it to twelve stories? Go big or go home! You know more authors than I've ever read. Ask them all!"

And with that, the birth of this anthology.

While the reception to this project has been overwhelmingly positive, some have made comments to the effect of, "…using horror to benefit tragedy victims…" or "…couldn't come up with a better group of stories than horror…". Well, I'm really not sure how to respond to those comments, except maybe, "Why not?" There's a big difference between "horror" as it pertains to the genre, and "horrific" as it pertains to the tragedy. When people hear the word horror, they immediately go to slasher – which couldn't be further from the truth. Written on these pages, you'll find love, loss, redemption, and of course, encounters with things that go bump in the night (or in the water, as the case may be). Yes, you'll also find tragedy – but doesn't every living being experience tragedy at some point in their lives? Of course they do. But there's something cathartic about knowing that you're not alone in that – or that what you have experienced can be much, much worse. And that, my friends, is why I chose horror.

It goes without saying that there are many people I need to acknowledge who have helped with this endeavor.

First and foremost, my heartfelt condolences to the families of the twelve who needlessly lost their lives: LaQuita C. Brown, Tara Welch Gallagher, Mary Louise Gayle, Alexander Mikhail Gusev, Katherine A. Nixon, Richard H. Nettleton, Christopher Kelly Rapp, Ryan Keith Cox, Joshua O. Hardy, Michelle "Missy" Langer, Robert "Bobby" Williams, and Herbert "Bert" Snelling. It's to them that this book is dedicated.

Next up, my wife of 30 years, Elaine. It's her encouragement, and understanding, that keeps me going. I have to mention my parents, Ann and Joe, who instilled in me a serious love of reading (although not really my love of horror), and always said I could do anything I put my mind to. To the talented Eugene Johnson, who's advice and contacts were an invaluable contribution. To Pete Federico, one of the nicest people I know (but I'd never tell him that directly). The gorgeous photos contained within are from his amazing photographic talent. They not only convey the beauty that is our city, but the history and emotion, as well. Of course, I have to give a huge thank you to all the authors involved, those who allowed me a reprint, and those who took the time to write original stories specifically for this book. Last, but most certainly not least, my publisher, and friend, Jason Stokes. It was his cliché comment that made me shoot for the moon. The mention in a preface that most people don't read is obviously nowhere close to the appreciation I feel towards all these people, but I hope they know how much they all mean to me.

So, there you have it. My very first foray into the editing world. I sincerely hope you enjoy the collection I put together; and have as much fun reading it as I did. I also hope you take a trip to our lovely city and see some of the sights presented within.

Until next time.

John J. Questore – Editor

Introduction

I N June of this year, John contacted me and stated he was "considering doing something crazy, that could turn out to be something wonderful." Of course, as an editor and writer, I was equal parts intrigued and confused. I have known John for a while, and he was not the sort of man to *cry wolf*. So, curiosity piqued, I asked him what was on his mind.

He told me of the tragic shooting that occurred in Virginia Beach and claimed the lives of twelve people. His "something crazy" idea involved him possibly editing a twelve-story collection of horror stories revolving around water or beaches. He wanted one hundred percent of the book's proceeds to be donated to the United Way of Virginia Beach who had set up a fund for the victims' families.

I thought it was an inspired idea.

The Virginia Beach shooting was the latest in an alarming number of mass shootings that have become far too commonplace in the US. Anytime something that distressing and tragic occurs it should grieve us all, but the Virginia Beach massacre hit me particularly close to home.

My father served in the Navy and I was born near Virginia Beach. Though we moved many times (as is common with military families), I have returned to that area many times to vacation with my family. For both of those reasons, it is a place that holds special significance in my heart. When I initially heard of the shootings, my mind blanked. It did not feel real and I had trouble processing the reality of the situation.

I can only imagine what went through John's mind. What I did understand was John's desire to do something for the families of the victims.

John wanted to channel his love of reading and the horror genre into something positive for the survivors of that terrible day. He needed to do more than simply post on social media or say a quiet prayer. John wanted to let that shattered community know they were not alone in such a very dark time.

Having edited several anthologies myself, I offered to help in any capacity or manner that I could. It was a genuine pleasure to stand alongside John as he brought this vision to life. It was more than a noble pursuit - it was a passion. He wanted to let those wounded people know that they were never alone and that even on the darkest of nights, there is light to be found.

I am both humbled and proud that he allowed me to join him on this journey. From brain-storming the title to producing the completed manuscript, John never lost sight of vision or his purpose. He inspired professionals within the genre to unite in helping the families of the horrible tragedy.

The talent presented on the pages that follow is extraordinary. Both in their craft and their giving spirits.

Everyone came together to assist John in assembling this amazing anthology. It was an honor to be part of this project and watch as John's dream became a reality. I hope that when reading this book everyone realizes just how special it is and how much of a difference, they have made in so many lives by simply picking up a copy.

Thank you all so much...

Eugene Johnson
Bram Stoker Award Winner

Terror From the Briny Depths

Elizabeth Massie

ANNA clutched the ship's railing and looked out at the foam-capped waves. The briny spray was refreshing, spattering her cheeks and arms with misty droplets. It was so good to be free of solid ground and sailing – well, by way of a motorized dolphin-watching ship – a half-mile off shore on the great Atlantic Ocean. There was something primal about the sea, something mysterious and moving and brilliantly powerful.

"Hey." Greg moved up to the railing beside Anna. He put his arm around her shoulder and drew her close. "Nice, huh?"

"It really is," said Anna. She brushed back a strand of red hair. "This is the first time I've been out on the ocean, and I love it. Strange, isn't it? I'm a mountain girl. I was raised by my dad in the Blue Ridge.

Yet, still, the ocean seems to be so familiar. As if it knows me. As if I have a connection to it."

"Ah, baby," said Greg, running his thumb along the back of Anna's neck. "You're such a dreamer. Head in the clouds, mind on such silly things. Don't worry. Once we're married you'll have enough to keep busy. Cooking. Cleaning. Planning parties. Raising our children. No time for crazy thoughts."

Anna grimaced. It was all she could do to keep from shrugging Greg's arm off her shoulder. Yes, she'd agreed to marry him. Yes, they had already set the date, a short two months away. Greg had even bought a brand-new 1958 Lincoln Premiere convertible to take on their honeymoon to Niagara Falls. The fact that he was recently graduated from law school and was now a freshman partner in the Virginia law firm of Fleming, Yaber, and Armstrong was certainly attractive. He would be able to provide all the creature comforts a newlywed couple could want.

Anna's own youth had been one of meager means, spent with her father in a three-room mountain house, tending chickens, milking cows, and swimming in algae-covered ponds. Financial stability was a big plus when it came to marrying Greg, whom she'd met while waitressing at the Conner Gap Diner in Tazewell County, Virginia. But recently, Anna had begun seeing and hearing parts of her fiancé's personality that set her teeth on edge.

"You'll never want for anything," Anna's father, once a poor traveling salesman and now a poor mountain farmer, had said of the relationship. "I'll be able to sleep soundly, knowing my daughter is well cared for."

And so Anna had done her best to endure Greg's irritating quirks.

"Dr. Pepper?" asked Greg, giving Anna's shoulder a squeeze.

"That would be nice. Thank you."

Greg sauntered off across the deck to the boat's enclosed cabin, where a white-capped ship's mate sold pretzels and soft drinks to the dolphin-watch customers.

"It'll be all right," Anna whispered to herself as she watched Greg disappear into the cabin. "I'll get used to it. He's not a bad guy. There is a lot a good in him, I know."

"Look!" shouted a little boy from the ship's bow. "Mommy, I see dolphins!"

"Yes, there they are!" his mother said.

The tourists hurried to the front of the boat, where they *oohed* and *ahhed* over the flashes of silver fins and tails.

Anna stayed put, enjoying her temporary solitude. She put her arms on the railing, her chin on her arms, and gazed down at the foamy water.

And there, staring up at her from inches below the water's surface was a huge, black, glistening eye.

The eye blinked.

Anna screeched and stumbled backward.

"Anna!" Greg was there, holding two bottles of Dr. Pepper, kneeling beside her. "What happened? Are you hurt?"

"I…" she began. "I saw an eye! A huge eye! Big, dark, almost as wide as this boat!"

Greg helped Anna to her feet. "An eye? Honey, you must have just seen some floating garbage."

"No, it was an eye. It was gigantic! It was *horrible!*"

Greg led her back to the railing. "Look," he said.

"I'm afraid to."

"I said *look!*" Greg's voice had lost its patience. Anna forced herself to look over the railing.

The water rose and fell, foam and brine and white caps. There was no giant eye below the surface.

"I saw it," Anna insisted. "I really did, Greg!"

"You saw a reflection of something, or maybe even a large jellyfish."

"No, it was…"

"It was not an eye."

5

But it was an eye! Anna thought but did not say any more. Greg wouldn't believe her and the discussion would only turn into a debate. He loved to be right.

"Now, let's go see the dolphins," said Greg. He took Anna's hand and led her up to the bow, elbowed his way through the crowd, and made room for the two of them at the railing. "There they are! Jumping, performing! Almost as if they know we're watching them. Do you see them?"

Anna nodded.

Greg pulled Anna close. "What a nice trip. I just wish this was our honeymoon, if you know what I mean."

Anna knew. She gave Greg a wearied smile. And as she looked back out at the dolphins, and then out across the vast expanse of the ocean, she thought she heard something whisper her name. It made the flesh on her arms prickle.

Anna....Anna.....Anna....!

But again, she said nothing. It would only lead to yet another debate.

* * *

The creature swam the sea, deep, where sunlight's tendrils were little more than faint ribbons, her long, massive, scale-covered body undulating and coiling as she moved, feeding angrily on anything that got in her way. She breathed as a land creature, rising up twice an hour to lift her giant head above the ocean's surface and draw in air before diving down again, exhaling blasts of gas and fire that boiled and scalded the waters around her. Her cavernous mouth, filled with spear-sharp teeth, could devour a whale in four bites. Two bat-like wings the size of a schooner's sails protruded from her flesh behind her mouth and served as fins.

Frustration and confusion drove her onward through the deep waters, from the tropical oceans to the frigid seas of the poles, back and forth, knowing she was cursed but not remembering why. On occasion she would rise up to the shallows and ram into a boat, overturning it and sending the occupants to their deaths. But primarily she was driven to swim, to move place to place, searching desperately, furiously, for something she could not find and could not recall.

But then, in the moderate, blue-green waters off the coast of Virginia, she felt it.

A bright, almost painful surge. There was something here she knew, something vague but powerfully familiar.

A name formed in her mind, and she rose up toward the daylight, her giant black eyes staring, looking, seeking.

And with all her might she thought the name that had come to her.
Anna! Anna!
Anna!

*   *   *

They were vacationing at the Cavalier Hotel in Virginia Beach, an elegant, seven-story, seaside establishment built in 1927 on a hillside overlooking the shoreline and a private outdoor dance pavilion on the sand. The hotel was five-star, serviced by stoic, white-jacketed and white-gloved waiters and bellboys, smiling concierges, and dutiful housekeepers in starched uniforms. Greg would accept nothing but the best.

As was proper, Anna and Greg had their own rooms. However, Greg had insisted that the rooms be adjoining. While he expected his bride to wear white during the wedding ceremony, he certainly didn't expect her to be a virgin. Anna found his lovemaking to be tedious and orchestrated, nothing like the passionate, clumsy coupling she'd experienced with her teenaged boyfriend, Barry, back in the mountains. But she would get used to it, she knew. She was resilient. She was a survivor.

They dressed for dinner; Greg in a tailored suit and Anna in a green silk gown Greg had bought for her. He ushered her around the dining room, making sure all the customers saw the red-haired beauty on his arm. A string quartet in the corner played tame versions of current favorites – "Rockin' Robin," "Lollipop," and "To Know Him is to Love Him."

Their table was next to a large window overlooking the hotel's wide, sloping lawn, the sandy private beach and pavilion, and the Atlantic beyond it. They dined on shrimp, filet mignon, and champagne. Anna didn't care for the shrimp and so dabbed hers with coatings of spicy sauce to mask the taste. The steak was perfect, however. The champagne, bubbly and delicious.

The world began to darken outside. The lawn, beach, and ocean took on the same evening-pewter hue. As Greg finished his last sip of champagne, he reached for Anna's hand.

"How about a stroll before retiring?"

Anna nodded. "That would be nice," she said. That seemed to be a pat answer these days. As long as he wasn't asking something beyond her ability to tolerate, she would agree. She would deem it "nice." That kept Greg happy and Anna out of an argument.

The night air was salty and damp. Dark clouds drifted overhead, obscuring the stars and moon. Greg said little, guiding Anna along the boxwood-edged pathways, past the koi pond, down to the patio and its white benches. They sat side by side, Greg looking at Anna, Anna looking down across the darkened lawn to the black sea. Faint strips of white became visible as the waves rose, folded over, and crashed onto the beach.

As Greg put his arm around Anna and leaned in to kiss her, the voice from the sea rose up on the salty air, an urgent whisper louder than before.

Anna! Anna!

Anna gasped and jumped to her feet. "Listen, Greg!"

"Anna, cut it out!" Greg glared at her from the bench.

"Didn't you hear it? It called my name! Something from the ocean called to me!"

"What the devil are you talking about?"

"Something…something out there knows me!"

Greg stood, grabbed Anna by the arm, and slapped her. Anna gasped.

"Some women claim they have a headache to stop their men from being affectionate," said Greg, "but not you, you and your blasted imagination!"

"No, that's not what's going on here. Honestly, I heard it call me. I heard it on the boat today, too, after I saw the eye in the water. I heard it, but didn't want to say anything to you."

"Why not?"

Anger roiled in Anna's chest, bubbling up, stronger than her fear. "Because…because of this very thing! Because you treat me like a child. You don't want to hear anything that is counter to what you think or want. If you loved me, you would hear what I have to say without needing to shut me up. If you loved me, you would care!"

"Oh!" said Greg. Even in the darkness she could sense the red of rage flowering on his cheeks. "So now I don't care? Give me examples of how I don't care. I don't care because I paid for that green dress? I don't care because I planned this vacation? I don't care because I gave you a diamond ring and asked you to be my wife?"

"Do you hear yourself? It's always about you! I didn't want this green dress, I wanted the red. But you said red didn't look good with my hair. I preferred a smaller ring but no, you got the one you liked best. But that's not what I'm talking about. I'm talking about what I think, what I feel! You always dismiss me, Greg!"

"So you want to break off our engagement?"

"I didn't say that."

"It sounds like it!"

"Greg!"

Bristling, Greg marched off up the pathway, heading for the hotel. Anna dropped down onto the bench, her head in her hands. What a mistake to accept his proposal! But, what a mistake to let him go. Her father would benefit as much as she would. And she loved her father more than anyone on Earth.

Maybe Greg was right. Maybe she was too fanciful, too imaginative. Maybe she was…

"Maybe I'm just insane."

The darkened clouds began to rain. Anna let the rain drench her, let them mingle with her tears, until she could take the chill no more. She went inside to warm up. And back up to the fourth floor to make amends with her betrothed.

* * *

She seethed in white-hot frustration, writhing angrily beneath the waves like a giant earthworm on a sun-scorched sidewalk. Her wings thrashed madly. She bellowed out great bursts of fire, feeling as if she would explode. Ocean creatures for miles fled for their lives.

Anna!!

She had seen Anna, there on the deck of a boat. Up through the rippling waters she had seen Anna's face, peering over the railing, and a memory had slammed back into her brain.

Anna, it is you!

Anna, you were stolen away from me!

Anna, my daughter!

* * *

Anna and Greg made love. It was as it always had been. Anna tolerant; Greg arrogant and boring. When it was done, he held her and told her how it would be even better once they were married. After a good twenty minutes, she excused herself to shower and return to her room. She wanted to lock the adjoining door, but knew that would only create a new slew of debates.

Clean and exhausted, she fell asleep.

And she dreamed.

She dreamed of an island; palmetto trees shading the sandy soil, crabs skittering amid the sea oats. Tar shacks. Clothes drying on lines and little roadside stands from which handmade baskets and quilts were sold. Small gardens enclosed with wire fences. Dark-skinned people singing and speaking in a language she couldn't understand. Kind people, smiling people.

But there was another shack. It was set apart from the others on a spit of land that had no trees, no sea oats, only rocky soil. It smelled bad, and even with no trees, it seemed to be in constant shadow.

Anna, now a very small child, stood outside the shed on the rocky spit, staring across the inlet to the other huts and the cheerful men, women, and children coming and going. She waved at them but they didn't see her. Or they didn't want to. She tried to call out "Hello!" but there was no sound to her voice.

"Anna!"

The command came from inside the shed.

Anna did not want to go, but her feet forced her to do so. Inside, on a stool, sat a thin woman with dull red hair and fingernails as long as claws. She was stitching a small cloth doll, and chanting and spitting on the fabric as she did. The cloth doll cried pitifully with each stitch.

Oh, my God! This woman is a witch, Anna thought.

"Bring me that jar!" the woman demanded. She pointed to a wooden shelf on which various glass containers sat, filled with oily liquids. "Quickly!"

Anna went to the shelf, but each jar she touched exploded beneath her fingers. When Anna looked at her hands, she saw that they were bleeding profusely, the fingers severed at the joints and lying on the dirt floor.

"Clumsy!" shouted the witch. "How dare you break my jars!"

"No, please..." began Anna.

"*Humbalan! Humbalan!*" wailed the witch.

With that utterance, Anna felt her body lock up, tightly, as if she were suddenly made of wood. Not a muscle moved. Even her lungs stopped working, and she stood there for many long, terrifying, painful seconds, afraid she would die.

Then the witch snapped her fingers. Anna could breathe again. As she bent over and sobbed, the witch laughed. A bellowing, screeching laughter that seemed to singe the very air.

* * *

Anna awoke to the sound of a screeching alarm and shouts from the hallway.

"What's happening?"

"Is it a fire?"

"No, no! Not a fire!"

"What is it?"

"Did you see it? Oh, my God!"

"We have to evacuate! Get away from here! Hurry! Hurry!"

The door to Anna's room blew open and Greg was there, his hair wild with sleep, his eyes huge with terror.

"Something's coming!" he screamed. "I heard them yelling from out on the lawn! Something's coming up from the sea!"

Anna stumbled for Greg, and they raced into the hallway, joining the river of hotel guests, some of whom were banging on the elevator buttons in an attempt to hurry them up, some of whom were pushing past each other and down the stairs, yet others of whom were heading for the plate glass window on the east end to see what had caused the sirens, the terror. Greg forced his way through the crowd, dragging Anna with him, up to the window.

Where they stood.

And stared.

The scream that formed in Anna's chest was stopped cold it its tracks.

In the ocean waves down below the lawn and beach, illuminated by a full moon that had broken through the clouds, there had risen the most enormous, horrific thing Anna had ever seen; a sea serpent two hundred feet tall at the least, as wide as a freight train, with giant, leathery wings battling the air. The mouth of the hideous monster opened to bellow, revealing vicious teeth. A column of flame shot from the mouth, out and down, igniting a nearby pier and the restaurant atop it. Then, the creature, propelled by its dreadful wings, lurched up and out of the ocean, its tail dragging the sand and crushing the dance pavilion like a bug.

It leapt again, heading up the hill toward the hotel.

"What is that?!" screamed Anna.

No one answered. No one knew. Some remained at the window and cried in terror as others turned and fled for the stairs and elevators.

The hotel alarm continued to blare, a mechanical wail that offered nothing to those who heard it but a sense of panic. No direction. No advice.

Just...*Help!*

We're doomed!

* * *

She remembered it all now.

Curses on them all, I remember!

She was a leviathan, the most horrifying of all sea creatures, created by one great collective *wudu* curse of the Gullah people on South Carolina's small, wind-swept Cootuh Island. Damned to swim the ocean in a state of constant confusion, anger, and misery.

She had once been a woman named Chloe, and a witch of great power. She lived in a shack on a rocky spit of land with her young daughter, Anna, whom she had been training to follow in her footsteps. Chloe had thrived on her magic, charming young men to her bed when she wanted them, bringing disease and crop failure to those whom she disliked, and causing "accidents" – broken bones, crushed spines, amputated fingers or limbs – to others on a whim.

But then the Gullah of many nearby villages had joined forces to curse and stop her. They had been jealous of Chloe's powers, of course, terrified of her spells, and unwilling to tolerate her any longer. Unable to destroy her, their combined spell had morphed her into the giant monster of the Atlantic, had scrambled her memories, and set her out to swim and suffer for eternity.

The leviathan did not know what had happened to Anna, but someone, somewhere had taken her and raised her. And now, Anna, full grown, was here.

She had seen Anna on a boat.

She sensed Anna in the grand hotel on the hill.

I will have my daughter back!

With a thrust of her powerful tail and flapping of her wings, the leviathan leapt farther up the slope toward the hotel, her body coming down atop vacationers who had made the deadly mistake of racing out onto the front lawn. She heaved a great bolt of fire at the hotel, at the roof went up in an instant. Screams could be heard from the building, and the sounds pleased her more than anything had pleased her in years.

Another flapping of wings, another leaping of her tremendous body, and she landed within yards of the hotel with an earthshaking thud. Now, with her huge black eyes, she could see inside the windows, see the terror in the faces of those who were frozen in place, staring out at the creature.

Where is Anna!?

Her gaping maw released another burst of fire that drove against the windows of the top two floors, blowing them inward, setting people aflame, flipping them backward in a writhing, wailing jumble.

Where is my daughter?!

And then she saw her. Anna, standing at the window on the fourth floor amid another clot of terrified humans, staring up in disbelief and horror.

*   *   *

She remembered it all now.

Living in the shack on the rocky spit with her mother Chloe, an angry, powerful witch. Anna trembling in her tiny shoes as her mother concocted potions, bearing brutal beatings for not learning spells and incantations quickly enough, doing her best not to cry, because crying only made things worse.

She remembered one bug-infested, humid morning. The Gullah people gathering where the rocky spit left the island, their voices rising in a deafening chant. Chloe racing from the shack, shrieking at the chant, morphing and growing into a hideous, gigantic, snake-like creature that they then drove into the ocean waters and away. A kind traveling salesman agreeing to take her far away from Cootuh Island and raise her as his own.

Yes, she knew now.

The creature out the window, raised up like a monstrous, winged cobra, was her mother.

Chloe, the leviathan, had come to claim Anna.

To keep her prisoner? To kill her? Anna couldn't know. But even as her heart thundered and her breaths came in jagged, painful gasps, she knew she had to do something to stop her. If she didn't, Chloe would continue to kill and maim innocent people. Much as she had when in human form.

The remaining people beside her at the window dispersed and ran, back to the stairs, the elevators, weeping, wailing. Anna turned to reach for Greg, but he was gone. Off with the others, escaping without her, his

15

selfishness no more clear than in that moment.

So be it.

Anna looked back at the window. The gigantic black eye lowered level to the window. Anna raised her trembling hand.

"Mother," she whispered.

The leviathan's mouth twisted in what could have been a smile, though Anna knew better. Anna jumped back as one wing slammed into the window glass, shattering it into flying shards. The wing then reached in, wrapped tightly round Anna's body, and drew her out into the night air.

With three powerful leaps, the leviathan returned to the ocean, her daughter in her cold, clammy grasp. Anna could feel its sense of victory as the monster breached and then dove into the water. Anna caught a breath before they went under, though the impact nearly knocked it out and away.

Chloe meant to drown her. Meant to kill Anna. Meant to punish her for existing and living upon the Earth even as Chloe was damned to live in the sea. Meant to punish her daughter for being what she could no longer be.

But I am a witch's daughter! I am not powerless!

I remember!

Oh, yes, I remember!

And so, as the leviathan swam deeper, Anna opened her mouth and in a muffled yet audible voice cried, *"Humbalan!"*

The creature turned its black eyes toward Anna and stared in shock.

"Humbalan!" Anna managed once more.

The leviathan's powerful tail ceased its moving. Though its eyes remained open in furious disbelief. Anna scrabbled from the grasp of the leathery wing and kicked her way to the surface as the mighty creature sank, paralyzed, like a stone.

No longer able to swim.

No longer able to come up for air.

And as she swam to shore, toward the light of the burning hotel and the flashing lights of the city fire engines, Anna thought back on what she'd remembered.

Her powers. They were still within her.

She would be fine. Her father would be fine.

She was resilient, a survivor.

And if Greg ever bothered her again, he would be sorry.

Anna smiled.

Pockets Full of Rocks

Justin M. Woodward

THE END

T
HOMAS stood on the beach with his toes in the sand, the pockets on his shorts filled with rocks. He gazed at the glassy black water with tears in his eyes as the cool night air picked up speed. He took a few steps forward, swaying as he did so. A few small orange bottles rattled against the rocks in his pocket as he walked.

When he reached the water, he stopped and stood staring into the night sky. There was a flash of light, a streak of lightning perhaps, and Thomas gasped in terror as he saw behind the clouds the outline of a shoulder and left wing of an enormous beast. He turned to run, slipping and falling in the cool sand.

When he glanced up, he saw an old man in a suit seated on a park bench in the middle of the beach.

"Who are you?" Thomas asked, approaching the stranger. "And what are you doing here?"

The man let out a dry chuckle and said, "I should be asking you the same thing, don't you think?"

The boy thought for a moment, his hand closing around one of the bottles in his pocket. "No," he said, "I shouldn't expect you should be asking me why I'm going for a swim in the ocean. It's a perfectly normal thing to do, unlike sitting on a park bench in the middle of the beach." He eyed the man with suspicion.

"Of course, of course," the old man replied, smiling. "It's perfectly normal to go swimming at dusk while fully dressed, and while there's a chill in the air, I might add."

"Well. . ." Thomas stammered. "I—" He glanced back over his shoulder at the towering figures behind the clouds. "What *are* they?" he asked.

"If you don't know," the man said. "Then you needn't worry about them just yet. Now," the man sat forward and spread his arms. "Would you like to tell me what led you to this place?"

"Like I said," Thomas insisted. "I was going for a swim." He crossed his arms in defiance, tears streaming down his face.

"I see." The suited man reached into his pocket and pulled out a handkerchief. Handing it to Thomas, he said, "Well then, perhaps I shall tell you a story of my own. That is, if you'd care to listen?"

Thomas folded his arms over his chest. He stared at the sand and watched a small crab as it scuttled away and back into its hole—as if it had also seen the behemoth-like creatures in the sea. "You promise they won't hurt me while I listen?"

"I won't let them," the man replied. "You have my word. If you'll listen, I won't let them hurt you." He patted the bench next to him and slid over a bit. "Now, come have a seat."

The man leaned back on the bench and drew in a deep breath of the salty sea air. "I'm going to tell you about a boy who felt so alone in this world," the man paused for a breath. "So alone and helpless, that he thought about doing something he could never take back. And I'm going to tell you how he overcame those thoughts."

Thomas stared out into the sea, watching as the monsters fought amongst themselves. "Okay," is all he could muster.

The old man smiled and nodded, "Okay."

THE MIDDLE

The boy sat on the edge of the freshly-made vacation house bed and stared into the sea through an open window. "Beautiful," he muttered. "Just wonderful." He reached over and picked up one of the many brochures his father had given him on the plane.

FLORIDA—the brochure promised, was **WHERE LIFE TRULY BEGINS.**

Retirement and all.

The boy's attention turned to a poster on the wall featuring a smiling family standing in front of the very house his family currently occupied. He saw the way they all smiled at the camera. So full of life. Lost in thought, the boy jumped when his dad burst into his room.

"Listen, bud," his father said from the open doorway. "If you don't get out there and enjoy this gorgeous day, well, I just might go crazy!"

"I thought about going to the beach," the boy said, still staring out at the water. "But I was hoping you guys could come too."

His father sighed and slicked back his hair. "I'm sorry," he said. "You know it's just not a good time right now. But you go and have fun! Hell, get into trouble! I just can't stand to see you stuffed up in this room! We're at the beach, you know!"

"I know."

How could he forget? Florida is where you go to die.

"Tell you what. Tonight we can order in from Sandman Sam's. Oysters, chicken fingers, whatever you want, we'll get it. Wouldn't that be great?"

"Yeah."

The boy's father slapped his hand on the wall, saying, "Good talk, son. Now get out there and have some fun, Dad's orders."

Quietly, he moved across the room, opening his closet and grabbing a change of clothes. He figured he might as well grab some swimming shorts, even if he was afraid to go out too far. As he made his way down the hall, he was tempted to peek into his parents bedroom, but thought better of it.

It was a short walk to the beach—the vacation house was just across the street, one in the giant multitude. It was easy to get lost coming back, at least until he'd memorized the number above the door.

The boy walked up and down the beach, watching the other kids play. He looked on as a brother and sister took turns covering each other up completely with sand, wincing every time the sand would cover them completely.

It seemed so final.

He continued on down the beach, hands in his pockets. Nobody seemed to notice him, and that suited him just fine. He noticed them, though. He watched them play their games, even managed to smile a little as he listened to the laughter of small children.

He looked out to the sea, and watched as the waves bobbed up and down. Sunlight glistened on the water, casting a bright shine over everything it touched. He forced a smile as a young couple walked by, swinging their young son by the arms.

The hair on the back of the boy's neck stood up as he heard pleading screams coming from the water, and before he saw who it was, he knew.

The boy's mother was drowning.

He cried for help. For anyone to help, to notice. But nobody did notice. They all continued on with their lives, seemingly unable to hear or see them. So the boy, barely able to swim himself, crashed through the water towards his mother

Again and again she cried out, and the boy struggled to reach her.

It didn't matter that the boy didn't know how to swim very well, because he tore through the water so fast that his body forgot he didn't know how.

Finally, he reached her. He grabbed her hand and pulled with all of his strength towards the shore. He kicked his legs and his one free arm flailed until he was exhausted, but he couldn't budge her. Tears streamed down his face and he screamed in frustration. He couldn't believe nobody would help.

He couldn't believe they wouldn't even look.

After what seemed like an eternity, the boy's mother was gone.

Gasping for air, he looked around in dazed confusion. Still, nobody from the beach took any notice of him at all. He let the tide carry him in, breaking into a clumsy run as soon as his feet hit the sand. Twice slipped and fell out of pure exhaustion, but he got back up each time, determined to make it back to the vacation house.

Back to his sick mother.

He knew the real reason they came this vacation spot. It was because there was nothing else left to do.

And when he saw the front door of the vacation home standing open, his father screaming his name from the doorway—he knew it was over.

He had missed it.

Failed her.

So he tore past his father, past the room with the long consistent beeping sound. He grabbed as many pain pills as he could manage to fit into his pockets, and—

THE BEGINNING

"I can't listen anymore!" Thomas shouted at the top of his lungs, tears welling in his eyes. "I don't know who you are, and I don't know how you know all of that, but I'm done listening to you!"

"But the story isn't over," the old man said. "That's what I came here to tell you. I wanted to tell you how the boy came across a man on a bench, a man who told him that it gets better. That the boy goes on to meet a beautiful girl, to raise a wonderful family, and to accomplish great things. I wanted to tell you that the boys father needed him more than he could ever know. And that he would start drinking, and that he would need the boy's help to overcome some dark things. But because the boy listened to the man, all of those things were made possible."

Just then, Thomas could hear father's voice calling for him. He looked out at the ocean and saw that the beasts were gone, and somehow, he knew they would stay that way.

Again he heard his father's voice calling his name, closer this time. Thomas turned to look at the old man, and smiled.

"I want to thank you for listening," the old man said as he hugged Thomas hard, releasing a flood of emotion in the boy. "Thank you so much."

Old Bastards

Tony Bertauski

THE world was swaying.

He thought there was firm footing beneath him, like the deck of a ship, with his nonslip rubber soles gripping the boards and salt spray coming over the bow.

Instead, he came up hacking.

Each retch brought a wave of pain. He crawled out of the surf and rolled in gritty sand. The receding headache revealed other agonies—a stabbing stitch in his side, stinging cuts on his feet and chest. A tropical jungle was behind him. Palm trees leaned over pristine dunes that were empty of tourists. Not a single umbrella. Just endless waves and a white-hot sun.

Glimpses of memory failed to start. There was the smell of hospital antiseptic, but he was wearing denim jeans without a shirt and a red bandana around his throat.

Out there, on the horizon, he sensed something. A wish or hope, something he wanted. Something he was never going to get.

"Thomas!"

Voices called from the jungle. His legs, cold and clammy, exhausted, surged with panic. The search party emerged down the beach, coming out of the jungle.

It was a golf cart.

A white roof with a windshield and wheels that reflected sunlight. There were two of them on it, one with white hair and the other one bald and hunched over the steering wheel. There were no golf clubs on the back. They saw him. Waved.

"Thomas!"

The front wheels buried in the soft sand. They took a wide turn. More of them followed. They came out in pairs, each on a cart, spilling from the dense jungle, a geriatric convoy slinging wet sand from silent tires.

Run.

Thomas flinched. It was a voice in his head, loud and clear. Like a cell phone reception. He looked around. It didn't sound like the search party shouting his name.

Fear flooded his legs.

His head was flashing again, a spotlight of pain swinging a blinding beam through his vision. He held the sides of his head; the crashing surf and his name became distant echoes.

Do you want to live? He heard. *Then run!*

His legs activated.

* * *

He crashed into the dense jungle.

A deer suddenly recognizing the scent, adrenaline surged. Pain irrelevant. There was no path for the carts to follow. Barely room to run. He grabbed at giant leaves and ropey vines. Sweat-drenched and burning, cuts old and new opened on his arms and chest. Dew fell like a spring shower.

Right. Turn right.

He veered to his right and ran across a fallen palm tree. It led to more jungle, dense and nearly impassable. He was climbing an unending slope. The thoughts drove him through it. There was full daylight ahead, a break in the jungle's shadow.

Stop. Stop, stop, stop!

Thomas slowed down. His chest an engine on redline, the fuel of adrenaline reaching empty. The headache was smashing his brain into oatmeal.

There. Next to the stump. Grab the shiny leaves.

Thomas saw a rotting stump, the tree trunk long since splintered and decayed. Sprouting next to it was a small shrub with red berries.

Start chewing on one of the leaves, but take the rest with you. Don't touch the berries.

Thomas reached for what the voice was saying. He was listening to it, like someone from above was watching him, guiding him. His hand felt foreign as he reached through the fog of exhaustion.

The foliage was bitter.

In minutes, the headache dulled. Pleasure rode beneath the pain like a riptide swelling up, neutralizing the burn and ache, filling his rubber legs. He tucked the leaves into his pocket.

Go straight.

Thomas didn't hesitate. He stepped out of the trees onto a cliff. The edge was sharp.

Don't look down.

* * *

Thomas crawled to the back of the alcove.

It was a deep recess in the granite cliff, a shelf that had naturally eroded. Somewhere far below, the remains of what had fallen out of the wall had crashed to jagged pieces.

The climb had been treacherous.

The footholds were rough but deep enough for a solid grip. He didn't look down, like the voice said. The shelter was only three steps down. It felt like a mile.

He wedged himself into the crevice as if the wind might suck him out. The sun glittered off the ocean. The horizon revealed the curvature of the Earth.

And the nothingness out there.

*   *   *

He was on a boat.

He was sure of it this time. A wooden deck beneath his feet. The subtle rocking of the hull on a relatively calm sea. He felt clean and dry. Fully dressed. Not strong though. In fact, he hurt all over.

Wake up.

Thomas opened his eyes.

His arm was numb beneath him. Somehow he'd fallen asleep. Now the moon, almost full, was casting shadows across the ocean. He crawled across the coarse floor. Fingers trembling, he gripped the edge.

The ocean sprayed plumes below.

He scurried back. Twigs and coconuts were stashed in the corners along with candy wrappers. He could feel the weight of the earth above him and the thinness of air beyond.

Eat another leaf.

The headache was returning. It was a distant call, a creature crawling back to life. It was important to stay ahead of it. Pain medication was always better when it was in the lead.

The bitterness was soothing.

Thomas was lithe and muscular, bronzed by the sun. His skin was smooth. Not a hair anywhere but on his shaggy head. He didn't know what to expect. He'd run all that way through the jungle and was hardly sore, except for the cuts. And his head. He reached for the source of pain on his forehead.

Don't touch it.

"What's happening?"

It was the first time Thomas had spoken out loud. His voice cracked with puberty.

Don't touch your head. It'll only make it worse.

"I-I-I-I…"

He stammered incoherence. None of this made sense. He couldn't remember how he got on the beach or why he was hearing a voice.

They told you there was an accident. Do you remember?

That was familiar. An accident. This was a place to heal. But what accident?

"Who are you?"

It wasn't an accident, Thomas. The old bastards aren't healing anyone.

The old men on the beach. They were looking for him.

"What are they doing?"

Eat another leaf. You need rest.

He did what the voice told him to do. So far it had worked.

*   *   *

Wake up.

Thomas had dreamed about a boat again. It was the same as before, only this time someone was with him. She was wearing a bikini with the top untied, her shoulders oiled. Actually, there had been two of them,

31

bronze beauty queens side by side. Strings undone.

He crawled to the ledge.

It had been two days since he'd climbed into the shelter. Mostly, he slept and chewed leaves. The voice taught him how to crack the coconuts and drink the water. He'd pried out the white meat and eaten a pile of berries.

The bandana was chafing his neck.

He pulled at the knot. The fabric was heavy against the back of his neck. He reached back and felt a tender lump beneath a fresh scar. There was something in the bandana. And something inside his neck. He began untying the knot.

Stop.

"What is this?" Thomas's fingers hovered.

They put something in your neck. The bandana has magnets to keep it from working. You have to keep it tight at all times. You got it?

"Or what… what'll happen?"

They find you.

Thomas did what the voice told him to do. He made the knot tighter. The knob on the back of his neck hurt more, so he ate another leaf.

Climb up.

Thomas crawled on his stomach. He didn't look over the ledge this time. He was never going to leave if he did. The sky was bruised by the setting sun. Shadows sank in the recessed handholds.

Thomas stopped.

You can't stay here. You'll run out of food. Just don't look down and focus on your steps. It's an easy climb.

That was all true. But tell that to his body. It had gone catatonic again. Fear petrified his legs into solid oak. He wrapped his arms around himself and began rocking.

Go!

Like the beach, the voice shattered the stalemate. He had a hold of the first step before doubt could stop him. And he continued, one hold after another, three steps to the top. He crawled across the ground, his heart pounding in his ears.

Go right. Stay in the trees.

"Where am I going?"

There was a pause. *To see what the old bastards are doing to us.*

To us. That was the first time the voice had said that. Thomas had begun to think he was hearing an imaginary voice. But it was telling him exactly what to do. And it was always right.

"What are they doing?"

There was no answer. Just directions. *Keep to the coast and stay in the trees*, it said. Whenever he ventured out to escape the humidity, the voice chided him to get back to cover.

It led him down a narrow path that descended the cliff. He found himself on a sandy abutment between a granite wall and rocky shore.

The tide was low.

Thomas walked for another hour. His headache was returning and he was out of leaves. He wanted to turn back and find comfort in the shelter.

There.

Thomas stopped. He saw it up ahead. The tide was just beginning to turn. There was still plenty of time to retrace his steps. Something was ghostly in the moonlight, the color of bleached hide. Thomas knew what it was.

He could smell it.

Go on. Take a look.

The voice bullied him to continue. He stumbled through the sand and over the rocks. It was exactly what he thought it was. Arms and legs twisted and broken into sharp angles by granite edges and the swelling tide. The flesh was puckered around wounds long drained, the exposed edges soft and white.

Thomas looked away.

Bobby killed himself before they took him. He wasn't going to escape, so he jumped. It's one way out of here, Thomas. One way the old bastards don't win.

Thomas shuffled through the sand. A lump swelled in his throat. The odor coated the back of his tongue. It was a smell that would stay with him for days.

Closer!

Thomas trembled. There were things crawling on the body. Little crustaceans picking at his flesh, flies on his face.

They're experimenting on us. And that right there, what Bobby did, is better than letting them win. You believe me?

Thomas nodded.

He tried to breathe through his mouth. Snot was leaking from his nostrils. He began retracing his steps. He believed. Hell yeah he did.

Not yet.

The voice kept him from escaping. It told him to get on his knees. It made him dig in the sand. He continued until the hole was big enough.

Then he dragged the body over.

* * *

Only one coconut left.

A ripple of clouds turned the sky into a washboard, like the sea had turned upside down. Thomas searched the piles of leaves and roots and berries. He'd eaten the tubers the night before.

Look for a box in the corner.

He found what the voice was talking about. It was small and velvety. But there wasn't an engagement ring inside. It was a jumble of paperclips. The voice told him to tuck it in his pocket.

He lathered salve from a succulent on his chest and arms. It kept the cuts from stinging and reduced the insect bites. He focused on the handholds and climbed to the top.

Turn left. Follow the path.

"Where am I going?" Thomas whispered.

The voice didn't answer. It only gave directions. He followed along, stopping to drink water pooled in the cups of tropical leaves and eat flowers when the voice told him to. They tasted like nectar.

The path ended at an opening.

Thomas was careful not to step into it. He crawled through the underbrush and peeked through ferns. Outlined against the lunar glow were the first edges of civilization.

Buildings.

A field stretched out like a playground. A two-story building was on the far side. And beyond that, rising out of the trees, was a cylindrical building with a chimney on top. The windows were reflective, like eyes wrapping around curved walls.

Someone emerged from the trees.

It was an old man followed by a line of kids. Teenagers, probably. Thomas's age. And they looked like boys, the way they walked. No one was talking. Heads down, they followed the old man across the field and, one by one, entered the two-story building.

The voice told him to be still.

Insects crawled on him. Something took cover under the bandana and began biting, mandibles testing soft flesh for something to eat or to lay eggs. Thomas, though, stayed locked. The image of Bobby kept him from moving until the voice told him to get up.

He stayed in the trees.

He worked his way to where the old man had led the line of boys out. The path was well established, the widest one he'd been on since waking up on the beach. It meandered through the forest and ended at a curved hut.

It was a small dome.

Thomas approached slowly. The door was open. Inside, it was

dark. There were circular windows on the roof like insect eyes looking at the moon.

Go on.

He reluctantly peeked in. There were iron bars inside. Cages. The concrete floor was damp with condensation. A stagnant fan was anchored on the ceiling, drips falling from the blades. Nothing else, though. No tools or weapons. No blood.

"Thank God," Thomas muttered.

God got nothing to do with this. Now go in the first one. Hurry.

He looked in the cell. There was a puddle in the center. It smelled like urine. He swallowed a rising lump, the image of Bobby returning.

"What are they doing?"

Look up. You'll see a little box at the top. You'll have to jump to pull it down.

A small black box was in the center of the cell. Thomas stepped around the puddle. He leaped a few times before snagging it. A strap unreeled on a cable like heavy fishing line. It looked like something that went over someone's head. It had a knob attached.

Look inside the knob. You'll find a small hole.

It was exactly like the voice said. The inside of the knob was shiny and smooth. Thomas's forehead began throbbing. He wiped the sweat from his eyes and found the small hole then followed the voice's directions, taking out a paperclip and jamming one into the hole.

Break it off.

It took some wiggling but eventually a bit of metal broke off from the paperclip. It was stuck. The voice told him to do it again in the next cell. Thomas did exactly what he was told until all the knobs were jammed.

"What do these things do?"

They get inside your head.

"Is that why I hear you?"

His fingers were raw from twisting the paperclips. He'd accidentally stuck one under his fingernail. Thomas finished the last one and sucked on his finger, feeling for his way out. The voice didn't stop him.

Yeah, it said. *That's exactly why.*

* * *

That dream again.

The one on the boat. The one where he was fully dressed. Only it wasn't a boat. It was a yacht. He was on a big-ass yacht with a drink in his hand. And there was something else that was different. He saw himself in the cabin's window—

Wake up.

A cool breeze rustled dried blades of grass. It had been a couple of weeks since he had been at the cells. His fingertip was still sore from poking the paperclips into the headsets. He'd had plenty of time to think about what he'd done and why. What those things did.

They get inside your head.

The voice offered no other explanation. In fact, there had been very little conversation ever since. At one point, he thought that was it. The voice was gone. But when he attempted to climb up, it would return.

Get back, it had said. *It's not time.*

Thomas had grown sore waiting. There was hardly room to stretch and none to stand or even squat. He'd finished his last coconut. The berries were long gone. He was going to have to go up soon.

Look in the corner, behind the leaves.

There wasn't really a corner in the crevice, just space that grew tighter. He searched on his belly and found a wad of dried foliage. It was shoved so far back that he had to squeeze his arm to get it.

There were two things in it. One was a key. The other was a sock full of seeds. Thomas began salivating. He imagined the seeds' bitter, starchy taste would be hard to swallow, but it would satisfy his hunger.

Don't eat them yet. Put the key in the sock and climb up.

"Where we going?"

Hurry. There's not much time.

Thomas didn't know how the voice would know what time it was. The moon hid behind a cloudy veil. He could barely see the handholds. He stuffed the sock in his pocket and scampered up.

The voice told him where to go.

Soon, the familiar sight of the cylindrical building came into view. His eyes had adjusted. A thin stream of smoke was pouring from the chimney.

The yard was empty.

Wait.

Thomas did like last time. He'd forgotten to douse himself with salve. The insects in the crevice were nonexistent. Here in the jungle they were all over him. He tried not to squirm each time something bit him. Something moved in the yard.

It was a golf cart.

The same one he'd seen on the beach. It looked like an old man driving it, the way he was hunched over. The way he eased out of the driver seat. He went over to the two-story building and tugged on the door. It didn't open. He got back on the cart and drove around the building.

The voice told him to go.

Thomas moved through the trees, occasionally stopping, looking. He worked his way around the yard until he was at the door.

Get the key ready.

"What are we doing?"

There was no answer. But the last time Thomas saw the yard, the boys were led into that very same building. This was where they lived. And Thomas had the key.

Now.

Thomas's heart thudded. The word was a starter's pistol. Before he knew it, he was sprinting. It felt good to stretch his legs, to press his body into action. Like he had all the energy, all the strength he needed to do anything. Like he could run.

Forever.

Key ready, he stuck it in the lock like a fencing expert. A quick turn and he slipped inside. It was silent. Clean. The floor was hard and the hallway dark. There were doors on each side. Thomas pressed against the wall. His breath echoed.

Third door on the right. Go now.

Barefoot, he barely made a sound as he counted down the doors. They were beige wood and looked heavy. When he reached the correct door, he turned the knob.

There were two beds, boxy dressers and walnut-colored desks. A large closet was lined with identical shirts. The bed next to the door was empty. The sheet was tucked in, the pillow fluffed.

The other bed was occupied.

There was a lump beneath the covers and a shaggy head of hair on the pillow. Thomas had pushed himself into the corner. He clung to the wall, afraid he was going to melt. It wasn't how this place looked that was so familiar.

It was the smell.

Like body odor and faint whispers of old-man cologne. It was soapy cleaning supplies and starched sheets. All the familiar smells tingled inside his head.

The boy stirred in the bed, turning his head at first then propping up on one elbow. His blue eyes blinked in the dark.

"Josh?" the blond boy squeaked.

If Thomas stayed still, perfectly still, he'd do what any boy did having a nightmare. He would ignore Thomas and hide his head under the pillow.

Go over there.

Thomas didn't listen, even when the voice repeated the demand and his legs twitched. His head began to throb, but he just couldn't do it.

The boy got out of bed.

Bare feet and big loops of straw-colored hair, he peered at Thomas like he was a ghost.

"I thought you got smoked," the boy said.

Smoked? Thomas felt a lump in his throat.

Tell Mikey, the voice said, *it's time to go.*

"It's…" Thomas swallowed, "it's time to go."

Say his name!

"Mikey," Thomas repeated, "it's time to go."

"Where?" Mikey said.

The voice told Thomas what to do. He undid the bandana against his throat. The weighted end swung off his neck. The voice had said it was magnets inside the bandana. Confusion was clearing on Mikey's face. He let Thomas wrap the bandana around his neck like the voice told him to do.

"Go to the place," Thomas said. "Get some coconuts and supplies. Don't leave for a week. Wait for the full moon when the ship arrives." He snugged the knot against his throat. "Then do what I told you."

Mikey listened. Nodded. Like he knew what any of that meant. Then Thomas told him what the voice told him to say.

"What you gawking at? Go."

"What about you?" Mikey said.

"I got a plan."

"Yeah, but they gonna—"

"I got a plan! Now go on."

Thomas struck him. It happened all of a sudden, like he didn't see it coming. It was a swift cuff to the side of the head. Mikey looked hurt, but it got him moving.

Wait!

Thomas told him to stop. The voice told him to grab the boy. He did. Then the voice said to hug him.

He did that too.

Mikey didn't hug back, but Thomas had him in a big bear hug and squeezed and didn't want to let go. When he did, he pushed him away. Diffuse light streamed through the window and highlighted Mikey, just for a second, and revealed a dark spot on his forehead. It was red and swollen.

They told you there was an accident, the voice had once said. *They were going to heal you. But they got inside your head.*

And then Mikey was out the door. All legs and arms, an adolescent gazelle awkwardly sprinting. The door down the hall slammed open. And then it was quiet. It was just Thomas in an empty room of familiar smells.

Eat the seeds. You need the energy.

As confused and scared as Thomas was, he was still hungry. He filled his mouth. They slid over his tongue like candy.

Chew them.

The seed coats were hard and, just like he expected, the starchy insides bitter. He swallowed them like aspirin and bent over the sink to wash them down. Hunger pains were already receding.

Now we wait.

Thomas wanted to argue, but the bed looked soft. The pillow too. The old bastards, though, would find him if he slept there. And he wasn't wearing the bandana. At the very least, he could grab some fresh clothes.

He yanked a shirt out of the closet and pulled it on. It was gray. In the dingy light, he saw a name stitched above his left breast.

Josh.

The hallway door opened. There was no patter of hasty footsteps, no quick breathing of a winded Mikey slinging himself into the room. The first of the slothy old men blocked the doorway. He grunted at the sight of Thomas. Even in the poor light, he could see the grin pull on the side of his face.

"I knew you'd be back," the old man said.

The silhouettes of others filled in behind him. Then one of them pushed through the doorway. He ran to Mikey's bed and threw back the covers, tossed the pillow and dropped on one knee as if he might find the boy hiding under the bed.

"What'd you do?" he said. "What'd you do?"

He hobbled after Thomas. The dry skin on his arthritic hands was at Thomas's throat. They tumbled onto the empty bed, and the others pried him off.

Thomas's headache was full throttle.

He was beginning to sweat. The old men smelled like wet leather and cologne.

"What'd you do with my Mikey?"

They tried to calm him down, walking him across the room. The doorway was open.

Run.

Another old man came into the room but was distracted by the wailing. They were frail and hobbled. The dim light made them look sickly yellow or gray. The voice was right. All he needed was a step on them and he would be in the trees.

He could join Mikey at the shelter. There was enough room for both of them. They could stay there until the ship arrived. Thomas wondered if it was the ship in his dreams.

Run!

The starter pistol had been fired. In two bounds he was in the hall. It was a clear shot. Adrenaline surged into his legs. He hit the door at a full gallop when the jolt came. It started in his neck.

Where the bandana magnets had been.

* * *

It was the ocean. Again.

The lovely ebb and flow. The slide in and out. Bubbles on sand, smooth and firm.

Below the surface, the thudding began. It rippled to the ocean's bottom and back to the roiling waves. In rhythm, it struck.

Thomas could hear it.

It settled in his forehead and spread behind his eyes. Perspiration leaked into the corners of his eyelids. He tried to lift his hand, to wipe the sting away, but found both wrists bound.

Things smelled antiseptic.

He had trouble focusing—the sweat, the cramping—but saw the low ceiling, the thick curtain next to him.

"Thomas?"

The deep voice was at his feet. It resonated through the fog. Thomas tried to lift his head. Pain shot from his neck. The bed, however, began to mechanically fold upright. He was effortlessly shown the man at the foot of it.

He didn't appear to be a doctor.

A wry smile grew in the wiry gray beard. "Like a little tornado when it goes off, I'm told."

The man tapped his own neck. The memory of escaping came to Thomas, of sprinting down the hallway, the blinding pain that started in his neck and tripped him into a very deep black hole. Now he was cuffed to a hospital bed with a disheveled long-haired man wearing a floral shirt.

He's not old, Thomas thought. *Not like the rest of them.*

Thomas tried to speak. His throat was dry. He swallowed and tried again. Nothing came out. Not because of his throat or the cramps shooting through his guts.

The words just weren't there.

"Director."

An old man came from behind the curtain. Now he looked more like a doctor, white lab coat and all. He showed an iPad to the man he called director, and they had a conversation in nods and points and murmured words. The director pursed his lips and nodded one last time.

"Give me a minute."

The doctor, if that was what he was, went behind the curtain again. The director stared down at Thomas. He dropped one of the railings and sat on the bed. It sank toward him.

"Can I get a washcloth?" he called out, and moments later, the doctor handed him a damp rolled-up washcloth. The director dabbed Thomas's forehead and wiped the perspiration from his cheeks. It was cool and forgiving. His lips were so dry.

"How'd you hide the tracker?" he asked casually. "Thomas? I know you're in there. You can hear me. I need you to tell me how you kept the tracker from giving us your location."

He reached behind Thomas's head and squeezed the scar on his neck. The room darkened. Thomas arched with pain, but a soundless gasp was all that came out. Tears flushed his eyes and mixed with sweat.

"You understand my urgency, Thomas? Vandalizing the headgear was one thing, but now Mikey has dropped off the radar. Just when you appeared on it. His investor is a bit upset. He's put a lot of money into the boy, just like you did. Where did he go?"

The director turned his head. Thomas had opened his mouth. His lips worked, but, still, there was nothing. He wanted to tell him about the cliff, where it was, the bandana with the magnets, the voice that was in his head.

The words just weren't there.

The director sighed and the smile returned. He leaned closer until Thomas could smell coffee on his breath.

"I know you're in there, too, Josh. Letting your little brother go sort of tipped your hand. I want you to know we'll scrub you out. And we'll find your brother. And Thomas will get what he paid for."

He patted him on the shoulder.

With a final sigh, he went to the curtain and slowly began to push it aside. There was another bed. The mounds of upright feet were beneath covers.

Thomas was confused by what he saw. He responded with a violent dry retch. The cramping had begun to wring out his organs, squeezing pain into his legs like juice from a lemon. A lead weight was in his chest.

"We're sending you back, Thomas." The director's voice was distant in the ringing. "You'll be stable till we clean up your investment. But you'll be back on your yacht in no time."

Thomas retched again. This time slimy bile spilled out and the lumpy remains of what he'd last eaten stuck to his chin. Something fell and danced across the hard floor. The director looked down then picked it up. He stared at the seed that had fallen out of Thomas's pocket.

The medical equipment sounded off.

Thomas's vitals were spiking. He retched a third time and nearly exploded. There was rushing in the room. More old men. A loud voice. The director was furious, his face right up against Thomas until their noses touched. His words were tangled, unintelligible.

There was nothing but pain.

Someone came to his side with a needle. In the dense fog, Thomas thought they were going to start an IV for surgery. But there was no anesthesia. He turned his head just before the seizures took his young and able body. There, in the other bed, lying with hands at the sides, was a very old man.

Memories of a yacht found their way through the confusion. Of standing on the deck, of the bikini-clad women, the drink in his hand. And he recognized the old man.

There was a needle in his forehead.

A flurry of old men tried to hold Thomas, but the seizures had him now. They tried to insert a needle into his forehead. They wanted to send him back, but spit bubbled on his lips and the numbness came. Sounds blurred together in a long hiss.

And just before the final darkness took him, the voice returned. Distant and weak.

You get nothing, Josh said. *You old bastard.*

Flange Turner

Gene O'Neill

THE blast of a high-pitched whistle momentarily quieted the noise in the bar.

Ian Sullivan glanced left past the Coors sign in the large picture window facing the Yard, then down at his watch: 4:10. "End of the day shift," he announced absently, thinking that for most of the twenty-two years he'd spent on the Yard his life had been governed by that whistle: Five minutes until work—Work—Lunch—Five minutes until work—Work—End of Shift. Sometimes he awoke at home dreaming he'd heard the whistle. As the noise in the bar resumed, he slipped off his stool, and pushed his nearly-full Bud and empty shot glass closer to his companion, Denny Rucker. "Be back in a minute, pal, watch my beer." Then Ian made his way through the small crowd around the pool table and stepped out of Tug's Bar into the fresh February afternoon, pulling up the collar on his Raider's windbreaker. He sucked in a deep breath and shuffled a little closer to the old ferry pier and the dark water, the hundred yards or so of strait that separated the city of Vallejo from Mare Island Naval Shipyard.

Directly across the water from where Ian stood, two shops ran side-by-side along a wharf; between the buildings a pair of gigantic cranes rested, resembling skeletal sculptures of two prehistoric monsters. No riggers moved around the cranes or nearby shops; in fact from his vantage point, Ian couldn't see anyone working on the Yard, as if it were Sunday or a holiday. He shuddered, the complete lack of activity creating a feeling of abandonment, adding to a lingering sense of unease that had plagued him since the big layoff in December.

The sun began to dip behind the shops, setting fairly early this time of year, rays extending between the two buildings and cranes, making a golden reflection across the dark water. For a moment Ian felt he could just walk right across the metallic pathway and down to Shop Eleven; then he blinked, and he realized that not only the path but the strait itself was an illusion, that the distance for him to the Yard was greater than the Pacific Ocean, because he might never cross again to work on any shift as a flange turner. He shook his head with a forced sense of resignation.

Flange turner: an elite specialty on the Yard—proud, highly-skilled, well-respected; but very specialized, a trade required to craft steel to the exacting tolerances needed in nuclear submarines; a handful of men, their unique skills utilized only at Mare Island, now that Hunter's Point was completely shut down. No, Ian knew that it was unlikely he'd ever again use a furnace, torch, or hydraulic hammer to bend, straighten, or shape a plate, shaft, or tube.

Despite his vow about not feeling sorry for himself, Ian let out a long, sad sigh. He'd left much more than his tools over there across the narrow dark waters.

Abruptly he turned and made his way back into Tug's, up to the bar next to his friend.

Rucker, a flange turner who'd retired from Shop Eleven last summer, was working on a fresh Bud. "Hey, Sully, you okay?" he asked, a concerned expression on his face.

Ian nodded, slipped back on his stool and signaled for another shot of Jack, then tipped up his bottle and took a long pull on the beer.

"Thought you looked kinda pale there for a minute," Rucker said over the sound of the jukebox, the group Lynyrd Skynyrd singing "Sweet Home Alabama."

"I'm fine," Ian responded, forcing a smile.

"Well, the times are tough on everyone," Rucker said. "All the lay-offs during the last couple of years. Now, the recession and the rumors of the Clinton administration completely closing down the Yard. Man, where's it gonna end?"

Ian drained the shot of whiskey, nodding absently. Yeah, the last round of RIFs had been a shock to him. He really hadn't believed any of this would affect him. But here he was drinking instead of going to work, and the way it looked, there would never be a Yard to go back to. He cleared his throat, remembering the vow he'd made to himself. At least Sadie, his wife, still had her secretary position with the law firm downtown. But even that didn't look too secure. And with Dana down at UC Santa Barbara and Liam out at Solano J.C., the old financial picture wasn't real rosy.

Rucker leaned over and bumped his arm. "I asked how'd the interview go up in Napa at the pipe plant?"

"Okay, I guess," Ian lied, knowing it hadn't gone well at all. They'd been looking for experienced pipe fabricators, and the personnel guy had even said: *You are, ah, fifty, Mr. Sullivan?* Ian had squirmed in his seat and nodded, feeling like confirming his age was admitting to having AIDS. But he wasn't about to tell his friend all that. Rucker kept harping about Ian taking advantage of the Yard's counselling and retraining program for those riffed. Dammit, he was a flange turner, period. He didn't want to be retrained as a machinist or a welder or a lathe operator. Now that he'd gone beyond technical skills, developing an intuitive, almost artistic sense in his craft, he wasn't sure he could be retrained at something else. Down deep Ian had to admit that despite all the signs he was really counting on the Yard not closing. He just knew he'd be called back. And if his friend couldn't understand his feelings, how could any retraining counselor at the Yard or this president for that matter.

Rucker was still rambling on, ". . .Hey, man, you better lighten up on the hard stuff, that Jack Daniels'll put you under, you know what I'm saying—"

Ian had enough lecturing and stood up suddenly, feeling a little shaky, his legs rubbery, and said, "I'm out of here, man." He glanced at his friend and hesitated for a moment, leaning against the bar for added support. Something looked funny.

In the gathering darkness that was creeping into the bar through the big window facing the Yard, Denny Rucker looked kind of fuzzy-like. . .shimmering for a moment, like a distant car looked through heat waves rising off a highway. Then, his image sharpened, outlined by a thin neon-blue line.

As Ian continued to stare dumbfounded, his friend's voice grew in intensity for a second or two then suddenly faded away, lost in the noise of the background; and simultaneously the neon outline flared up, like a light bulb before it blew, then grew dimmer, as Denny Rucker's features faded away into the gloom—

Jesus, Ian swore silently, feeling a sense of growing panic. Abruptly, he turned away and stumbled clumsily through the crowd of unemployed shipyard workers, rubbing his eyes. *What the fuck is going on?* He asked himself, blinking repeatedly.

At the door to the place he stopped, still not feeling too steady on his feet; and even though he knew there was something wrong with him, he couldn't resist a quick look back at the bar.

The two stools where he and his friend had sat were empty, now...

"Ah, I'm just drunk," Ian finally whispered unconvincingly, forcing himself to leave, not giving in to the impulse to check the bathroom or the rest of the crowded room for his friend. "Too much Jack Daniels."

*   *   *

Later that evening at home, Sadie asked Ian to go upstairs and tell Liam it was time for dinner.

He trudged up the stairs, his legs still weak, feeling twice his age. He'd had a couple more drinks after getting home and listening to Sadie bitch about money—the lack of it; and he knew he was indeed three quarters in the bag. He would quit going down to Tug's during the day, Ian promised himself, as he reached his son's door. Yeah, time to ease up on the hard stuff. His friend, Rucker, was probably right. He pushed open the bedroom door and looked around, saying, "Hey, Bud." The room was empty, but the reading light at the desk was still on.

Ian stepped over the clothes and junk on the floor, thinking Liam must be in the bathroom. At the desk, before turning off the light he glanced down at the closed book, wondering what his son was studying. Ian didn't think Liam really did any studying…at least his grades at the J.C. didn't reflect it. But it was a library book from the college: LORD JIM. Ian recalled reading the book by Joseph Conrad, remembered that it'd been difficult going, wading through dense sentence construction; but he'd really enjoyed the story. He'd even taken Sadie to see the movie. Peter O'Toole had been great as Jim.

As he lifted up the book it fell open, marked by a small hand mirror and some other stuff. That's strange junk to mark your place with, Ian thought, putting the book down carefully and staring at a razor blade and straw. He closed the book and flipped off the light.

In the dark it hit him.

"Hey, Pop, what are you doing sneaking around my room?" the voice asked from a figure highlighted in the doorway. It was Liam.

Surprised, Ian stammered defensively, "I-I-I. . ."

Liam remained in the doorway, hands on hips, his face shadowed.

51

Finally, Ian managed to explain in a heavily-slurred voice, "I just came in to get you for dinner."

"Okay, let's go then."

"No," Ian said, not moving, "we gotta talk."

"Now?"

Ian nodded, then gestured weakly at the book by Conrad. "I found your stuff. You know, the drug paraphernalia."

"Ah, Pop," Liam began in a dismissive tone. "That straw and stuff?" he asked rhetorically. "Not mine," he added with a humorless chuckle. "I found them in that book, you know."

It had been a long time, but Ian was getting really angry with his son. "Hey, look, Buddy. What do you think I am, huh? Just fell off a potato truck from Idaho?"

They stood in silence for a long time, then the boy seemed to kind of straighten, growing taller in the doorway of light, as if gathering strength. "Naw, I don't think you're stupid, Pop. But this really isn't a big deal, you know."

"Not a big deal?" Ian said stiffly. "You're snorting some kind of crap isn't a big deal. What the fuck is the matter with you, Liam? You're becoming a drug addict, a bum, a—"

"Hey, what do *you* mean," the boy responded, a suggestion of irony in his tone, "coming off with that kinda shit? Look at you right now. You're about ready to fall down, man. You're drunk. In fact, that's about all you're good for anymore, feeling sorry for yourself and sucking up the sauce. So, where you coming from, calling me names?"

Ian was stunned.

Feeling sorry for himself?

A drunk?

He just stood there next to the desk, not really hearing the words as his son continued tearing him apart...

Then the dark figure in the doorway suddenly became fuzzy, its shimmering outline gradually compressing to a pencil-thin, neon-blue edge; and abruptly, the outline flared briefly as the voice increased in volume then everything began to fade away.

Before his son completely disappeared, Ian squeezed his eyes shut, as if to magically halt the weird process.

Jesus, he was drunk on his ass.

He blinked, refocused, but Liam had gone; and by the time Ian shuffled through the litter on the floor, the boy must have gone down the stairs. "Liam, wait," he whispered in vain.

Then, stumbling quickly down the stairs in pursuit, he shouted frantically, "Liam?" At the foot of the staircase he listened, but heard no car pulling away. "Liam," he repeated hoarsely.

From the kitchen, he heard his wife explain, "It's okay, Liam, he's going over to Tom's. He'll eat there."

* * *

After pushing his dinner around on his plate and ignoring Sadie, Ian remained in the kitchen by himself. He'd considered another drink of whiskey; but, thinking about what Liam had said, he settled for a can of Bud.

He wasn't really a drunk. No way. He could quit or at least cut back any time he wanted. Sipping the beer, he decided he'd better have his vision checked though, maybe even a complete physical Something strange was going on here with him, with people shimmering and then disappearing from sight. He'd known this welder at the Yard who developed seizures, apparently triggered by the arcing of his torch. The guy would fade out in the middle of a conversation for just a second or two, then come right back, but confused by what he'd missed. Ian wondered if it was possible that maybe he was experiencing some kind of petit mal seizures, too. A neurological problem brought on by the lay-off, the strange vision episodes triggered by any additional stress, like Denny's yapping about his drinking or Liam calling him a drunk—

Brring!

The phone interrupted his thoughts. Ian stood and picked up the receiver. "Hello."

"Daddy, it's Dana," his daughter announced, excitement evident in her tone.

"Hiya, Babe," Ian responded.

"Got some news, Dad," she said, her voice a little more measured. "Are you sitting down?"

"I am, now," he answered, finding his chair and can of beer.

"I'm getting married next Saturday."

"What--?" Ian asked, almost choking on the sip of Bud he'd taken to fortify himself against the impending news.

"It's not a regular marriage, Daddy, not like you think" Dana explained, laughing. "This guy in my apartment complex, he was a student, but got some bum grades and dropped out. Anyhow, he needs to get married to stay in this country, because they're jerking his student visa. Are you following me?"

Ian took a long pull on the Bud, then said, "Sorta." Keeping the receiver on his shoulder, he stood and poured himself a shot of Jack as his daughter continued.

"He's really a great guy, and this will just be a ceremony of convenience, you understand?"

Ian nodded dumbly.

"He's from Uganda—"

"Uganda?" Ian repeated as if he'd never heard of the country. "That's in Africa?"

"You're right, Daddy," Dana said, laughing again. "Robert is an African. You know, like black."

"Ah, isn't Uganda the country with a major AIDS problem, Babe?" asked Ian, unable to keep the slurred words apart or hide the concern in his tone.

"Daddy have you been drinking again?" Dana said, more of a condemnation than a question. "You promised that all that. . ."

Ian squeezed his eyes closed as her voice suddenly flared in intensity then began to gradually fade away, finally replaced by a hum—the dial tone.

He sat there at the table for a few moments until he got tired of listening to the humming phone.

Jesus, I'm really fucked up, he thought. But he wasn't sure what to do about it. Then he dug Sadie's address book out of the junk drawer under the phone, found Dana's phone number and dialed. The line rang four times, then his daughter's voice came on: *Hi, we're out of the apartment now—If it's Mom or Dad, we're at the library studying. Ha, ha, ha. Anyhow, leave your name and number and we'll get back.*

It was only her recording machine.

This wasn't his eyes this time. And he didn't think it was a seizure either. It was something else.

Had he imagined the call?

He didn't think so.

Maybe he was just going nuts, the booze finally getting to him? Again, he recalled Denny Rucker's lecture about the hard stuff.

Jesus, what was going on?

His chest felt tight, like he was about to have a heart attack. He had to talk to someone. But who–?

Sadie!

Ian stood and almost fell over. Man, he was really in the bag.

Still, he managed to make his way from the kitchen and into the rec room. The room was empty, the TV staring back blankly. The clock on the VCR read: 10:30 pm. She must've gone upstairs, Ian thought, making his way up the staircase.

Sadie was in the master bathroom getting ready for bed. She was wearing her leopard skin shorty nightgown; and that almost made Ian groan when he saw it. Her *special* signal. No, not tonight, he thought, sitting down on the edge of the king size bed. "Hey, Hon, can we talk?"

he asked, speaking in a measured way.

She leaned out of the bathroom door and gave him her fake smile. "Sure can," she said, winking. "Not exactly what I had in mind, but what's up?"

"Well, it's about something funny happening to Dana—"

"You mean this wedding thing," she interrupted impatiently, turning back to the mirror, sitting down on her stool, and starting her face cleansing routine that prevented wrinkles. "What about it?"

"Well, you know, a Ugandan, a black?" he said, but realizing after he said it, that wasn't the immediate thing bothering him. Jesus! Dana's voice had faded out—

"For crissake, Ian," she chastised him, "don't be so melodramatic." She shook her head, standing up off the little stool, smoothing out her nightgown provocatively and glancing out where he sat. "Dana's not going to go through that whole process, including the questioning by immigration for some black kid she hardly knows. It's a passing thing, like most of her big plans." She stared at him with that look: *Don't you dare disagree with me.*

He froze for a moment or two, his mind going blank, the alcohol adding to his focusing problem.

"I'm not so sure," Ian finally said, attention redirected now. "She sounded pretty committed to me."

"Uh-huh," Sadie nodded, giving him a derisive look. "How about the Peace Corp thing in her freshman year or quitting school and joining Greenpeace last year. She sounded serious then, too, right?"

Ian thought for a moment, realizing his wife might be right about their daughter…But what about the rest, the fading out business? What about something being physically wrong with him? He stared at her, collecting his thoughts, trying to think of some way to introduce the subject without sounding silly. But his mind was fuzzy, his tongue too thick. So he just nodded. It was easier to just agree with her.

Sadie shrugged, dismissing the subject, then smiled and licked her full lips. "Hmmm, time for bed, don't you think." She came close to where he sat, leaned forward and kissed him on the mouth, then made a nasty face. "Yuk, how can you drink that terrible stuff." Despite the continuing frown, she kissed him again, forcing her tongue into his mouth. Then she helped him undress.

Ian knew it was too late now for any more discussion.

Naked on the bed, they wrestled for several minutes, Sadie not giving up easily, but working up nothing more than a little sweat. It was no use. Ian couldn't get an erection.

"Hey, Hon, I'm kinda in the bag, you know," he finally said, the weak apology heavily slurred.

Silently, Sadie got up, slipped on her nightgown, trod back to the bathroom. After snapping on the nightlight, she stood framed in the dimness, her chubby body only a hint through the thin negligee. After a moment she nodded. "Guess I won't be needing my diaphragm, tonight," she said, not even trying to hide the disappointment in her voice. She glanced his way. "You know, Ian, I haven't needed it but once or twice since the layoffs. Three months. I'm still a fairly young woman, only forty-one. And you're not really an old man, but you got to do something about *your* problem, and the drinking isn't helping either. You know?"

Ian knew. And he knew she was right. But it was much more than the drinking. He wondered if now was a good time to tell her about Denny and Liam fading away, and what happened on the phone with Dana? That maybe he had something wrong with his eyes and ears…or maybe all of his perception of reality.

No, he could see Sadie wasn't in the mood for a serious discussion about his problems. She was more concerned about her own needs at the moment. So Ian said nothing, just nodded his head again. Then he stared with disbelief at what was beginning to happen to his wife.

Sadie seemed to be coming unglued, her image in the doorway blurry, dim, as if she were shrouded in fog. Ian blinked, trying to focus clearly, as the now familiar neon-blue light framed her outline—

She had flipped the door shut.

Still completely naked, Ian jumped up and cried out in a panic, "No, no, wait, Sadie."

Unsteady on his feet, he reeled across the room, his pulse racing, and grabbed the knob; then, he hesitated, afraid of what he would not find in the bathroom.

"Sadie?" he said, his heart sinking.

No answer.

Of course, like the others, she had faded out, too.

At that moment Ian Sullivan realized the truth. He knew now this was really happening. People close to him were disappearing, right after they said something he didn't want to hear, almost as if he were willing them out of his life.

They were all gone!

Minutes ticked by…

Numbed, defeated, and exhausted, Ian finally let his hand slide weakly from the door knob, sighed deeply, and shuffled back to the bed and his clothes.

In a kind of dazed stupor, he dressed.

On automatic pilot he left the house, driving slowly through a thickening mist toward the waterfront.

*   *   *

Tug's was still fairly crowded but kind of quiet, subdued, the juke-box not even playing.

Eerie.

Ian managed to find an empty stool near the picture window at the left end of the bar. Coming in he hadn't seen Denny or anyone he knew; but then he really didn't care. Maybe it was better if he drank alone tonight, thought things out. After he ordered he glanced at the headline of today's *Times Herald* lying on the bar top:

IT'S OFFICIAL: MARE ISLAND TO CLOSE

Jesus, no wonder everyone is subdued.

Ian glanced out the window, but could see nothing in the fog. It was gone, too, like everything else. The Yard, his job, his wife, his kids, his friend. He drained the double in one belt, the whiskey burning his throat, bringing tears to his eyes; then he took a long pull of Bud to dull the hurt. But he could think of nothing to cure the pain in his chest.

It was like he was living in a kind of mirage or dream. Yeah, a dream. Nothing was real. It was all an illusion.

He twisted left and stared out the window into the night again, searching, hoping to spot something over there, anything to anchor reality; but the thick fog shrouded even the lights of the Yard.

Ian shrugged and ordered another drink.

Then a revelation hit him.

Maybe it wasn't the others who were gone after all; maybe the problem was really only him.

He wasn't a flange turner anymore. He was nothing. Maybe he didn't even really exist.

Sure that was it!

He grinned wryly to himself and glanced up into the mirror behind the bar, knowing what he would see now. With a sense of acceptance Ian Sullivan lifted his shot glass in a mock toast to the neon-blue light beginning to outline his shimmering reflection.

NIGHTSWIMMING:
A Creepy Little Bedtime Story

William F. Aicher

THE steady hum of the mosquitos and intermittent chirp of cicadas did little to dispel the utter quiet blanketing the evening. Less than an hour ago, the sun had dipped below the skyline, its sherbet orange and cotton-candy pinks melting the horizon into a contused twilight as the day ended and night began. For Susan Jamison, this type of silence went with secrets, and tonight was no different. A night of secrets and chicanery with a pure and simple goal: fun.

For what good was fun when it was done wide in the open, with a healthy public to witness it. That fun was vulgar and cruel. Fleeting moments of delight cheapened by the spectator. For those who got off on the exhibitionism, perhaps things were different. But for Susan, the purity of delight when gained under subterfuge was considerably more invigorating.

Not that she didn't mind a bit of exhibitionism. From time to time, life called for spectacle. Tonight, however, was not one of those times. No. Tonight was for simplistic wicked debauchery. Nothing sinister, nor hurtful to others. That kind of fun tended to be against the set of internal rules Susan had built over the last nineteen years of her life. Just something a bit *naughty*.

She'd been nightswimming before, of course. Her parents had a pool of their own. On more occasions than she had fingers and toes, she and some friends had slipped off into the pool in the dead of night, while her parents slept. At first, it had just been with the girls, a bit of fun stretching the boundaries of *propriety*. Then she and her friends discovered alcohol, and the excursions became more frequent. Soon boys became part of the mix, and that's when the exhibitionist part came into play.

Still, never anything more than a show. And absolutely never any touching.

At least, not unless the boy was special.

Unfortunately for Susan, that special boy never showed up. Not until two weeks ago.

When Bobby Keller and Susan Jamison first met, no sparks flew. Just a boy her little sister Katie's friend, Johnny Holiday, dragged along to their house the Friday night her parents took that trip to LA. Other than that he was one of the few boys not to get drunk and encourage her to take her clothes off, there was nothing particularly notable about him … even though he did get drunk, and Susan *did* take her clothes off. But that was par for the course at a summer weekend at the Jamison house when the parents were away. He just wasn't an asshole about it and managed to keep his hands to himself without first having to be slapped away like a pesky, horny fly.

Two weeks and a half-dozen dates later, Susan and Bobby were a thing. Almost an item. But not quite.

Susan planned to change that tonight.

"I don't understand why we can't just go to the pond over at Shaker Park," Bobby said as he backed his red and rusted '94 Camaro down Susan's driveway. His left arm hung out the window, taking in the late afternoon sun and further baking in his summer trucker's tan.

"Because it's gross," Susan replied. Her floppy, wide-brimmed hat threatened to blow from her head as the car took off East on Clarence Avenue, the street Susan had called home ever since her parents brought her back there from the hospital as a newborn bundle of promise. "You know what I heard?" she asked as she rolled up her window. "I heard they've got that flesh-eating bacteria there."

Bobby laughed. "I sincerely doubt that, Suze. Maybe some leeches and a bit of swimmer's itch, but flesh-eating bacteria? I'm sure we'd have heard that one on the news."

"Well, that's what Karen Slattery told me. Said her cousin's best friend's nephew went swimming there back in July—I think maybe over the holiday—got real sick afterward and died."

"You Google that?" Bobby took his left hand from the steering wheel and clicked the passenger-side window button, rolling it back down to let in the late summer breeze. "Go ahead, search it on your phone. You show me the news story and I'll … well, I'll go swim with you wherever you want."

"And if I'm right?"

"If you're right, you have to kiss me. On the lips. And with tongue."

"Bobby Keller, I will do no such thing," Karen replied. Though in the back of her mind, she knew she would already do just that—even if she lost the bet. After all, that's what tonight was for. "And roll up the window," she continued. "It's too windy."

Bobby grunted but rolled up all the car windows and turned on the air conditioning. "So, you gonna check? Or what?" he asked.

"Doesn't matter," Susan replied as a smile crept across her face. "You already know where we're going, and if you don't like it, you can take me home right now."

Bobby didn't reply. He knew darn well he'd do just whatever his new lady friend wanted. Such was the case in a bad case of young lust. Instead, he just reached for the stereo, turned up the radio, and continued to follow the GPS to the address Susan gave him before they left.

Four-and-a-half songs and a few bits of flirtatious conversation later, they turned on to Lakeview Boulevard. As they passed by one multimillion-dollar home after another, many of them closed off with electronic gates, their foundations built at least an acre or two back on the lot, the mechanical voice of the GPS spoke.

"Your destination is on your right."

Bobby pulled the Camaro to the side of the road, the dusty gravel crunching beneath tires as it slowed until they stopped in front of a sign with "4815 Lakeview Blvd" marked in gold-flecked lettering. A formidable wrought-iron gate with an electronic keypad blocked the drive, while a stately colonial two-story brick mansion, with a footprint large enough to house at least 10,000 square feet, a half dozen bedrooms, and probably a movie theater, full-sized gym, and even its own bowling alley cast a long shadow across the perfectly-kept yard.

"This is the place?" Bobby asked. He leaned across Susan and the front seat and lowered his sunglasses. "You've got to be shitting me. How do we even get in? That place is locked up tight."

Susan smirked. "That's the place alright but keep driving. This isn't how we're getting in. I have a different way—a secret one."

Bobby frowned but put the car back in gear and pulled back onto the street. As he brought the car up to speed, the streetlights began to turn on, one by one, as if they were following the two young lovers with their own goal to find out just what kind of shenanigans these kids were up to.

After driving about two miles, Susan pointed to a parking lot and said, "There. Pull in there."

"I thought you wanted to go to a pool, not take a dip in the ocean."

Bobby slowed the car and turned on his blinker but stopped before turning into the parking lot. "Besides, sign says the beach is closed after sunset."

"Since when has that stopped you?" Susan laughed as she unbuckled her seat belt. "That spot, over there, behind the dumpster. Park there."

Bobby pulled the car into the empty space and killed the engine. But he did not unbuckle his seat belt. Instead, he sat still, or as still as he could. Whether Susan noticed his anxious trembling, he didn't know. But he hoped he hid it. As he killed the engine, Susan lifted her handle and pushed her door open with a creak that hit her like fingernails on a chalkboard.

When Bobby didn't open his door, she leaned in and put her hand on his upper thigh. He kept his face forward, staring out the windshield at the breaking surf. "You coming or what?" She asked.

"I know I laughed at you when you talked about that flesh-eating virus, or whatever it was," he began. "And now you can laugh at me if you want to, but there's no way I'm going in there. I've seen Jaws, and The Shallows, and 47 Meters Down. And I also saw the news the other day. Someone got attacked by a shark out there less than a week ago."

Susan squeezed his thigh, leaned in further, and pressed her lips against his cheek with a small kiss. Then, with her free hand, she flicked his earlobe and laughed again. "I told you we're going to a pool, and that's where we're going. That house back there? You can get into the yard from the beach."

As Bobby rubbed at his stinging earlobe, a look of relief spread across his face. He turned to Susan, forced a smile, unbuckled his seat belt, and got out of the car.

In the half-hour it took to walk the two miles back up the beach, the sun went down, sinking slowly into the ocean. The last remaining beach-goers packed up their towels, umbrellas, and coolers and headed back to the parking lot. In the back of his mind, Bobby wondered how conspicuous his car would be once the other cars cleared out. Dumpster or no dumpster, any cop or security guy who turned in and even took a cursory look at the parking lot would notice it. Whether they'd do anything about it, that was a different question. Worst-case scenario, he'd come back and find a ticket slapped on the windshield.

As for if police patrolled the beach at night or not, that was a question he didn't have an answer to. He considered asking Susan, since she'd obviously been here before, but decided against it when he realized how uncoolly paranoid such an inquiry would sound.

"Here it is," Susan said at last and turned up a path leading through the dunes away from the ocean. In the murky glow of twilight, the mansion from earlier loomed ahead. Not a window was lit, though a soft radiance emanated from the ground behind the columns of evergreens planted against the fence lining the back of the property. "He doesn't keep the gate locked. Probably figures no one's dumb enough trespass on his land."

"Just whose house is this, anyway?" Bobby asked hesitantly.

But Susan didn't answer. She just swung the gate open on its silent hinges and stepped from the beach into the private yard. Sensing Bobby's hesitance to follow, she quickly flipped up the back of her skirt, exposing her bare buttocks in a milky white flash of temptation, then took off again along the path, up to the hill to the house.

As any other teenage boy hopped up on hormones would do, Bobby, of course, followed.

On the other side of the gate, the sand of the beach ended, transitioning to a thick, full, and perfectly-kept lawn. Large enough to fit an entire football field, and still have room to spare, Bobby had never seen so much green space outside of the city park. Up ahead, the mansion became fully visible, its immaculate landscaping tastefully illuminated by thoughtfully-placed lighting. A hedge of low-cut holly bushes marked the edge of a large stone patio. It was at the outer edge of this perimeter that Bobby spied Susan stripping off layer after layer of clothing, until her naked body silhouetted against the glow of the mansion, beckoning him to join her.

"Hide your clothes here, stuff them behind the bushes," she commanded. With one hand she snapped the elastic of his boxers against this stomach, while she draped her other across her body, blocking her more enticing bits from Bobby's view.

Bobby slipped his shorts down his legs and onto the ground, all the while willing his growing erection to go away. He'd never been skinny-dipping before, but he had a feeling that presenting a rock-hard boner before even dipping into the water surely wasn't the way to win a woman over.

"Point that thing somewhere else, would ya?" Susan laughed, and Bobby felt his face turn hot as he bent to grab his clothes and add them to Susan's pile. Before Bobby could respond, Susan was already on her way to the pool, her bare feet slapping against the stone deck as she ran.

Bobby expected to hear a splash as she jumped into the pool, but when the sound of Susan's feet stopped abruptly, with no splash to follow, Bobby looked up to find her standing at the pool's edge. He padded over, hand over his crotch. When he saw what held her from jumping in, his jaw went slack.

"Does it open?" he asked, pointing to the pool's closed cover.

"Of course, it opens," Susan replied with a hint of frustration in her voice. "We have one of these at home. Just need to find the button to open it."

Bobby twisted his neck in a quick scan of the deck area. "What if it's in the house?"

"Then, we're fucked," Susan replied. "Go see if you can find it."

"And what will you do?"

"I'll keep watch."

"I thought you said there was no one home…"

"There isn't," Susan snapped. "Just go look for it. Maybe over by the equipment shed."

Sure enough, there it was—a silver metal box with a flip-open silver door with the words "CoverProtect" engraved on it and a keypad beneath.

"Uh, Suze," Bobby began. "I think we might have a problem. This thing needs a code."

"Try 1234," Susan whisper-shouted across the deck. "That's the code that came with ours, and my dad never bothered to change it. Could be they didn't either."

Bobby punched in the code and pushed the "open" button. The sound of an electric motor started up, and a twinkling reflection of stars began to unfurl as the cover opened to the night sky. Next to the touchpad, a single switch marked "lights" beckoned, and Bobby flipped that one as well. The pool came to life in a brilliant blue, illuminating Susan's shocked face.

"Turn those things off!"

"You said no one's here," Bobby repeated.

"Still," Susan huffed. "Better safe than sorry. Besides, it's more romantic this way."

Bobby considered his shrinking erection and agreed.

Susan slipped into the dark water, and Bobby followed. For the first five minutes, the two didn't speak—the only sounds the gentle waves lapping against bare skin and the staggered, yet soft, breath of two trepidatious lovers in the night.

"You can come closer, you know," Susan whispered from across the pool.

Bobby didn't answer, but instead dove under the water and swam in her direction. As he reached her, his fingers touched upon her bare skin, and he pulled away instinctively. His head broke the surface, and she cupped his cheeks in her hands and kissed him.

His erection was back, but he didn't even notice. He was too lost in the softness of her lips against his. She pulled herself closer, pressing her breasts against his chest, and Bobby yelped.

"What's wrong?" Susan asked. "I thought you liked me."

"I do," Bobby stammered. "But something touched me."

"That was me, silly," Susan replied and leaned in to kiss him again.

Only this time Bobby didn't kiss her back. Instead, he shoved her away, almost violently. In the moonlight, Susan could see his fear as his pupils enlarged and his eyes opened as wide as the moon above.

"I'm serious," Bobby answered, almost shouting now. "Something touched my leg."

"Probably just the filter," Susan said. "But we can go home if you want." She shrugged and made to swim away to the stairs at the shallow end of the pool.

Bobby considered this, but only for a moment. To go home meant to get out and get dressed. And that also probably meant no more kissing. No more … whatever came next. None of those sounded like good options, so he wrapped his arms around Susan, pressing his body against hers, their skin mingling with such voltage he almost worried he'd electrocute the two of them. In the brilliant glow of the moonlight, her hair slicked back, lips still wet from their last kiss, he leaned in for another.

Only this time it was Susan's turn to get scared.

"Quick, go under," she whispered. "Swim to the other side and stay low. There's someone here."

Bobby did as commanded, slipping under the water without a noise. Opening his eyes did little to help in the dark, so he reached out with his hands as he swam until they touched upon the side of the pool. There he surfaced, finding Susan already there next to him.

"What do you mean there's someone here?" Bobby whispered. "I don't hear anything."

"The lights. In the house. Some of the lights turned on."

Bobby exhaled a breath of relief. "Probably just on timers. You know, for security. Make it look like someone's home."

"Maybe…"

"Besides, you said no one's ever here except on the weekends, and it's Thursday."

Just then the unmistakable sound of a door latch opening sounded, followed by the sliding of a large glass door.

"I told you to take care of it," a voice echoed in the air. It came from the direction of the house, near where the patio door would have been, and it sounded pissed. "No, this is your problem," the voice continued. "I'm down at the beach house."

A pause.

"I had to get out of town. They're not pinning me for your fuck-up."

Another pause.

"Who is that?" Bobby whispered, his voice broken and frantic.

Susan pressed her finger against his lips, silencing him.

"Just get it done, Mark."

Bobby brushed her hand away. *Who's Mark?* He mouthed.

"I don't care, and I don't want to know. Just text me when it's over," the voice continued.

Bobby's breath now came in ragged, worried spurts, and it scared Susan. It scared her that this stupid boy's failure to *just shut the hell up* would get them caught—and who knows what would happen then. She clapped her right hand over his mouth, forcing him to breathe through his nose. But it didn't matter. His next question didn't need words. She could see the question in his eyes.

Whose house is this?

A quiet beep from the direction of the voice signaled the end of the phone call.

"Press yourself up against the side, and stay as low as you can," Susan ordered in a barely audible whisper. "If he sees us, we're dead."

Again, Bobby did as told. And again, his penis responded. Only this time instead of hardening into another massive erection, it let out a steady stream of hot piss. The sudden warmth spread from his groin, and he was certain Susan felt it as well, but he didn't care.

The heavy sound of hard-soled shoes thumped on the stone of the deck. With each step, their sound became louder, as the man with the phone and the bad attitude made his way to the pool's edge.

Bobby clenched his eyes shut and sunk beneath the surface. In his mind, he imagined what it would feel like to get shot in the head while underwater. He pictured the cloud of red from the bullet in his skull mixing with the yellow from his urine to create a sherbet orange to match the one that had graced the horizon only a few hours earlier.

Under the surface, the thud of footsteps disappeared. Whether it was because the man had stopped, or because the concrete and water deadened the sound, Bobby had no idea. He held his breath until his lungs burned, then he held it some more, all the while careful not to let a single bubble of air escape.

Meanwhile, Susan did the same. She'd slipped under just after Bobby, sticking around just long enough to see the tousled mop of hair atop the man's head peek over the pool's edge. Struggling against her body's natural buoyancy, she resisted the urge to expel a breath of air to help herself sink. Her fingers scrambled against the slippery tile of the pool wall, fingernails scraping and searching for any crack or crevice they could latch on to. Her eyes, meanwhile, remained focused on the rippling surface of the water, fully expecting a meaty hand to plunge in, grab her by the hair, and pull her kicking and screaming from the pool.

She counted to twenty. When no one appeared, she felt her body relax, just a little, and she turned her eyes to Bobby. The boy was terrified, that much was clear. But other than a loose bladder, he'd kept it together. So far.

Thirty.

Forty.

Fifty.

She could hold her breath for minutes if she had to. Bobby, as it turned out, could not.

Susan's heart flinched as Bobby began to twitch, and a small bubble escaped his nose. She placed her hand on his shoulder, partially to calm him, and partially to hold him under should the desire to surface get the best of him.

CPR, she knew. How to fix a bullet through the brain? That, she did not.

But that was part of the fun, wasn't it? The danger. The fear of getting caught.

And then there was the phone call. The one he'd know they'd overheard.

Maybe it could have been innocent. Maybe.

If this were someone else's house.

Bobby pushed up beneath her, a desperate struggle to escape the dominating pressure of her rigid arms on his shoulders. His hands clawed at her own, clutching at fingers. Prying. A fingernail caught the skin on her right pinkie, tearing it loose.

A muffled scream ripped through the dark water, followed by a rush of bubbles ... then a high-pitched squeal, like a garage door motor starting up. A shaky rumble joined in—one felt in the vibrations of the water more than heard.

After a few final spasms, Bobby's struggles subsided. She looked beneath her, and his wide, lifeless eyes stared back at hers, twinkling like dead sapphires in the moonlight.

And then they were gone. Not just his eyes, but his wavering hair, the pale glow of his skin. All gone. Into darkness.

But still, she felt him. There beneath her, her hands still on his shoulders. Though they no longer struggled against her, the dull pressure of his natural buoyancy persisted beneath her touch. Whether the man remained on the pool deck was of little consequence now. Unless she wanted to have the guilt of boy's death haunt her the rest of her life, she'd have to pull him up, onto the deck, and use those life-saving skills she'd learned but never dreamed she'd use.

She took her right hand from his shoulder while keeping the left in place to make sure she didn't lose him in the dark. Her free fingers clutched at the ragged mop of hair wavering atop his head, and up she swam.

Only up didn't look like up anymore. The darkness that devoured Bobby devoured everything. No stars. No moon. Just darkness above. Perhaps a cloud.

But a cloud doesn't form a physical barrier. Not like the one she met as she met where the surface should have been. Her right hand still clinging to Bobby's hair, she took her left and reached above and found nothing but a thick layer of plastic.

The man had closed the cover.

Susan's mind raced. The boy. The boy she'd brought here and *drowned.* There was no way to get him out. Hell, there was no way for her to get out. At least not here. Maybe at the edge. Maybe where the cover closed against the end of the pool. Maybe she could pry it open. Maybe she could escape.

Maybe she could drag his body out, save him, and not have murder forever on her conscience.

Susan kicked off in the direction she thought the stairs would be, dragging Bobby behind her.

Then, with a sudden, violent tug, Bobby was gone.

Her lungs burned, and head spun. Two kicks, maybe three. That's all she'd be able to manage if she didn't find some air quick. Wherever Bobby went, she could find him. But only if she was alive to do so.

Her head crashed against the wall with a muffled thump. Darkness turned to stars, shifting and twisting like a new sky in her mind. Between the impact and the lack of oxygen, a new dimension beckoned. An eternal one, where she'd be certain to find Bobby.

But she fought the delirium, allowed her body to right itself, and her feet found the solid floor of the pool. As she stood, her head broke through the surface into a pocket of air between the water and the cover. A little wedge of relief between the pool's edge and the surface. Nowhere near enough space to accommodate her head, but enough to tilt it back on her neck, and expose her desperate mouth to the air.

She breathed deeply, sucking in a mouthful of water, coughed, and froze. If the man on the deck hadn't noticed her before, frantically fighting against the cover, the alarm blare of her cough was sure to get his attention. When no shouts or thunder of footsteps followed, she breathed again. Perhaps he'd gone back inside the house already. Nonetheless, she wasn't about to risk getting his attention. For now, she had to find Bobby.

Another deep breath and down she went, blindly feeling along the pool floor for any sign of where he had gone.

Her fingertips brushed against the rough plaster of the floor, and the pool floor began to slope away, taking her deeper and deeper into the diving end of the pool. Her ears throbbed under the pressure as she reached what she felt must have been over ten feet of water, and the floor leveled out.

There she stopped, listening intently in the vacuous watery womb for any sound. Any hint of where the boy might have gone. But dead boys don't speak. And they certainly don't scream.

Up, down, left, right. It wouldn't matter where she went. Bobby'd been under too long already, and she knew it. Even if she found him, he'd be beyond saving.

Hell, she didn't even know how to save herself.

Then, to her left, a ripple in the water. Something there, in the darkness beyond. She kicked off in its direction, again feeling before her for any hint of the boy. A clump of hair, a patch of skin. A foot.

She shuddered.

And that's when she found it Not Bobby, but something else. Something *else*.

Something slick but wiry, like tentacles of hair. Strands of seaweed. But seaweed doesn't move, and it surely doesn't twist itself around you. Not like this did.

Her outstretched fingers found it first, and at that first touch, she'd felt a glimmer of hope. It had to be Bobby. Had to be that stupid mop of hair on his head. Something she could grab again and drag his body to the side and then burst through the cover, toss his body onto the deck and breathe in new life.

The hair, however, as she clutched it, it clutched back. Wrapping around her fingers and hand, eagerly slithering up her wrist until within seconds, it felt like she'd shoved her hand into a wet, fur-lined glove. Only gloves don't sting. They don't burn like fire and electricity and a thousand tearing teeth.

With a sudden yank, it pulled at her, attempting to drag her further into the deep end of the pool. Reflexively, she pulled back, freeing her hand with a horrible ripping pain, and swam off in the other direction as fast her body would take her.

As she swam, she imagined the wiry tentacles tickling at her feet, wrapping themselves around her toes and ankles and calves and thighs. Grabbing hold, dragging her back down. Down into the depth where she prayed she'd run out of air and drown like Bobby before it did whatever it was slimy monsters did to kids who went places they weren't supposed to go.

But nothing touched her. Not even a brush against the skin, though she couldn't be certain as sometimes imagination and reality can become one and the same. But when she reached the other end of the pool and scrambled up the steps, squeezing herself into the narrow space between the top step and the heavy shroud which kept her trapped, she knew she'd outswam the thing. At least for now.

As she surfaced, she inhaled a deep breath of air, blew it out, and inhaled again.

Then out.

Then in, then out.

In, out, in out.

Inoutinoutinout.

She clawed desperately at the cover. Hopeful that just *maybe* she'd catch a loose piece of fabric. A tiny tear. One she could rip and pull and slash into a gash big enough to slither through.

Of course, she found nothing of the sort. Just a slippery wall blocking her from freedom and keeping her trapped in the water with that *thing*.

"Help!" she screamed. "Help! Help! Help!" She continued until her throat burned and she couldn't scream any more.

* * *

In the water, out in the deep end, far from the stairs and that little pocket of air and chlorine gas where she hid, something moved. It moved silently and stealthily, its tendrils searching the pool, eagerly snapping up any tiny bit of food it could find.

The big meaty thing, that had been quite a meal. Enough to satiate it for a long time.

But it didn't eat because it was hungry. It ate because it was its job. It was its nature. To eat and clean and scrub.

That was the deal, as it understood it. Clear out the garbage, and the nice man would let it stay. A place to live, deep in the pipes and plumbing. Like the deep caves and tunnels it had once called home.

Free from the predators that had taken so many of its kind.

It thrived in the dark. And it thrived on its purpose.

And above all, it knew never to come out until the sky went disappeared.

Something was there with it, in the water. Something that shouldn't be there.

It would find it, and it would get rid of it.

And in the morning, Master would be proud of his sparkling clean pool.

Hell, Master might even go for a swim.

By the Seaside

Kevin J. Kennedy

ARAH'S excitement had reached its peak as they pulled into the caravan park. Her family had gone to the same place every year since she had been born, for their holidays and she loved it. There was always lots of other children to play with and she was given a little more freedom than she got at home. Her parents could sit on the porch of the caravan and watch her play on the beach, where she spent most of the day if they weren't going anywhere but her mother and father worked hard, so they were quite happy to relax and let her play.

Normally, as they got closer to their destination the sun would start to shine around the time the sea came into view, over the side of the cliff. They would often stop somewhere for lunch. This year however the sky was grey, and the rain pelted the car windows and drummed on the roof on their approach. They didn't stop on the way there and just made do with the sandwiches her mother had made. Peanut butter and jam, her favourite.

Sarah hoped the rain would stop soon. If it didn't, there would be no other children out playing, and she would be stuck in the caravan with her parents. She always had fun with them but not as much as she did with other kids her own age, on the beach.

They stopped at the caravan site office and got their keys, then quickly found their new abode for the week. Sarah's dad brought their luggage inside. Sarah unpacked her own case and then started rummaging through the food bags. She found herself a packet of crisps, then flicked on the TV. For the next hour and a half, she looked over her shoulder out of the large front window that faced the beach. The sky just kept getting darker as the fading sun slipped below the horizon. Her hopes of playing outside died.

As Sarah and her father watched TV, her mother prepared them a meal of cheeseburgers and fries.

"I'm bored. Are we going to do anything tonight?" Sarah asked, looking to her father.

"Well, we could go to the little amusement arcade on site, but I don't think it's an evening for going into town honey. We will do something fun tomorrow."

The look of disappointment on Sarah's face melted their hearts.

"Or maybe we could turn all the lights off and I could tell you a scary story?" Sarah's dad said, knowing this might brighten Sarah's mood. She had always loved scary stories.

"Yay!" Sarah replied, her frown turning into a smile.

She disappeared from the main area into her room and came back carrying her little stuffed fox and her She-Ra cover. It was worn n faded and it had originally belonged to her mother, but she had taken it everywhere with her, ever since her mother had shown her old episodes of the cartoon. Both her mother and father smiled at her cuteness. Sarah's mother went around the caravan, turning off the lights, closing curtains and then turned on the coal effect fire for a little atmosphere, before she made them all some hot chocolate with little marshmallows.

"If it was a little nicer outside, we could have done this around a campfire, but I think as things are, this will work perfectly well." Sarah's father commented, looking around the caravan.

It was very early in the season, so a lot of the other caravans were still empty, meaning that there wasn't a whole lot of light outside and their van had thick curtains.

Sarah's father shone the torch he had grabbed, onto his face, casting shadows before making an exaggerated evil laugh. Sarah went into fits of giggles, rolling around in her duvet.

"Okay, everyone ready?" he asked, before switching the torch off and setting it down.

"I am," Sarah said, excitedly.

"Me too," her mother said, giving her father a sly smile. Sarah had always liked her father's scary stories but sometimes he took it too far. He lived for a big scare, never happy with just having a creepy ending to his stories. He always had to go one step further and organise something stupid that would have them all jumping out of their skin and set them up for a sleepless night. No matter. Sarah's mum missed her sleeping in with them so a night with them all snuggled up together suited her just fine.

Sarah's dad started to tell his story, bringing her mother back to the present.

"A long time ago, not very far from this very caravan park, there was a family of cannibals, said to live in the cliffs and feed on passing travellers. Their leader was a man called Sawney Bean. He had once been a normal little boy, just like you."

"I'm not a boy," Sarah piped up.

"No, I mean… oh, never mind." Sarah's father continued. "Legend tells that Sawney and a girl he had met and ran away with, lived in a cave along the cliff side near Girvan. It was a long time ago and people went missing all the time in those days, so no one suspected anything at first, allowing time for Sawney's clan to grow in numbers and feast on the blood and bones of those they kidnapped, sometime even keeping babies they stole to add to their ever-growing family. As time passed by the family started to have problems. They only left the cave to catch their prey, so they would all pair off and have children with each other. Children were born with misshapen heads and extra fingers and toes. Some had no noses or two sets of teeth, some had scaly skin and others were born missing limbs."

Sarah wrinkled her nose in disgust. Her father had paused for effect, looking between his wife and daughter, trying to look serious but failing to keep a smile from spreading across his face.

"It is said that by the time the townsfolk began to worry about the number of people going missing, and started to believe that the rumours about a cannibal family living nearby, that the family had grown to over forty members, all living in the one cave and all surviving off of human flesh."

"So, what happened, did the town people catch them?" Sarah asked, her voice sounding higher than it had the last time she spoke.

As the rain continued to drum on the roof the thunder clapped. Sarah's father continued. "The townsfolk got a lynch mob together and searched the cliffs until they found the cave where the Bean family had been hiding. It stunk of death and was filled with bones from more humans than you could possibly imagine. Now, this is where parts of the story seem to differ. Some people say that the townsfolk killed every last one of the awful clan. Others claim that only Sawney survived, having somehow known that his time was almost up and having left before the townsfolk arrived. Ask someone else and you will hear that they moved further into the heart of the cliff, going further into the caves and caverns than normal people would ever dare and there are even those who believe that some of the clan moved to Wales and set up in a new set of caves. I've looked into it and there is information to support several of the views."

"But they would all be gone now anyway, right?" Sarah asked, with a twinge of fear in her voice.

Her mother pulled her in tight against her. "See, you always need to take things too far."

"What?" Sarah's father said, proclaiming his innocence.

Just at that point there was a bang on the side of the van, followed by some giggling.

"Daniel. Did you pay some kids to come over and scare us at the end of your story?" Sarah's mum asked.

"What no. How could I know when I'd finish? I didn't even know we were going to be telling scary stories. I'll go check. It's probably just some local kids having fun," he replied.

"No, you can't go outside and leave us here ourselves."

There was genuine fear in Sarah's mother's voice, causing Sarah to cuddle in close to her leg.

"Oh my god, woman, did the scary story get you all wound up? I'll be two minutes. You two find a movie for us to watch, and make some popcorn" and with that, he pulled his jacket on and was out the door, holding his flashlight.

Sarah and her mother had barely looked towards each other when they heard a scream from outside and then silence. It even seemed as if the rain had quietened down. Sarah's mother turned off the fire, which was the only light inside the van and crept up to the curtains next to the door. She peeled them aside and looked outside. There was no movement and no sign of her husband. After making her way around the van, peeking out from each curtain she knew that there was no way her husband would take a joke this far. She rushed to the room and dug her mobile phone out of her bag and called the police and then the site manager.

When the site manager got to their door he had to speak to Sarah's mum through the door for several minutes before she decided to open it and let him in. He had searched around outside and found no signs of Sarah's missing father. The police arrived shortly after and searched the area and come up with nothing else. All either of them could tell Sarah and her mother was that there were several sets of childlike footprints outside their caravan and it appeared that, even in the horrible weather, the kids had been barefoot. Sarah's mother went into hysterics. "He wouldn't just leave us. We heard a scream and then he was just gone. You have to find him."

While the police officers tried to calm her mother down, Sarah grabbed the spare torch and sneaked out of the van. She quietly closed the door behind her and walked a few steps before turning it on, but she knew the curtains were still closed anyway so she should be okay. It only took her a minute of searching before she came across some of the footprints. The rain was already beginning to wash them away but as she crouched closer, she gasped. Some of the footprints had six or seven toes.

The Burdens of the Father

Mark Matthews

JANIS placed his hand on his wife's belly and was certain he could feel the heartbeat of his baby inside. Tiny signs of life, *boom-boom*, beat inside each swirl of his fingerprints. He kept his hand wrapped around her navel until his whole body felt enveloped by the same warmness of her womb. He was already together with his child, both of them just waiting for birth, waiting to start their new life together. That day was coming soon.

"Go. Take your walk," Kathryn said. "Because once I cut this umbilical cord, you'll be the one attached to me."

It wasn't just her white robe that made her seem to glow, her aura radiated.

He took one last breath of his home air before opening the front door, and the outside air engulfed him like a sour pool. Deadness of the ocean filled the air, remnants of the dying seas, and each breath he took made him struggle for the next, hoping more oxygen might be inside.

Each step brought him closer to Mount Trashmore park, where the Nu-Air, rich with oxygen, was being released soon. He was just moments away from bliss, but this morning the serenity was shattered by the screeching words that got louder with each step.

"The hooves of the four horseman have trodden! Dust from barren ground will rise with the Lord's spirit. His light will shine life into the forgotten."

The man's screams hung over the park like a storm cloud. His wiry arms waved in the air and spread his words for all to hear. An unkept beard grew on his face, hiding the grime of one who could clearly not afford clean water. Janis squinted his eyes and braced himself for the heavens to eliminate this man. The **No-Nanny-State** drone high above was surely being alarmed by his brain waves and the toxic CO_2 being omitted by such a non-industrious being.

Yet nothing happened.

This should be an easy one. How had the old man even lasted this long without the **NNS** eliminating him? ***Capacity to be Fruitful and Generative,*** less than null. ***Capacity for Industry,*** gone. ***Capacity for Rageful Transgressions***, high. ***Degree of Stagnation,*** beyond repair. All of this certainly put him below the null state needed to live in this limited oxygen environment.

But the man could preach:

"Disease so strong it has infected the air. The new air coming is not like the new air of old. Skies will rain down and the dead shall rise up."

The nu-air was coming, he was right about that, it would be pumped through the vents at the crux of mid-day, the way the nation-state of America Redux had promised. Janis lived for this spot, this moment, right before it began, when the nu-air was about to start its cycle, and the clean oxygen would flow to his lungs. He imagined tiny little fila branches in his lungs, swaying back and forth like a sea anemone with each breath, to and fro, in and out.

"The Nu-Air is a spirit sedative!" his dad had warned him with words poetic, but Janis couldn't help but crave the clean rush to his lungs, the life in his blood, and the dreams it let grow in his head. It was unlike the old air that seemed full of sewage, clogged his nasal passages and made him cough up globs of black stained mucus.

The park of plastic greenery was crowded with others who shared this same craving. Janis imagined his wife, Kathryn, by his side, but didn't want her blissful spirit contaminated by the ash of the dead that dusted the ground. Tiny flakes of those who had been eliminated by the NNS always swayed in the wind when the Nu-Air is released.

"Don't let them know you are expecting a child," his dad had told him, "Let your child breathe at home, let him be born at home. A home birth delays facial and cardiac recognition by the NNS database. Keep him hidden long as possible."

Kathryn was growing either an Adam inside her, his choice of names, or a Noah, her choice. Both had the sounds from a better time gone by, and a new world coming, and ashes of the dead had no place at her feet.

"*Thus, says the LORD of hosts; behold, disaster shall go forth from nation to nation ... And at that day the slain of the LORD, shall be from one end of the Earth even to the other end of the Earth . . .*"

Janis wished the preacher man would spew his words elsewhere. A laser strike during mid-day right before his face would wreck this clean air moment. Elimination started with the tiniest of sparks, just an electric blink from the NNS in the clouds. Then the man would collapse into a pile of dust that stank like burnt hair. The remains of the haggard man would fall to the ground, and over the coming days, the wind would blow his ashes and mix him with others. The tiny flakes of the dead gathered on corners, on the bottoms of feet, and at times kicked up in the air to float. Janis didn't need that in his nostrils when the nu-air came.

"Elimination doesn't hurt," his dad had told him. "Consciousness is lost immediately. An atomic implosion occurs from your heartbeat. It takes a beating heart for them to make you implode, then we become anti-matter. Just atoms of God, just a spirit. But Janis, remember this: don't say *spirit* in public, **NNS** doesn't like that. And don't say *God*."

Janis never knew for sure if his father was eliminated due to **capacity for crime** or **uncorrectable stagnation** or some other perceived evil. His dad just didn't come home one day. "When you're in bliss, you don't want to work," his dad had warned, "you are no use to the state. Spiritually free is a null state to the material world, and you are no longer of use to the nation, for you waste oxygen."

When his dad spoke on this, he seemed to know his end was coming. "We must bear the burdens of our forefathers," were his last words spoken, but his edict to Janis, to have a home birth, to keep the green plants hidden, and to tell the true history of the nation to others, remains:

"The nation is trying to erase our history of the days before the Terraform when states polluted one another, wars were fought over clean air, and air purification forests were obliterated. Gas masks became a staple of the rich. The continent had to be nu-cleared, America Redux was born, and we are all a threat to the oxygen supply if we don't produce. They feed us so we keep the machine running, but these Nu-organic meals they give us are not food. They are not nourishment; they are an opioid for the soul that starts in your stomach. You ache when you don't have it, because it's a drug."

The gaunt preacher who danced and howled before Janis clearly had not eaten in a long while. His garments were a patchwork of rags and they hung on his slight frame as if he was a skeleton. Janis felt for a second that the man was an illusion, something that he alone could see and hear. His voice was a high pitch reaching different octaves than the droll humans who sat idly around him. The No-Nanny State drone in the sky seemed to ignore the haggard man as well, and Janis just watched as the ragged man hopped about and preached. This insane man had been left to live too long despite losing his mental capacity.

"You breathe the air of the state and become the state. Plants made of plastic turn us into plastic."

Janis was one of the rogue few who had seen real plants. Touched and lived with real plants. His dad grew one unregistered with equipment he called hydroponics used by underground plant growers for hundreds of years. The stem had such fresh greenness, and the bud was like a slowly opening eyelid peeking at him. As a child, he liked to caress it with his fingertip. It felt scratchy on his thumb but nice. More plants would come in its place, and Dad had grown a small bed of greenery, hidden out of sight.

"The plant releases oxygen, real and true, and that is why the state wants to control it. If all the females of the land could breathe such air, our race could start anew."

You were an enemy of the state, Dad, but what did it get you? You are gone, and I have no father. His dad had left him alone, forever. Janis saw his father only in a reoccurring dream. His dad would point his skinny finger in the air like there was an idea that Janis was missing and needed to look at. When Janis turned to look he would be shocked out of sleep and awake again to his fatherless world.

A world full of ash.

Janis shuffled his feet across the ground and imagined the ash on his feet was dad, come to say goodbye. Sometimes when he coughed up soot from the ashes of those who had been eliminated, he looked at the blob on the piece of tissue and wondered if it was parts of his father.

I'm about to be a dad myself, but I won't leave my child alone. I will learn how to get by living within the rules of the state. I will do enough to avoid elimination.

The sound of gears shifting rumbled through the park like a soft earthquake. Janis's head felt a sweet buzz from anticipating the fresh oxygen. Gears clicked and the hum of the blower began. The excitement started with a beat in his chest and spread warmth through his veins. The new air was seeping in. Glorious, glorious! Like a return to birth! Being reborn in a pool of freshness. Janis breathed in, smiled with contentment, and the dirty preacher man began to sing.

"*Thy dead shall live, my dead bodies shall arise. Awake and sing in triumph, ye that dwell in dust; for thy dew is the dew of the morning.*"

The air was indeed like the opiate that his dad had promised. Janis sucked through his nostrils like they were straws, and the air was an elixir of youth. A clean gas of ecstasy went deep into his lungs, filling them and expanding his chest cavity. He felt his blood with new oxygen reach his brain, and imagined it seeping into every tiny capillary, spreading fresh life into the nearly dead grey matter. The energy of the park was alive. People were smiling, softly swaying in unison. An orgy of fresh oxygen air over the next 30 minutes would be like a fantastic symphony.

If only Kathryn with child in womb could be here with him. Someday soon they would all be here, his son the newest CO_2 producing entity, but loved with such might, safely in his arms.

The machine churned the air, and the aging preacher man stopped bounding about, as if also silenced by the fresh oxygen. His skin pulsated with energy, beaming with power, well beyond any of the other pale, droll humans in the park. The power wasn't stopping, it was growing, ascending to higher pitches, new octaves, until an aura of deep blue rays shot from his flesh. He flapped his arms as if trying to fly. Small jet streams hit Janis's cheek. Dust and ash from the ground began to whirl. Tiny tornadoes began to spin in the park.

The park became full of tiny cyclones whipping up from the ground and rising towards the sky. Everything was sucked up within them. Whirlwinds of ashes congregated in the middle of each twister, the grey ash got darker, collected and gathered, until finally shapes appeared—human shapes, like mannequins. The bodies were first faceless but after the tornado spun faster and tighter a complete being appeared inside each one. Bodies made of ash came to life.

The first born had a face twisted in anguish and a mouth born of hunger. It snarled like a dog and turned to its side, where a bystander stood, oblivious, her nose turned to the air to breathe, her eyes closed, and her jugular exposed. The creature bit into her neck, blood sprayed forth, and the crimson red was the brightest color in the park.

The winds whipped and a dozen more beings appeared from the ashes. Their blank eyes were grey with anguish, their skin seemed broiled from fire. Their teeth nibbled on the necks of the remaining park dwellers like over-eager lovers. Their teeth seemed as sharp as sharks, slicing through skin. Blood dripped off their lips and colored their ash-grey bodies in red.

Janis sat silent and stunned, surrounded by the sounds of crunching bones and screams of terror. He saw families watch their loved ones destroyed. He saw human meat become fodder. He saw a small army of ash slaughtering the minions of the state too drunk on fresh air to scatter to safety.

And from the heavens, the **NNS** drone struck down with rapid fire shots, but the laser bursts had no effect on these beings reborn without a beating heart. Creatures kept springing forth from the swirl of ashes, and not a single zap from the NNS could bring them down.

The sight made him sick, and for the first time, Janis prayed the NNS would cause instant death, that these creatures could be zapped to ash, but they were immune, and the slaughter continued. The blood from the deaths made the new air stink.

If he wanted to live, he had to move. He needed to get home. He sprang into action, but after just one step, the aged preacher man stood before him and blocked his path. The pores of his skin became vast caverns. One eyeball bulged out of his socket and looked into his soul.

"You, you! You will finally know your purpose. This judgment is not just a passing notion but an action that is sweeping the cosmos."

The preacher had a shaky finger pointed at Janis, right at his heart, and he felt like an electric bolt would come not from the NNS in the sky, but from the man's finger, and it would end his life.

But it did not, and so he ran. The wind whirled in his ears. Urgency beat in his heart. The swooshing noise seemed to get into his skulls and explode. He felt in the middle of a storm front, cooler air in front of him, warmer behind. He sprinted with arms and legs blazing, and his lungs gasped for air. Sucking in all this oxygen and releasing CO_2 while he was not being industrious put him at risk of elimination, but none of that seemed to matter now for something bigger was happening. Behind him the cloud of ashes was swarming like a plague of locusts.

The wind fueled him home. He dashed the 200 yards to the front of his dwelling, yanked open the front door, and there was Kathryn right inside.

My God.

No.

Every fear he ever had was erased, his head emptied, his heart stopped.

There was Kathryn. Her brown hair was wet with sweat and stuck on her forehead. Her head was bowed. Her white robe was red and bloody, and so was the lifeless infant she cradled loosely in her arms. The scent in the room was foreign. Foul, even. Janis coughed, and a splattering of brown went into his mouth. He swallowed it down

There would be no crackling infant tears to announce the birth of his son. In its place was death. The silent terror of a stillbirth

With their dead son in between, he hugged Kathryn, but she herself seemed dead and absent from her body. She was beaten, her soul and backbone hung near lifeless in his arms. And she certainly had no idea what was going on outside their door

I forced this at-home birth. I killed my son. Dad, why did I listen to you?

At a state-facility this would have been done in a clean, well-lit place with equipment and monitors and a perfect excision. Even had his baby been entered immediately into the software of the state, he would at least be alive.

Janis stayed there lost in time. Seconds passed, or maybe centuries, it mattered not, until his front door swung open and the chaos of outside came pouring ins. A whirlwind of ashes and beings were sucked into his dwelling, a small group with the preacher man at the lead. The haggard man pulsated with energy like he was a celestial star. He stood before Janis and muttered one word.

"Son"

Janis was beaten, motionless, nauseous. The word SON hung in the air and Janis stared at the preacher in a trance. *Was he human or God? Was he made of flesh or ash?* Skinny nose, gaunt cheeks, deep-set passionate eyes. He seemed wise enough to call anyone younger than him SON.

"Son," he repeated.

Janis shook his head in disbelief.

"Yes, my dear son. You thought I had died. No lasers could stop my beating heart. We are here to start a new species and take back our land."

"Dad? That's you?"

"Yes, and you knew it was me from the start. You knew it the moment you saw me. Do not pretend you did not. And do not pretend you did not know what kind of child you were making here at home. A new set of lungs to help lead us. A new set of lungs to breathe in a new air, with a heart that is not registered, and will lead when I cannot. My lungs could not make it in this world. We needed someone new, born from a mother who breathed of the fresh, green plants. You did as I said, my son. The mindless followers who breath this Nu-air will be destroyed, and the children such as the one born from your wife will prosper"

"Dad, he's dead. It's too late. He did not live at all."

"His death was expected, but you can give him life. He may be dead, but he can be resurrected."

"What?" Janis felt his body turn from defeat to rage.

"We made this happen, you and I. We knew he would die at birth, but we can save him. Together. Channel your anger to strike me down. Kill me, kill your father. Act on that impulse. That is the way to help your savior child. Strike out against your father in rage, try and commit the ultimate crime, for we need ashes of his father's flesh, your flesh, to save him and make him one of us."

Kathryn was holding the carcass, rocking him as if bringing him back to life, but it was hopeless. Janis felt his lungs bleed and he coughed spastically.

He was done here. His life was over. His Dad's eyes said as much. Janis had been his dad's puppet all along.

Anger to murder wasn't hard. He imagined his fist smashing against his father's cheek. He thought about a sharp object at his dad's neck slicing through his aging skin. He thought of the head this nation-state of America Redux and how he wanted to destroy this whole complex of nu-air generating deities. He concentrated with all his might as if holding his breath and letting blood rush to his head. And then swung with the aim of killing the decrepit father.

His arm couldn't make impact before the NNS from the heavens struck.

His father had been right, elimination did not hurt, and consciousness of his body was lost but energy of his soul moved on. The explosion was indeed glorious, a wondrous freedom beyond what any nu-air oxygen could ever give him. To not have to breathe, to be one with the air and free from poisonous impurities. It was orgasmic. He felt as if he was a gas emitted by the purest of plants. Just the exhale of a green bud giving birth. Inside he cackled with tears of infinite joy.

And then he couldn't say if he saw it or felt it, but the remains of his ashes swirled in a cyclone. They whipped and whirled and spread through the air, and found their way into the airways of his infant child. Flesh of the old mixed with flesh of the new, and when his child's eyes opened, his body was not fueled by a beating heart, but by the burdens of his father.

The march of the revolution of ashes was led by a grey-haired leaping preacher and his newborn grandchild. They called him Adam.

Black Mill Cove

Lisa Morton

T was still dark, forcing Jim to pick his way through the treacherous thistles and spider webs by the narrow beam of his flashlight. He stumbled once, his boot caught in an overgrown rut, and then he found the dirt track that ran along the shoreline. Even though the season had just opened and this morning was one of the lowest tides of the year, he realized he was completely alone on the path, and he thought, *Maybe Maren was right – maybe this isn't such a good idea.*

He'd left his wife in the warm bunk back in the camper, but he knew she was only pretending to sleep; they'd argued the night before, and now she was giving him the well-honed Maren Silent Treatment. She'd read an article in the paper last week about two divers who had been attacked by a shark while abalone hunting. One man's arm had been ripped off and he'd bled to death in the boat before they'd made it back to shore.

"It says this happened about twenty minutes from Fort Ross, north of San Francisco," Maren had told him. "It's where we go, Jim."

"Honey, you know I don't dive," he'd tried patiently to remind her.

"You wear a wetsuit."

"You've been with me, Maren. We go at low tide and shore-pick. I've never been in water deep enough for a shark."

"But you always go alone, Jim. It's not safe."

Maren had already decided that she didn't want him to go, though, and the argument had ended very badly. She'd come with him on the winding three-hour drive from San Jose, but he knew she wouldn't make the two-mile hike down to the cove in the pre-dawn chill, and he hadn't asked her to. He just hoped that when he returned to the campground with a full limit of the rare shellfish, when they'd been cleaned and it was her turn, the sweet scent of the delicacy frying in butter would cause her to forget the argument.

It'd happened before. Too many times.

When they'd married, he'd made it clear that he was a hunter. Sure, he had a job, family, friends, other interests – but his life was about that oldest and most sacred of sports. Nothing made him feel so connected, so *pure*, as putting meat on the table, meat he'd taken with his own hands. The hunt was usually difficult, sometimes even tedious, but that always made the final victory that much more satisfying. In fact, Jim could have said that when he was out in the field, in pursuit of his prey, was the only time he really felt alive.

Maren had endured his hunting trips, but she never actually picked up a gun or fishing pole or catchbag. He supposed it was just the difference between men and women; men were by nature the hunters, women the gatherers. Still, he was constantly left mystified by her desires. Maybe a child…but when he'd suggested that, she'd told him she wasn't ready. He didn't understand what she was ready for. After five years of marriage, he still didn't understand.

He tried to stop thinking about Maren and their failing marriage as he hiked another mile along the thin dirt lane worn between the weeds. The sound of the surf was somewhere off to his left, and its quiet, without the pounding of an incoming tide, soothed him. The path veered to the right, but Jim spotted the fallen, gray tree limbs that he used as a signpost. He left the trail behind, once again picking his way through nettles and dying grass. He knew from experience that he would walk about two minutes before he came to the cliff, and he moved slower now, swinging the flashlight beam until he spotted the edge.

That was another thing Maren had argued with him about – the difficulty of reaching Black Mill Cove. After a three-hour drive on hair-pin curves along the frightening Highway 1, the cove was still another forty-minute trek from the campground. It was bounded by steep cliffs on three sides and open sea on the fourth; only one narrow ravine, half hidden by brush, offered a way down that didn't involve actual climbing. Jim liked to hunt alone; what if he got hurt down there, couldn't get back up? He'd tried to tell her, of course, that the cove's isolation was what made it ideal; in the three years since he'd found Black Mill Cove, he'd seen only one other hunter working it, and he'd been scuba diving. He knew he could always get his limit of the elusive abalone in the small cove.

By the time he pulled up at the cliff top above the sea, all thoughts of Maren had fled his mind, as he focused on the task before him. First he had to make his way cautiously along the edge until he spotted the patch of shrub that he knew marked the ravine. He stepped carefully around the brush, and lowered himself down onto a boulder three feet below it. He was in the ravine now, and he knew he'd have to find the rest of the way down by touch alone. He put the flashlight into his belt, and started down.

The ravine was choked with boulders that formed a natural, al-though steep, stairway down, and he made it to the bottom without inci-dent. The pungent smells of salt and exposed seaweeds and the volume of the surf noise, amplified here by the cliff walls, hit him as soon as he left the ravine, and he pulled the flashlight out again. By its light he saw the tide pools a few feet ahead of him, black water surrounded by encrusted rocks and gleaming, slippery kelp. He felt the thrill of the hunt gathering in him as he quickly lowered the backpack onto a hip-high flat rock, took off his outer hiking boots, checked his catchbag and iron, and, lastly, turned off his flashlight.

There was just the faintest hint of gray in the sky as he began picking his way over the slimy rocks and slick kelp. He heard tiny scuttlings around his feet, and the occasional sharp *pop* as he stepped on a floater bulb in the exposed seaweed. His eyes were already beginning to sting from the salt spray, so he lowered his mask, ignoring the snorkel. He walked until he thought he was about forty feet from shore and could just make out the darker shade of a large pool to his left. He lowered himself into the water until it was up to his waist, then began feeling under the rocks.

His gloved fingers brushed past spiny urchins and sucking anemones, and within minutes he was rewarded with the feel of a large shell. The creature was wedged several feet under the water, and to reach it with the iron he'd have to either hold his breath or use the snorkel. He decided to try the former, took a gulp of air, got a good heft on the iron, and ducked beneath the water.

He chipped the abalone's shell getting the iron under it, but finally jammed it under and began to pry. The abalone was strong and the position precarious, and his lungs were about to burst before he felt the strong shellfish foot give way. The abalone fell into his waiting hand, and he threw his head up out of the water.

It turned out to be only a medium-sized abalone, but it didn't pass through the gauge and he knew it was a keeper. With a feeling of satisfaction he placed the creature into his catchbag, and then continued hunting.

The first pool revealed no more treasures, and so he clambered to the next. This one was separated from the ocean by only a thin wedge of rock and weed, and it was a large, promising pool. He entered it, and began feeling under the outcroppings, keeping one hand on the exposed rock near his head. He didn't flinch when a crab as big as a salad plate sidled across his fingers.

He had found nothing under the first rock, and now turned to the next. This one had a long underwater slope away from him, and the water was up to his chin as he struggled to reach the back. He was working his way left to right when he felt something that was long, thick, with jointed shreds on one end.

It felt, in fact, like a bony human arm.

He jerked back as if bitten, his breath catching. He'd felt what he'd sworn were wristbones, then fingers, with some flesh still attached.

That was ridiculous. A severed arm in a tide pool? It had to be a strange weed, or driftwood branch, trapped there at the last high tide. Or it could be (*shark*) –

He looked around, panicked for a moment, suddenly wishing he'd waited until sunup to come down here. No, he'd wanted to be hunting while the tide was still going out, before it began its mad rush back to land. He'd had to come down here in the pre-dawn salty blackness. Alone.

It was just light enough now so that he could make out his own fingers, if he held them up close before him. He pulled the mask away, squinted painfully until tears welled and washed the brine from his eyes, then he forced himself to reach back under the rock.

He found the thing again, got a good grip around it and pulled. After a brief struggle it came free, and he brought up out of the water, held it up before his eyes.

It was, without question, a human arm.

He involuntarily cried out and dropped the thing. It was mostly bones, just a few tatters of skin or tendon still attached. The fingers seemed to be complete, and it ended about where the elbow would have started.

He backed frantically out of the pool, and up onto the rocks, his heart pounding, eyes tearing. He tried to scramble back more and fell flat as his feet slid on the kelp. The impact with the crusty rock, the pain as his gloves tore on the sharp facets of limpets and barnacles, jarred him enough to make him stop and consider the situation.

What the hell..how did…that get here?!

It had to be Maren's shark, right? He suddenly looked around and realized he was on the ocean side of the tide pool, peering out into barely-seen, gently sluicing waves. Seawood and driftwood bobbed here and there in the surf, sometimes breaking the surface like a head coming up out of the water. Or a fin.

He scrabbled backwards on all fours and into the pool again. The *plosh* of his own body hitting the water startled him, and with fresh panic he realized the arm was in this pool – wasn't that it brushing against his ankle? He cried out, throwing himself at the nearest rock and hauling himself up over the edge of it, then turning to the shore and crawling towards it.

He crawled a few feet before he was calm enough to think again, then he stopped to catch his breath (*fuck, I'm about to pass out!*), and think.

Okay, obviously I've gotta get back to the camper, wake up Maren, and drive to the campground offices. They'd tried their cellphones before from the campground, but there was no signal out here. Then, he supposed, he'd have to come back here and show the authorities where he'd found the arm. Of course the tide would be in by then, and they'd probably have to send out their own divers.

He hoped they had shark protection.

He had a plan, he knew what he had to do. He realized he'd somehow gotten to the far left edge of the cove, and from here the easiest way back to shore would be to simply wade through several large pools.

Several large pools which could hold more pieces.

He knew instantly he couldn't do it. What if the next pool held something worse than an arm, like a head, a half-skeletal head with a terrible grin…

He forced himself to think again. By the dreary light he could just barely pick out a path back to where he'd left his backpack – and the flashlight. He told himself to move slowly and cautiously, but he was shaking and it was harder to keep his balance –

His foot slipped and one leg went down into a pool.

Even though it was only up to his ankle, he snatched his foot back up as if it'd been thrust into liquid fire. He found himself peering into the water, then at the rocks around him. Any of those lengths of stripped, whitened wood could have been bone instead, those broken shells bits of nail or teeth…

He tried to stop shaking, but couldn't. Instead, he reached for a large driftwood branch (*too big to be anything human!*), which would serve as a walking stick. Using his newly acquired staff, he thrust into tricky patches of kelp or rock before setting foot there, and so finally came to the bottom of the ravine.

He let himself fall onto the flat rock as he threw the makeshift staff away. For a moment he just lay there, feeling relieved, feeling safe and alive. After a moment he stopped shaking. He was away from the tide pools and the terrible secrets he'd found there. He only had to climb the ravine, and he'd be safe.

He sat up, quickly opened the backpack long enough to get a towel to wipe his agonized eyes with, and was briefly surprised to see a black patch on the white towel; he was bleeding badly from a cut in his hand. He wrapped the towel around his palm, then pulled on his hiking boots, thrust his arms through the backpack straps, and started up the ravine.

It was light enough overhead now to see the top of the cliff as he clambered up over the rocks. He stopped occasionally to orient himself, then went on to the next rock. He was almost to the top when something blocked the light overhead. He looked up –

– and saw the shadow of a man standing there.

He started to call out, grateful for the presence of another (*living*) human being, but then something froze the shout in his throat, and he just stared instead.

The man overhead was carrying something, something big. It was black, and Jim thought it was probably a forty gallon plastic trash bag, the kind Maren used as a liner at home. Except this bag was stuffed, bulging with something.

What the hell, is this guy dumping his goddamn trash out here?!

The man hefted the bag, and Jim saw that it was obviously very heavy.

And then he knew.

Oh my god. Oh Jesus fuck, fucking hell –

The bag was full of body parts.

And the man was stepping down into the ravine with it.

Jim didn't know if the man knew he was there; he thought he didn't, yet. Jim's ascent had been quiet, and he was in the shadow of the ravine, in a black wet suit. But if the man hadn't seen him yet, he would certainly discover him in the narrow ravine –

– because he was coming down now, and was only five feet above Jim.

Jim instinctively began scrambling down backwards. There was no place to hide in the ravine, but maybe if he could get to the cove, to a boulder or a tidepool …

At least maybe he could reach the thick branch of driftwood he'd thrown aside, the one that had made a nice staff…or club.

The man above him was moving slowly, trying not to rip the overfilled bag, and that gave Jim a slight advantage, even though he was moving in reverse. He reached the big flat rock where he'd rested only moments before, dropped beside it in a crouch, and felt around until his fingers closed on the reassuring bulk of the branch. Then he started working his way to the left, pressed against the rocky slope of the cliff.

He heard a small rattling of pebbles and jerked to a stop, his stomach in his throat, until he realized the sound had come from the other man, losing his footing and tearing a few pebbles loose from the wall of the ravine. He heard the man curse under his breath, then saw him emerge from the ravine, stepping onto the large flat rock and setting the bag down there to rest.

Jim's heart was pounding in his ears as he dropped to a crouch, although there was no boulder to hide him. He could see the man because he was outlined by the sky, and because the man had now removed his own small penlite from a pocket. If the man turned the penlite in Jim's direction…

He didn't. He turned the ray on the tide pools before him, hefted the bag, and stepped off the rock, evidently intent on his task.

Jim knew he had two options now, the classic dilemma of fight or flight. He could try to wallop the man with his branch, but if the guy heard him and was armed, Jim would be dead. Or he could try to make it up the ravine before he was discovered; he knew that if he waited much longer, the lightening sky would point him out like a spotlight. He had to choose quickly.

He decided to opt for the latter, but thought he should wait until the man was as far away from the ravine as possible. Jim was young, and could probably outrace the man even if he were discovered, but again – if the man were armed…It was the only real choice. Jim slid out of the cumbersome backpack, since it would slow him down. Then he waited, kneeling beside the cliff wall, his eyes riveted to the man with the bag as he picked his way down to the first large tide pool. Once there, he set the bag down, reached in, pulled something out –

(*oh jesus it's a leg, it's a fucking leg*)

– and put it carefully down into the tide pool. Once he'd placed it there, he reached behind him, and Jim guessed he was finding another rock to use as a weight, to hold the limb down under the water. Where it would be when the tide came again, bringing with it the sea creatures that would quickly and efficiently dispose of the evidence, leaving only a few bones that would probably never be found in this isolated cove...

Jim suddenly sprang to his feet and ran for the ravine.

It was a bad, clumsy run, and he knew it, knew it with the same certainty that told him he was about to die. Still, he had a chance, clumsy didn't matter if he was just quiet –

He slipped sideways and banged against a rock. The forgotten ab-alone dying in his catchbag rattled loudly, so loudly.

As Jim scrambled desperately to his feet, the penlite beam flickered across him.

For a moment he was paralyzed, and the only thought in his head (*deer in the headlights!*) was ridiculous. Then he realized the man was turn-ing towards him, trying to run across the unstable tide pools. The man was also reaching into a pocket, and the penlite flickered across – not the barrel of a gun, but a knife blade.

Of course he has a knife. You don't carve people up with a gun.

Jim started to run, but saw he'd never make the ravine in time. So he stopped and hefted his club up in both hands –

– and the man advancing on him stopped.

Jim had only one brief second of surprise before the man seemed to re-evaluate him, and started forward again. Suddenly the penlite beam stabbed into his eyes, blinding him. He nearly reached up to block the light, but instead swung the branch blindly.

And felt it hit something solid. He heard a grunt of painfully ex-haled air from the other man, and a clatter as the man went down. But when he heard the man curse ("Fuck!"), he knew he hadn't knocked him out, and the man would be on him in a second, with that knife.

Jim backed away – towards the tide pools, since the other man had fallen between him and the ravine – and raised the branch again.

The other man turned off the penlite now and tossed it aside, and Jim realized there was enough light now that he could make out some of the man's features. He was slightly older than Jim, but not much, and was wearing dark sweats and sneakers. His most noticeable feature, of course, was the knife in his hand.

He suddenly jumped forward, and Jim stepped aside, the knife slicing the air where Jim's body had just been. Jim tried to swat at the man with the branch, but he missed and was thrown off-balance. He caught himself just as the other man came down above him, and Jim tried to roll aside but wasn't fast enough. The knife caught him in the shoulder.

The pain was immense, but not paralyzing, and Jim swung the branch at the other man's feet. The branch connected and the man was thrown sideways. He went down in a jumble of rocks, and groaned. Jim got to his own feet, teeth clenched against the pain in his torn shoulder, and he staggered backwards. Then his boots caught on something and he went down –

– into the plastic bag.

He cried out as the bag burst around him, releasing an acrid stew of gore and limbs. He batted and kicked and clawed his way back from the gruesome mess, and this time was grateful when he fell into a tide-pool, of cleansing saltwater. He splashed up out of the pool as he saw the other man rise. He wasn't sure, but he thought there was something black on the man's head that might have been blood.

He started to heft the branch, and realized, with fresh horror, that it had cracked somewhere along the line and was nothing but a useless, footlong piece of lightweight driftwood. He tossed it aside and frantically looked around for something else he could use – another branch, a boulder, even a sharp piece of shell…

And the other man was on him then.

Jim caught his arm as he swung it down with the knife, and they both went down on the rocks, Jim's back colliding painfully with a grapefruit-sized boulder. Their elbows slipped on a length of kelp, and the knife blade drew sparks as it ground along an outcropping. Jim found enough strength to throw the other man off, and his hand found a weight at his side, a weapon he'd forgotten about: The abalone iron. When his opponent regained his feet, Jim was waiting. He brought the iron down on the man's head as he rushed Jim. There was an especially gratifying *crack*!, and the man went down.

This time he didn't groan or move, and Jim knew that, at the very least, his blow had knocked the man out, maybe killed him.

He didn't wait to find out.

He took off for the ravine, regardless of how many times his feet slipped or stumbled. He reached the ravine and forgot about his backpack or his wounded hand and shoulder. He hauled himself up out of the ravine, and before he knew what had happened, he was running down the dirt track towards the camper, out of breath but aware that he'd made it.

He paused long enough to turn, to be sure the man wasn't behind him. His lungs were burning, and when he saw that there was no pursuit, he stopped, doubled over to catch his breath. And before he knew or understood, he was laughing. He laughed at the sheer sense of relief, of victory. This time he'd been the hunted, and he'd escaped. He'd confronted death and lived to tell Maren about it.

Maren…wait until he told her. He turned and started running for the camper again, a smile still creasing his face.

Maybe I'll be a hero. Maybe there's a reward. Won't Maren love that, when her friends see my picture in the paper…?!

He finally turned and ran unthinkingly through the brush, heedless this time of stinging nettles and grasping roots. He saw the campground in the dawn light, his camper truck the lone resident.

"Maren!" he started calling, even though he knew he was still too far for her to hear.

"Maren!" he called again, as he jogged up to the truck and around the driver's side to where the camper door was.

And then he staggered and stopped.

The camper door was hanging open, creaking slightly in the morning breeze, and there was blood. Lots of it, great gouts around the door and the stepdown and the pavement. A thick swath of it led off a few feet and then disappeared. After that there were only a few bloody footprints leading off into the brush, footprints made by a pair of men's sneakers.

Jim couldn't bring himself to look inside. It wouldn't do any good, because he knew Maren wasn't in there, at least not most of her. He knew where she was, and what had happened to her.

And as he realized just how badly he'd lost he began to scream in the chill morning air.

Down to a Sunless Sea

Neil Gaiman

THE Thames is a filthy beast: it winds through London like a snake, or a sea serpent. All the rivers flow into it, the Fleet and the Tyburn and the Neckinger, carrying all the filth and scum and waste, the bodies of cats and dogs and the bones of sheep and pigs down into the brown water of the Thames, which carries them east into the estuary and from there into the North Sea and oblivion.

It is raining in London. The rain washes the dirt into the gutters, and it swells streams into rivers, rivers into powerful things. The rain is a noisy thing, splashing and pattering and rattling the rooftops. If it is clean water as it falls from the skies it only needs to touch London to become dirt, to stir dust and make it mud.

Nobody drinks it, neither the rain water nor the river water. They make jokes about Thames water killing you instantly, and it is not true. There are mudlarks who will dive deep for thrown pennies then come up again, spout the river water, shiver and hold up their coins. They do not die, of course, or not of that, although there are no mudlarks over fifteen years of age.

The woman does not appear to care about the rain.

She walks the Rotherhithe docks, as she has done for years, for decades: nobody knows how many years, because nobody cares. She walks the docks, or she stares out to sea. She examines the ships, as they bob at anchor. She must do something, to keep body and soul from dissolving their partnership, but none of the folk of the dock have the foggiest idea what this could be.

You take refuge from the deluge beneath a canvas awning put up by a sailmaker. You believe yourself to be alone under there, at first, for she is statue-still and staring out across the water, even though there is nothing to be seen through the curtain of rain. The far side of the Thames has vanished.

And then she sees you. She sees you and she begins to talk, not to you, oh no, but to the grey water that falls from the grey sky into the grey river. She says, "My son wanted to be a sailor," and you do not know what to reply, or how to reply. You would have to shout to make yourself heard over the roar of the rain, but she talks, and you listen. You discover yourself craning and straining to catch her words.

"My son wanted to be a sailor.

"I told him not to go to sea. I'm your mother, I said. The sea won't love you like I love you, she's cruel. But he said, Oh Mother, I need to see the world. I need to see the sun rise in the tropics, and watch the Northern Lights dance in the Arctic sky, and most of all I need to make my fortune and then, when it's made I will come back to you, and build you a house, and you will have servants, and we will dance, mother, oh how we will dance…

"And what would I do in a fancy house? I told him. You're a fool with your fine talk. I told him of his father, who never came back from the sea – some said he was dead and lost overboard, while some swore blind they'd seen him running a whore-house in Amsterdam.

"It's all the same. The sea took him.

"When he was twelve years old, my boy ran away, down to the docks, and he shipped on the first ship he found, to Flores in the Azores, they told me.

"There's ships of ill-omen. Bad ships. They give them a lick of paint after each disaster, and a new name, to fool the unwary.

"Sailors are superstitious. The word gets around. This ship was run aground by its captain, on orders of the owners, to defraud the insurers; and then, all mended and as good as new, it gets taken by pirates; and then it takes shipment of blankets and becomes a plague ship crewed by the dead, and only three men bring it into port in Harwich…

"My son had shipped on a stormcrow ship. It was on the homeward leg of the journey, with him bringing me his wages – for he was too young to have spent them on women and on grog, like his father – that the storm hit.

"He was the smallest one in the lifeboat.

"They said they drew lots fairly, but I do not believe it. He was smaller than them. After eight days adrift in the boat, they were so hungry. And if they did draw lots, they cheated.

"They gnawed his bones clean, one by one, and they gave them to his new mother, the sea. She shed no tears and took them without a word. She's cruel.

"Some nights I wish he had not told me the truth. He could have lied.

"They gave my boy's bones to the sea, but the ship's mate – who had known my husband, and known me too, better than my husband thought he did, if truth were told – he kept a bone, as a keepsake.

"When they got back to land, all of them swearing my boy was lost in the storm that sank the ship, he came in the night, and he told me the truth of it, and he gave me the bone, for the love there had once been between us.

"I said, you've done a bad thing, Jack. That was your son that you've eaten.

"The sea took him too, that night. He walked into her, with his pockets filled with stones, and he kept walking. He'd never learned to swim.

"And I put the bone on a chain to remember them both by, late at night, when the wind crashes the ocean waves and tumbles them on to the sand, when the wind howls around the houses like a baby crying."

The rain is easing, and you think she is done, but now, for the first time, she looks at you, and appears to be about to say something. She has pulled something from around her neck, and now she is reaching it out to you.

"Here," she says. Her eyes, when they meet yours, are as brown as the Thames. "Would you like to touch it?"

You want to pull it from her neck, to toss it into the river for the mudlarks to find or to lose. But instead you stumble out from under the canvas awning, and the water of the rain runs down your face like someone else's tears.

Devourer

Andrew Lennon

PETE and his family were on holiday in Malta. It was the second day of their escape to the sun, one the family rarely experienced together.

A true family holiday.

Pete's father spends his days as an accountant, working long hours, so Pete was lucky to see him for an hour or two at night. His mother was a hairdresser; luckily her salon closed early so Pete was one of the fortunate kids who could go home from school and his mother would be there waiting. They decided to go and spend the day at Golden Bay beach. It was one of Malta's most popular beaches, set among the countryside and is relatively undeveloped. It has a café-restaurant along with a games room. The beach itself is renowned for its beautiful view of the sunset. Pete didn't know it, but his cousins had also gone on holiday to Malta with their parents. Both sets of parents had arranged to meet up; it would be a nice surprise for the children.

When they arrived, Pete's aunt, uncle and cousin were already there. They hadn't been there long as they began putting down towels on sunbeds and trying to adjust the parasol so James, Pete's uncle, could sit in the shade.

* * *

"*Sarah!*" Pete shouted when he saw his cousin, a huge grin of excitement washed over his face. He sprinted over to her, leaving his parents to carry their bags along the sand. Sarah shared Pete's excitement. When she saw him, she clutched him in a big hug and lifted him from the ground, partly a sign of affection, but also a slight reminder to him that she was older, and still bigger. Pete didn't care. He was just happy to have someone on holiday that he knew. Holidays were always fun, but not when you have to go on days out and leave the few friends you have made behind at the hotel.

Pete greeted his aunt with a hug and his uncle with a handshake as was always the custom. It had to be a firm handshake as well. His grandad had always told him that you can judge a man by his handshake. Never trust a man who shakes with a limp hand.

* * *

"Hello, Melanie," Pete said, looking curiously at the man that was rubbing sun lotion on her back. Melanie was Sarah's older sister. She had turned twenty-one a few months ago so to Pete she was really old. He didn't recognise the strange man with her, though.

"Hi, Pete." Melanie looked up and smiled from the sunbed. "This is Roger."

"Nice to meet you, Pete," Roger smiled and shook his hand, with a firm but slippery grip. Pete looked at his hand in disgust and wiped it on his shorts.

"Sorry about that," Roger laughed, holding up his slick hands. "Sun cream."

"Oh, yeah," Pete laughed as well. "Well, nice to meet you."

Sarah threw the beach ball at Pete's head. It bounced off and knocked her mother's drink over, soaking her towel in cold Pepsi.

"For God's sake, Sarah! Now there's going to be ants all over the place."

"I'm sorry," Sarah pouted. "I was just throwing the ball to Pete to see if he wanted to play for a bit."

"Well you should..."

"Hey, I'll play with you," Roger butted in quickly, defusing the scalding that Sarah was taking. He picked up the ball and ran over to an empty space in the sand. "Hey, Pete. Are you playing?"

Roger and the two children were laughing and joking while throwing and kicking the beach ball to each other. They had asked Melanie to play, but she refused, telling them that she had to lie down to ensure she got a full, even tan. They laughed at her and continued their game.

"You know, Melanie. He's great with kids," Jenny said.

"He's just perfect, isn't he?" Melanie smiled as she gazed at Roger.

"So, when is yours coming?"

"*What!*" Melanie shouted loud enough to make everyone stop what they were doing for a second. Jenny laughed.

"I'm not having kids until I'm at least thirty." Melanie said, matter of factly.

"Well, just putting it out there."

"Well I'm *not* putting out," Melanie confirmed with a giggle.

Roger kicked the ball so it flew over Pete's head and rolled into the waves coming onto the beach. Pete ran to retrieve the ball. Speeding along in front of him, with water firing behind it, was a red jet ski. It bounced and bobbed along the waves.

"Whoa." Pete stood with the beach ball in his hand.

"*Pete, bring the ball back!*" Sarah called, but Pete didn't hear her. His eyes didn't move away from the jet ski. It was the coolest thing he had ever seen. It was like a motorbike, but on water. He imagined himself as James Bond chasing after bad guys, no chance of anyone escaping in a speedboat. He would catch them on his jet ski.

"Cool aren't they," Roger said, suddenly standing beside him and bringing Pete out of his daze.

"Yeah, they're amazing! I want to go on one."

"You can," Sarah said. "There's a guy over there that you pay for a ride."

"Really?" Pete asked. He looked in the direction Sarah was pointing. She was right, he couldn't believe he hadn't noticed them earlier. There, just sitting on the shore were a whole bunch of jet skis. Pete didn't even look back at Sarah, let alone say anything else to her. He sprinted to ask his parents if he could go and rent one of the jet skis.

"Please," Pete begged.

"I said no!" His father, David, scowled.

"Well, perhaps if we just…." Jenny, Pete's mother started.

"No. I don't have a good feeling about them." David responded then continued to read his book.

"Sorry, Pete," Jenny said. "If Dad says no, then its no."

Pete looked at his feet in disappointment. Melanie looked at Pete's face and felt sorry for him. She stood up from her sunbed.

"You know," Melanie whispered, but so loud that everyone could still hear. "Roger is a lifeguard. So he can take him. He'll be perfectly safe."

Pete's mouth opened from ear to ear with a huge grin.

"Roger is a lifeguard?" He asked in a high pitch screech of excitement. "Can he take me, please, please, please?" He dropped to his knees and begged. He could feel the sand burning them but he wouldn't rise. Not until he was given an answer.

"Well it's not fair to dump it on Roger like that is it?" David said.

Roger picked up his drink, only arriving at the tail end of the conversation. "What's not fair on me?"

"For you to take Pete on the jet skis," Melanie said. "I told them that you're a lifeguard so he'll be safe."

"Yeah, I'm fully qualified." Roger said. "Starting my own business soon to train lifeguards and swim teachers. He'll be fine with me, David. Plus, there is a jet bike we can rent, specifically designed to have two people on it."

"See, Dad! *See.*" Pete silenced quickly at the glare from his father.

"I'm not happy about this," David mumbled.

"Come on, love." Jenny put her arm around David "It's all part of the holiday isn't it. Just let them have their fun."

"If anything happens I…"

"Nothing will happen, they'll be fine," Jenny re assured.

"Fine," David spat.

"Fine? As in yes?" Pete asked.

"Yes! Fine!" David shouted. "But be bloody careful."

Roger smiled. "Come on, Pete. Let's go and see how much it is."

After paying the man in charge of the jet skis they were led to a roped off area where they waited for the man to pull the jet bike into the water. Roger climbed on first and then, with a little help from the man, Pete climbed on too. As instructed, he wrapped his arms around Roger's stomach. It was difficult at first as they were both wearing life jackets, but once he'd gotten himself seated comfortably, Pete was fine.

* * *

Roger revved the engine and before he knew it, Pete was speeding across the water. The wind was blowing in his face, along with a salty spray of water from the sea. The adrenaline rush was fantastic.

"*Woohhhhoo*," Pete screamed.

"*Are you having fun there, Pete?*" Roger shouted above the roar of the waves, but Pete could barely hear him over the wind.

"*Wooo hooo!*" Pete screamed again.

He looked around to see that there were other people on jet skis racing across the water as well. Pete thought about waving for a second but then decided against it as he was too scared to let go in case he fell off.

They rode into a wave which sent the ski bouncing into the air. Pete giggled and screamed with excitement. Roger let out a manly yell. "Yeah!"

The pair laughed as they sped along. Pete glanced to the side; he could see another one of the skiers pacing along the water with them. The man riding it had long black hair. It was flying about in the wind behind him. A spray of water went into Pete's eyes forcing him to close them. The salt stung and he had to blink repeatedly until the sting calmed down a bit. He was able to look to the side again just in time to see the other jet ski crash into the side of them.

Pete flew through the air like a rag doll. He was unconscious before he hit the water. The life jacket, which now became evident was bought on the cheap from the jet ski vendor, had ripped and simply slid off of Pete's floating body. Pete slowly began to sink. By the time Roger came to, his life jacket still intact, Pete was nowhere to be seen.

The long talons gripped tightly around Pete's ankle, pulling him further down into the depths of the ocean. Pete slowly started to come around. He looked to his surroundings, he could see that he was under water. But then why wasn't he drowning? He felt something tight on his ankle.

*   *   *

"Ouch! Let go of me!" he screamed.

Again, Pete felt shocked and confused at the fact that, not only had he not drowned, but it appeared that he was able to both breathe and speak under water. His attention returned to the thing around his ankle.

It definitely looked like a hand, of some sort. The finger nails looked really long. Pete tried to learn forward to get a better look but suddenly he was surrounded by complete darkness.

"Ahhh, Help! *Help!*" He cried "*Where am I?*"

"This is the meeting space," something slurped in response. "You'll pass through soon enough."

"What do you mean the meeting space?" Pete asked. "Let me go!"

"Oh, I don't have hold of you," a slurped wet giggle followed. "I don't even have any hands."

"What's got me then? Can you get it loose? And why can't I see anything?"

"So many questions at once. You do not want to know what has got hold of you, it's best you don't know. It's easier that way, for you at least. I cannot get it loose, I am not so stupid as to even try. And you cannot see because you are in the meeting space. As I've already told you."

Pete tried to swim away, but whatever it was that had hold of him was strong. His efforts amounted to nothing. He didn't even feel the momentum in his movement shift slightly. He gave up almost instantly, he didn't need any longer to see that it was useless.

"OK, so what's the meeting space?" Pete asked. As he did, his surrounding gradually started getting lighter.

"That darkness above you is the meeting space."

"Yes, but why is it *called* the...." Now the light had returned to normal, Pete was able to get a good look at the thing he'd been talking to. He tried to scream, but nothing came out. He was frozen with fear. The face, which was mere inches away from his own, was like nothing he had ever seen. It had teeth like long pointed fingers. They curled up around its mouth with more entwined curling below. It had small beady black eyes. As it had already told Pete, it had no arms. Only small fins. It looked like a fish, but its face was almost human. Besides the long teeth and beady eyes, the rest of the features were the same. A normal forehead, what looked to be normal lips, cheeks, chin? It even had ears.

"Please don't hurt me, please, please," Pete cried.

"I am no threat to you," The thing slurped. "Please do not judge me by my appearance, down here. It is you that looks strange."

"I, I suppose," Pete said. Now composing himself a little bit.

"Anyway. It's not me you need to be scared of, it's him." The thing gestured with its head.

Pete looked down to the thing that was dragging him. He couldn't see anything except for a large, muscular arm and fin, but it was a large fin. The only thing Pete could think of that had a fin of that size was a shark, which meant whatever was dragging him was at least the size of a shark. He tried again to swim away, but it was no use.

"I thought you would have learned by now that it's too strong for you."

"What is it? And what is this place? Is this still the meeting?"

"No, the meeting is that dark bit up there. It's where your world meets our world. You people never usually see it because once it gets so dark then there appears to be nothing. You assume there is nothing. Your ignorance keeps us safe down here."

"Well, where is *here?*

"Here is our home. There is no other name for it."

"OK, and what is that thing dragging me. And why the hell am I not dead then if I've been dragged all the way to the depths of the ocean?"

"We call it Boreas. I don't know why you can breathe, all of the things it drags from your world can breathe down here. I think it's something to do with the long talon that he stabs into your misshaped hand."

Pete looked at his hands. He couldn't see any markings at all.

"What did he stab into me? I can't see anything, and what the hell does Boreas mean?"

"Not those hands, stupid. Those ones down there."

"Oohhh, you mean my feet. Well what the hell did he stab me with?"

"I already told you, its talon." The being slurped.

"Well I can't feel anything?"

"That does not mean it hasn't happened."

"Yeah, I guess. OK, so why do you call it Boreas? What does that mean?"

"Devourer."

Pete's eyes widened with fear. He realised now that whatever this thing was, it was dragging him down here so that it could eat him.

"*Please! Please let me go. I don't want to die!*"

"It's no use. It, unlike me, does not have ears. That's why it does not speak."

"Where is it taking me?"

"To its lair. We're not far now."

Pete cried. He couldn't think of anything else to do. There was no point in struggling because this thing was too strong. No point shouting because it couldn't hear him, and if it could, Pete was sure that it wouldn't care about anything he had to say anyway.

"What are you called?" the thing slurped.

"Pete. My name is Pete. What about you?"

"I am Sqonk. You don't look like the last Pete that it dragged down here. And that one didn't say it was a Pete."

"Huh, what do you mean? What did it say I was?"

"It said *it* was a Michael. But it looked just like you. Had the weird bottom hands and everything."

"You mean it's had more than just me!"

"No, you are the first Pete. Do you taste the same as a Michael?

"What? What the hell do you mean do I taste…"

* * *

Pete's sentence was cut off when the creatures large curved teeth ripped into his cheek. He clutched his face and screamed out in pain. He could see the water around him changing colour. A mix of blood red added to it.

"What are you doing?" Pete cried.

The creature attacked again. Pete tried to protect his face, but the large teeth were so sharp. When he put his hand out, a finger was ripped off. Pete stared at his hand in shock, looking at his missing digit. It was too late before he could see the next attack coming. Again another chunk was taken from his cheek, but this time his eye was taken with it. Pete howled like a wild animal. The pain was too much to bare.

"Ahhh, why? *Why? Please.*"

A loud growling noise came from below him.

"Have to eat," his attacker slurped.

For a second, Pete heard a crunching sound. Was that his eyeball? He couldn't think anymore. The pain was too great. He could feel himself slipping out of consciousness, perhaps it was better this way.

"No," Pete encouraged himself. No matter how hard it seems. I'll survive this."

He looked down below him, as best he could, his vision being greatly impaired now. Even with his remaining eye, flashes of white came with searing pain. The nerves within his socket were still very active. He managed to get a glimpse further down again.

Past the huge fin, he couldn't see any sort of end, but there was a strange hole in the water. Had it been land he would have guessed it was a tunnel. But this just seemed to float in the middle of the water. The Boreas disappeared into the hole. Before Pete knew it he was also dragged in and then was surrounded again by complete darkness.

The grip left Pete's ankle, but before he was able to move something was strapped across the top of his body and pinned his arms to his side. Pete could see nothing, he could hear nothing. He had no idea as to where the Boreas was or what it was doing. How long until he was going to be devoured.

It's fine. I've just been knocked unconscious in the crash. Any minute now I'm going to wake up lying on the beach, or in the hospital after being saved. It's fine. Soon enough I'll wake up.

CRUNCH.

The loud noise was followed by excruciating pain in Pete's legs, he couldn't feel anything below his waist.

CRUNCH.

Another blinding pain, this time in his stomach. He knew now that he was being eaten. He managed half a scream before he was gone completely, devoured.

*   *   *

After days of search and rescue teams looking for Pete. Helicopters with heat searching radars, a team of diving squads. They gave up, there was no way he could be out there that long and survive.

They gave his family the only thing they had managed to find. His lifejacket.

A Quickee

John Skipp

RIGHT, wide-open and china-blue, her eyes were the first things they went for. Then she tried to scream, and her mouth parted wide, and a few of the larger ones rifled down her throat.

In less than a second, they had her name. Barbara.

She started to flailing, in liquid slow-motion: long hair and long limbs, wafting and waving in what bordered on grace. She choked, and they went up her nose as well.

They listened to her panic: the only thoughts she had.

In less than three seconds, the poison began to take effect; her body, and all of its openings, went slack. They had open access to all the doorways in her skull, no restrictions on the tight gaps in her scant bikini bottoms, absolute liberty with all the portals of her flesh.

Her dying mind was numb and softly sinking, like her body. They listened, while her gentle tongues of memory lapped over them in waves...

...and Larry was still looking at her like that, with those fuck-me eyes and that connoisseur smile. And Bob was still back at the cottage, no doubt; suspecting everything, sure of nothing, trying to drag himself through a Mack Bolan novel that was over his head while her first bar room Romeo in fifteen years stripped down to his Speedos on the damp wooden planks...

The blood was coming now, copious and thick, absorbed and concealed by the blackness that surrounded her.

They filled her brain. They filled her belly.

And just as her life began to flicker out entirely, they made her rise up from the depths.

*   *   *

It was dark, with only the half-moon's mellow light to shine upon them. The cottage-window gleamings from across the lake might just as well have been sent from the stars.

Larry wavered at the edge of the pier, looking down. The night was not warm, and the goosebumps that speckled his flesh were not entirely from anticipation. *An hour, on the outside, before hubby comes a-hunting,* he mused, *and she has to jump in the goddam water. I can't believe it. She must want to get caught!*

It was just stupid enough to be true. He didn't like it. She was gorgeous, yes. And hot to trot. But she wasn't worth fighting over.

None of them were.

He was thinking back to the bar, and the blonde he'd passed up on, when Barbara's head broke the surface. Backlit by the moon, her features were indistinguishable. He couldn't make out her toothy grin, the nipples she exposed to him with softly-kneading hands.

He couldn't see that her eyes were gone.

NO SWIMMING AFTER DARK read the signs that ran up and down the length of the beach. Larry deferred to the bulge in his Speedos.

"How's the water?" he asked.
And she said it was fine.

Dark Skies

Jason Stokes

Dark skies. Clouds gathered, turning the horizon a grayish black mass even before the train reached the station. On the platform, he checked his phone. Early droplets smattered the screen, distorting colors, gathering along the crack that bisected the glass. The radar had shown an hour before rains reached this part of the coast. Now it showed thirty minutes. Forecasters had moved up their warnings.

The winds were already here, pushing him around the sidewalk, tearing at his clothes as he crossed the empty intersection. The bell of the train was lost in its roar as it left the station, making the final run of the night. He was alone, windows boarded up, doors locked, the streets were abandoned as the sky turned prematurely dark. The firehouse was quiet. Even emergency crews had made their final rounds, retreating once again to safety until it was over.

Safety is exactly where he would be if the mechanic had bothered to finish the repairs he started over a week ago on schedule. A dented hood and a busted headlight were not exactly an overhaul, but the man, with a slow manner and greasy tone, insisted there was paperwork to sign for insurance purposes and parts to order. The parts were bullshit and he had told him that. The paperwork, they avoided, with an extra hundred bucks on the bill. It was robbery, but if he wanted to deal with insurance companies, he would have gone to a reputable shop, not one recommended through a friend with experience in these matters. Insurance agents asked too many questions.

The hundred was enough to get a promise to finish by the weekend. This weekend. But that was before the hurricane made an unexpected turn north and placed Norfolk square in her sights, wasn't it?

The first time in his adult life without a vehicle to drive and there was a hurricane. Figures. He knew the route, had been walking it every day for a week. A straight shot down Colley, through the park and right on Graydon. If he went quickly, it would take twenty minutes at the most. He checked the time on the cracked screen. Twenty-five minutes to landfall but that was several miles south of here. There was time. The wind gusted, pushing from behind, as if urging him on.

The first two blocks swiftly passed, blending to the colonial era architecture of the Ghent district. What rain there was stung his skin, perhaps hail starting early. Head down, he fought against the swirling wind that came at once from behind, then the side, pushing him around the sidewalk, redirecting tiny bits of icy rain to pelt his face and neck. The jacket, though leather, protected against rain but only weakly battling the biting cold that rushed in off the ocean. He kept his head low, hiding as much as possible from the chilly wind and stinging rain.

He didn't notice the woman on the sidewalk, a dark figure standing still against a fast fading light, until they were a block apart. Head bowed, she looked like a lamp post, another piece of scenery bracing for the incoming assault. She hadn't seen him approach, hadn't moved at all. At the corner, he turned right, took a side street that would redirect

136

through an area known as "the greens" but not add any significant time to the route. Better safe than sorry.

The side road ended at a block-wide swath of manicured green park down the center of an upscale neighborhood. Rebranded and sold as a park, there were giant old-growth trees and benches for watching the ducks, or whatever it was people did over here. It was truncated by a spillway for the Elizabeth river, at least a hundred feet or more wide, designed to protect from the kind of surges they would see today. The man-made waterway, its low cement walls already sloshing high with water, forced him to turn left and start towards home. He found himself entranced by the normally serene surface as ribbons of wind snaked from one side to the other. Breaking free, he shook it off and trudged uphill.

The rain thickened. The steady patter shifted to a consistent plopping of larger drops that burst on the concrete and ran down his neck, creating icy rivers on his spine.

He should have called out of work. Approaching the top of the first hill where the ground leveled out, he regretted the decision to go in. But that would have drawn attention, wouldn't it? People would start asking questions, questions he could do without. Joke was on him of course, half the office had called in, the other half left early to beat the traffic, to be home with family in warmth and security. How much had he stood out, being the last to leave? Who would notice, would wonder why he wasn't in a hurry to get home?

He forced the thoughts away. No time to worry about possibilities. At the corner he checked both ways, out of habit, knowing it was pointless. No cars braved these streets. To the left he eyed the corner where the woman had been. Empty. She was gone.

Maybe she was never there.

A chill swirling wind shook him free of the curb and he started across the street. No time to be worrying about ghosts. Across the street the park took over, the soaring tower of St. Luke's imposing against the slate sky, blocking out daylight as if night were already on him. A row of equally stoic buildings, one with large marble columns, made up the right side of the park. His side, a series of row houses with barely enough space to walk between them, filed past one by one. Brick and wood structures built in classic style, painted every color imaginable, with mortgages he could only dream of, all were locked down, windows dark, brass hurricane lanterns — for show only — swinging creaky on their chains.

He had managed to avoid this neighborhood for the few months he lived on this side of town. Until a week ago, he had only seen the park from the freeway, where it was another part of the scenery, seen but not noticed every day. A place that didn't concern him. Since then he had avoided looking at it at all.

A drum roll of thunder curled across the atmosphere overhead and reverberated underfoot, signaling that time was short. He wouldn't bother checking the phone, difficult to see, even impossible, in the rain. He figured it had been fifteen minutes so far, with four blocks left, maybe five. At the end of the park, he crossed, took a turn on the crossing street and headed up another, two blocks from home. In ten minutes he would be inside. Able to dry out; spend the night drinking while the hurricane raged against the shores. A thunder crack heralded the skies opening up. A wall of water fell. It came from behind, followed by a second and a third, a never-ending wave that drowned whatever part of him wasn't already soaked. It was here, no time left.

*　*　*

The bottle would come first. He needed a drink, bad. Next would come drying off. If he was lucky, the Irish triple-blend would outlast anything this squall had to offer, and they could all deal with the consequences in the morning. At the corner he looked up, trying to peer through the deluge that ran down his face, dripping from his hair, nose and chin. The street looked right. Ancient brick buildings, nothing but the façade. Renovated and rented out at inflated prices, his was the least modern of them all. Except his building wasn't there. He flicked his head, throwing rain and hair that had matted down out of the way. His street looked exactly like his, except none of these buildings were the ones he had grown accustomed to. Somehow, he'd made a wrong turn. Backing up he glanced at the sign, covered his face to read the letters clearly.

He read the sign, white letters against reflective green, difficult to make out with his eyes forced shut, but he knew immediately it was wrong. Too many letters. Princess Anne. One road too far. Spinning around, he spotted the large expanse of green, the northern end of the park. He'd gone too far. Somehow, he had walked right past his own road to the next one. Flustered, he turned, bowed his head and set back off down the sidewalk. Wet clothes clung to his skin. Streams worked their way down the jacket's lining, chilling the flesh with its icy touch. At the next corner he had to brace against winds that picked up, screaming down the narrow roads, colliding at the intersection like runaway trucks. They rocked him in place as he struggled to focus on the sign post rocking on its anchor. The letters, bright white even in the darkness, sent a chill worse than the rain.

Westover. He read them twice to be certain. The road before his. He had gone too far again. He twisted, squinted into the wall of water that continued to pummel the ground all around. The green of the park was still behind him. A distant blob of color, but unmistakable still.

Only one solution: he had somehow turned himself around. That park, the one he was looking at, *had* to be the south park. Which meant his road, the right road, was still one block up. It tugged at him as he splashed through the intersection, puddles already inches deep where the city's inefficient drainage system struggled to keep pace with the sudden influx of water.

He was on the wrong side of the street. If he was going north, or had been, then this would be the left hand side, right?

He shook his head. It didn't make sense. It didn't need to as long as he could get out of this weather before it got any worse. How could it possibly get any worse?

*　*　*

His fears were realized long before he noticed the road take a dip, headed downhill. He raised his head from the cracked and aged concrete of the sidewalk, shoes splashing as he stepped. He craned and squinted to the end of the block where a street should be, a street he knew too well, a street he'd give almost anything to see again. It wasn't there.

A large, wide expanse of carefully maintained green faced him. Old growth trees and a wrought iron fence waited at the bottom of that hill. The gutters were becoming rivers with swift currents that rushed towards the park, the grass soaked through so that water stood in massive puddles. Where there had been dirt, mud and tangled roots poked out of the ground. It was impossible. But he knew it was true. The sign on the corner verified what he knew beyond a doubt. This was the south end, the same row of homes he had trudged by not more than five minutes ago. The towering steeple of St. Luke's in the distance erased all doubt.

A street couldn't disappear. The storm couldn't pick up an entire road and blow it out to sea. He huddled inside the jacket, pushed back as massive offshore winds roared down the alley and down the roads behind until he had to grab a street pole for balance. It wasn't possible. Yet, somehow…

The first inkling that this might turn serious had started to gnaw at his intestines. A parasite chewing away, reminding him that people could die in storms. Accidents happened, all the time.

Forcing them out, he focused on a plan. The only explanation, the only logical reason was that, unfamiliar with these surroundings, avoiding the overpriced show-offs that bought homes on that street, he had gotten lost.

That's not why.

"Shut up," he replied, realized he was talking to himself.

The only explanation was that he had gotten lost. Simple as that. In the rain, in the dark, in gale force winds, it could happen; it would happen.

He needed to get back to somewhere he knew. To start again.

To the right, the cross street started again in another neighborhood, identical to his own. Two blocks down he would find the main artery, Colley, follow it to his own road and turn there. It was a path he'd taken a thousand times coming home from work or the bar. He could do it blindfolded.

Or drunk, the voice whispered.

Turning right this time, pushing towards Colley, he could see the main throughway in the distance. Two blocks down.

Nothing to it.

*   *   *

The wind died down as a new row of homes rose to the left, blocking the arriving gale. It did nothing for the rain, now an inch deep, and he stepped heavy, splashing in puddles as he marched towards the road, the one he knew for certain couldn't change. Every window was dark, every blind pulled as he pushed on. No one saw him, their eyes turned from the battle being waged. One with increasingly higher stakes. You could live through storms, right? Surely someone had gotten stuck outside during a hurricane and lived to tell the story but as the sky boomed, rolling low and heavy, he jerked, twisted and fell. His knee came down hard, sending jolts of pain like lightning as it traveled up the bone into his leg and hip.

"Fuck," he shouted. The words swallowed by the roar that swirled around him.

He repeated the curse three more times, cradling the injured knee. How was this happening? What had he done to make the world start fucking with him?

Lightning flashed for the first time by way of response, another booming crack of thunder. A wall of wind pushing him back told him he knew what it was.

"No," he said defiantly, unable to hear his own words. "Not today."

The downpour increased, making it difficult to see. Reports be damned, the storm was here, the outer bands at least.

Standing gingerly, he hobbled on.

*   *   *

Colley was, perhaps to his surprise, exactly where it had always been. As he approached, using his jacket to break the wind from the wide passage, he couldn't help but recognize the corner. Now empty. Tree-covered and shadowed by the buildings around, it was difficult to make out anything, especially in the darkness that had descended upon the city, almost as black as any night. Anyone could blow right through here, take him out if he stepped into the road. No one could blame them. There were no cars and there was no figure standing in the rain and he didn't have time to worry about it.

Time is short. The voice whispered. He brushed it off.

Around the corner, he moved at a near run. Brisk, splashing as he went, jacket pulled over his head to block what it could so he could see, could make no mistake this time. He crossed over Westover, without looking beyond the sign, and on to the road ahead. Everything looked familiar, exactly the same as it always had. Relief flooding more than the gutters that had overflowed, spilling onto the sidewalks, washing across the roads. At the next corner, he should turn right, two blocks back and he'd be home again. Rid of this nightmare, ready to kill a whole bottle in an hour if need be to wash away this day. When he reached the road, he paused, only long enough to double check, certain it was right this time, certain it couldn't be anything else. At a jog he glanced up, stopped, breath caught in his chest.

It was the right street. There was no way around it, but for some reason the signs were wrong. Someone had switched them. That had to be it, because the white letters, glaring back at him, mockingly read, "Princess Anne." He gaped at the sign, sure it was a mistake, and started up the road anyway, but no more than two houses passed, two stark, indifferent facades, completely unfamiliar to him before he knew it was true.

It was gone. Somehow, inconceivable as it was, wherever he was, the street he came home to every day, returned to every night after blowing off steam downtown, the apartment he could barely afford but stuck with for appearance's sake. It was gone.

You should run, the voice whispered.

He resisted its urge. Unwilling to panic, unwilling to let himself come undone so easily.

He turned again, retraced his steps and looked both ways. To the right, a road he had seen too many times, with its rows of bars and restaurants. Downtown, unmistakably. To the left, calling to him, the corner, the one he knew perhaps better than his own. It told him to return, that there was no sense running, that there was no escape from this. He shook it off.

"No!" he denied even to himself. "Impossible."

He was lost.

Yes, lost and no one will ever find you.

The panic was rising. He could feel it, his composure slipping away like leaves from a tree. He forced himself to stay calm. Reasonable explanations were slow to appear. Somewhere a tree branch snapped, unable to withstand the onslaught of rising winds any longer, and landed with a crash. He did run, back towards the corner, back towards that road, but he didn't give in to its call. Instead he turned, retreated to the safety of the close-grouped buildings. He found the first one that wasn't boarded and ran up the cement steps. Under shelter of the porch, he could catch his breath. Large brick columns blocked the wind, providing refuge for now. Old gutters rocked as they poured torrents of water onto the ground. He struggled to slow his breathing, to bring his heart rate down. The water gushed forth, somewhere above. A leak rained down a steady stream on his head. He thought about drowning, pictured it until his breath caught in his throat.

"Stop it," he shouted again, this time hearing the sound of his own panicked voice echo in the enclosed space. He banged on the door, seeking distraction, seeking refuge, seeking anything but to be left out in this storm. To face what was coming.

No answer from the door. He pounded until his fists hurt, shouted over the sound of rushing water, howling winds. Screamed into the splintered wood. Finally exhausted, he backed off, searching the facade for signs of life. Four windows on the front, two on this floor, were empty. Seeing the others meant backing out into the rain. The downpour hit like a heavy curtain, flooding him all over again. Standing on the top step, craning to see the windows above. Too dark to tell. He saw nothing, started to turn but paused at a sign of movement. Someone inside. Something had definitely moved on the other side of the glass. The angle was wrong. He backtracked down the steps, stepped back to see if anyone might be there, someone who could take him in, provide sanctuary.

Nearly in the street, he squinted to see through darkened glass, the shape of a head and shoulders, unmistakable. A flash of lightning off the pane blinded him, sent a white light through the sky, but when it receded he saw her again. A woman, no doubt, closer now, looking down on the street below. He knew that she saw him as clearly as he saw her, a face he recognized.

* * *

He was five houses away before he stopped running, slowed enough to give himself time to think. Heaving, struggling to breathe, he risked another fall to put distance between himself and the window.

It was an illusion. Nothing more. A trick of the light. But it had sent him running and he wasn't going back now. A deep unsettling tension in his gut quickly became nauseous sickness. He wanted to hurl. Even in the ice cold grip of the storm, he was hot, sweating, struggling to take in enough air. Again it felt like he was drowning, like he was being held under as the water rose. His chest thumped hard enough to feel it against ribs that were sore from the struggle. He could feel himself, dying slowly, drifting away beneath the surface, unable to stop the crush of water that sucked him down and squeezed the life from him as it invaded his mouth and lungs.

He snatched at his phone, pulling it from his pocket, seeking anything to break the spell of anxiety that was going to drive him to the edge. The screen was soaked, impossible to read. He swiped at the glass, brushing over the crack that distorted everything around it.

You knew this was coming.

"Shut up." He said it out loud, maybe. His mouth was moving, but the words came too fast, like a prayer. "Come on. Come on. Come on."

He prayed for a signal. Any signal and he could call for help. Emergency services, they would find him. Pick him up. Tell him where to find shelter. Something. It didn't matter. He needed to see another person, he needed to get out of the rain.

The screen filled too fast with fresh droplets to respond to touch, not even the weak shelter of his jacket was enough cover to work with. It didn't matter. The icon of a cell tower, with its little gray *X*, said there was no signal. Where the data should be, only a circle with a line through it. The lines were down. He cursed.

Absorbed in the screen, not watching ahead, he stepped off the curb, landed in a puddle that swallowed his foot and ankle whole and flung him forward, slinging the phone as he scrambled to catch himself. He landed hands-down on the pavement, ankle twisted, the sting of rock in his palms, the faint clatter of his phone on pavement somewhere ahead.

"Fuck!"

This time he screamed the word loud enough to hear over the gale. Scrambled up and started the search for his phone. Gone, nowhere to be found in the rushing water that surrounded him, he felt blindly, sticking his hand deep in the torrents of runoff racing down gutters to drainage holes and coming up empty, only loose twigs, leaves and debris in his fist.

Screw it. It was covered; no way could they tie *that* one back to anything important. He looked over his shoulder, verified the face in the window hadn't manifested on the sidewalk behind him, hadn't in fact pushed him from the curb, and then got to his feet, bullied by the billowing wind but defiant. He was alone, the streets empty, and if he didn't find shelter soon he'd be riding out category-three winds and flying debris in the open. The rising water levels alone would be enough to do him in. Norfolk hadn't flooded for years, but he began to think that was about to change as the ground disappeared beneath his feet. Only the centers of the road, raised to create runoff, still poked above the water like a corpse just under the surface.

Move, the part of him that wanted to survive urged.

He splashed back down the street, no destination in mind, working blindly towards something familiar. Visibility had reduced to just a few feet ahead, the storm's intensity raising at alarming speed. When he reached the street's end, confronted once again with that hated park, he knew there was no hiding from it. He crossed the street to it. Maybe he could huddle under one of the massive trees, cling close to the trunk, long enough to come up with a plan. Wait for rescue. But who was coming?

No one, the voice whispered. *Well . . . almost.*

The ground, saturated with rain, was slick and slippery as he slid past the wrought iron gate and stumbled across the open green field. A giant oak, fifty-feet-wide at the top, promised at least temporary shelter, that is if one of the massive branches, swaying to and fro, bending but not breaking, didn't snap off and crush him where he stood. Its roots, gnarled and old as time and concealed under several inches of standing water, conspired to trip him, to bring him down before he could reach its safety. Lightning traced the sky, reminded him that nowhere was safe if the storm wanted to reach him first.

He prayed the towering buildings around were enough to offset the natural lightning rod he cowered beneath. There were too many other hazards if he didn't seek shelter immediately.

The rains came sideways now, blowing in from every direction so the tree did nothing to stop them, but he managed to avoid the highest winds, the trunk pressed firm to his back offered a shelter against their sudden fury. Their wails had grown so loud it was impossible to hear anything but their shrill warning. Pressed tight enough to feel the grooves of the rough bark in his back, he let himself look again, once more toward the road he had come down, obscured by a single sheet of water, a gray wall that let only pinpoints of light peek through.

She wasn't out here. It was impossible. So many things were. If he was losing his mind, he'd picked the right night to do it.

It could not be past five but the skies had turned a black so dark the clouds were no longer visible. Everything beyond twenty feet disappeared, a fallen shadow too deep to penetrate. The shelter gave him a chance to catch his breath, but it wouldn't hold. He had to get indoors. Somehow, he had to find safety before the real storm arrived.

There was a firehouse a few streets over. He had passed it on the way in. It was far but if he could make it, retrace his steps back out to the train station, they would have to let him in. He tried to remember, his brain a jumble from getting so lost, something he was starting to suspect might not be his own fault.

But he couldn't think like that. He had to concentrate.

It was possible. Even in limited visibility, ten minutes. Ten minutes and this would be over. If he could make it. He looked over his shoulder, peeking from behind the tree, confronted with a blast of coastal wind, a spray of salt and ice cold water churned up from the depths of the Atlantic. He would be working on instinct, unable to see through this surge of weather, but it was possible.

Lightning flashed and its roll of thunder was barely audible over the screeching wind. There was no option.

She's waiting.

"Fuck off," he told the voice, and broke free of his sanctuary. Immediately his jacket flipped up, caught in the wind, exposing him to a pelting of thick heavy drops that stung his chest and ribs. Every step an effort, the gales raged, whipped around him, tugged at his feet, threatened to uproot him from the ground that slid, wet and thick with mud under his feet. But he pushed on, seeking the edge of the green, hoping to land the next heavy step on concrete, to find the road and follow it to safety. Frequent flashes lit up the sky, showing him the world bent to the will of nature, her fury unmatched. Head down, he forced himself through her rage. When he touched cement, the surface uneven, it sent him over before he caught himself, buoyed by the forces against his body, and stumbled forward. It seemed the wind doubled, screamed, denying passage. Something sharp cut his cheek, whipped by too fast to see. An object, heavy and large, slammed against his leg, cracked into bone, then was gone. Across the street a shape, ominous, dark, stood out against the flashes of lightning playing tricks on his eyes, creating monsters in the sheets of incoming rain. He recognized it even though he didn't want to. The structure, a wooden gazebo, built by the city, was a miracle to be still standing. Bracing as best he could, he used the structure to block the wind and forced his way towards its silhouetted structure.

The thing was solid, buried in a base of concrete and screened in, at least on most of its eight sides. He found the steps slick but the screen door open, flapping on its hinges, slapping against saturated wood. Without thought, he hurried inside.

The mesh wire wasn't enough to block the wind but it stopped the rain, reduced what made it through to a fine mist that swirled in the air. The shape of the thing, though it creaked and rocked, water pouring through where a piece of the roof had come free, managed to direct most of the air around it, creating a void, a sense of false security. He huddled on a soaked wooden bench, ignoring the unspoken poetry of this situation. It wouldn't hold. Already the timbers were twisting, threatening to pull apart, but the battering drum roll of rain on the roof signaled a grand finale. Soon the roof would tear loose completely and the structure would disintegrate in the violence that followed. He couldn't stay here but for a minute. He could gather himself for what came next.

Instinctively his eyes searched the area outside, the streets ravaged by a force of nature so large it defied understanding or control. Visibility reduced further to a few feet beyond the meshed windows, one of which was now hanging loose, letting in water by the bucket load. He saw nothing, but it didn't matter. He didn't need to see it.

She's out there.

It was not true. He wouldn't believe it. He had seen her though, hadn't he? With his own eyes, twice. What else was there to explain it?

Hysteria, came the answer. Guilt and hysteria and panic. He was trapped in a life-threatening situation and his mind struggled to find a reason for it. But there was no reason, sometimes shit just happened. Sometimes things didn't go your way.

Sometimes people die.

"No. Not this time," he said, as much to himself as to the storm that pounded on the door, demanded to be let in. Shook the structure so it appeared to tilt sideways. Time was running out.

Some people died because they didn't know any better, weren't careful, weren't smart enough. Others survived. That's what he had done. He had survived. Done what was necessary in a world that wouldn't understand, couldn't allow the laws to be broken, couldn't comprehend the way of nature. He hadn't made the choice that decided who lived and who died, he had made one that ensured he would survive. He would keep living. It was too late for anything else.

He looked out again, expecting her face to emerge from the depths of darkness, soaked to the bone, hair stringy, clinging to her throat, like the last time he'd seen her, but she wasn't there. She wasn't out there and he knew it. He knew exactly where she was. The wind gusted, took hold of the screen door and ripped it open, slammed it shut again on cheap hinges. One broke loose, leaving the door to hang crooked as the storm clawed at it, trying to tear it free completely.

She wasn't out there. But she had been here. The wood floors, standing with water now, the last place she had lain before the decision was made. Before the decision *had* to be made. He gaped at the empty spot now. Suddenly aware he'd never leave this place. The storm wouldn't let him. There was no sanctuary.

"I had to choose," he said, then shouted. "I had to choose!"

He broke from the space, unable to stand its confines any longer. In the raging winds again, he didn't fight their wrath, he welcomed them. He pushed through their grip and stumbled, down a hill to the edge, to where the overflow reached land. As predicted, it had crested the weak embankments, already several feet above the landline. He splashed in the shallow pool the overflow created. He reached the edge where the flooded banks dropped off into the spillway, where it would only get deeper on its way out to sea.

He stood at the edge, huffing, heart pounding, searching the surface, a mass of waves and distortion. He knew where she was and it wasn't out there, not in the storm. He searched the surface, finding nothing.

"You're dead," he shouted after the search turned up nothing. "That's not my fault! You're dead," he said again. Willed himself to accept it.

She was dead. She had been, even before now. She was dead before she ever stepped off the curb. Before she hadn't thought to look. Hadn't considered there might be anyone else in the world. Like a driver, on his way home.

He cursed her, as he had when she had stared at him with lifeless eyes, on her back, in the middle of the road.

She was dead. That was fate, that was life. It was her time to go. Before he had left the bar and climbed in his car. Before she had stepped on the street that night, her number was up. It wasn't his doing. No one would have seen her, not like that.

He repeated his shout. Added for emphasis, "You're not real!"

A blast of thunder, an array of lightning lit up the sky, argued that he was wrong. The flash knocked him back off balance and he landed on his ass in the water. Three, four more flashes, and he caught a glimpse of something on the water. Something that hadn't been there before. He squinted, dared it to be true, knowing it was impossible.

"Bullshit," he said.

Thirty yards out, a shape, black and humped, barely breaching the surface. It wasn't there a minute ago, he was sure of it, but it could be anything. It didn't mean anything. Even if it was, so what? Why shouldn't she be there, why wouldn't she fucking be there, turned up from the bottom in swirling currents? It didn't prove a thing. He'd put her there. Why wouldn't she still be where he put her, not carried out to sea like he'd hoped, not whisked away with the tides. He hadn't been thinking clearly. The cloud in his brain had barely lifted when he realized what had happened. Realized the dumb bitch had stepped in front of a moving car. Thoughts, panic, anger swirled as they drove, fighting through the haze of adrenaline, fear, and three fingers of fine scotch. One shot and a couple of beers. Legally he would be blamed for this, they would make it his fault but he hadn't done anything different. Nothing that didn't happen a thousand times a night anywhere in the world. He knew his limits. This dumb piece of shit had dropped off an unlit sidewalk and landed on his hood. It was a miracle he hadn't crashed the car. Just a busted headlight, some cosmetic damage.

He knew she was dead though. She hadn't moved, only stared at him with those blank, lifeless eyes. When he loaded her in the passenger seat, strapping her down so she wouldn't flop forward at stops. He knew she was dead.

They drove for what seemed like forever. Circling the streets, the yellow lamps reflecting off the dent in the hood, tracing over the car, lighting up her face, staring, accusing in his direction. They couldn't keep it up. He had to do something. Had to make a choice. One life ended that night. If a cop got nosy, pulled him for driving with one light, searched the car, they'd both be over.

Twenty-six. Too young for prison. One mistake, but it wouldn't matter. His life would still be over.

He made a choice. The spillway was as good a place as any. He had dragged her to the gazebo, thought about leaving her there; let someone find her, alert the next-of-kin. He wanted to, so someone would know, but forensics, right? People always asked questions and it wouldn't take long to piece it together, especially if anyone had seen him driving that night. The roads, empty, like they were now. If anyone had seen him, it was over. He had to make a choice. Her life or his. He chose his. Hers had run its course.

Near waist-deep, knowing for certain that the mass in the lake was a body risen from its watery grave, he shook for the first time.

"So what," he spat. "What can I do?"

Defiant, he forced himself up and spun, intent on climbing the hill, freeing himself from this once and for all and making for the safety of the firehouse before he did something stupid, too, and got himself killed.

When he turned, his heart stopped, seized in his chest, unwilling to believe what he saw. The overflow, its churning surface, the bands of rain and the ocean in the distance all stretched out before him, a scene too surreal to comprehend. He shut his eyes, ordered himself to breathe, to calm down. But when they opened the lake was still there.

Frantic, he spun again, a complete one-eighty, no more. Still there, waters raging, the unquenchable beast of the hurricane bearing down on him. There was no escape.

"Stop it!" he shouted but the noise was stolen from his lips, snatched away by the wind.

No matter how he turned, it was still there, the expanse of spillway leading to the ocean, the body floating, bobbing on the growing waves. He shivered, expecting her to appear any minute, no longer floating in the depths, but alive and seeking revenge.

"What do you want?" he argued with himself. Still not ready to accept it. She was there, but that was a body, a shell, dead meat. It had no more life in it than when she rolled off the bank and splashed in, sinking, thankfully, to the bottom. It had taken a knife blade between the ribs, to deflate the lungs, to ensure she would sink, but he had done it. And it was over. His conscience was making him think up things that weren't there.

How could he explain it though?

A violent wind whipped him sideways, knocked him into the water. Waist deep on his knees, he caught himself. Staring down the dark shadow at the drop off. The black impenetrable.

"What do you want?" he shouted. "Leave me alone!'

The storm increased.Charging like a rabid animal, saving the worst for last.

Struggling to stand, fighting against the waves that crashed against him, pulled him toward the edge, feeling the adrenaline rise, the panic sink in, the fear of drowning, his throat tightened, swelled shut. He tried to breathe, fought for air that wouldn't come. He knew what she wanted as sure as he knew he needed air or he would die. The darkness would rush in and crush him as the depths had taken her.

His vision clouded. Not long now.

He screamed, but nothing came out.

"Alright," he rasped. His throat unclenched, allowed the first passage of desperately needed oxygen, his brain coming alive, the shadows receding. "Alright," he coughed.

It was stupid, crazy but… he allowed himself to consider it.

He allowed himself to assess the distance between shore and the body. Impossible, like so many things tonight. He'd never make it. It couldn't be done. After the storm, after he saved his own life, maybe.

He turned, looked up the hill, and it was there again. A way out. A short climb.

Lightning flashed, a silhouette, then gone.

He blinked. Nothing there.

"Fuck me," he said.

The water was rising. He could feel it getting higher as he bent over, on hands and knees, inches from its ink black surface. He could see himself as a dark outline, a shadow passed over blocking out his own image.

Another flash. He jerked, flipped over, pushing himself back. Had he seen her face? Had she been standing over him, or was he losing his mind? It was too close to call. The current wrapped its fingers around him, tugged him into the deep water. They didn't need to. He got to his feet, wobbled in the undertow that begged for his sacrifice, and stepped to the edge.

"I'll do it," he said. "I'll bring you back. I'll pull you out but then, you leave me alone."

The wind howled. Unwilling to make a deal. It demanded repentance.

"You leave me alone," he said. "It's not my fault. I had to choose."

No answer came and, eyes closed, speaking a prayer that was drowned out before it could leave his lips,he stepped forward, sinking deep into the darkest waters.

At first he thought he wouldn't come up again. The current grabbed his ankles, dragged him out at least ten feet before he realized what was happening. The undertow, stronger than he could have thought from the surface, tugged his body like a doll straight to the bottom. He clawed at the cement foundation, struggled against its pull, but couldn't free himself.

At last it relented, let him loose and he bobbed to the top, lungs burning, nose full of water, coughing up filth and fluid that tasted like garbage. It was a fight to maintain his position. The black water churned, tossed him and tugged at his legs, trying desperately to pull him under again, to finish what it started. He kicked wild, slapped the water with his arms, flailing at first, then managing a half-assed stroke. He pointed himself towards the floating mass, one he recognized before he was even close, constantly redirecting, adjusting for the current that seemed to pull him away until he was exhausted.

"Help me," he shouted to the storm, to the dead girl in the water. "Help me reach you."

The storm raged but the waters calmed. He was able to make progress. By the time he reached the body, its chest poking up, the holes he made too small to see in the dark, he felt more confident. He could drag her back, pull her to shore and leave her there. Someone would find her in the morning. Forensics would never be able to find usable evidence after this long. Another victim of a tragic accident. He was confident five days underwater and a hundred year storm were enough to clear his name.

If not, he'd fight it. He'd find a way.

An arm floated on top, delicate fingers uncurled, skin turned an awful shade that made him sick. He reached for the wrist, content to pull her back behind with one arm. The skin felt slick, covered with slime like a dead fish. The sensation made him gag. She had been warm before. Not yet fully dead.

"She was dead," he asserted to himself. As dead as could be, especially after his impromptu surgery.

Was she?

"Shut up!" he shouted. Squeezing the wrist, he kicked hard, pulling the body with him. He pushed as hard as he could but got nowhere, the arm straightened, limp, but refused to budge. The body jerked, bobbed in response to his repeated tugs, but nothing moved it. He swam closer, the head underwater, covered by a mask of thick tangled hair. He slid his arms under hers, gagging at the smell that invaded his nose. She had decomposed or picked up sewage or both, but it was impossible to breathe as he kicked hard with his legs, forcing as much weight as he could to bring the body along. It refused to budge.

"Are you fucking serious?"

When he let go she bobbed, hair flowing free, partially revealing a washed out face, one blank white eye, staring at him, accusing.

"Fuck this," he said and started towards shore. Two good strokes and he stopped.

She wouldn't stop. He had to finish what he started. Working back towards the body, the current ripping against his legs, tugging him like a shark testing a meal, he swam around, looking for something that might be stopping progress, something she was caught on. Too dark to see he dove under, found nothing but stinging pain in his eyes, and came up again.

"You have to come with me."

His legs burned, his arms ached, exhaustion setting in. The lactic acid building up would turn to cramps soon, and they would both be dead in the water.

"I'm sorry, now come on." He grabbed the body, slinging one arm over his shoulder, the weight enough to force him down in the water, to fill his mouth as he struggled to keep his head up. He kicked hard, he thought she moved but they stopped. She jerked free, the wet hand smacking against his face as it slid back into the water. Slowly the body disappeared, sinking into the darkness.

"Fuck it. I tried!" he shouted. "I tried."

He turned, kicked, but his leg didn't move. The current, wrapped around his ankle, pulled him off course. But when he fought to get free he realized it wasn't the current. Something had a hold of his ankle. Something tangled itself around his leg and refused to let go.

He shouted. Screamed as the weight dragged him under water

and he came up again spitting.

"Help!"

He splashed the surface. Clawed at the seawater lake that rushed in and sucked him further down. The weight that had him, constricted and forced him down refused to let him up. Too tired to keep swimming, losing the battle with exhaustion. But it held like an anchor until he could no longer strain to get his head above the surface. Water rushed in his mouth and nose, making him panic. Making him flail, the wrong thing to do.

He wore himself out, kicked, screamed pleas for help that came out nothing but bubbles until his ineffectual spasms weren't enough. He went under.

The blackness rushed in, closed around him, squeezed the air from his lungs. It was too heavy, too much, to fight. Tossed in the current, he lost sight of which way was up. He squeezed his mouth shut, held his nose, fought the urge to inhale deep, to seek air that was out of reach, a foot overhead now. So close, too far to save him. The anchor released, reattached itself higher, clawed up his legs, pulling him down. The current under here shook him, yanked him towards the open mouth of the storm, the waiting, raging sea. But the anchor held tight, refused to let it be that easy.

As the narrow biting bones of fingers dug into his skin, pierced his side, sliding effortlessly between the ribs. The water rushed in, filling up the vacuum of his chest. Choking from the inside out, he couldn't fight any longer. The fear realized, darkness flooded in, rushed through his mouth and lungs, blocked out all else. When the cold fingers wrapped around his throat, the air was already gone. They squeezed anyway. All went black.

Cycles

Chad Lutzke

WHEN I was only seven, I came upon the bloated body of Stanford Willems, his engorged head resting on the muddy bank of the Cascade River. Finding him was the catalyst for my paralyzing fear of water, but it was my grandfather who made sure it remained.

My grandfather and I had been fishing in his rowboat—a rusty thing that sported two small holes where rivets eroded, and every hour we would take to emptying the boat by way of scoops made from old milk jugs. He assured me "Old Emily" was safe, but the decrepit thing set the mood for an anxious trip down the Cascade that ultimately ended with lifelong scars.

I was the first to spot the body, and I'm not embarrassed to say I screamed. I think it's what any boy my age would have done. My grandfather on the other hand used the corpse as a lesson in biology, as though pointing out the decomposition of Mr. Willems might teach me something, other than how to retain an image you wished you'd never seen.

"I'll be damned," he'd said, poking Mr. Willems with the oar as we moved closer, rather than frantically paddling away like we should have been doing.

Flies were darting about, and there was stench the likes of which I'd never smelled before, so potent I could almost taste it.

At the time, we had no idea who it was—and I gather even his own mother wouldn't have either—but once I saw the name in the local paper, I never forgot it. He'd worked at the hardware store. I'm sure I'd seen him in there before, because Grandpa would send me in for birdseed and fertilizer once a month, and Mr. Willems probably waited on me more than a few times. We may have even talked. And just knowing that put a chill in my spine whenever I thought of it.

There was talk around town of suicide, and some spread word of foul play, while others claimed that's what happens when you fish at night by yourself in a rickety old boat while toting a six-pack. Each one of those scenarios just as haunting as the next.

* * *

"I figure this poor guy's been dead for a good two weeks." Grandpa stared at the man, fascinated, like he was watching a hen lay glitter-covered eggs. "Marty, I want you to see this." He reached for me, barely taking his eyes of the dead man. "Now, this is nothing to fear. This here is science at work. If we hadn't come along and found this gentleman…" He squinted, studying the corpse. "Yes, this gentleman…then, a whole lot of critters, not only from the land, water, and air but also those invisible to the naked eye, would benefit from his death. Some would feast on him, some nest within, and some use him as a birthing place for their young. It's a beautiful thing, really…unfortunate for him, but a captivating thing to behold, the cycle of life. To think just how much life could spawn, or sustain itself, from what this body offers."

And then he urged me to look again, and I did. But I wish I hadn't. Not only was it hard to tell if it was a man or a woman, there was no real human resemblance at all. The man lay face up, his eyes shut tight behind mounds of puffed flesh, his lips the same. I imagined it's what Billy Johnston would look like without his EpiPen should he stick his head in a wasp's nest.

The man's shoes and socks were gone and his feet just as plump as his head. His flesh shined under the midday sun, glistening a pale white and speckled brown. And I felt if Grandpa poked him too hard the skin would split and he might explode, covering us in death juice.

Not only did Grandpa not paddle away, we lingered while he broke out sack lunches, going on about the cycle of life and how important it was, all the while still within poking distance of the corpse.

When I refused to eat, Grandpa told me I'm missing out on a valuable lesson and that it was all about perspective. He said I needed to find the beauty in everything, even death. But I learned nothing good that day, and my perspective never swayed. Death was death. It was ugly and it stunk, and it was downright terrifying. But it was the subtle splash of waves while staring at the body that truly instilled my fear of water, because it was the water that created the nightmare before us. And after that day, it seemed to me water was downright evil in every way.

That was the last time I ever went fishing with Grandpa. And when he died of pneumonia, I went to his funeral and realized he too died with fluid-filled lungs—a thought that secured my fear all the more.

Outside of sitting in six inches of grass-littered water in a neighbor's kiddie pool, I never went swimming after that day either. I never even so much as stood beachside. Those crashing waves that others find so tranquil were like screams of the dead for me, each lap of water a reminder of that engorged face with its plum eyes. So, when my new girlfriend asked if I would take her to the boardwalk one Saturday evening, my heart raced at the thought of being so near the ocean. If there was ever anything to give rationale behind my fear, that vast body of water was it.

Without thinking, I immediately said I'd take her—a kneejerk reaction driven by the excitement of having my first girlfriend. We'd spent nearly two hours a day on the phone for the past two weeks, and I was smitten. No way was I about to do anything that would sabotage us. I'd be getting my driver's license in a few years and I pictured us driving around, holding hands and listening to music with the windows rolled down, the wind in our hair, driving to our next destination where we'd kiss for hours, fogging the windows and blocking any view of the outside world. Nothing else would exist but us.

This is what falling in love must feel like.

Which includes making sacrifices.

I spent the next few nights mentally preparing to lay eyes on my arch enemy, to be within grasp of its briny scent, and to finally face my fear. I looked at pictures of ponds, lakes, and finally the sea itself. My mouth would go dry and I'd even tremble, there in the safety of my bedroom. I debated whether I should go at all. What if I made a fool of myself? If fear struck me so easily in my own home, what will happen when I'm face to face with it? And if I don't confront it now, would I live my entire life avoiding what so many others found enjoyable? Even into adulthood?

Friday night came much too fast. Allison and I spoke on the phone for an hour before our date. She was excited for the evening ahead, and I did my best to hide my worry, which I'd gotten good at over the years.

My mother dropped us off at the boardwalk. The salty odor was masked by the smell of fried foods, its monstrous body hidden by shops, restaurants, and the massive crowd of people. But the time would come when Allison and I would walk hand in hand within eyeshot of the beast and I would need to maintain control.

I bought us ice cream cones and forced myself to eat. I kept a smile and a joyous demeanor, when all I really wanted to do was go home and talk on the phone for hours, until we both fell asleep. And maybe we'd talk long enough and deep enough that I'd share with her my secret, and maybe she'd have one of her own she would trust me with, and there would be no teasing, no judging. Only understanding. But there we were. And all I could think of was the water and just how ridiculous the fear, just how debilitating.

As we made our way toward the boardwalk, my hand in Allison's began to sweat. I could see Mr. Willems being picked at by fish, carrying away bits of his gelatin skin. Allison let go of my hand and wiped hers on her jeans. "Are you nervous?" She smiled.

"Sorry." I wiped my hand too.

"Don't be. Tonight is special. It's our first official date."

"It's just…" I almost told her right then and there, spilling it all. But the look in her eye. I swear there was a twinkle in it, and if I started talking about corpses and fears and long-passed demented grandfathers that the twinkle would leave, and I couldn't let it. That twinkle felt like everything I'd ever been missing. It reminded me of before the fear. When the waves carried light like glitter on its crests, and I loved the sight just as much as anyone.

And then in that very moment, the water seemed as beautiful as it should be, and the fear felt weaker.

Then the crowd parted as we came upon the boardwalk, and my stomach dropped. But I did not pause, and I did not tremble. And I kept my mind on Allison's twinkling, blue eyes and how if I play it cool, I just may get to kiss her.

We held hands again, and I listened as she talked about how she used to come here when she was young, before her parents divorced and her father moved two states away. She said it felt good to be back again, making new memories with me. We locked eyes, and I almost kissed her, but I wanted to make sure it's what she wanted. I wasn't good at reading tells. This was my first time.

While the sun fell, we kept our backs to the water and played carnival games. As hard as I tried, I failed to win even the smallest stuffed toy for Allison, but she seemed to be having fun anyway. We drank soda and ate elephant ears and counted how many fanny packs we saw, with extra points if the wearer sported socks with sandals.

Then two young girls gloating over their new seashell necklaces caught Allison's attention. And that was the beginning of the end.

"Those are beautiful! Where'd you get them?" Allison asked the girls.

"There's a vendor at the end of the pier. He has bracelets, too."

"Ohh!" Allison looked at me with wide eyes. "They have bracelets! We could get matching ones!"

The excitement she displayed should have been contagious, but all it really did was stop me from wetting my pants. I looked toward the pier. It was congested with people and a million miles long, reaching right into the eye of the storm, like a gangplank to Hell.

"I have to use the restroom," she said. "Then we'll go get some!" She leaned in and kissed me on the cheek. I could smell her hair and makeup, and something stirred within me that never had before. It wasn't like seeing a pair of tits on HBO or stumbling across your father's magazines. It was different, and I felt it in my gut, swirling and fluttering. It was like medicine that masked the fear, and I knew what I had to do.

I'd go to the vendor, buy the bracelets, and return before she was back. I could never be on the pier with her. If I needed to run, if I needed to sweat or scream, if I needed to dig my nails into my palms, I would do it without her around.

I turned toward the pier and saw the bleeding blue between the moving people. I looked back, searching for Allison. I could still see her, making her way to the restrooms. I needed to move now. Before thinking any further, I commanded my feet toward the pier. They moved, but slowly. I took longer strides and hummed a favorite song. I mumbled the lyrics, doing what I could to keep my mind off the idea that I wasn't just nearing the water, but walking high above it. My feet hit the weathered wood of the pier, and I kept my eyes fixed on my shoes. I sang louder. A song no one could hear, my voice lost in a hundred conversations by a thousand different people.

I picked up the pace as much as I could, but the darkened sky and crowd of people made for an obstacle course that demanded a civil stride. I bumped into others, making my way further, further. I looked up from the ground only slightly and saw the vendor ahead, surrounded by customers, checking his wares, trading bills for jewelry.

The further I went out, the more the smell of fried foods gave way to the salty reek of ocean. I wanted so badly to revel in it like so many did, to be normal and live truly free, even carelessly so, if only to make up for time lost in my self-imposed prison. But in that moment, it didn't really matter, because I was in the middle of slaying the dragon, sword drawn, and I was melding with normal people, ones who never gave the liquid a second thought.

I was becoming free!

Thankfully, there was no waiting in line at the vendor, only people browsing, so I quickly asked the man how much for two of the bracelets.

"Six bucks a piece, or two for ten."

Ten was all I had left for the rest of our date, but I wasn't going to make the trip in vain and so forked over a ten-dollar bill. He handed me the bracelets and I put one on, holding onto the other.

That's when I made the mistake of looking up and directly at the sea. It was never-ending. Other than behind me, there were no shores, no banks, no islands, just a vast, black void with waves painted white with moonlight, hiding a multitude of man-eating creatures of varying sizes. My heart pounded harder than I ever thought possible, and I nearly threw up. My knees grew weak, and my vision went dark.

I turned away from the water and toward the crowd that filled the pier. I panicked, pushing through, watching only my feet as I ran for safety. I hit several people on the way, disorienting myself, and losing all sense of direction. And then I hit the safety rail and sent myself over, plummeting twenty, perhaps thirty feet, into the belly of the beast. It happened so fast, though time seemed to slow as I watched the black death approach, until finally it smacked my face with a ferocious blow.

My eyes shut tight, and the impact of the sea drove the air from my lungs as I submerged. For only a moment, I was unable to move. Still disoriented, I drew in a deep breath, filling my lungs with the fear that kept me prisoner, the thing which stopped me from enjoying even swimming in a pool with friends.

This was no longer facing my fear. This was dying because of it.

I opened my eyes and saw my arms waving frantically in slow motion against the mighty strength of the sea, my hand still holding the gift I'd bought Allison, its shells glimmering under the glow of the moon.

I kicked and screamed, and my lungs filled all the more. It was never how I thought drowning would be. There was no bobbing in and out of the water, flapping my arms in the air for help, while heroes quickly disrobed and dove in to save me. The water I'd breathed was an anchor in my lungs, holding me captive and pulling me deeper while I held firm to Allison's bracelet as though it would somehow save me—a reminder that love and life had only just begun.

I contemplated how it wasn't the water that killed me, but my fear of it. And as I sank to the bottom, I wondered who would find me and if my head would swell into a bulbous nightmare, my body used by the cycle of life. Or perhaps it would play a role in a different type of cycle altogether. One that gave birth to fear. Would I be the subject of a failed lesson taught by an old, deranged man, scarring an impressionable young child?

Which cycle would my body feed?

They Came from the Sea.
They Went to the Stars.

Hanson Oak

O LIVER West felt that the statues of the cemetery, with their cold white eyes and indifferent expressions, were derisive at best, malevolent at worst. These were forgotten Gods, demoted to caretakers of the dead, who mocked the visitors that strode between the weathered grave markers. Oliver was certain if he turned at the right moment, he would catch one of these statues in motion. Of course, he told himself this was a paranoid impossibility, but never tested the theory either, not wanting to risk discovering he was right. But, as he passed under a granite angel perched atop a mausoleum, the hair rose on the back of his neck, pulled for his attention as the statue did indeed turn away to weep for this broken man.

The September winds whispered their condolences as well, rattled dry leaves and left a chill on his cheek as they passed. Rain fell on the bare trees and dormant grasses, like boney fingers that tapped on their own tombstones in a macabre serenade, a minimalist symphony. Even the animals of the forest paused at the tree line and lowered their heads as Oliver approached the graves of his family.

Heartbreak is a condition collectively suffered by all left in death's wake, but never had a person suffered loss as Oliver had. The sorrow he felt at the departure of his wife and three children was felt by every living thing. The tears he cried were toxic, bitter, and poisoned the ground they fell upon. His depression, so all-encompassing, drove strangers around him to take their leave of life. His screams of despair tore from him with no more control than a river that falls over a cliff, and deafened some hundreds of miles away. In fact, the first night he'd come here, his fists that pounded the ground in rhythm with his grief-stricken heart, caused earthquakes and tsunamis on the opposite side of the Earth. Of course, no one knew or would believe this, least of all Oliver — but it was true.

Oliver's guilt for not attending his family's funeral was a fog that would not lift. It was understood that him surviving the crash at all was a miracle, and none held a grudge for his absence aside from himself. Almost a year after, with aid of a wheelchair, Oliver did visit but never forgave himself for not saying goodbye — even if was just to well-dressed corpses in high gloss caskets. He came to the graves every night since. Five years fell away, Oliver's body healed while his heart withered. Each visit hurt as much as the first, always coming at night to ensure he would be alone and free to shatter into as many pieces as there were stars bearing witness. However, Oliver was never alone in the darkness. As he fell across the grass of all four graves, the only other living thing in the cemetery, as far as living things are understood, could no longer hold her tongue.

"Where do your tears come from?" A gypsy woman stepped from the shadows behind him. Her voice was silky, warm and comforting as bisque. Her skin was pale as unglazed porcelain, hair and eyes black as the inside of fist. Oliver was quick to his feet, frightened and embarrassed to be seen as a fleshy sack of broken bits. "I would think you would have none left by now, but then I think the same of the rain, and both still fall all too frequently."

He wiped the tears and rain from his face; she seemed not to be bothered by the rain at all, but by his presence. Oliver tried to ignore her, thinking his silence would help her move along. Instead, the gypsy came closer.

"I fear I may have done something wrong." Her cadence was strange, like the words held to her lips for a moment too long. The gypsy looked up as streaks of lightning slashed the sky. Oliver found it hard to take his eyes off her, but not because of her beauty. She was odd. The way she moved, jerky and unpracticed. Her eyes were wild and hungry as they darted around, unable to maintain focus on any one thing longer than it took to see it. She seemed uncomfortable on her legs, always moving, looking for better footing. "I've watched you come on many nights, from under the ground and now above it. But tonight, I am more certain that what I have done should not have been done, but it is done, and I might say I'm sorry if I was the sort to say such things, which I'm not."

"Do I know you?"

She pointed at the inscription on the headstone shared by the four graves, words leaked from the fractures of Oliver's heart early on: *Maggie, Timothy, Tylor, and Samuel. A mother and her beloved sons. Forever mourned by the man they left behind.*

"They're yours?" The woman asked. "You left them here?"

"Buried." The word was bitter and stabbing, Oliver choked on it. "I buried them here."

"Discarded like trash," she corrected.

"What do you want?"

"To help you," she said. "I help you and you help me. I keep what I've gotten, you get what you mourn, he gets what he searches for."

Oliver turned back to the wet grass that separated him from his family. The woman was drunk, drugged or both. "Fuck off."

"I like that." A smile emerged from under her thin lips. "It's good to see there's still some fight in you. You'll need it."

"For what?"

"To get them back."

Oliver moved his fingers along the headstone, whispered goodbye, and walked away. He was not interested in arguing with a lunatic in the rain. Come morning, he'd tell the cemetery management about this, ask why there was no security at night. The woman watched him go, looked to the statues that surrounded her, the gods in the sky and the forest in the distance. None were satisfied with this resolution. She felt it; their judgment squeezed the air from her lungs, forced her to speak. "I traded them!"

The words were like a hook in Oliver's back. "You did what?"

"People throw their dead here like trash in a heap," she said. "Most of them aren't worth the flesh the worms work through, but sometimes, as rare as a crow's smile, you find something The Collector might want, and he traded deeply for your family."

Oliver started on again, the gypsy ran in front of him, falling in the mud, unsure on her legs. "You can be with them again. The ropes that bind you to your family tighten like a noose after death. They will not cut, will not break or stretch, only tighten. That is why your heart can not heal, why their memories take your breath."

"You said you were sorry—"

"I never said I was sorry," she defended. "I said if I was the sort to say such things, I might say it, but I never did say it, and I won't."

"But if you did, what would you be sorry for?"

She bit her lip as if to hold her thoughts hostage for a moment longer, to think them through, but they escaped. "I knew they were still bound to you and I traded them anyway. But he'll realize soon that the set is not complete, then he'll take back what he's given me."

"Who?"

"A creature called The Collector of Very Odd Things."

"Why is he called that?"

"He collects things."

"What kinds of things?"

She cocked her head. "Odd things."

"What does he want with my family?"

"You have to ask him," she said. "And you can, but you must go."

Oliver's mind turned into itself like kneaded dough, dismissing and reconsidering all that was happening. "What did you get for them that you're so scared of losing?"

She pointed across the landscape, an arched back with headstone spines, to a mound of fresh dirt beside a deep hole. "A second life, another chance. So rare to cross back and forth, rarer still to remain in between, and that is where your family exists."

*　*　*

Oliver dug, scratched, and pulled at the wet earth until his fingers were raw and bloodied. With each fistful of mud, he moved deeper. The deeper he went, the more loudly his better judgment questioned his predicament. What was he doing? Had he gone insane? Why was he allowing himself to burrow into the earth like a dog after the promise of a bone? Why was he listening to this gypsy and entertaining her impossible possibilities?

The gypsy watched as he excavated. She sat on the edge of the hole, her legs dangled over him as he gasped for breath and threw the dirt into the night. He reached in for more, using both hands, this time they did not find dirt but something impenetrable; the first casket. The rain washed away the mud to reveal the wood lid, as vibrant as the day it was buried.

He rested his palms on the lid to steady himself. "You lied. She's still here."

"Lied? I never lie!" The gypsy stood, kicked a mound of mud over Oliver. "I would close you in and spit on the grave if I thought for a moment you weren't too dumb to die."

He examined the dirt and blood on his arms. "Look what you've made me do."

"Your wife is not in that box, Oliver," she said. "You are standing at the front door. She's gone out the back. Go on. Open it."

Oliver considered this. While it didn't make sense, neither did anything else, and he'd come this far. He dug out a nook next to the casket to kneel, placed his fingers under the rim of the lid. He closed his eyes and pulled it open. The smell of rot, of old air and mildew, rushed into his nose, he gagged and turned away.

"See?" The woman said.

Oliver opened an eye just enough to see that the casket was empty, the satin lining had been pulled away to reveal a door on the back. He ran hands over it to convince his mind it was real, that other senses agreed with his eye's assessment. Oliver fished out a piece of paper that rested in the corner of the vacant box, it read: *"We're sorry to inform you of your death but are pleased to welcome you to what comes next. Please turn around to exit the casket. Good luck."*

"What is this?"

"The other side," the woman said. "Comes standard. Hurry now."

"Where does it go?"

"It will take you to exactly where you need to be, exactly when you need to be there."

Fear and adrenaline mixed in Oliver's body and became excitement, he felt alive for the first time since before his family had died. If the gypsy had been right about this, maybe he could believe all she had told him. He held his breath, the one that would tell himself to stop and think this through. His family was waiting for him somewhere on the other side of this grave, and he had to suffocate that voice of doubt if he was to go any further. He turned the knob and the door dropped away, dangled in blackness so absolute it pained his eyes. The void made him dizzy, sick. His body was revolted by it like the stench of rotting meat. He knew at a very primal level that he should climb from this hole, cover it over, and never return. But he did none of those things.

Instead, he forced his fingertips into the blackness, and it was cold. Not a chill of weather or water, but death. The taste of living flesh caused it to ripple inward, towards his hand, the inky pane leaping up further on his hand and arm. Again his body heaved back, tried to fight, but he forced his arm in deeper, than the other. The void met his enthusiasm and engulfed him. He felt a chill that began on his flesh then soaked through him. In a moment, he felt nothing at all. He was still aware of himself but could not see or feel anything. He was comfortable here, not lost in an abyss but afloat in his own consciousness. When the cold had run its course, the warming began. He felt it building, moving down his body which was not there a moment before. He felt as if he was being constructed, pieced together again, then a flash of heat and his eyes opened to a blinding light. He examined his hands that shielded him from the light and the arms they attached to. His body and clothes were as they had been but felt newer, and that was not all that had changed.

He stood on a path, surrounded by groups of thick, thorny vines that wrapped themselves into giant trees which carried into the sky. It was daytime and there were no clouds, no rain. In the distance, a great house stood on a hilltop. There was nothing else in all other directions but the forest of strange trees.

It must be where I am meant to be, Oliver thought. But as he moved forward, the trail he walked moved back, making his movements useless and feeble. He watched his steps now, examined his feet and the earth below them, began moving ahead on the straight path. When he looked up at the house, it was on his left, the trail had turned but he knew there were no curves when he started. Oliver stopped, confused at his lack of progress.

"She's moving it." Behind Oliver, a little creature watched him. It was both as intangible as shadow and solid as stone, with emerald eyes and large ears that twitched, changing direction to take in all the sounds of this Thorned Forest. The small animal was not one thing, but many. Its fur was a soft brown giving way to a striped pattern on its back. Its belly was golden and soft and a formidable, with a rigid barbed tail, like the stinger of a bee, on its backside. It was a quilt of a creation.

"Who's moving it?"

"The Seeded Girl." The creature's voice echoed, though not by reverberation but repetition. More of the animals emerged from the sides of the trail, walked out on the vines of the trees. "She moves them around."

"Around." They staggered their repetition. "She twists the paths."

"Why?"

"To try and make them right again." The first of them walked to Oliver's feet, admiring his boots, smelling and pressing them. "What have these poor creatures done to you?"

Oliver looked at his shoes. "Nothing."

"Then why make them carry you?"

"They're *shoes*," Oliver said. "They're not alive."

A collective gasp was released by the whole of the creatures. The one at his feet turned, lifting its barbed tail high. "You walk on corpses!"

"No! It's called 'leather'. It's just the skin..." The creatures began to retreat into the forest, their large eyes held on him. He looked at the house. "Wait! Tell me where I can find the Collector of Odd Things!"

They stopped their retreat, curious at the question. The first of them lowered its stinging end.

"Why?"

"He has something of mine," Oliver said.

The creature turned back. "If he has something of yours, then it is his."

"Is that his house? The one on the hill?"

"Yes."

"Then that's where I have to go." Oliver was about to take a step but thought better of it. "How can I get to the house when the path is being moved?"

"We can tell you." The creature extended a finger toward Oliver's shoes. "But you can't see The Collector of Odd Things, one who cherishes life, being carried on death."

Oliver looked at the ground beneath his offensive footwear. The vines that formed the Thorned Forest were deeply rooted, but smaller, thirsty offshoots were close to the surface. They had fine thorns, like kitten teeth, that crisscrossed the path. Just the thought of pressing his fleshy heel into the biting thorns locked his jaw, but if his family was in that house there was no other choice to be considered or deal to be made.

Oliver pulled a shoe off, placed his foot down to not delay the agony that waited. The thorns stabbed through his socks and into his sensitive flesh. He screamed, spit, released a thundering of profanity. He removed the other shoe, pressed his foot against the soil beside the first. The pain was too much and his vision drifted, he lost his footing, the vicious little points drove into his knees and palms when he fell. He closed his fingers around the soil, began to pull the dirt and roots out until the hole was deep enough to bury his shoes. He pushed the dirt back over them and got stood, slow to adjust to the pain of the thorns. Oliver wiped the tears and sweat from his face. "Tell me."

The creatures came forward, their expressions joyous, the first one that came to him walked on the mound covering his departed footwear. "To get to the house, you can't look up because the trail below will never allow you to move forward. But you can't only look below you because you will become so consumed with walking the path, you will lose sight of where you are going. To stay on course, you must be mindful of now but focused on then."

"Be mindful," Oliver said to himself. He focused on the path ahead, making sure to see both the house and the trail. The first steps buckled his knees and drew a hiss from his mouth, but the ground did not push him back or shift him off course. Another step, mindful of now and then, his goal and the moment he existed in now. It was working. He whispered on the wind, hoping it would carry his words above this Thorned Forest, to the house on the hill and his family. "I'm coming."

*　*　*

For countless miles, he walked and his feet became numb to the pain. The sun did not move in this place, making it useless to tell time by. The sun only changed phases like a static moon, so while the light of the world dimmed to dusk, it soon began again as bright as a spark. He just focused on avoiding the satisfaction of the now and the anticipation of the then, until he stood at the doors of the immense home.

While from the distance it appeared as a solid and uniform home, it was anything but. The outside was a patchwork of this and that, brick and stone, shingle and board, cloth and mortar. It was as beautifully mismatched as the creatures he'd left the company of.

Even the front doors disagreed with one another. The right, dark mahogany, carved with patterns of flowers and leaves. The left, a bowed yellow steel mass, a bit rusted, reminding Oliver of the underside of a rowboat.

A rope swayed above him that carried up to a bell mounted ominously over his head. The brass colossus was two dozen feet tall and twice as wide across its mouth. Oliver thought to knock, the humbler approach to announce his arrival, but feared it would go unnoticed. The Bell, which looked large enough to shake the sun from the horizon, was also large enough to shudder the house to pieces. *Still,* Oliver thought, *if it's here, it's meant to be used.*

He gripped the rope and pulled, the great bell tilting to one side, the clapper rested against the mouth, waited to swing. Oliver released the rope, pressed his palms against his ears as the bell dropped with a deep woosh of air — then the sound. Oliver did not hear it but felt it. It moved his teeth, deflated his lungs, rattled his bones and ground his joints. Dust and loose bits of the house fell all around him, The dirt and sand below him jumped and danced in the vibration. Then the bell broke from its timber holds and dropped over Oliver.

The vibration stopped, and there was nothing. No light, no sound, not unlike the bleak void he'd crossed through to come to this world. He pushed the brass walls, but they would not budge. He wiggled his fingers under the rim, but it was too thick to grasp, too heavy to lift. He tried to dig his way out, a decision protested by his abused fingers, but the ground was solid stone below only a few inches of soil. There was nothing to be done but wait to die or be discovered, but it was the darkness that began to bite at him. He sat unable to even see himself in this cast tomb, but visions and memories require no light, more vivid in the blackness now than they ever had been, and they took his mind far from this bleak grave.

He was laying in the snowbank, a moment so clear to him that he felt he was living it and not simply remembering. The brightness of the clouds above was overwhelming, made his head throb. All he wanted to do was rest but knew he shouldn't. He had to do something. A popping sound came to his ears. It was repetitive, annoying. The cold kiss of snowflakes teased their affections on his skin before they melted away. It occurred to him that he didn't know where he was or how he'd gotten there. He let his head drop to the side, seeing a car with its engine burning. He realized he was on the shoulder of a road. The side of the car that faced him was smashed in, the doors pressing into the vehicle. The opposite side was pinned against a stone outcrop. A sticker on the rear hatch, *Once a Marine, Always a Marine, Semper Fidelis* stirred a memory. That was *his* sticker on *his* car, but how did he get out here?

Another car rested on its roof thirty feet from his. There was blood on the shattered windshield and the driver's door, the glass was fogged. A face was pressed against the window, body crumpled on top of it as broken as the car's frame. He remembered now. The car on its roof had hit him, spun the car around, he'd been ejected.

"Maggie!" He voiced his horror before his mind fully grasped that she was still inside the car, so were the boys. He tried to get up, willed his body to move, but it wouldn't. Something was wrong inside him. Something was broken. He lifted his head, looked over his body, and saw it was all wrong. His legs were facing the wrong way, his feet pointing opposite ways. His arm was twisted behind and under him. "Maggie!"

A face appeared in the back window of his car. It was Samuel. The boy looked out into the bleak winter dusk for his father. A release of air, excitement to see life in the vehicle, sounded almost like a laugh starting in Oliver's throat. He waited a moment for his other boys to pop up next to Samuel, for Maggie to open the door and lead them away from the wreckage, but it none of that happened.

"The window!" Oliver's own voice startled him, with its tones of desperation. "Break the window!"

Oliver felt a chill as his son's eyes found him, sparking a smile on the boy's face. His gaze was distant, weak, but his brightened when he looked at Oliver. He knew his father would save him now, knew it was going to be okay because Oliver always made everything okay. The fire was spreading back towards the cabin now, moved quickly, the flames first taking a lick then jumping to fresh fuel with bursts of satisfaction. Oliver wept, knowing all he could do was watch, and that's what he did. He watched his family burn. He watched his son scream and beg for help until the fires exhausted themselves with him. He refused to turn away until the night swallowed the day.

"Hello?" A man called, pulled Oliver from his memories. The voice was amplified by the bell that surrounded him. Oliver put his hands in front of him, feeling for the side of the bell.

"I'm in here." Oliver regretted the volume of his reply, as it was ten-fold amplified back to him.

"Why?" The voice asked.

"Because I can't get out."

"Is it dark in there?" Oliver didn't answer. The questions were so ridiculous that his mind refused to process it. There was a knock-on bell. "Hello?"

"Yes, it's dark," Oliver said, mindful of his anger and volume. "It's the inside of a bell, what else would it be?"

"If you can't see where you are, you can be anywhere," the voice said. "Perhaps you're in a closet. If you were in a closet, you could just open the door."

"This is not a closet," Oliver's skin prickled with anger. "It is a fucking bell, and bells are not closets, and have no goddamn doors."

"But *if* you were in a closet," the voice pressed, "You could simply turn the knob and open the door, couldn't you?"

"Yes," Oliver admitted.

"So, know that you are in a closet, find the knob and come out already."

Oliver's hands dropped down along the side of the bell in defeat. It was his luck that this rescuer would be as senseless as the gypsy in the cemetery. But she wasn't insane after all, was she? If she wasn't insane then maybe this man speaking to him wasn't either—Oliver's fingers bounced off something protruding out from the bell and his hands recoiled. He felt for it again, wrapped his fingers around what felt like a knob. He twisted his wrist and it turned freely, sounding the click of a latch unlatching. A line of light appeared all at once, a rectangular glow about the same height and width as a door, and when he pushed it open, he found himself looking into a hallway at the silhouette of a man waiting for him. "There you are. Welcome."

*   *   *

Just as the outside of the house was a patchwork of small, unrelated things, the inside was as well. The Collector of Odd Things was himself just a bit of this and that, sewn and piled together until it became altogether different and whole. At first glance, it looked like a man in a costume of cloth rags, old pictures, twine, candy, gold coins and so on, carefully woven together so not a space separated any of it. But through the center of this form was a hole that one could look clear through to the other side, proving that The Collector of Odd things was not just *wearing* his collection but *was* his collection.

Oliver followed him through hallways that twisted, turned, and branched off in all directions, filled with doors of all descriptions. They came to a room that felt impossibly long and unattainably high with only a small table in its center, beside a single chair, and that is where The Collector of Odd Things sat. On the table was an empty apothecary bottle, corked at its mouth. At once, Oliver explained the extent of his journey that began with five years of mourning and ended in that room, at that moment. The Collector of Odd Things said nothing.

"I have them," The Collector of Odd Things said after some time.

"I want them back," Oliver stated.

The Collector of Odd Things tapped his mismatched fingers (a twig, finger from a glove, bundled rose stems, a long claw, and a stout mushroom for a thumb) against the side of his mouth in rhythm. He dropped his hand and looked at Oliver with hollow eyes. "You never asked why I wanted them."

"It doesn't matter," Oliver said. "I want them back."

"You must always know why someone wants what they want, especially if you want it," The Collector of Odd Things said. "That way you know how to proceed in getting it or if it can even be gotten at all."

"Why do you want them?"

"Because they are perfect," The Collector of Odd Things said. "I have yet to see one perfectly alive, yet curiously dead human, let alone four, and I have traded from deep in my collection for them. I gave that rotting gypsy a second life, and life is terribly rare itself. I'm unsure if I'll ever replace it."

"What do you mean they're alive?"

"Not alive. Not entirely," The Collector of Odd Things corrected. "Few things are as simple as that. Life and death, on and off, this and that, all have a path to one another. If I blow out the flame of a candle, while it no longer burns, it smolders for a bit before resting. Even then it is not entirely as it was before the fire and, if you wanted to, you could relight it, though it would not burn as it had the first time."

"What does this have to do with my family?" Oliver asked.

"When I acquire something, I bring it to this room, Oliver," The Collector of Odd Things said. "It's free of distractions so I can focus on my new additions, try and decide where they fit. Do you know what happened when I brought your family here?"

Oliver's heart forgot a single beat as he thought of them standing where he stood now, that they might indeed be alive, or some variation of such, and he could hold them again and weep out the final pools of sorrow left from his guilt. "Tell me."

The Collector of Odd Things leaned forward, pointed the claw finger at Oliver. "They asked for you. Your wife questioned nothing of what happened, only asked, 'Where is Oliver?' to which I said nothing because I did not know what an Oliver was then. That is what is so special about them, the connection. There's no bond I know of that death, given time, cannot break. But the bond between you and your family has not degraded in the slightest. Even their physical forms would not decompose because they remain so close to life. They are precious to me for that reason."

"They are my family," Oliver said.

"They *were* your family, Oliver."

"You said we are still connected. I feel that."

The Collector of Odd Things sat back in his chair, tapping his strange hand against his mouth once more. "I am not unreasonable; I am a collector, and a collector's collection is never complete. I'm always searching. Always looking. Always wondering if the next new piece will be *the* piece, a punctuation to it all. It never is."

"All I want is to be with them," Oliver said. "I'll give you anything."

"It would have to be something of equal value," The Collector of Odd Things pondered. "It would need to be a trade for something I've longed for."

"I doubt I have anything that might interest you."

"No, but perhaps you could find me something." His hand moved from his lap, hovered slowly until it settled on top of the apothecary bottle at his side. "This."

"But that's right there."

"It is, but it's not," The Collector of Odd Things said. "A long time ago a traveler came to my home, said he'd been searching for me, been wandering for ages, which is no exaggeration when you consider how The Seeded Girl arranges and rearranges the paths. He told me his dog was ill—"

"There are dogs here?"

"Of course," The Collector of Odd Things laughed. "No place is worth being in without dogs. I have dozens, he had one, and it was dying. In exchange for something to save his dog, he offered me this."

"A bottle?"

"Not the bottle, it's what it contains."

"It's empty."

"It's not."

Oliver walked to the table, stared into the glass vile. "So, what is it?"

"I don't know. The traveler said it was what sits in the core of all living things. He claimed it was what drove mankind from the water and took them to the stars. It was what sustained him for his journey, and he would give it away for the life of his dog."

"You agreed without knowing what it was?"

"He swore he'd tell me once he knew his dog would be well. I was intrigued, gave him a balm of EddleBee honey and Black Jay tooth grindings, very rare, I still have not found a replacement," The Collector of Odd Things said. "When he arrived back, he was with his dog. He said his companion was better than before he was injured. He handed me this bottle and promptly died."

"Died?" Oliver asked.

"Before telling me the answer to his riddle." The Collector of Odd Things took the bottle in his hand, looked through it, the glass distorting his view of Oliver on the other side. "If you can tell me with certainty what this bottle contains you can be with your family once more."

"Fine," Oliver said. "But I want to see them first."

* * *

The Collector of Odd things led Oliver deeper in the house, passing rooms and common areas that seemed endless in their number and variation. The walls were covered in paintings, ribbons, sticks, skins, horns and so on to infinity. There were rooms filled only with birds, some familiar to Oliver, and others so strange that they paused his steps and stole his focus. Most creatures were not confined to an area and roamed freely. Some were so small they went almost unnoticed, others so large Oliver had to move from the hall to allow them to pass.

"Where do they all come from?" Oliver asked.

"Everywhere," The Collector of Odd Things swelled with pride in Oliver's tone, sensing his awe at the living museum. "Some of them, like the small Pulfers you encountered on your arrival, I make myself from what's on hand."

They came to an open room under a great stained-glass dome that overlooked another room below it. The Collector of Odd Things stopped at the iron railing, gestured for Oliver to come closer and look down. When he did, his knees went weak. The Collector of Odd Things had to grab Oliver, pull him away from the rail to prevent him from toppling over. Oliver pulled away, crawled back to the overlook and gazed between the iron balusters. Below them, Maggie sat in a chair reading a book. Oliver realized the mind's eye was cursed with poor vision, precious memories are reduced to fleeting blurs. Maggie was more beautiful than those insufficient recollections painted her. He felt like he was seeing her for the first time; her strawberry hair and narrow eyes, thin lips above a soft jaw. She chewed the corner of the nail on her small finger, as she always did when she read a good book. Around her, Timothy, Taylor, and Samuel played with cars and trains spread out over the floor. They laughed. The sound of it paused his pounding heart so his ears could hear more clearly. They were alive — or at least something acceptably similar. "Thank you."

"For what?"

"Taking care of them," Oliver said. "When I heard they'd been traded away, told they were part of some collection, I was angry. But if they had to be anywhere, I am grateful they're here."

"My pleasure."

"Can I go to them?"

"No." The Collector of Odd Things watched Oliver's face wilt. His response was like a blade between Oliver's rounded shoulders. "Understand it's for them. If you go to find my answer after your reunion and do not return, they will forever taste misery waiting."

"When can I start?" Oliver asked.

"Now."

Oliver asked to be alone then, to begin his search for the words to describe the nothing inside the apothecary bottle. He wandered the house, thinking through the riddle again and again. The man said it sits at the core of all living things. What was that? A soul? Life was so diverse; did everything have a soul? Does anything have a soul? And what did it have to do with the evolution of humanity? The pressure to discover the answer concentrated into a single point inside his head, began to throb, and made it impossible to contemplate any further.

Oliver could not say how much time passed but it was enough that he felt it leave him like sand being blown off a dune. He wondered what time was in a place like this, then cursed himself for letting his mind be pulled off course. Like the trails that led him here, the more Oliver tried to focus, the more it seemed impossible. The Collector of Odd Things found Oliver laying on the floor below the great dome, listening to his children laugh and his wife talk below. "You need to go."

Oliver stood, rushed to The Collector of Odd Things with clenched fists, desperate eyes. He bit his lip so he wouldn't scream, as he begged for more time. "I'm trying!"

The Collector of Odd Things placed his hands on Oliver's shoulders. "know this in your heart if you doubt everything else; I want you to succeed, Oliver. I tell you to leave because I have watched you pace these halls and rooms for months."

"Months?" His voice sounded surprised, but in truth, he would have guessed longer.

"Obviously the answer is not here."

"I don't know where I am," Oliver said. "Where will I go?"

"You need to trust where the path will take you," The Collector of Odd Things said. "Fear will hold you captive in a moment, only courage pulls you into the future."

"But the girl will stop me."

"What girl?"

"The Seeded Girl," Oliver said. "The one who keeps changing the paths. Who is she?"

The Collector of Odd Things motioned for Oliver to walk with him down the hall. "A long time ago, two druids conceived a daughter who was more of the natural world than the human world. As she grew, all the trees and flowers, the animals and the winds, fell in love with her. Wherever the druids traveled, she would bring new life. It was said that she once stepped foot in a desert and the sands were so grateful for her touch that they sprouted dense grasses and trees, generous wells of cold water, forever an oasis."

He turned to a door that came up to his waist, knelt and opened it. He crawled through; Oliver followed his host. As he did so, the warm wood of the hallway relented to soft grass. While he thought they were outside, this was another room with an earthen floor, shrubs, and glass walls to allow the sunlight to fall on them.

The Collector of Odd Things looked out over the Thorned Forest. "Of course, not all things were so in love with the girl, as nothing is in love with everything and some things love nothing at all. The vipers that once lived in those desert sands were angry that their home was gone. They followed the druids as they moved, waiting for an opportunity to take revenge. One night, when the girl was asleep and the other druids circled the fires, one viper struck, biting and killing the girl."

"All the forests and creatures in them wept and begged the druids to give the girl back to them. So, they buried the girl and moved along, as druids do, in their pursuit of knowledge and magic. Now, since the girl was so loved, no worm or maggot would feed on her, so the girl simply lay beneath the ground in wait, until one day, show woke up."

"She came back?" Oliver asked.

"The bond with life was not broken, like your family," The Collector of Odd Things said. "But the creatures that loved her could not bear to tell the girl she was dead, so the girl thought she was lost instead. She waited for her parents to come for her, to find her in the dark woods, but they never came. Over time, the trees twisted and wove their limbs and roots into a home. The plants all bear her fruit and the animals sacrificed their meat so she wouldn't know hunger. Then, she began using her magic and connection with nature to shift the trails in hopes that one day the combination would be just so, and her parents would come back."

"If she is changing the path," Oliver asked. "How can I trust it will lead me the right way?"

"An answer is always obscured by questions, and not all of them will be your own," The collector of Odd Things said. "If the answer is not in here, then it is out there, and if you don't know where to look, it doesn't matter where the trail will lead. You must simply trust it will lead you to right where you need to be, exactly when you need to be there."

* * *

Oliver looked over his family once more, offered a silent goodbye and promise of his return, then left the house and walked back to the edge of the Thorned Forest. He prepared himself to enter, for whatever might happen or wherever the path might bring him, mostly he braced for the ache in his heart as he moved away from his family. He took a moment to make peace with death, or an eternity searching for an answer as unobtainable as alchemist's gold.

As he moved forward, the path began to twist and writhe like a wounded snake, but he did not stop. Trees withered and died, others grew from seed to maturity in a blink and a breath. The Seeded Girl was not just moving the path, but time. Oliver looked at his hands, they grew older, feeble. Then his skin tightened, and he was younger, stronger. The power manipulating him was terrifying, but he kept moving ahead. At once, time returned to the present and the path went stiff as a corpse. Oliver began to run, relieved he could see the trail ahead so clearly, but a wind lifted from whisper to a howl. It bent the trees, threw leaves and branches in all directions. The dirt and sand of the path blew into Oliver's eyes and he stumbled forward blind, hands outstretched. The thorns in the ground stabbed his feet deeper, he screamed out, his agony swallowed by the wind. He charged on, blind and deaf, screaming the names of his children, his wife, all swept away with the tears from his burning eyes.

Then it stopped.

Oliver fell to the ground. He rubbed the sight back into his eyes and took in his surroundings. He'd made it into a clearing. Oliver felt the sun on his flesh, a warmth like a comforting touch, soothing his body. He took inventory of the new bruises and cuts on his exposed skin.

In the distance, a small, humble house stood. He hobbled toward it, every inch of him begged for rest. He hoped whoever lived in this place would show pity on him and offer him shelter, but the closer he came, the slower he moved. While this structure was shaped like a normal home, it was woven of roots and limbs. He knew where he was, what this was, as The Collector of Odd Things had described it very clearly. This was the home of the Seeded Girl.

Nature had done a striking job mimicking a human home. There was even a small covered porch, a combination of branches and vines, all alive with leaves and flowers carrying to the top, forming a watertight roof. There was a door made of moss and stone with windows of spider silk instead of glass, a cozy home by any standard. A humming danced on the breeze and into his ears, a happy song of a child. Oliver rounded the side of the home, and at the tree line he saw her.

She faced away, crouched down and tending to a patch of saplings. They were not in a row, growing where the seed had found soil naturally. Her dress was filthy, frayed, her flaxen hair a series of knots and wild braids. She continued with her song as her hands caressed the young trees and scooped water to their bases from a bucket beside her.

"Hello there," Oliver announced himself.

The girl spun and fell back, flattened one of her plants. She looked at Oliver, then begin tending to the broken shrub. "Who are you?"

"My name is Oliver," he said. "I didn't mean to---."

She tried to lift the broken stem, to balance it, but it was no use. She pushed two small mounds of dirt over the tree, held her hands on it. "How did you find me?"

Oliver moved closer. "Your trail brought me here."

"It did?" Her head lifted, excited. "Did you see anyone else?"

"No."

"I'm waiting for my parents to come," she said. "They'll be here soon. The trail isn't right, I don't know why, but it can't be, because they haven't come. If they're searching that way, I need to lead them this way. Then I can leave this place and go wherever the trails want to take us instead of where I want them to take others." She turned to Oliver with a furrowed brow and tight lips. "Are you sure you haven't seen any others?"

"Only the Collector of Odd Things," Oliver said. "That's where I've come from."

The Seeded Girl stood; her mask of suspicion clung to her face. She had eyes like the sky reflected in black water, and while all the things of the natural world loved this child enough to keep her alive, time was not such an admirer. Even though her size and features were that of a young girl, her skin was wrinkled and dry. "You should go."

"Why?" Oliver asked.

"I want to be alone when my parents come. I want to show them my home and my garden."

Oliver looked around the forest, this one of real trees and undergrowth, and saw there were dozens of trails entering the clearing. "How long have you been here?"

The Seeded Girl opened her mouth to answer before she realized her mind had no answer to voice. Instead, she knelt back beside her garden and ladled more water with her hand. "One day or a thousand are equal when you live them alone. Life will start its clock again when my parents come, but I need to give them the right path. It's my fault they can't find their way."

The Seeded Girl's hands fell to her sides, her hair dropped over her face. She stared at the grave of the sapling, a fragile and pathetic heap. He saw himself in her, the years he wept over the graves of his own family. There was a moment Oliver considered ending the girl's misery, telling her that it does not matter how she arranges the trails because her parents were not walking them, that they were not looking for their dead daughter. Instead, Oliver walked back to the trail he'd come from. "I hope they arrive soon. It's a nice day for a reunion."

"Aren't you going to ask?" The girl called.

Oliver turned back. "Ask what?"

"You're not the first to come here," she said. "The Collector of Odd Things has made a bargain with others to find the answer to his riddle. The ones that make it here are quick to ask me if I know. Some even get mad, try to tell me I'm dead, if you can believe that."

"Outrageous. No sense in asking," Oliver said. "If you knew the answer then, I wouldn't be here now."

"I suppose not," the girl said. "Do you know why it's so important to him?"

"No."

The Seeded Girl turned, sat beside her garden, looked at Oliver with softer eyes now. "The Collector of Odd Things once had a family that he loved very much, but his heart was conflicted. For all his good intentions, greed was at his core, and it was that need to have things that blinded him to what things were needed. His wife pleaded for him to take in not one more thing, not even a grain of sand."

She paused to examine one sapling that had a pair of brown leaves, she pinched them off and tossed them aside. "The Collector of Odd Things was convinced it was the things in his life that gave him joy, so he was confused at the hole cut through him when he woke to find his family gone. That was when he began to collect anything and everything to fill the void, the strange and odd, the unique and unexplainable, he even began to create things to collect. You are here, like the others, because he believes what is inside that bottle is what he needs to be happy."

"But what is it?" Oliver asked. "I need to find out so I can be with my family again."

"Your family?" The Seeded Girl sat rigid. "Are they waiting for you?"

"Yes," Oliver said.

"For your family? Not for gold or power? Well, that does change things," The Seeded Girl said to her saplings. She brushed the back of her hand against one, it bent at her touch. "I feel a connection with them. These little trees try so hard for the attention of the sun, but where does it get them? I wonder why they keep reaching for it, knowing the canopy above them takes it all for themselves. The sun's rays are their food, and they get so little. I often wonder what else is nourishing them. That is my connection to them, why I care for these throwaways."

"What is?" Oliver asked.

"That is just one of the questions you must answer." The Seeded Girl stood, brushed the dirt from her tattered dress. "That answer will answer another question, and another, and that answer is the connection of all living things, from these saplings to me, to the Collector to you, and why you're even here at all."

The Seeded Girl went inside her home, offering only a kind smile before the door closed. Oliver paced the clearing and admired the saplings until he grew tired. The trails leading into this clearing moved again, the girl rearranged them in spite of seeming to know the truth of her situation. Oliver considered all the questions, trying to find the lynchpin at their center. What was it that drove the creatures that became men from the sea? Why were men driven to the stars? What connected all things, plant, and animal?

Why was the Seeded Girl unyielding in her pursuit to change the paths and how did that connect with her sapling garden starved by the shade? How did that connect with Oliver? How did all of it connect with The Collector of Odd Things' obsession to discover what was in that bottle? Why did giving whatever it was away killed the man who did so? He pondered the questions as individual problems but a collective mystery. What did any of it have to do with why Oliver had come here?

Oliver stood in front of the sapling garden. A breeze emerged from one side of the forest and dove into the other, washing over him and the young trees as it went. The plants were not orderly, but they were healthy, even if their existence in the shade starved them. It reminded him of Maggie, the garden her and the boys had decided to make in the shade of the large maple behind their home.

When they first planted the vegetables there, Oliver was quick to point out the Maple would make it impossible for anything to grow. Maggie and the boys insisted it stay and Oliver said no more, letting what he thought was the inevitable failure grow where the seeds had been sewn. To his surprise, and his family's delight, not only did the vegetables grow, but they yielded the largest and most delicious offerings he'd ever seen. After a humble apology for his doubt, Maggie kissed him and said, "Sometimes everything can be against you, but you'll come through it if you have—"

That was it. That was the answer.

The thought turned electric, moved through Oliver like a strike of lightening. Its simplicity was beautiful, profound, and humbling. He felt lighter, as if the sunlight of the clearing had been collected in his heart and filled his lungs. He ran to the nearest path, unsure and uncaring of where it would take him, knowing that it would bring him right where he needed to be, exactly when he needed to be there.

Just as the first of his steps fell on the bath, the earth shivered and the world began to swirl again, to change. But this time he did not let it shake him, he was one with all of it as he always had been, but only now he understood. The winds, the movement of time, life and death. The weight of the questions shattered and forced its way out of him as laughter. Just as the sound of his own voiced rose high enough to mix with the winds that danced around him, all was still.

*   *   *

Oliver pushed the doors open to the great hall to find the Collector of Odd Things sitting in the lone chair, staring into the nothing inside the bottle on the table beside him. The brash entrance took The

Collector of Odd Things to his feet. "Oliver!"

"I know what's in the bottle!" The words that fell from his lips were tied to his breath, came forth with the frantic pace of his beating heart. "Hope!"

The Collector of Odd Things stopped his approach, the word entering his mismatched ears and unwrapping itself in his mind like a gift. "Hope?"

"Yes. Hope is what drove the man to you to beg for the life of his dog, what killed him when he gave it away. It is why you collect and make all these things, it is why the Seeded Girl moves space and time, why the saplings push higher, why I dug up my family's grave, why I'm here. What took men from the sea and to the stars. It is what drives life forward even though it might be driving off a cliff. Hope."

"Hope," The Collector of Odd Things whispered. "Of course."

"Now we can go. My family, right? We can all go?"

"Yes." The Collector of Odd Things walked to the apothecary bottle on the table and lifted it in line with his eyes. He twisted the vile back and forth, trying to catch a glimpse of the intangible inside it, thinking now that he knew its secret it could be seen. "I mean no. No. You can't leave."

Oliver felt sick. "You said if I—"

"I said you could *be* with them," The Collector of Odd Things said. "Not that you could *leave* with them. While knowing what is in this bit of crystal will help me place it on my shelf, *you* are what will complete my collection." The Collector of Odd Things put his hand over the hole in his center, waved his fingers inside it. "You and your family are what I've been searching for." He paused a moment. "What I've *hoped* for. A love that defies, endures. That can't be broken, that can't be traded away or squandered."

Oliver thought he should be mad, feel the betrayal overtake his better judgment, charge across the room and tear all the bits and pieces that formed The Collector of Odd Things into a blizzard of floating debris. Instead, he felt weightless, content, even happy. Even if he silky the chance to take his family from here, where would they go? He couldn't take them back into the world he'd come from, and without them in that world, it was not one he would want to stay in. This was exactly where he needed to be, exactly when he needed to be here. "Can I go to them?"

The Collector of Odd Things placed the bottle back down, gestured to the door. "This is your home now, Oliver. You can do as you wish."

Oliver left the room and started down the hall, feeling the energy of this house and the living collection all around him. The sounds of birds, the visceral charge of the countless pieces of art, the musk of the animals as he passed made him feel alive. Then he heard a loud shriek, a joyous call of children at play, followed by laughter. He knew it was one of his boys and that carried his feet faster. He was running, weeping and laughing.

Inside this strange place, concealed in a strange world, Oliver was unsure of where it would lead or how it might end – but he had hope.

Night Surf

Stephen King

AFTER the guy was dead and the smell of his burning flesh was off the air, we all went back down to the beach. Corey had his radio, one of those suitcase-sized transistor jobs that take about forty batteries and also make and play tapes. You couldn't say the sound reproduction was great, but it sure was loud. Corey had been well-to-do before A6, but stuff like that didn't matter anymore. Even his big radio/tape-player was hardly more than a nice-looking hunk of junk. There were only two radio stations left on the air that we could get. One was WKDM in Portsmouth — some backwoods deejay who had gone nutty-religious. He'd play a Perry Como record, say a prayer, bawl, play a Johnny Ray record, read from Psalms (complete with each selah', just like James Dean in East of Eden), then bawl some more. Happy-time stuff like that. One day he sang Bringing in the Sheaves' in a cracked, mouldy voice that sent Needles and me into hysterics.

The Massachusetts station was better, but we could only get it at night. It was a bunch of kids. I guess they took over the transmitting facilities of WRKO or WBZ after every-body left or died. They only gave gag call letters, like WDOPE or KUNT or WA6 or stuff like that. Really funny, you know — you could die laughing. That was the one we were listening to on the way back to the beach. I was holding hands with Susie; Kelly and Joan were ahead of us, and Needles was already over the brow of the point and out of sight. Corey was bringing up the rear, swinging his radio. The Stones were singing 'Angie'.

'Do you love me?' Susie was asking. 'That's all I want to know, do you love me?' Susie needed constant reassurance. I was her teddy bear.

'No,' I said. She was getting fat, and if she lived long enough, which wasn't likely, she would get really flabby. She was already mouthy.

'You're rotten,' she said, and put a hand to her face. Her lacquered fingernails twinkled dimly with the half-moon that had risen about an hour ago.

'Are you going to cry again?'

'Shut up!' She sounded like she was going to cry again, all right.

We came over the ridge and I paused. I always have to pause. Before A6, this had been a public beach. Tourists, picnickers, runny-nosed kids and fat baggy grandmothers with sunburned elbows. Candy wrappers and popsicle sticks in the sand, all the beautiful people necking on their beach blankets, intermingled stench of exhaust from the parking lot, seaweed, and Coppertone oil.

But now all the dirt and all the crap was gone. The ocean had eaten it, all of it, as casually as you might eat a handful of Cracker Jacks. There were no people to come back and dirty it again. Just us, and we weren't enough to make much mess. We loved the beach too, I guess — hadn't we just offered it a kind of sacrifice? Even Susie, little bitch Susie with her fat ass and her cranberry bellbottoms.

The sand was white and duned, marked only by the high-tide line — twisted skein of seaweed, kelp, hunks of driftwood. The moonlight stitched inky crescent-shaped shadows and folds across everything. The deserted lifeguard tower stood white and skeletal some fifty yards from the bathhouse towards the sky like a finger bone.

And the surf, the night surf, throwing up great bursts of foam, breaking against the headlands for as far as we could see in endless attacks. Maybe that water had been halfway to England the night before.

'"Angie", by the Stones,' the cracked voice on Corey's radio said. 'I'm sureya dug that one, a blast from the past that's a golden gas, straight from the grooveyard, a platta that mattas. I'm Bobby. This was supposed to be Fred's night, but Fred got the flu. He's all swelled up.' Susie giggled then, with the first tears still on her eyelashes. I started towards the beach a little faster to keep her quiet.

'Wait up!' Corey called. 'Bernie? Hey, Bernie, wait up!' The guy on the radio was reading some dirty limericks, and a girl in the background asked him where did he put the beer. He said something back, but by that time we were on the beach. I looked back to see how Corey was doing. He was coming down on his backside, as usual, and he looked so ludicrous I felt a little sorry for him.

'Run with me,' I said to Susie.

'Why?'

I slapped her on the can and she squealed. 'Just because it feels good to run.'

We ran. She fell behind, panting like a horse and calling r me to slow down, but I put her out of my head. The wind rushed past my ears and blew the hair off my forehead. I could smell the salt in the air, sharp and tart. The surf pounded. The waves were like foamed black glass. I kicked off my rubber sandals and pounded across the sand barefoot, not minding the sharp digs of an occasional shell. My blood roared.

And then there was the lean-to with Needles already inside and Kelly and Joan standing beside it, holding hands and looking at the water. I did a forward roll, feeling sand go down the back of my shirt, and fetched up against Kelly's legs. He fell on top of me and rubbed my face in the sand while Joan laughed.

We got up and grinned at each other. Susie had given up running and was plodding towards us. Corey had almost caught up to her.

'Some fire,' Kelly said.

'Do you think he came all the way from New York, like he said?' Joan asked.

'I don't know.' I couldn't see that it mattered anyway. He had been behind the wheel of a big Lincoln when we found him, semi-conscious and raving. His head was bloated to the size of a football and his neck looked like a sausage. He had Captain Trips and n6t far to go, either. So we took him up to the Point that overlooks the beach and burned him. He said his name was Alvin Sackheim. He kept calling for his grand-mother. He thought Susie was his grandmother. This struck her funny, God knows why. The strangest things strike Susie funny.

It was Corey's idea to burn him up, but it started off as a joke. He had read all those books about witchcraft and black magic at college, and he kept leering at us in the dark beside Alvin Sackheim's Lincoln and telling us that if we made a sacrifice to the dark gods, maybe the spirits would keep protecting us against A6.

Of course none of us really believed that bullshit, but the talk got more and more serious. It was a new thing to do, and finally we went ahead and did it. We tied him to the observation gadget up there — you put a dime in it and on a clear day you can see all the way to Portland Headlight. We tied him with our belts, and then we went rooting around for dry brush and hunks of driftwood like kids playing a new kind of hide-and-seek. All the time we were doing it Alvin Sackheim just sort of leaned there and mumbled to his grandmother. Susie's eyes got very bright and she was breathing fast. It was really turning her on. When we were down in the ravine on the other side of the outcrop she leaned against me and kissed me. She was wearing too much lipstick and it was like kissing a greasy plate.

I pushed her away and that was when she started pouting. We

went back up, all of us, and piled dead branches and twigs up to Alvin Sackheim's waist. Needles lit the pyre with his Zippo, and it went up fast. At the end, just before his hair caught on fire, the guy began to scream. There was a smell just like sweet Chinese pork.

'Got a cigarette, Bernie?' Needles asked.

'There's about fifty cartons right behind you.'

He grinned and slapped a mosquito that was probing his arm. 'Don't want to move.'

I gave him a smoke and sat down. Susie and I met Needles in Portland. He was sitting on the kerb in front of the State Theatre, playing Leadbelly tunes on a big old Gibson guitar he had looted someplace. The sound echoed up and down Congress Street as if he were playing in a concert hall.

Susie stopped in front of us, still out of breath. 'You're rotten, Bernie.'

'Come on, Sue. Turn the record over. That side stinks.'

'Bastard. Stupid, unfeeling son of a bitch. Creep!'

'Go away,' I said, 'or I'll black your eye, Susie. See if I don't.'

She started to cry again. She was really good at it. Corey came up and tried to put an arm around her. She elbowed him in the crotch and he spit in her face.

'I'll kill you!' She came at him, screaming and weeping, making propellers with her hands. Corey backed off, almost fell, then turned tail and ran. Susie followed him, hurling hysterical obscenities. Needles put back his head and laughed. The sound of Corey's radio came back to us faintly over the surf.

Kelly and Joan had wandered off. I could see them down by the edge of the water, walking with their arms around each other's waist. They looked like an ad in a travel agent's window — Fly to Beautiful St Lorca. It was all right. They had a good thing.

'Bernie?'

'What?' I sat and smoked and thought about Needles flipping back the top of his Zippo, spinning the wheel, making fire with flint and steel like a caveman.

'I've got it,' Needles said.

'Yeah?' I looked at him. 'Are you sure?'

'Sure I am. My head aches. My stomach aches. Hurts to piss.'

'Maybe it's just Hong Kong flu. Susie had Hong Kong flu. She wanted a Bible.' I laughed. That had been while we were still at the University, about a week before they closed it down for good, a month before they started carrying bodies away in dump trucks and burying them in mass graves with payloaders.

'Look.' He lit a match and held it under the angle of his jaw. I could see the first triangular smudges, the first swelling. It was A6, all right.

'Okay,' I said.

'I don't feel so bad,' he said. 'In my mind, I mean. You, though. You think about it a lot. I can tell.'

'No I don't.' A lie.

'Sure you do. Like that guy tonight. You're thinking about that, too. We probably did him a favour, when you get right down to it. I don't think he even knew it was happening.'

'He knew.'

He shrugged and turned on his side. 'It doesn't matter.'

We smoked and I watched the surf come in and go out. Needles and Captain Trips. That made everything real all over again. It was late August already, and in a couple of weeks the first chill of fall would be creeping in. Time to move inside someplace. Winter. Dead by Christmas, maybe, all of us. In somebody's front room with Corey's expensive radio/tape-player on top of a book-case full of Reader's Digest Condensed Books and the weak winter sun lying on the rug in meaningless window-pane patterns.

The vision was clear enough to make me shudder. Nobody should think about winter in August. It's like a goose walking over your grave.

Needles laughed. 'See? You do think about it.'

What could I say? I stood up. 'Going to look for Susie.'

'Maybe we're the last people on earth, Bernie. Did you ever think of that?' In the faint moonlight he already looked half dead, with circles under his eyes and pallid, unmoving fingers like pencils.

I walked down to the water and looked out across it. There was nothing to see but the restless, moving humps of the waves, topped by delicate curls of foam. The thunder of the breakers was tremendous down here, bigger than the world. Like standing inside a thunderstorm. I closed my eyes and rocked on my bare feet. The sand was cold and damp and packed. And if we were the last people on earth, so what? This would go on as long as there was a moon to pull the water.

Susie and Corey were up the beach. Susie was riding him as if he were a bucking bronc, pounding his head into the running boil of the water. Corey was flailing and splashing. They were both soaked. I walked down and pushed her off with my foot. Corey splashed away on all fours, spluttering and whoofing.

'I hate you!' Susie screamed at me. Her mouth was a dark grinning crescent. It looked like the entrance to a fun house. When I was a kid my mother used to take us kids to Harrison State Park and there was a fun house with a big clown face on the front, and you walked in through the mouth.

'Come on, Susie. Up, Fido.' I held out my hand. She took it doubtfully and stood up. There was damp sand clotted on her blouse and skin.

'You didn't have to push me, Bernie. You don't ever —' 'Come on.' She wasn't like a jukebox; you never had to put in a dime and she never came unplugged.

We walked up the beach towards the main concession. The man who ran the place had had a small overhead apartment. There was a bed. She didn't really deserve a bed, but Needles was right about that. It didn't matter. No one was really scoring the game any more.

The stairs went up the side of the building, but I paused for just a minute to look in the broken window at the dusty wares inside that no one had cared enough about to loot -stacks of sweatshirts ('Anson Beach' and a picture of sky and waves printed on the front), glittering bracelets that would green the wrist on the second day, bright junk earrings, beachballs, dirty greeting cards, badly painted ceramic madonnas, plastic vomit (So realistic! Try it on your wife!), Fourth of July sparklers for a Fourth that never was, beach towels with a voluptuous girl in a bikini standing amid the names of a hundred famous resort areas, pennants (Souvenir of Anson Beach and Park), balloons, bathing suits. There was a snack bar up front with a big sign saying

TRY OUR CLAM CAKE SPECIAL.

I used to come to Anson Beach a lot when I was still in high school. That was seven years before A6, and I was going with a girl named Maureen. She was a big girl. She had a pink checked bathing suit. I used to tell her it looked like a tablecloth. We had walked along the boardwalk in front of this place, barefoot, the boards hot and sandy beneath our heels. We had never tried the clam cake special.

'What are you looking at?'

'Nothing. Come on.'

I had sweaty, ugly dreams about Alvin Sackheim. He was propped behind the wheel of his shiny yellow Lincoln, talking about his grandmother. He was nothing but a bloated, blackened head and a charred skeleton. He smelled burnt. He talked on and on, and after a while I couldn't make out a single word. I woke up breathing hard.

Susie was sprawled across my thighs, pale and bloated. My watch said 3.50, but it had stopped. It was still dark out. The surf pounded and smashed. High tide. Make it 4.15. Light soon. I got out of bed and went to the doorway. The sea breeze felt fine against my hot body. In spite of it all I didn't want to die.

I went over in the corner and grabbed a beer. There were three or four cases of Bud stacked against the wall. It was warm, because there was no electricity. I don't mind warm beer like some people do, though. It just foams a little more. Beer is beer. I went back out on the landing and sat down and pulled the ring tab and drank up.

So here we were, with the whole human race wiped out, not by atomic weapons or bio-warfare or pollution or anything grand like that. Just the flu. I'd like to put down a huge plaque somewhere, in the Bonneville Salt Flats, maybe. Bronze Square. Three miles on a side. And in big raised letters it would say, for the benefit of any landing aliens: JUST THE FLU.

I tossed the beer can over the side. It landed with a hollow clank on the cement walk that went around the building. The lean-to was a dark triangle on the sand. I wondered if Needles was awake. I wondered if I would be.

'Bernie?'

She was standing in the doorway wearing one of my shirts. I hate that. She sweats like a pig.

'You don't like me much any more, do you, Bernie?'

I didn't say anything. There were times when I could still feel sorry for everything. She didn't deserve me any more than I deserved her.

'Can I sit down with you?'

'I doubt if it would be wide enough for both of us.'

She made a choked orwardng noise and started to go back inside.

'Needles has got A6,' I said.

She stopped and looked at me. Her face was very still. 'Don't joke, Bernie.'

I lit a cigarette.

'He can't! He had -, 'Yes, he had A2. Hong Kong flu. Just like you and me and Corey and Kelly and Joan.'

'But that would mean he isn't —'

'Immune.'

'Yes. Then we could get it.'

'Maybe he lied when he said he had A2. So we'd take him along with us that time,' I said.

207

Relief spilled across her face. 'Sure, that's it. I would have lied if it had been me. Nobody likes to be alone, do they?' She hesitated. 'Coming back to bed?'

'Not just now.'

She went inside. I didn't have to tell her that M was no guarantee against A6. She knew that. She had just blocked it out. I sat and watched the surf. It was really up. Years ago, Anson had been the only halfway decent surfing spot in the state. The Point was a dark, jutting hump against the sky. I thought I could see the upright that was the observation post, but it probably was just imagination. Sometimes Kelly took Joan up to the point. I didn't think they were up there tonight.

I put my face in my hands and clutched it, feeling the skin, its grain and texture. It was all narrowing so swiftly, and it was all so mean — there was no dignity in it.

The surf coming in, coming in, coming in. Limitless. Clean and deep. We had come here in the summer, Maureen and I, the summer after high school, the summer before college and reality and A6 coming out of South-east Asia and covering the world like a pall, July, we had eaten pizza and listened to her radio, I had put oil on her back, she had put oil on mine, the air had been hot, the sand bright, the sun like a burning glass.

Anniversary

John R. Little

I T was 60 years ago to the day when they first met.

Jimmy Lamars didn't need any help remembering, because it was not only the anniversary of the day they met, a year later they married on the same day. August 1.

To add to that, August 1 was also his birthday.

He'd wandered down to the beach that day when he turned 23, expecting nothing but an afternoon of reflection and peace.

Jimmy had just changed jobs, and the new one wasn't really working out for him. They expected him to work long hours and to be available on weekends.

He wasn't too into that, because he was finding he had almost no time to himself.

Who wanted to be locked into a career that left him no free time to enjoy his life?

He was 23 for Christ's sake. His life was just beginning, and he knew it.

"Not me," he said as he took his sandals off and walked slowly out to the water. The beach sand was squishy between his toes, and he loved the feel of the blistering sun beating down on him.

It was a hot day, maybe the hottest of that summer.

Hibbon's Cove was off the beaten path. He had driven fifty miles from Bangor to reach the secluded area just south of Bay Harbor. He'd found the place by accident two summers earlier while wandering along the Maine coastline.

Jimmy never told a soul about Hibbon's Cove. He'd been there a half dozen times since then, to walk in the refreshing water, watch the tides come in and out, and to just be alone with his thoughts. It was the perfect place to go when he needed to make a big decision.

He was already a heavy man, more than 220 pounds, and when he was walking his beach alone, he never had to worry about anybody laughing at him.

It was his own private paradise. Until that day.

* * *

Gail Sommers had also tripped across Hibbon's Cove by herself. Well, in her case, it was her and two girlfriends who had found the quiet little beach together. She was 21 and her two besties were both leaving Bangor to move to New York City.

They'd only given her two weeks notice that they were going to the Big Apple to find themselves. Whatever that meant.

They hadn't asked her to join them, which hurt, but she also knew she wouldn't have gone. Maine was where she'd been born and where she would probably live her entire life.

"I'm going to miss you guys so much," she said as they walked the lonely beach. Trish and Amber smiled and nodded. It was during that walk that Gail realized that although they were her besties, she wasn't theirs.

Secretly she couldn't help thinking it was the same as always.

According to her daddy, Gail was big-boned. That sounded like something she was born with, so it wasn't her fault she was bigger than the Barbie dolls walking with her. They were twigs compared to her, and when they didn't invite her to go to New York with her, she knew it was because they didn't see her in the same league as them.

Walking on the deserted beach and understanding that fact made Gail horribly sad.

Ten days later, Trish and Amber left with a small trailer dragging along behind Trish's car (the one her own daddy had given her for her 18th birthday), and they hit the road.

They never answered her phone calls or letters. This was before emails and texting, but she later knew they would have ignored those too.

Hibbon's Cove should have been a sad place for her, but it wasn't. It was a place of transition for her, moving from being a dumb girl who had no clue to a woman who was starting to understand how the world worked.

From that day, Gail thought of the Cove as a place she could just be herself, without worrying about what anyone else thought about her.

* * *

On August 1, *that* August 1 sixty years ago, Jimmy and Gail both walked on the sand at Hibbon's Cove, each expecting to find nobody else to share the beach with, and so each was shocked to see another person there.

Jimmy saw Gail first, and his initial reaction was to want to cover his belly, but he had left his T-shirt in the car. He had nothing to hide behind, and his belly fat spilled out over his bathing suit like always.

He wanted to just turn around and leave, but he could tell that

Gail saw him. If he left now, he'd look like – what? – like a freak? A coward? He didn't even know, and he didn't have much time to think about it.

The girl was walking toward him.

He looked at her and tried to smile. He felt trapped, mentally as well as physically, since his feet were being sucked into the wet sand as waves spilled over his toes. It felt like quicksand, and for a moment he was afraid he'd be sucked right down, but of course no such thing happened.

After hesitating, he started to walk toward her. She was smiling at him.

When they got closer to each other, she said, "I thought I was the only person who knew about this place." She laughed.

He felt a wave of relief wash over him. Something about that laugh just set his mind at ease.

"And I thought that, too."

They stared at each other, as if they were the only two humans left in a dead world.

Jimmy didn't know what to say. He just wanted to see that smile again.

Gail had smiled because she was afraid. It was an odd habit she knew she had, but there was nothing she could do about it. She smiled in lots of other circumstances, too, but this time it was due to fear.

Who was this strange man who was encroaching on *her* beach?

"I'm Gail," she finally said.

"I'm Jimmy."

He didn't know if he should offer to shake hands. That might be weird.

Gail was calming down. She liked the sound of his voice. It wasn't scary. In fact, he seemed as nervous as she was.

It took them ten minutes before they both shook their jitters and were able to be comfortable.

ANNIVERSARY

Neither one knew that this was the start of a lifetime together.

*   *   *

Now, Jimmy was turning 83 on this August 1.

Gail was 81, going to turn 82 on December 14.

They'd woken that morning, full of the normal pains and problems they woke up with every day. Growing old is not for the meek, especially when serious health problems come along for the ride.

Jimmy was taking a chemo-break. It'd been two years since the cancer first showed up in his bowel. At times he considered himself lucky to have lasted until then without any serious problems, but once that bit of cancer showed up, everything changed.

Hastily arranged surgery removed part of his bowel, along with his prostrate and his bladder. Those organs were collateral damage since they couldn't get the bowel cancer out without taking those, too.

Since then he wore a couple of bags stuck to his body all the time, taking care of his piss and shit.

Maybe that would have been okay if that was all there was to it, but oh no, the cancer had other ideas. After some initially promising check-ups, the cancer showed up again. This time in his liver and a spot on one of his lungs.

Jimmy was subjected to radiotherapy and lots of chemo sessions. Lots.

Sometimes the chemo made him nauseated, and he wouldn't eat for days on end, even when pushed to it by Gail.

The last rounds, though, were different chemicals, and these ones made him want to eat non-stop.

Weird.

He'd ballooned back up to 275 pounds, and he supposed he would die one day soon, way too big for a standard casket.

Have to make those arrangements before it's too late, he'd often think to himself. But he hadn't ever followed through on that. He didn't want to leave the funeral details to Gail, but it felt like if he went to chat to the local undertaker, he'd be giving up.

Gail's health problems weren't life-threatening, but they were equally debilitating.

She'd had her right knee replaced ten years earlier, and now she'd had to have the left one replaced. She could barely walk, even with crutches, but at least she knew that was temporary. After a few months, she be waddling along the same as she always had.

Gail never commented about Jimmy being so overweight. After all, from the day they'd met, she'd never been slim, and now although she knew she tipped the scale at 204, she wouldn't ever mention that to him.

Jimmy loved Gail with all his heart.

Gail loved Jimmy just as much.

Sixty years together didn't seem nearly enough, but both knew they'd be lucky to celebrate 61.

*   *   *

That morning, Jimmy creaked to life when the dawn sunshine reached down from their bedroom window. He'd been dreaming about that long-lost day when they first met.

It hurt to move at all, and it took a lot of energy just to roll over to face Gail. He was breathing hard and took a moment to catch his breath.

Gail smiled. She knew the effort it took him. It was almost as bad for her.

"We should go to Hibbon's Cove," he said.

She frowned and said, "What are you talking about? It's been years."

Jimmy nodded. "I think it's been twenty years since we were there."

He wondered how that was possible. It was their special place, but somehow, they seemed to have forgotten all about it.

Twenty years? Really?

Yes, maybe twenty-one or twenty-two. He wasn't sure.

"It'd be awfully hard on us," Gail said.

Jimmy shrugged. "Easier today than next year." He paused and added, "I think we deserve to see it one last time."

Gail nodded, knowing she would do anything for the man she loved.

"Should we pack a lunch?"

"Yes. Tuna sandwiches and Coke."

She smiled. That was the same lunch they'd taken almost every time they'd gone to visit the Cove when they were young.

She remembered them running out to meet the tide, catching the waves that crashed over their bodies, laughing as the powerful water pulled them every which way, and grabbing each other's hands to help them stay stable.

Jimmy leaned over and gave his wife a long kiss. He didn't care how much it hurt.

*   *   *

Jimmy had given up his driver's licence a year earlier, and Gail couldn't really drive with her new knee still in training mode, so they called an Uber to take them to Hibbon's Cove.

It took them more than a few minutes just to get themselves out of the car. The Uber driver had to help pull each of them out in turn, and he asked, "Are you sure you folks will be okay? You don't look too... "

Stable? Healthy? Alive?

Jimmy didn't know how he had planned to finish that sentence, but he supposed any of those words would fit.

"It's okay," he said. "We come here all the time."

"Okay, well, you can request me when you want to go back

home if you want."

Jimmy nodded and didn't look back as he and Gail shuffled down the skinny little path that led through some trees and eventually down to the Cove.

"Think anyone else has found our little paradise yet?" he asked Gail.

She smiled and looked at him. He still loved that smile.

There was nobody else on the beach, which is what they expected. They set the bag of sandwiches and cans of Coke down and looked out to the water.

It was as beautiful a day as either could remember. The sky was pure blue, a deep blue that somehow seemed to reflect the deep color of the water below.

The beach was empty of people, empty of garbage, empty of all signs of humanity.

Jimmy liked that.

They looked out to the water. It was low tide, so the ocean seemed a very long way from them.

He hesitated, not sure he could walk that far. He didn't have to look at Gail to know she was thinking the same thing. She had brought a single crutch to use on her left side, but it was as hard for her to walk as it was for him.

It wasn't just his cancer or her knee. Their bodies were old, and they just couldn't support their heavy weights like they used to.

Fuck it, he thought. He looked at Gail and smiled.

"We'll never come back. This is our only chance. We can't miss this last chance."

Gail didn't answer for a moment, and he was afraid she was going to say no.

Finally, she nodded and said, "It's our life."

The first steps were easy enough. The sand was mostly dry, and they didn't really sink in. Jimmy's feet seemed to have some kind of memory, as if they were young and happy to be in the sand.

Twenty years? Really?

Gail used her crutch but was struggling to move. He wanted to take her hand and help, but with him being a bit unstable himself, he was afraid he'd make both of them fall.

They moved slowly, occasionally glancing at each other and smiling support.

The sun bounced off Gail's hair, and it almost brought tears to Jimmy's eyes. She was beautiful.

He had dropped his shirt, so he was wearing only shorts. He no longer owned an actual bathing suit. Gail was wearing an old dress she didn't care about. It was bright yellow, perfectly matching the sun.

The sun itself was beaming down and was hotter than Jimmy could ever remember. Was it always this hot? He was sweating, rivulets of water flushing down the rolls of his upper body.

He didn't see any sweat falling from Gail. *Figures*, he thought.

Gail didn't notice any of that. All she could think of was trying desperately to put one foot in front of the other without falling. She didn't want to look like a fool in front of Jimmy. She'd done that quite enough times in her life, thank you very much.

She never would have tried this without his encouragement. She wanted to look back, to see how far they'd walked out, but she was afraid that if she did, she'd lose her nerve.

She had to be strong for Jimmy.

Jimmy was breathing hard. He was already worn out, and they'd only covered about half the distance to the water.

"Wish it wasn't low tide," he said softly.

"We would have come no matter what," Gail said.

He grunted.

She added, "Back in the day, we'd have run out to the water in seconds. At least this way we get to enjoy the walk."

Jimmy burst out laughing in spite of himself. "Yes," he said, "It's a beautiful walk."

And it was.

His one and only love was walking with him on an amazing afternoon. How could he complain about that?

"It would have been nice to have a cool breeze," he said.

"Sure would."

Jimmy wondered how long they'd been walking, but he wasn't wearing his watch. It wasn't waterproof and he was firm in his belief that he'd be out sitting in the water very soon.

Another ten minutes passed, and they reached the water.

It started with little pools that had held the last of the retreating water. Jimmy wondered if that meant the tide was still going out or if it was coming in now. He hated that his memory was failing. Even ten years ago he would have known how the damned tides worked. Now it was just a big puzzle.

"Oh, it's cold!" said Gail.

"It always feels that way," Jimmy answered. "But, you're right, I'd forgotten that, too."

"It's nice on my toes."

He nodded. "Let's keep going."

They walked more, and Jimmy tried to convince himself it was getting easier. His feet were all wet now, water up to his ankles. The cool water was soothing the pain in his feet, but it wasn't helping the pain in the rest of his body.

He felt weak, and he gritted his teeth to try to gain control of himself. He would *not* fall down in front of Gail.

"Should we stop here?" she asked.

"Just a little farther," he whispered. He wanted to stop there, too, but it would be like they were little two-year-olds splashing in the water on their first trip to the beach.

He was a man, not a baby.

He walked another step and Gail followed.

"Just up to our knees," he promised.

She didn't answer, and he wasn't sure if she was okay with that decision or not, but he really needed them to go a little farther. Just a bit. Far enough that he would leave the toddler area behind him.

"Remember we'd come out here with our Frisbee and stand fifty feet apart throwing it to each other? Other times we'd toss a football," said Jimmy.

"We'll not be doing that today, my dear."

"Oh, I know. It's just the good memories flooding me."

"Me too."

"Sometimes we'd go a bit deeper and you'd stand on my shoulders, looking like the Statue of Liberty. I'd crouch down and then push you up as high as I could, and you'd do a freedom dive into the water."

She smiled, and this time she reached out and took his hand.

"I remember," she said.

They stood still and looked out together. The water wasn't up to his knees, but they'd gone as far as he could manage. He was exhausted.

He turned to her and smiled. A tear fell down his cheek.

"Jimmy? What's wrong?"

He was choked up with emotion and couldn't answer her. He just shook his head. Then he sniffed and tried to get control of himself. He made a downward motion with his hands and both of them took some very cautious movements to lower themselves to sit on the sand.

Jimmy was almost out of breath. He tried to take a deep long breath, but it was hard. *That* was the effect of the chemo, he was sure.

He looked back to shore. From the perspective of sitting there, the shore looked forever away.

"Are you okay?" Gail's voice sounded concerned.

"I'm fine. I just needed to catch my breath. "How are you doing?"

"Well, I don't know how I'm going to get back up, but right now I feel fine!" She laughed. She'd used her crutch to get herself down to the sandy ground. Now she set it on the other side from her. She kept a hand on it so it wouldn't float away.

Jimmy watched the waves lap at them. When they slapped his belly, it sounded like a tiny cheering section.

Clap, clap, clap.

He tried to shimmy himself a little bit closer to Gail, but he couldn't manage it. The sand was sucking his body down, and his 83-year-old muscles didn't have the strength to argue.

Gail said, "I think we were sitting right around here when you asked me to marry you."

Jimmy opened his mouth in surprise. He'd forgotten proposing to her here, but that was right! That's exactly right!

"You're as beautiful now as you were then."

She smiled and then looked out to the water.

"I think the tide is coming in."

Jimmy glanced over and saw waves that looked a little bit bigger than he'd expected. They continued to slap at his belly.

"I think you're right. Might make it easier to walk back."

"I'll take all the help I can get!"

If I can't move my whole body over . . . he thought. He lay down and supported himself on his right elbow. Then he could reach her with his outstretched left arm. He just wanted to touch her.

"Sixty years," he said.

She was lost in thought and didn't reply.

They sat for thirty minutes, each swimming in their own memories of the many wonderful times they'd spent in this same water. They'd make comments occasionally, but all they really needed was to touch hands.

Gail was also lying down now, trying to regain some of the strength she'd lost by walking out this far. Her knee throbbed and screamed to her brain to not be so fucking stupid, but she ignored that, preferring only to think of wonderful memories with her husband.

* * *

"Do you think we should go back?" asked Gail.

Jimmy really didn't want to, but he knew she was right. They'd done what they came for, and the memories of this day would have to satisfy them in the future.

That's not such a bad thing, he thought.

He was still lying down, and he pulled his legs toward himself.

They hurt and didn't want to move. The tide was indeed coming in, and he was surprised that his legs were totally covered. How did that happen?

He took a different strategy and leaned over to his right, bringing his left arm around as if he was going to do a push-up.

As if.

That didn't work, either. He didn't have the strength to push himself up.

Not even close.

"Sweetie, I think I'm going to need you to help me up."

Jimmy was embarrassed at having to ask for help.

Getting old really sucks.

He kept trying to move his body around to get some traction, but nothing seemed to work. He was stuck lying in the water and had no way to help himself.

"Good thing I've got you here," he said.

He glanced over at Gail, but she was struggling, too. That's when he noticed her crutch had somehow gotten loose and was floating independently toward shore.

He'd have to help her walk, once they got up.

That's okay. I'm still her knight in shining armor. I can do that.

Now, Gail was struggling with her own breathing. She'd pushed and pushed but she was too frail to get her own body lifted off the sandy bottom.

Stupid fat woman.

She never called herself fat out loud, but she'd used that term her whole life in her deepest, most private thoughts. Now, she was glad the word hadn't slipped out. She felt totally useless. What kind of a woman can't even stand up?

She was out of breath and hadn't moved an inch.

In frustration, she looked over at Jimmy. He was squirming around, having as much trouble as she was.

She needed his help, but he needed hers.

"This is ridiculous," she said.

The water lapped on her belly, and she wanted to yell at the damned ocean. It was like the tide was laughing at her.

How the hell could we both be stuck out here?

More importantly, how can we get back to shore?

Gail tried to turn herself over, to try to crawl, but she couldn't make the transition. She had no muscle power to push her body over. It was like trying to use a pitchfork to turn over Mount Everest.

"Jimmy, what are we going to do?"

Jimmy had no answer for her. He kept squirming as much as she was, but he wasn't having any more luck than her.

Finally, he stopped. He was overcome with the effort and saw black spots in front of his eyes. He knew he was about to faint, but he couldn't allow that. The water was only a foot or so deep, but it was enough for him to drown.

He pressed his eyes closed, as if that would somehow stop him from blacking out, and maybe it worked. He kept conscious. Barely. In a corner of his mind, he heard Gail calling to him, but he couldn't make out any of her words.

Jimmy wanted to just turn back the clock and not have this crazy idea of going out into the water.

What was he thinking?

Water splashed onto his face, and he flashed his eyes open.

"The water," he mumbled.

"What?"

He took as deep a breath as he could. "Water is rising. Fast."

Gail noticed for the first time. The water level had been rising so slowly, it hadn't registered, but she could see it was higher now. *Much* higher.

"Oh, God . .. "

"Don't panic," said Jimmy.

"But, what can we do?"

"I . . . I don't know."

Gail tried to look back toward shore, to see how far away her crutch was, but she couldn't see it. Water was lapping in her face, too.

"Jimmy, I'm afraid."

He didn't hear her. A larger wave had splashed onto his face, and he'd started choking from the water he'd swallowed.

With the tide coming in, his body wasn't as pinned to the sandy bottom, but it didn't seem to matter. He still couldn't find the energy to move his body around or to sit up. He was paralyzed, with no energy reserves. The cancer treatments had sucked all the life from him, and now it was leaving him for dead

The next wave came quickly and then the next.

Gail couldn't really see much, because she was battling her own fight. It seemed like the waves had just started a battle that only they could win.

Her knee was killing her, but she knew it was old age that had sapped all her strength.

After another dozen waves splashed over her harder and harder, she knew she wouldn't last long.

All she wanted was to hold Jimmy's hand one more time.

She reached out, but she wasn't sure if she was touching him or if it was just her imagination.

The waves kept rolling over the two lifelong lovers, and eventually they both stopped fighting.

*   *   *

It was three days later when Allan and Theresa Gilson walked through the pathway to find their way down to Hibbon's Cove. It was their own private beach. As far as they knew, nobody else ever came here.

This was their third wedding anniversary. They'd made a habit of coming to the beach each August 4, and they hoped it would be that way their entire lives.

After all, this was where they had met, five years earlier.

They laughed and ran down to the beach. As they got close, they flipped off their sandals and kissed, a long loving kiss that would start their little anniversary off on the right foot.

As they broke the kiss, Theresa pointed out a bag that was sitting on the sand. They went to look and found there was some sandwiches and a couple of cans of Coke.

"That's odd," Allan said.

"I guess somebody else knows about this place after all."

"I guess."

They looked around. It was Theresa who saw them.

"Over there."

They ran two hundred feet down the beach and out toward the water. As they got close they could see the two bodies. A man and a woman, partly eaten by birds and crabs.

Some of their bodies were under sand, and great patches of skin were peeled off.

Their faces were horrible. Grotesque. Barely recognizable as human. Theresa and Allan couldn't help tears falling from their eyes when they saw that the corpses were holding hands.

Beneath the Tides

Kelli Owen

LYDIA had ended their engagement with little more than a sob. She'd placed the diamond ring on the kitchen counter and disappeared out the door and out of Trevor's life, the gut-wrenching conclusion to their months-long debate about having children. Needing time away to accept what had happened and adjust to life without her, Trevor felt escaping the city seemed like a solid plan. The beach house was the perfect solution.

The small rental at the end of the pothole-filled road came fully furnished, unlike the forgotten town housing it. An abandoned post office, a dilapidated cemetery, a one-pump gas station doubling as a grocery store, and two taverns dotted what the listing referred to simply as Town—unincorporated and apparently unnamed.

With nothing but a suitcase holding more books than clothes, Trevor smiled at the silence. Retrieving a Neil Gaiman novel from the outer pocket, he left the luggage at the bottom of the stairs and dropped into a well-worn armchair without bothering to even tour the cottage. Trevor became lost in the pages, and as the sky began to bruise and the horizon darkened, evening crept into the stillness. There were no interruptions. No jet skis. No party boats. No other houses on the lonely stretch of rocky shoreline. It was exactly what Trevor needed.

And then the screaming started.

Trevor dropped the book as he stood and spun in one fluid motion of fear. The shrill high-pitched anguish was so clear, so loud, he expected to find someone standing behind him.

The empty kitchen stared back at him.

Faintly reverberating in his mind, the scream had all but faded when it began anew. Trevor covered his ears and looked frantically around the kitchen and living room of the small cottage. The cry became something akin to wailing, the kind punctuated with heaving shoulders and gasping breaths. The silence of the beach house was then shattered in a sustained, keening cry, and Trevor began desperately looking for the source.

Checking every room, every closet, under beds and behind furniture, his hesitation grew and convictions faltered. He reminded himself he didn't believe in nonsense, and tried to blame the sounds on some strange natural phenomena.

Animals? Are there bobcats out here? I've heard they sound like a woman screaming.

It definitely sounded female. Almost dainty, had it not been so disparaging. The sound faded again and the quiet of the house seemed unnatural.

"What the—" His words were cut off by another wail.

Pipes? Could pipes sound like this?

Not a squeal or squeak, it didn't seem metallic at all. Nor was it feral—neither a natural call nor an injured cry for help. It absolutely sounded like a woman unabashed in her agony. Whether she was being actively attacked or crying out afterward, there was a pain and fear to her tone. And it was contagious, filling Trevor with dread as he continued to search.

Having checked the entire second floor during another long wail, Trevor stood in the bathroom and looked up. While the sound appeared to come from everywhere, he felt it was louder up here than on the main floor.

The attic?

The idea someone may be squatting in the cramped space of a dusty cottage attic panicked him.

"Hello?" He tentatively called out. "Are you hurt? Do you need help?"

Trevor tried to follow the sound. He checked the ceilings in each of the two small bedrooms, inside their closets, and returned to double-check the bathroom. There was no attic. No door, no dropdown steps, not even a crawl space to shimmy into.

The screaming stopped.

He swallowed uncomfortably, the dampened noise of his saliva too loud in the abrupt silence. The sudden nothing in the air made his ears feel as if they'd popped from a change in pressure. He looked around the little cottage and waited with bated breath. Trevor slipped from the bathroom and looked again into each bedroom.

"Hello?"

Nothing.

He returned to the well-worn overstuffed chair where his novel lay and glanced at the empty kitchen.

"Hello?"

Still nothing. Trevor swallowed hard and tried his best to dismiss the noise as some strange fluke of wind and wood and pipes. Something logical.

Trevor's vacation returned to its intended peace and he spent the next several days reading, walking along the water in the afternoons when the overcast skies occasionally cleared. He carried rocks and bits of drift-wood back to the cottage, adding them to a growing collection in the chipped ceramic bowl on the porch. The beach was made up of tiny pebbles and broken bits of shell, rather than soft sand. The days were warm but the northern coast offered a breeze to counteract the heat. The nights were cooler but not *cold* by any stretch and he pulled an old fan from the closet to blow on him while he slept.

The scream jolted him from sleep while the moon rode high in a sky speckled with dodging clouds. He checked the second floor, calling out as he opened closets and looked under beds.

"Hello? Is someone there?" It had to be a person rather than pipes.

Halfway down the stairs, it stopped, and did not resume. After a time, he crawled back into bed and fell asleep, where his mind wandered at the edge of reason and dropped him into dreams of violence.

He finished the Gaiman novel and two others by the end of the first week, without further interruptions. His self-imposed therapy of reading things much worse than the heartbreak of his little life seemed to be working. He paused for dinner, a smile of satisfaction on his face for both finishing another novel and for feeling genuinely okay about his situation. He knew his healing was only beginning, but he felt it was a solid start.

Trevor pulled out the last of the frozen meals and popped it into the microwave. His mother had called them TV dinners, but had never let him sit in front of the television to eat one. During his childhood, the bland, prepackaged portions were a convenience for busy parents. Nowadays, while they were equally convenient, they seem to be marketed to single people rather than families. Trevor fit the demographic. He had no reason to cook lavish dishes, or even simple ones at that. Since he's arrived, he had been surviving on the frozen meals at night with simple ham and cheese sandwiches for lunch. He noted the dwindling pile of apples on the counter and realized he'd have to at least check out the gas station store for supplies. If necessary, he'd run up the road to the next town for another week's worth of Salisbury steaks and turkey medallions in watery gravy with taste-leached soggy vegetables.

He watched the time count down on the microwave, but didn't hear the ding over the scream. As loud as it had been the first night, and just as startling, Trevor could almost feel the vibrations on his exposed flesh. He flinched, pulling his arms tight to him, and looked around the room, eyes wide, brow furrowed.

Again, there was nothing. No one. But the wailing continued. Long and forlorn, the breathlessness of it pulled at his heartstrings. The desperation of the cry made him clench his fists.

Trevor ran up the stairs, hoping to pinpoint where the sound was coming from. It broke, staccato, as if someone gasped between sobs. Nothing. Nothing but the sorrow and anguish the sound imbued. Trevor ran back down the stairs, grabbed the keys from the counter, and left the cottage.

He jumped into his car and headed back down the pot-holed stretch toward town.

He had purposefully avoided alcohol after the breakup, knowing his addictive personality could easily drown in a new problem. But right now, more than anything, he wanted a drink. He pulled into the first of the two bars, The Rusty Bucket, and parked next to the only other car in the lot. Inside the quaint building, he wondered if the other car belonged to the bartender or the grizzled elderly gentleman at the end of the bar setting down his empty, iceless glass. Trevor bee-lined to the line of stools and sat dead center. The bartender looked up from his conversation, watched Trevor make his way to the bar, and met Trevor as he settled in.

"Can I get a bourbon?"

"Jim or Jack?" The bartender pulled a tumbler from below the counter.

Trevor cocked his head at the man and squinted, wondering if the question was a trick.

"Ah, so you have discerning taste and *know* Jack is whiskey. Jim it is then."

Really? Trevor blinked away his irritation, remembering that his plan to avoid the locals and any of their quirks had been squashed by an unseen screaming woman. "Make it a double, would ya?"

The bartender raised an eyebrow and continued his pour. Trevor watched the amber liquid raise higher in the glass.

"Name's Rusty. That's..." He nodded toward the end of the bar. Trevor followed the man's indication to an empty bar stool. The front door shut with a whisper. "That *was* Milton."

"Rusty, eh?" Trevor looked at the wood burnt sign above the bar reminding him of the tavern's name. *Of course.*

Trevor threw back the warm Jim Beam, the ice clinking in the glass, and set it down. Rusty lifted the bottle, but Trevor put a hand over the glass, remembering he had to drive back.

"How much for the bottle?"

"Bad day?" Rusty rested the half full bottle against the rail.

Trevor pulled his wallet from his pocket. "Serious. How much to just take that and go?"

"Driving?"

"Nah, just down to the cottage at the end."

"Ohhh..." Rusty nodded and his expression changed, the snark melted to some sort of concern. "A ten spot'll do. You can get more at the Gas 'n Go during business hours if you prefer to drink by the bottle."

"This will do, thank you." Trevor slid the bill across the polished bar and Rusty set the bottle down in response. Trevor took it and left.

Trevor parked at the cottage and sat for almost an hour, fogging up the car windows with anxious breath. He couldn't hear the screaming, but didn't know if it had stopped or simply didn't exist outside the house. He alternated burning swallows of bourbon with memories of Lydia and thoughts of the wailing from the cottage. He stared at Lydia's engagement ring, dangling among the keys hanging from the car's ignition, but didn't touch it, wondering if Lydia cried about their breakup. *Did she sound like the screaming? Or was it a more restrained sobbing?* Half a bottle wasn't much to a drinker, but it blurred both Trevor's broken heart and his bewildered mind. He stumbled inside, collapsed onto the couch, and slept uninterrupted.

The mild hangover had faded by noon. A quick trip to the Gas n' Go later and Trevor had several more meals and another bottle of Jim Beam—though he put the liquor in a cabinet and hoped it wouldn't come to that. By the end of the day, his nerves had settled and he regretted purchasing it.

After dinner, he sat in a tall rocking chair on the porch and watched the peaceful water. The getaway had indeed been just what he needed to calm his mind and work through his feelings.

It had simply been interrupted with occasional screams.

He huffed, almost laughing at the ridiculous thought. Three times in a week, what had sounded so explicitly like a woman screaming had shattered his silence. There was no rhyme or reason to it. It wasn't at the same time every day. Hell, it wasn't even every day. But every time, the sound was the same—a high-pitched, frantic, emotionally laden scream followed by sorrowful wailing. And it always happened at night, which felt cliché to Trevor. He shook his head and shrugged the phenomena away.

He kicked his shoes off and wandered down to the water. He walked close enough for his feet to be occasionally swallowed by the gentle ebb and flow of the fading waves stretching onto the pebble beach. The night was calm. A cluster of clouds blocked the nearly full moon, but the orb's brightness was strong enough to light the surrounding sky and give the water a surface glow.

His mind drifted back to Lydia and their ugly ending. She'd never adequately explained her sudden stance on remaining childless forever, and Trevor still believed something had triggered it. They'd often talked of having children. Over the course of their six-year relationship and into their engagement, they'd even named their children.

233

Trevor plucked a medium sized flat rock from the shoreline, his mind battling between contentious anger at Lydia and sadness at her absence. Turning to the water, intent on skipping the rock, he closed his eyes and took several deep breaths. As he opened his eyes, the clouds moved and the moon reflected on the water. Trevor squinted at something large out on the surface.

"Is that a ship?" He questioned the quiet around him, noticing the list of the hull. "My God, is it sinking?"

There were no lights on the boat. No yelling of men or the sounding of alarms on deck. And the style was old. Too old. It wasn't a yacht or cruiser or anything modern.

What's the boat they put in bottles? A schooner? Around here? What the... oh my God, it is sinking.

The front of the boat dipped into the water, but rather than run for the cottage to get his phone, Trevor stood still, watching the ocean behind the schooner. He stared at the watery horizon he could see *through* the wood of the ship. He would have believed the boat to be real, to be solid, if not for the impossible reflections which gave away its secret.

Trevor cocked his head, trying to reconcile the scene. The schooner hadn't been there before. He was sure of that. The clouds moving hadn't illuminated an *existing* ship, but rather had allowed this one to materialize in the moonlight.

He didn't believe in ghosts, but had no other explanation for what he was seeing, or rather, seeing *through*. The deck dipped lower, the boat's many sails stretched out against the sky in protest. The tall center post, its flag hanging limp in the still evening, pointed down the shore as the schooner tilted ever further. Trevor gasped as the boat slipped beneath the waves, the sails and posts sliding slowly as they followed into the darkness.

As only the reflection of the moon shone on the calm surface, Trevor heard the keening of a woman's scream behind him. He spun, and this time could *see* the source.

A woman in an old-fashioned white nightgown floated above the house. He squinted to focus, disbelief fighting reality. She gripped a railing attached to nothing. The widow's walk materialized below her. Beneath it, the roof formed, and then the house itself, shimmering like the boat had. Within moments, Trevor could make out the details of a grand three-story home, translucently engulfing his little rental cottage.

He watched as she collapsed to the roof, sobs wrenching her body—just as he had imagined. He glanced back at the black water where the ship had sunk from sight, and then slowly walked toward the house, unsure of what he was going to do.

He looked up at her as he approached, watching her use the railing to pull herself back up to her feet. Trevor stopped at the sudden appearance of a patio in front of him—a stone patio with faintly formed flowers along the edge, the stones placed in an intricate pattern. Trevor wasn't sure if he should try to walk through the shimmering boundary or not. He looked up and flinched when he saw her looking down at him.

The wails had died down to the familiar rhythmic sobs, and he swallowed hard realizing he knew the pattern of her screams.

"Hello?" He called up to her and waited. She wasn't looking *at* him, but had her eyes downcast, turned away from the water.

"Hello?"

She stopped crying and looked out to the water. Her face, clearly visible in the exposed moonlight, was full of pain. Her eyes held a lost look. She opened her mouth wide and the sharp high-pitched shriek filled the air. It was hard for Trevor to see the anguish that went with the cry. She held the scream, sustained for several seconds as if yelling at the water or the moon or both. Then she let go of the railing and leaned forward, tipping over the edge of the widow's walk to fall toward the flagstones.

Trevor's eyes widened as she sped toward him. Unable to move, he stood dumbfounded as she slammed into the stones, Trevor flinched at the expected sound of impact—none came. He watched in horror as the moon reflected in the spreading blood for a few moments before she shimmered and disappeared. The flagstones faded away, the blood gone with them. The house dissipated, leaving only his rental cottage behind, still and silent.

Realizing he was holding his breath, Trevor exhaled into the emptiness of the moonlit night. The gentle lapping of the water seemed suddenly loud. The cottage was foreboding. He looked up to where the widow's walk had been and wondered how long she'd been screaming. Dying. *How many years had it been since the ship sunk? When did they tear down the house?*

Trevor stepped into what he now knew was the boundary of the other house. He crept across the unseen flagstones, walking around the area where he'd watched the woman land. He made his way into the cottage and grabbed his car keys. He didn't need bourbon, but he did need the bartender.

The locals had to know something, right?

Ginger ale in hand, he told Rusty what he had seen. The ship, the house, the woman—all of it spilled out in an excited, rushed-breath tale. It sounded absolutely insane when spoken out loud and he braced for disbelief. The old weathered man at the end of the bar answered, staring into his glass.

"Oh yeah. Poor ol' Rebekkah. Rebekkah Tucker, captain's wife and widow."

Trevor looked from the man to the bartender. "Did you know about this last time I was here?"

"Sure." Rusty absently wiped the rail. "But not everyone sees her."

"And almost no one sees the ship." Milton pushed his glass toward the back of the bar and Rusty plucked the bottle of Smirnoff from the shelf to refill the man's glass.

"So why did I see her?" Trevor's brow furrowed and both men answered with a shrug. "Okay, then how do I make it stop?"

Rusty turned to Trevor, his face twisted into an expression of confusion. "Why would you wanna do that?"

"Why not? Why not help her move on? I mean, if we can, we should."

"I never—"

"Would *you* wanna do that for decades, or *centuries*?" Trevor cut Milton off.

"I reckon not. Though it never dawned on nobody else to do anything about it, other than suffer through it or leave."

"What can you tell me?" Trevor swallowed the remains of his ginger ale and nodded to Rusty. "Can I get a refill, with a splash of Jack this time?"

Milton leaned on the bar, and nodded slowly, as if agreeing to a plan he'd been hesitant to support. "All anyone really knows anymore is that Captain Tucker's ship sunk there, just right off shore but in the strongest part of the undercurrent. Not a single crewmember made it out of those waters. When I was young, there were tales of them all being dead before it sunk, but that was just urban legends and exaggeration building on top of ghost stories." He took a sip of vodka. "And then there's Rebekkah. Screaming and carrying on, and then jumping to her death. She weren't found for almost a week, the crabs and birds having had their way with her."

"So, she's buried in the little cemetery then? With the captain?"

"Oh Lord, no. A suicide? Buried in the Catholic cemetery? No way, not back then." Milton took another swallow of his drink. "She's buried out on the property. Somewhere between your cabin and the point where the swamp begins, there's a small stone marker. And the captain? He has a watery grave, and ain't no seaman ever wanna be removed from that."

"She's buried by the house? My god, no wonder she haunts it."

"Only when the moon is out." Rusty leaned against the back bar.

Trevor cocked his head at the bartender. "Is that it? That's why it's random?"

"Not random. Supposedly she originally watched the ship sink by moonlight, so she and the ship are only there when the clouds either part, or you get a clear night. Which isn't all that often around here."

"Buried on the…" Trevor's voice faded as a thought began to form. Finishing his drink in two swallows, he paid Rusty and slipped from the barstool. "Thanks, fellas."

During the short drive home, his mind spun with possibilities. Having never been a believer, he needed to get to his phone and the Internet and do a bit of research.

Trevor first thought to consecrate the grave by sprinkling holy water over it. Google disagreed. He read at length about a team of ghost hunters who had calmed many spirits by salting and burning the bones within the grave. He felt ridiculous when he realized it was a fan site for the television show *Supernatural*. He crossed off as many ideas as he wrote down for several hours. When his phone flashed LOW BATTERY, he stopped for the night. He plugged it in and headed to bed, drifting off to bones and ghosts and the tales of hauntings.

Trevor took his coffee with him in the morning and wandered the property looking for the small stone. His cup eventually empty and dangling from a bent finger, the ground beneath him became more grass than sand, and there she was. Several feet from a thin tree, the exposed portion of the cylindrical stone jutted from the grass—a foot tall, tilted with age, and clearly marked R.T. He turned back toward the cottage. It was less than a football field to the house and Trevor wondered just how close to the original flagstones and gardens the grave had been placed. He sat in the grass next to the stone and sighed.

Running his fingers over the carved initials, Trevor thought of the anguish in her screams. The Internet had provided him with no help to end her pain. No way to stop her suffering.

"I'm sorry. I wish I could ease your tired bones…"

Bones.

He gasped, the idea forming faster than he could process it. Trevor looked from the little stone out to the section of water where he'd seen the ship sink.

"Can't move the captain's bones, but what if…"

His expression changed from pondering into a slowly widening smile.

"I'll be back." He retrieved his coffee cup from the grass and headed back to the cottage with a lilt in his step, the idea swirling until it solidified.

I'll bring her to him.

He set the coffee cup on the counter and fetched the small folding shovel he'd seen in the closet next to the cheap metal detector—both meant for vacationers rather than grave diggers. Dumping the beach toys from the cloth bag, he headed back to desecrate the grave intent on helping a forlorn soul.

The grave wasn't as deep as he expected, and hitting bone rather than wood took him by surprise. Instead of a coffin, he found the skeletal remains wrapped in a rotting, canvas tarp. He carefully collected the bones and put them in the oversized beach bag. Trevor sat back and rested, looking around him with trepidation.

He felt no qualms about what he'd done, no raised hairs or gooseflesh to give him guilt or send his imagination into overdrive. He smiled at the hole in the sand.

This will work.

Dragging the small dinghy from the side of the cottage to the shoreline had been easy enough. Waiting for the moon to hit the water had been the hard part. Generally a calm, reserved man, his excitement gnawed at his patience. He'd eaten a rushed dinner of microwaved Salisbury steaks, and then settled into the porch chair. Watching. Waiting. *Willing* the moon to break through the clouds and show him the ship. To show him the exact spot the schooner had gone down.

The second night his patience was threadbare and raw. He removed Lydia's engagement ring from his key ring and spun it on the tip of his finger, absently fiddling with it while he remembered their beginning and their end. The parts between were filled with happiness, he *knew* that, but for whatever reason, he could only remember the less than perfect times. And the arguments at the end. He slipped the ring onto his little finger before he drifted to sleep in the cool air of the moonless night.

The third evening he pushed Lydia from his mind and tried to read. He fingered the white gold on his pinky and reread the same paragraph three times before setting the book aside with a sigh. He stood, prepared to go into the house to fetch the bourbon. But on the water, moonlight slowly crept across the darkness, exposed as the clouds thinned and broke.

"Finally." Trevor grabbed the beach bag, and ran to the small rowboat. Pushing off shore, he jumped in a step too late and soaked his left shoe. The wetness registered, but he didn't care.

The schooner materialized as if through a haze, and he rowed straight for it. Pulling the oars through the water, he urged the dinghy forward, hoping to reach the doomed ship before it disappeared beneath the tide. The ship tilted and the sails reached skyward. Trevor rowed faster, leaning forward. The bow of the sinking ship dipped into the water, and Trevor swore under his breath. He lifted the oars from the water and flipped them into the rowboat, the ship slipping below the surface as he drifted into the boundary where it had been. Up close to the ship's resting place, he'd expected to see ghostly seaman swimming, treading water, or drowning. But there were no men in the water, and the ship itself had sunk into the darkness.

Behind him, Rebekkah's wails pierced the night. Floating above the cottage, she had watched for the millionth time as her captain sank to his death just off shore. The railing and roof and house appeared, as her cries ebbed and flowed like the gentle waves beneath Trevor's dinghy. He turned away from her and looked over the side of the little boat, considering the dark waters for a moment.

Lifting the bag, Trevor took a deep breath, lowered the bag of bones into the water, and let go. The fabric opened like a great yawn as it soaked up the ocean, and the moonlight pierced the water to illuminate the white bones tumbling free. Trevor thought he could make out the highest point of the schooner's waterlogged mast, long ago swallowed by the waves.

The screaming stopped mid-cry and Trevor looked back toward the ghost house to find only the present-day cottage.

Did it work?

Returning his gaze to the waters, Trevor saw a flash of swirling white nightgown as it dove to meet the still-sinking bones. The bones, the mast, and the gown drifted further down, out of sight.

The house is gone. The ship is gone. The woman is gone.

Trevor smiled and exhaled with a sense of satisfaction.

And the screaming has stopped.

The night was calm again. The waters were still. And the racing of Trevor's heart slowed. He reached for the oars and saw the ring on his pinky, the stone sparkling in the moonlight. He pulled the ring free and turned it over in his hand, a sense of peace spreading through him. He dropped it over the side to let it sink beneath the tides.

Eternal Valley

John Palisano

May we walk this Eternal Valley
May we walk this land in peace
May we find the Place We're looking for
May this Eternal Valley ever be

THE railroad men sang as the first cold winds blew across Diamond Creek, carrying smells of earthy grass, leaves, and dirt. Looking out over the sunny valley, past the men working on laying the tracks, my head overflowed with memories of little Jesse and me: us diving and playing up near the mouth of the Wabash River. Mary and me brought him, day before last, us exploring our new Missouri home, the place that would save Jesse's life.

Our place in New York sold high and left us a comfortable cushion. It was more than that, though, that made us move. Our Jesse didn't much do well in the cold or crowded city streets. Hell, none of us did, but reacted unnaturally toxic. His throat closed so tight he couldn't breathe. Probably had something to do with the factories sprouting coal smoke all around us in New York. Doctor Faith said Jeese'd probably wouldn't make it unless we moved somewhere with lots of space and clean air. Sounded good to me; I harbored no love for the City because it made my son ill. Top of that, my school smarts were not enough to land me inside a brownstone building writing on papers for a living like Mary's daddy. I made my living on the shores of the Hudson with my hands unloading and packing ships. Living off the land would suit me just fine.

Work in Diamond Creek turned out to be fulfilling. Doctor Norton managed his own grape vineyard and I did everything he'd let me. Most my days were spent training the vines and making sure the condition of the fruit remained reasonable. We worried about the grapes catching powdery mildew or black rot, although the good German Doctor earned his name as horticulturist after cross-breeding the varieties so they'd grow more resilient than their European cousins. America turned out to be a harsher environment for grape growing. The seasons, like the people, showed no mercy.

My life was simple. My life was good. My life tore apart in an instant. One moment little Jesse played the part of a healthy six-year-old, running, playing, eating, laughing…the next minute his skin turned gray, his lips turned purple, his eyes glossed over. He wouldn't rise. He hardly moved. It took all we had to feed the boy sustenance. We were scared giving him water. Jesse barely swallowed and we were afraid he'd drown.

Jim Longforth, our neighbor to the south, rushed over with his case of potions. He wasn't a doctor, but he was all we had. Rubbing a whitish, oily concoction across Jesse's forehead, he said, "Scott? I think the Devil has captured his soul. This will draw the monster out."

I was skeptical. Mary nodded, said, "Maybe we should bring him to Hermann and see Doctor Wallington– Hermann being the nearest big town."

We cleaned Jesse's head off and tried to move him. He moaned like a hellhound.

"He break something, you think?" asked Jim. "If you move him might make it worse: might even kill him."

Mary looked to me. "I don't know," I said. "He seemed just fine all day."

"He'd just laid down for a nap when this started." She put a hand to her mouth. Her eyes watered. "I don't know what's happening."

"Could be consumption," Jim said. All the color drained from his face as though he'd stumbled across the answer and was embarrassed about it.

I put an arm on his shoulder. "If it is consumption, you best get going. Make sure you ain't around the boy enough for it to rub off."

"What about you and Mary?" he asked.

"We're his parents. We'll do what we have to," I said. We walked to the door where Jim snuck a last long look at Jesse. "Don't stare at him like he's not going to be here next time you come down," I said. "Don't you dare."

After Jim left I sat on Jesse's bed, looked at him until I couldn't look any more. "Was Jim right?"

Mary said, "Where would Jesse catch consumption? He's not coughing."

"There's got to be a treatment for him." I looked out the window. The valley had grown dark. It'd be hours until the moon was at its highest.

"Tomorrow you can talk to the Good Doctor and see if he might know of something," Mary said.

I shook my head. "He's a doctor of plant life, not people. His skills will be no fit for this."

She said, "Still—he may have recommendations."

I turned my face to Mary's. "I will leave in an hour, soon as there is moonlight to light my way."

"No. It's too dangerous at night." Mary clutched her cross around her neck. "There are demons outside."

"Nothing will bother me," I said.

She shook her head. "The Conner boys over the hill? They hear you coming and don't see you they're ripe to shoot. They might fire just for the game of it."

I stood up. "They don't frighten me and no creature of the night can get in the way of saving our son."

"Won't you be better useful here? What if he needs you?"

I squeezed Jesse's hand; his was limp and cool and barely squeezed mine back. "He won't miss me for a few hours. If he does, you tell him his Daddy went to find him a special medicine that will make him better."

* * *

Long purple trails of light stretched across the valley. The grass seemed painted and alive as it swayed from the nighttime wind. I pulled my jacket closer and tightened my scarf. For a late September night, the weather was colder than I remembered.

Far below, stretching across the flat lands, fires from the rail worker's tents glowed. I could make out the long black railroad lines near the camp. It wouldn't be long until the big steamers raced across our valley on their way across Missouri. The peace and tranquility we had known would now be forever broken. Mary and me spoke about the trains coming through. A new century loomed. We were both concerned because we didn't want noise and crowds they'd bring.

"It's like the city is following," Mary had said, and I'd agreed.

There was a rustle near me. I looked round and saw nothing but knee high grass. The nearest trees were still a ways off, and there were no big rocks for hiding.

248

I stopped and listened for a moment. Whatever it was would spot me. I was the tallest thing in the field. My mind raced because I knew some of the railroad workers liked to drink a little too much and wander the hills. I hoped it wasn't one of those boys laid up in the field waiting for something dumb to stumble on by.

"Hello?" I asked, knowing I was taking my chances. If someone were hiding they'd see me.

Something rustled behind me and I turned full on. "Hello?" I called.

Training my eye to where I thought I heard the sound, I saw only the tops of the grass swaying gently in the night wind.

I smelled something burning— reminded me of sweet natural tobacco. *Someone was with me.* Nothing burned all by itself— that's for sure.

Who could it be?

"Who's there? My name's Scott Robertson and I'm just passing through."

"So am I."

A woman's voice—she appeared from nowhere behind me, all slinking and sure of herself like I've never seen a woman before or since. She was striking. Long hair flowed down halfway down her body. Her eyes were dark and glinted in the moonlight. She held a wooden pipe. Smoke trailed from its end. With a hand on her hip, she raised an eyebrow.

"Who are you?"

She smiled. "My name is…Mary."

I was taken aback. "You're name can't be Mary," I said. "You're an…"

"Indian?"

"Yes. You need to have an Indian name like *Sunwater* or *River*, right?" I asked.

"Says who?"

249

"Well…I don't know. Ain't that just the way it is?"

She shook her head. "Does the name Mary upset you?"

I stepped back. "Why would it?"

Mary shook her head. "You know someone else named Mary?"

"Sure," I said. "That doesn't mean anything. Look: who are you and what are you doing up here? You scared me half-way back to Jesus."

She moved closer, raised the pipe and took a pull. When she was done, she handed it over. I waved it away. "I don't smoke."

She exhaled. "Fine with me," she said. "I already told you."

"Told me what?"

"That I am passing through here," said Mary. "Same as you."

"Ma'am? I don't mean to be rude, but I have a sick child waiting on me and I need…"

She put up her hand. "A sick child? Is that what makes you walk alone so late on such a night?"

"Such a night? What the heck you getting at?" I asked. "'Tis the same as any other night, maybe a bite colder, might be all."

Mary said, "This is the night when the animals feast."

"Okay? You know what? I don't believe in any of that Indian smoke. I'm a dyed-in-the-wool Christian," I said. "I sure wish there was a church up here. You believe we got a theater for actors, another one for musicians, but we got no church. Not enough people would go. I guess that's what happens when you're in the business of spirits."

Mary nodded. "Business of spirits?"

"We grow grapes," I said. "For wine. Gets you drunk. Kind of like that pipe you've got there." I pointed.

"I know what wine is," she said.

"Good Christians would probably frown upon our livelihood."

Mary looked around. I guessed her smoke was playing its fun little effects on her. "This is a special place," she said. "Don't you think so?" She shut her eyes and breathed as loud as she could. "You can just hear the animals and the spirits around you. It's safe. I could live here forever and never grow tired."

"That so?" I said. "I do need to move along. My son's going to need me to get back real soon." I started walking past her.

"May I walk with you?" she asked. "I wouldn't mind just for a little bit?"

I shook my head and put out my hand. "I don't know," I said. "That probably wouldn't look right. If anyone sees us together it could mean trouble for me."

"I thought none of the Christ-inns cared?" she asked.

"That's different," I said and stopped in my tracks. "They all on the same page so far as God is concerned. They ain't all going to look kindly on a man if he's walking around with another woman while his wife's home tending to his sick child, are they?"

She pulled a hood over her head. "I could wear a disguise," she said, "lower my voice, pretend to be a man." Mary laughed. "What if I were an old woman lost in the fields?" Her face changed before my eyes. "And you were just being a good Christ-Man…" Mary looked older and slighter and her hair went grey, all in a blink. "You might be leading me somewhere warm." By the time she'd finished speaking she again looked far too beautiful for her to be safe.

"You blow some of that stuff at me?" I asked. "That what it is? You got a trick up your sleeve? A couple boys hiding somewhere to hit me on the head and rob me?"

Mary laughed again. "You find me very threatening," she said. "I find that touching." She stared me in the eyes, looking back and forth inside mine several times to make sure she had my attention. "I am here to help you, Scott Robertson," she said. "I am here because of Jesse."

All the blood in my body froze.

The only thing I could think to say was, "Your name ain't really Mary, then, ain't it?"

She smiled.

"How am I supposed to know you ain't talk to the Longforth clan before you found me? How do I know this ain't some elaborate trick?"

She shook her head. "I am not asking you for anything," she said. "I have no weapons with me."

"There's still something about this I don't trust," I said. "I'd feel better if I could go talk to Doctor Norton about this. I bet he's got some ideas about what we could do."

"You can do that," she said. "But Jesse is in trouble, is he not? What if it is something much worse than you know? What if he only had hours left?"

"You know something I don't know?"

"I know where we can go to find him something that will take it all away."

Mary looked up and to our left, to where the hill grew steep, to the top of Diamond Creek. "There is a point where the Wabash holds magic and power," she said. "I know of a place we can find his medicine."

"The Wabash River?" I asked. "You want to head on up there at this hour, on this freezing night?" That moment I noticed something peculiar. No longer was I shivering. In fact, the air felt just as warm as a summer evening. "Well damn me—- did we hit some kind of hot spot or did the wind stop blowing?"

Mary looked right through me and I just sensed that she was the reason things were a lot more comfortable. How could something like that be unless she was a witch of some kind?

She must have heard what I was thinking because the next thing to escape her mouth was, "you need to let go of some things you're holding close to your heart—at least for the next few hours."

"This ain't natural at all," I said. "It's all going against God."

"Is it?" she asked. "God would not let things happen if they would harm you, would she?"

"God's a man."

"Does it matter?"

"Sure as hell does."

"Your son's life is hanging on by breaths," she said.

Bugs crawled all over me. I felt them crawl up from the grass, up through my pant legs and right up onto my chest. I pulled my shirt away from my stomach and scratched at the little bugs. Only thing is there weren't any. I still felt them crawling. They'd reached my hair, my scalp, and nose. The itching was maddening. "Excuse me, Miss," I said and dropped to the grass and started itching like mad.

"This is the disease that's befallen your son," she said, her tone serious and forceful.

The itching burned; the sensation became more unbearable. I felt what seemed to be spiders crawling all over me, biting me, nipping me, burrowing inside. Once inside I rubbed at my skin to try to free them, but they would not come back out. I fell on my back. As I lay in the grass, I found I could no longer move my limbs. The hand that scratched at my belly froze; my fingers curled into a stiff claw. My sight blurred and the night sky felt like it might fall and smother me.

My heart slowed and I could hear its beats, which sounded to me very much like the easy tides of the Hudson River back in New York City. It sloshed in and out, steadily. With each pull, a new wave of pain surged through my veins, beginning at the soles of my feet, gathering and intensifying inside my head. My stomach tightened and I wanted to throw up, yet, I could not even move. Blinking hurt, believe it or not.

It seemed as though I might die shortly. Jesse was in bad shape if what I was experiencing was the same for him. I was a full-grown man; feeling that horrible as a young child scared me silly.

In my head, I willed Mary to stop what she was doing. *She might be a witch, all right. Maybe she cast this same spell on Jesse when he was outside and made it a trap to catch me.*

"No," Mary said, kneeling down and looking me in the eyes. Her lips were shut but they still formed a smile. "I am not trapping you or your son. You must believe that I was called here to help you and your son."

Another wave washed over me, but it was warm and lessened the pain, as if it were being cleaned from my insides. After several seconds, I was able to move my fingertips. Soon, my hands and arms moved and I was able to lift my head. Blessedly, the itching was gone. All that remained was a numb tingle in my hands and feet. I sat up and rubbed my eyes.

"You have only felt that way for a few minutes," Mary said. "Your son has been feeling that way for much too long already. We have to be quick. There is a point where the body will no longer tolerate pain and will stop."

"What does he have?" I asked.

"The curse of the wind," she said. "Which was what called me."

"Why?"

"You are here in a sacred place," she said. "And not everyone is happy about it."

"He is a child!"

I stood.

She said, "Gods do not discriminate."

"If God has done this than how can we stop it?"

"We will ask."

*   *   *

After we turned left and made it through the prairie, we arrived at the bottom of a steep hill. The hill turned into the base of the mountain. There was a path, carved out by many of the town's folks. We climbed the side of the mountain's trail, me following Mary. "Good thing the moon is high," I said. "We can see our way."

"The Gods work in our favor," said Mary. "It's of great importance. They must know what we are doing."

"I sure hope so," I said.

As scared as I was about my son's well being, I could not help but

254

find myself deeply intrigued with Mary. Of course, she was beautiful and strong, but she also possessed a kind of magnetic pull. "I don't understand why so many people hated the Indians," I said. "I'm looking at you and you look just like a person to me." Her back was turned to me and I was embarrassed because her curves were quite wonderful and made my thoughts race. Quickly I remembered that she might have somehow been hearing what I was thinking.

"The earliest people who came to this land and met with the Lakota were our friends," she said. "They lived with us. They dined with us. Our women loved their men."

"I can see why," I said, my mouth opening before I could stop it.

She paused, briefly, and kept walking. "You are right in believing all of what makes us people would be the same."

The path steepened. We passed a small tree, no larger than either one of us. I recalled being struck by the same tree when I'd brought Jesse and my Mary to the Wabash's mouth to play only a few days earlier.

"It just seems silly to me that people always seem to want to fight over something," I said. "Especially the color of our skins. I mean, I kind of like all the different ways people look. If we all looked the same it'd be like that field down there all covered with one kind of flower and one kind of tree and nothing else. That seems awfully uninteresting to me."

She stopped. "I believe that may be part of the reason why I was called to you," Mary said. "You see the world not like most of the men around you."

"Come on," I said. "I can't believe I'm the only one who ever thought of that."

She shook her head. "I'm sure many others have. I'm not so sure many others would allow themselves to believe so."

* * *

High on the hill, where the grass gives way to the towering granite of the mountain, the Wabash River curls around a bend and forms a large lake right before it all rolls down toward the valley on the other side. The land is flat surrounding the lake, and large enough for several houses. Trees and brush rim the lake. The water swirls gently and slowly round and round.

"I know this place," I said. "We brought Jesse here the other day. He loved it."

Mary stood still, her eyes fixed on the water. "This is where it began," she said. "He caught it here."

I stared at the water, too, searching for some kind of sign. I saw none. "You mean the water's poison? Is that it?"

"Something in it," she said. "Something's living inside."

"A fish?"

She shook her head. "Not quite." Then she turned to me. "You must go inside. You must clear your mind and you must ask for your son to be taken back."

I was confused. "Your son's spirit was taken," she said, her eyes glanced back to the swirling water. "It needs to feed."

Mary handed me her pipe. She reached inside a pocket, found a match, struck it, and as I lifted the tube to my lips she put the flame near the opposite tip.

I inhaled. My mouth filled with smoke, its sweet flavor reminding me of nutmeg and leaves. My lungs opened and warmed. Immediately I felt dizzy. The top of the lake seemed to glisten more than any body of water I'd ever seen. Every reflection bloomed and glittered. Mary took the pipe from me and smoked some herself. We shared her pipe for several minutes. Each pull brought me deeper and deeper under its magic spell.

The earth moved under our feet. I crouched slightly to keep my balance. "What was that?" I asked. My voice sounded as though we were inside a cave. It was difficult to keep my eyes open, despite the shaking ground.

"Look inside the water," she said, and pointed.

The bottom of the lake moved. The edges of the lake grew lighter as the creature curled its sides and revealed the true bed beneath. Its body was as dark and smooth as the night and it floated effortlessly. While the waves rippled, the creature at the bottom seemed to blend in with the water. If I broke my stare for even a second I lost track of where it was and what it was.

"You must go inside," Mary said. "It can only hear you when you're in the water with it."

"It will kill me! It will devour me and have its supper! I'm no fool! Are you sacrificing me to this creature?"

"This is your choice," she said.

My instinct told me I couldn't go in the water. The thing filled nearly the entire lake. I pictured walking into the water and it covering me, smothering me, dragging me underwater with it—- bringing my limp body toward its beak-shaped mouth. That had to be its plan.

"It has no mouth," Mary said.

"I don't want to be in this world if Jesse can't be here with me," I said. My mind seemed to flip in on itself. "If this thing took him then I guess I'll have no choice."

What happened next was a blur. As I put one foot in the Wabash Lake, the dark thing in the water moved back. When I'd swum in the lake with Jesse and Mary, the bed was dark. We'd been stepping on this thing the whole time and we hadn't even known it. Damn. Maybe Mary was right. I still was not sure how she came to be or how any of it was happening to me, but I knew, somehow, deep within, that I needed to have faith.

In no time I was up to my waist. The water was warm, which it hadn't been the other day. The air was warm, as well. The thing still moved away from me as I stepped inside. I imagined it was as scared of me as I was of it, although that changed as soon as I ducked my head under. I turned one last time and my eyes met Mary's. She smiled and blinked once. I nodded and lowered myself under the water.

Once I turned around, I saw nothing but darkness. The thing was going for the kill. It was smothering me. I was soon going to die.

Only I didn't. Instead, I took a few steps forward and saw that I was on a ledge. An endless cavern dropped down into the earth as far as I could see, ending in what looked like a bottomless black hole. The thing had covered the hole. I lowered myself into a sitting position so that I wouldn't step over the ledge and drop down. There was a tidal pull I could sense coming from the tunnel and I didn't want to be pulled down inside.

I felt something watching me and looked up. The thing was above me and I met its stare. Two flat grey eyes, each as big as my head, scanned me. Mary was right: I saw no mouth, although I did see two slits just under its eyes. Its movements were graceful and slow. Around its edges, I saw dark nubs like fingertips rolling across its rim—they looked to me a lot like they might be playing piano.

Then I lost my breath. I gasped and swam, but found the water difficult. I looked up and found I was much deeper than I'd thought. When I first stepped inside the lake, it felt as though I were only a few feet under. Somehow, I'd fallen several men deep.

I thought of Jesse sick and in bed and I didn't want to die. *He's going to need me. He needs to get better. He shouldn't be suffering like this. Take me, if that's what it takes. Take me in his place.*

The things eyes met mine.

It was just us swimming in here and having a good time. We didn't want any of this. We didn't need any of this. We didn't want to bother you none. Please. Let him be. You can have me if you need something. He'll miss me but he still has the world in front of him. He can do things I'll never be able to do. He can make things better. I can't. I'm just taking up space here now. I'll tell you what? I'll trade you, big guy, and maybe you can hear me the same way she can hear me. So just take me and throw me down that big hole you got there or whatever you need to do, but just let little Jesse free.

My mind raced with memories of my son. I remembered our room in New York where he was born, Mary's parents standing around, our friends. I remembered his first few nights as clear and as real as new. I felt his little fingers curling around my thumb. I heard his baby cries blending into his laughs. The smell of his hair so vivid I swear he was right there with me.

I saw him on the train jumping on the seats to get a better view as we rode from New York and across the plains. I heard his voice asking me if we were going to be okay. "We're always going to be together, right Poppa?" he asked.

"Of course," I told him. "Of course. Ain't nothing going to get in the way of that."

But it had.

Pictures of him racing across the field chasing some creature or another filled my head. It seemed I saw something just like that every day of my life in Diamond Creek as I passed him and went to work for Doctor Norton in the vineyards. Oh, to just have one more day! To have endless days!

I looked upward at the thing floating above me. It lowered itself onto me and as soon as our skin touched, I felt fire and pain worse than anything I can ever tell. My head filled with colors, exploding as if the heavens were on fire. I couldn't help but wiggle and try to break free. No matter. I was stuck in its grasp and nothing I could do would fix that.

* * *

When I woke, I was on the shore and I was alone. I sat up and got my bearings. I was soaked through. All my limbs were there. Everything worked. Nothing was out of place. I had a headache from all hell and I was sore, but that came as no surprise.

Mary was gone. I stood and poured out my canteen. Then I went to the edge of the lake. The bed was dark. The water rippled, but the river bottom did not move. I searched for its eyes and could find none, them being on its underside.

259

Kneeling down, I filled my canteen with water from the lake. I stared at the dark bottom, and when I pulled the canteen from the water, I saw the slightest twitch.

Then I turned and took the first steps back home. Beneath the fading night, the stars shimmered against the deep blue sky.

Far below in the valley I heard the railroad workers singing again.

May we walk this Eternal Valley
May we walk this land in peace
May we find the Place We're looking for
May this Eternal Valley ever be

I pictured Jesse and knew soon I'd raise my canteen to his lips, and knew its lake water would cure him, and soon thereafter I'd hear his laughs and watch him run, and knew one day soon all I'd seen would just be a curious story I'd tell.

Widow's Point

Richard Chizmar & Billy Chizmar

Video/audio footage #1A (5:49pm, Friday, July 11, 2017)

The man holds the video camera in his left hand and grips the steering wheel with his right. The road, and calling it a road is charitable at best, is unpaved dirt and gravel, and the camera POV is unsteady. Mostly we see bouncing images of the interior dashboard and snippets of blue sky through a dirty windshield. The Rolling Stones' "Sympathy for the Devil" plays at low volume on the radio.

After another thirty seconds of this, we hear the squeal of brakes in need of repair and the car swings in a wide circle – giving us a shaky glimpse of a stone lighthouse standing atop a grassy point of land – and comes to a stop facing rocky cliffs that drop perilously to the Atlantic

Ocean below. The ocean here is dark and rough and foreboding, even on this clear day.

The man turns off the engine and we immediately hear the whine of the wind through his open window. In the foreground, an old man with thinning gray hair, thick glasses, and a wrinkled apple of a face, shuffles into view.

The man recording exits the car, still pointing the camera at the old man, and we see a hand enter the top corner of the screen as the driver flips a wave.

"Hello," he yells above the wind, walking toward the old man.

Up ahead, we watch the old man shuffling his way toward us through the blowing grass. His body is so frail, it appears as if the wind might steal him away and send him kiting over the distant cliffs. At first, we believe he is smiling. As we draw closer, we realize we are wrong, and the old man is scowling. It's not a pretty sight — like a skeletal corpse grinning from inside a moldy coffin.

"Turn that damn camera off," the old man growls.

The picture is immediately replaced with a blurry patch of brown and green grass as the camera is lowered.

"Okayyy, we'll just edit that out later," the man says to himself off-camera.

And then in a louder voice: "Sorry, I didn't think it would—"

Video/audio footage #2A (6:01pm, Friday, July 11, 2017)

The screen comes to life again and we see the stone lighthouse off in the distance and hear the muffled crash of waves pounding the shoreline. It's evident from the swaying view of the lighthouse and the intense howl of the wind that the camera is now affixed to a tripod and positioned somewhere close to the edge of the cliffs.

The man walks on-screen, carrying a knapsack and what looks like a remote control of some sort. He appears to be in his mid-forties, shaggy blonde hair, neat dark-framed glasses, artfully scuffed boots, pressed jeans, and a gray sweatshirt. He stares directly at the camera, green eyes squinting against the wind, and sidesteps back and forth, searching for the proper positioning.

He settles on a spot just in time to witness a particularly violent gust of wind defeat the tripod.

"Shit," the man blurts, and sprints toward the camera – as it leans hard to the left and crashes to the ground.

There is a squawk of static and the screen goes blank.

Video/audio footage #3A (6:04pm, Friday, July 11, 2017)

The video switches on, and we see the man standing in the foreground of the lighthouse, pointing the remote at the camera. The image is steadier this time around. The man slides the remote into the back pocket of his jeans and clears his throat.

"Okay, only have a few minutes, folks. Mr. Parker is in quite the hurry to get out of here. He's either playing the role of hesitant and anxious lighthouse owner to the extreme and faking his discomfort, or he's genuinely unnerved and wants to be pretty much anywhere else but here on the property his family has owned for over a century now."

He leans over, his hands disappearing just off-screen, and returns holding the knapsack, which he places close on the ground at his side. He stands with an erect but relaxed posture and folds his hands together in front of him.

"My name is Thomas Livingston, bestselling author of *Shattered Dreams, Ashes to Ashes*, and eleven other bestselling non-fiction volumes of the supernatural. I'm here today on the windswept coast of Harper's Cove at the far northern tip of Nova Scotia standing at the foot of the legendary Widow's Point Lighthouse.

"According to historical records, the Widow's Point Lighthouse, originally named for the large number of ships that crashed in the rocky shallows below before its existence, was erected in the summer of 1838 by Franklin Washburn II, the proprietor of the largest fishing and gaming company in Nova Scotia."

Livingston's face grows somber.

"There is little doubt that the Widow's Point Lighthouse led to a sharp decrease in the number of nautical accidents off her shoreline – but at what cost? Legend and literally centuries of first-hand accounts seem to reinforce the belief that the Widow's Point Lighthouse is cursed...or perhaps an even more apt description...*haunted*.

"The legend was born when three workers were killed during the lighthouse's construction, including the young nephew of Mr. Washburn II, who plunged to his death from the lighthouse catwalk during the final week of work. The weather was clear that day, the winds offshore and light. All safety precautions were in place. The tragic accident was never explained.

"The dark fortunes continued when the lighthouse's first keeper, a by-all-accounts 'steadfast individual' named Ian Gallagher went inexplicably mad during one historically violent storm and strangled his wife to death before taking his own life by cutting his wrists with a carving knife.

"In the decades that followed, nearly two dozen additional mysterious deaths occurred within the confines – or on the nearby grounds – of the Widow's Point Lighthouse, including cold-blooded murder, suicide, unexplained accidents, the mass-slaughter of an entire family in 1933, and even rumors of devil worship and human sacrifice.

"After the final abomination in 1933, in which the murderer of the Collins' family left behind a letter claiming he was 'instructed' to kill by a ghostly visitor, the most recent owner of the Widow's Point Lighthouse, seafood tycoon Robert James Parker – yes, the grandfather of Mr. Ronald Parker, the camera-shy gentleman you glimpsed earlier – decided to cease operations and shutter the lighthouse permanently.

"Or so he believed...

"Because in 1985, Parker's eldest son, Ronald's father, entered into an agreement with the United Artists film studio from Hollywood, California to allow the studio to film a movie both inside the lighthouse and on the surrounding acreage. The movie, a gothic thriller entitled *Rosemary's Spirit*, was filmed over a period of six weeks from mid-September to the first week of November. Despite the lighthouse's menacing reputation, the filming went off without a hitch...until the final week of shooting, that is...when supporting actress Lydia Pearl hung herself from the polished iron guard railing that encircles the catwalk high atop the lighthouse.

"Trade publications reported that Ms. Pearl was despondent following a recent break-up with her professional baseball-playing fiancé, Roger Barthelme. But locals here believed differently. They believed with great conviction that, after all those long years of silent slumber, the Widow's Point curse had reawakened and claimed another victim.

"Regardless of the reasoning, the lighthouse was once again shuttered tight against the elements three years later in 1988 and for the first time, a security fence was erected around the property, making the lighthouse accessible only by scaling the over one-hundred-and-fifty-foot high cliffs that line its eastern border along the Atlantic.

"So...in other words, no human being has been inside the Widow's Point Lighthouse in nearly thirty years..."

Livingston takes a dramatic pause, then steps closer to the camera, his face clenched and square-jawed.

"...until now. Until *today*.

"That's right – tonight, for the first time in over three decades, someone will spend the night in the dark heart of the Widow's Point Lighthouse. That someone is *me*, Thomas Livingston.

"After months of spirited – pardon the pun –negotiation, I have been able to secure arrangements to spend an entire weekend inside the legendary lighthouse. The ground rules are simple. Today is Friday, July

11, in the year of 2017. It is..."

He checks his wristwatch.

"...6:09pm Eastern Standard Time on Friday evening. In a matter of minutes, Mr. Ronald Parker, current proprietor of the Widow's Point Lighthouse, will escort me through the only entrance or exit to the lighthouse, and once I am safely inside, he will close and lock the door behind me..."

Livingston bends down and comes back fully into view holding a heavy chain and padlock.

"...using these."

He holds the chain and padlock up to the camera for another dramatic beat, then drops them unseen to the ground below.

"I will be permitted to take inside only enough food and water to last me three days and three nights, as well as a lantern, flashlight, sanitary supplies, two notebooks and pens, along with this video camera and tripod, and several extra batteries. In addition, this..."

Livingston backs up a couple steps, reaches down into his knapsack, and quickly comes up with a small machine in his right hand.

"...Sony Digital Voice Recorder, capable of recording over one thousand hours of memory with a battery life of nearly ninety-six hours without a single charging. And, yes, please consider that an official product placement for the Sony Corporation."

He laughs – and we get a glimpse of the handsome and charming author pictured on the dust jacket of one of his books – and then he returns the voice recorder to his knapsack.

"I will not be allowed a cellphone or a computer of any kind. Absolutely no Internet access. No way to communicate, or should anything go wrong, no way to request assistance of any kind. I will be completely cut off from the outside world for three long and hopefully eventful nights."

We hear a car horn blare from off-screen, and a startled Livingston's eyes flash in that direction. He looks back at the camera, shaking his head, a bemused expression on his face.

"Okay, folks, it's time to begin my journey, or shall I say, *our* journey, as I will be recording all of my innermost thoughts and observations in an effort to take you, my readers, along with me. The next time I appear on camera, I will be entering the legendary – some say, *haunted* – Widow's Point Lighthouse. Wish me luck. I may need it.

"And cut..."

Video/audio footage #4A (6:22pm, Friday, July 11, 2017)

Livingston is carrying the video camera in his hand, and we share his shaky POV as he slowly approaches the lighthouse.

Mr. Parker remains off-screen, but we hear his gravelly voice: "Eight o'clock Monday morning. I'll be here not a minute later."

"That will be perfect. Thank you."

The lighthouse door draws nearer, large and weathered and constructed of heavy beams of scarred wood, most likely from an ancient ship, as Livingston had once unearthed in his research. The men stop when they reach the entrance.

"And you're certain you cannot be convinced otherwise?" the old man asks.

Livingston turns to him – and we finally get a close-up of the reclusive Mr. Parker, an antique crone of a man, his knobby head framed by the blue-gray sea behind him – and Livingston laughs. "No, no. Everything will be fine, I promise."

The old man grunts in reply.

The camera swings back toward the lighthouse and is lowered. We catch a fleeting glimpse of Livingston's knapsack hanging from his shoulder and then, resting on the ground at the foot of the entrance, a dirty white cooler with handles by which to carry or drag it. Livingston leans down and takes hold of it by one plastic handle.

"Then I wish you Godspeed," the old man says.

The camera is lifted once again and focused on the heavy wooden door. A wrinkled, liver-spotted hand swims into view holding a key. The key is inserted into an impossible-to-see keyhole directly beneath an oversized, ornate doorknob and, with much effort, turned.

The heavy door opens with a loud *sigh*, and we can practically hear the ancient air escaping.

"Whew, musty," Livingston says with a cough, and we watch his hand reach on-screen and push the door all the way open with a loud *creak* – into total darkness.

"Aye. She's been breathing thirty years of dead air."

Livingston pauses – perhaps it's the mention of "dead air" that slows his pace – before re-gripping the cooler's plastic handle and stepping inside.

At the exact moment that Livingston crosses the threshold into the lighthouse, unbeknownst to him, the video goes blank. Entirely blank – with the exception of a time code in the lower left corner of the screen, which at that moment reads: 6:26pm.

"I'll see you Monday morning," Livingston says.

The old man doesn't respond, simply nods and closes the door in Livingston's face. The screen is already dark, so we do not see this; instead, we hear it with perfect clarity and finality.

Then we listen as the key is once again turned in the lock, and the heavy chain is wrestled into place. After a brief moment of silence, the loud *click* of a padlock being snapped shut is heard, followed by a final tug on the chain.

Then, there is only silence...

...until a rustle of clothing whispers in the darkness and there comes the *thud* of the cooler being set down at Livingston's feet.

"And so it begins, ladies and gentlemen, our journey into the heart of the Widow's Point Lighthouse. I will now climb the two hundred and sixty-eight spiraling stairs to the living quarters of the lighthouse, lantern in one hand, camera in the other. I will return a short time later this evening for food and water supplies, after some initial exploration."

We hear the sound of ascending footsteps.

"Originally built in 1838, the Widow's Point Lighthouse is two hundred and seven feet tall, constructed of stone, mostly granite taken from a nearby quarry, and positioned some seventy-five yards from the sheer cliffs which tower above the stormy Atlantic..."

Video/audio footage #5A (6:41pm, Friday, July 11, 2017)

We hear Livingston's heavy breathing and notice the time code – 6:41pm – appear in the lower left hand corner. Once again, the rest of the screen remains dark.

"Two hundred-sixty-six...two hundred-sixty-seven...two hundred-sixty-*eight*. And with that, we have reached the pinnacle, ladies and gents, and just in time, too. Your faithful host is feeling rather...spent, I have to admit."

Even without a video feed, we can almost picture Livingston dropping his knapsack and holding up the lantern to survey his home for the next three nights.

"Well, as you can certainly see for yourselves, Mr. Parker spoke the truth when he claimed this place was in a state of severe ill repair. In fact, he may have managed to actually underestimate the pathetic condition of the Widow's Point living quarters."

A deep sigh.

"I believe I shall now rest for a moment, and then venture upward and explore the lantern room and perhaps even the catwalk if it appears sturdy enough before returning downstairs for my food and water supplies. Once I've straightened up a bit and established proper housekeeping, I will return to you with a further update.

"I also promise to discuss the mysterious incidents I referenced earlier – and many more – in greater and more graphic detail once I have made myself at home."

The sound of shuffling footsteps.

"But, first, before I go...lord in heaven...just gaze upon this magnificent sight for a moment."

Livingston's voice takes on a tone of genuine awe. The phony theatrics are gone; he means every word he is saying.

"Resplendent mother ocean as far as the eye can see...and beyond. The vision is almost enough to render me speechless." A chuckle. "Almost."

The time code disappears – and the video ends.

(Voice recorder entry #1B – 7:27pm, Friday, July 11, 2017)

Well, this is rather strange and unfortunate. After I last left you, I returned downstairs and brought up a day's ration of food and water, then spent considerable time cleaning and straightening in preparation for the weekend. Once these tasks were completed to my satisfaction, I settled down for some rest and to double-check the video footage I had shot earlier.

The first batch of videos was fine, if a little rough around the edges, but then I came to the fourth video...and discovered a problem. I was shocked to find that while the audio portion of the recording worked just fine, the video portion seemed to have somehow malfunctioned once I entered the lighthouse. And I do mean as soon as I stepped inside the lighthouse.

I proceeded to check the camera lens and conduct several test videos, all with the same result – the audio function appears to be operating in perfect order, while video capabilities are disabled. I admit I find the whole matter more puzzling than troubling or unsettling, even with the rather bizarre timing of the issue.

Perhaps, something inside the camera was broken when the wind knocked it down earlier by the cliffs. Or...perhaps the otherworldly influence that dwells here inside the Widow's Point Lighthouse has already made its presence known. I suppose only time will tell.

In the meantime, this Sony – hear that, folks, *Sony* – digital voice recorder will serve my purpose here just fine.

(Voice recorder entry #2B – 9:03pm, Friday, July 11, 2017)

Good evening. I've just taken my first dinner here in Widow's Point – a simple affair; a ham-and-Swiss sandwich slathered with mustard, side of fresh fruit, and for dessert, a thin slice of homemade carrot cake. Next I finished organizing my copious notes.

Now it's time for another brief history lesson.

Earlier, I referenced more than a handful of disturbing incidents that have taken place in and around the Widow's Point Lighthouse. I also promised to discuss in further detail many of the lesser-known tragedies and unexplained occurrences that have become part of the lighthouse's checkered history. In time, I will do exactly that.

However, for the sake of simplicity, I will first discuss the three most recent and widely-known stories involving the Widow's Point Lighthouse. I will do so in chronological order.

I referenced earlier the 1933 mass murder of the entire Collins' family. What I did not mention were the gory details. On the night of September 4, 1933, lighthouse keeper Patrick Collins invited his brother-in-law and three local men to the lighthouse for an evening of card-playing and whiskey. This was a nearly monthly occurrence, so it did not prove particularly troublesome to Patrick's wife, Abigail, or their two children, Stephen, age nine, and Delaney, age six.

One of the men whom Patrick invited was a close friend of his brother-in-law's, a worker from the nearby docks. Joseph O'Leary was, by all accounts, a quiet man. A lifelong bachelor, O'Leary was perhaps best known in town as the man who had once single-handedly foiled a bank robbery when the would-be robber ran out of the bank and directly into O'Leary's formidable chest. O'Leary simply wrapped up the thug in a suffocating bear hug until the authorities arrived.

According to Collins' brother-in-law and the other two surviving card players – Joshua Tempe, bookkeeper and Donald Garland, fisherman – the night of September 4 was fairly typical of one of their get-togethers. Collins and Tempe both drank too much and their games became sloppy and their voices slurred and loud as the night wore on. On the other hand, the brother-in-law ate too many peanuts and strips of spicy jerky, and as usual, there were many complaints voiced about his equally spicy flatulence. O'Leary was his quiet, affable self throughout the evening, and if any one observation could be made regarding the man, it was agreed by the others that O'Leary experienced a stunning run of good luck throughout the second half of the game.

By evening's end, a short time after midnight, the vast majority of the coins on the table were stacked in front of O'Leary, with a grumbling Donald Garland finishing a distant second. The men shrugged on their coats, bid each other goodnight, descended the winding staircase in a slow, staggered parade, and returned to their respective homes and beds.

All except Joseph O'Leary.

When he reached his rented flat on Westbury Avenue, O'Leary went directly to his kitchen table, where he sat for just over an hour and composed the now-infamous, lengthy, rambling, handwritten letter explaining that earlier in the night while taking a break from card-playing to visit the bathroom, he had experienced an unsettling – thou admittedly, thrilling and liberating – supernatural occurrence.

To relieve yourself in 1933 in the Widow's Point Lighthouse, you had to descend to what was commonly (albeit crudely) referred to as the Shit Room. Once you found yourself in this isolated and dimly-lit chamber, you tended to do your business as quickly as possible for it was a genuinely eerie setting and not designed for one's comfort.

It was here, inside the Shit Room, that O'Leary claims the ghostly, transparent image of a young beautiful woman wearing a flowing white bed-robe appeared before him – at first frightening him with her spectral whisperings before ultimately seducing him with both words and embrace.

Afterward, O'Leary returned to his friends and the card game in a daze. His letter claimed it felt as if he had dreamt the entire incident.

Dreamlike or not, once O'Leary finished composing his letter, he rose from the kitchen table, took down the heaviest hammer from his workbench, returned to the Widow's Point Lighthouse, where earlier he had purposely failed to lock the door behind him as was usually the custom, ascended the two hundred-and-sixty-eight steps – and bludgeoned the Collins' family to death in their beds.

Once the slaughter was complete, O'Leary strolled outside onto the catwalk – perhaps to rendezvous with his ghostly lover now that the task she had burdened him with was complete – and climbed over the iron railing and simply stepped off into the starless night.

O'Leary's body was found early the next morning by a local fisherman, shattered on the rocky ground below. Shortly after, the authorities arrived and a much more gruesome discovery was made inside the lighthouse.

(Voice recorder entry #3B – 10:59pm, Friday, July 11, 2017)

It's late and I can barely keep my eyes open. I'm rather exhausted from the day's events, so I bid you all a fair goodnight and pleasant dreams. I pray my own slumber passes uninterrupted, as I am planning for an early start in the morning. Exciting times lay ahead.

275

(Voice recorder entry #4B – 4:51am, Saturday, July 12, 2017)

(Mumbling)

I can't. I don't want to. They're...my friends.

(Voice recorder entry #5B – 7:14am, Saturday, July 12, 2017)

Good morning and what a splendid morning it is!

If I sound particularly rested and cheerful for a man who has just spent the night in a filthy, abandoned, and reputedly haunted lighthouse, it's because indeed I am. Rested and cheerful, that is.

Trust me, folks, I'm as surprised as you are.

My night didn't begin in very promising fashion. Although I tucked myself into my sleeping bag and dimmed the lantern shortly after eleven o'clock, I found myself still wide-awake at half past midnight. Why? I'm not exactly certain. Perhaps excitement. Perhaps trepidation. Or perhaps simply the surprising coldness of the lighthouse floor, felt deep in my bones even through my overpriced sleeping bag.

I lay there all that time and listened to the lighthouse whisper its secrets to me and a singular thought echoed inside my exhausted brain: *what was I hoping to find here?*

It's a question I had been asked many times in the days leading up to this adventure – by Mr. Ronald Parker and my literary agent and even my ex-wife, just to name a few – and never once had I been able to come up with a response that rang with any measure of authenticity.

Until last night, that is, when – in the midst of my unexpected bout of insomnia, as I lay there on the chilly floor in the shadows, wondering if what I was hearing...the distant hollow clanking of heavy metal chains somewhere below me and the uneven scuffling of stealthy footfalls on the dusty staircase...were reality or imagination – the answer to the question occurred to me with startling clarity.

What was I hoping to find here?

Inarguable proof that the Widow's Point Lighthouse was haunted? Incontrovertible evidence that nothing supernatural had ever dwelled within the structure, all the stories and legends nothing more than centuries-old campfire tales and superstition?

The answer that occurred to me was none of the above – and all of the above.

I realized I didn't care what I found here in the Widow's Point Lighthouse. For once, I wasn't looking for a book deal or a movie option. I wasn't looking for fame or fortune.

I was simply looking for the *truth*.

And with that liberating revelation caressing my conscience, my eyes slid closed and I fell into a deep and peaceful sleep.

(Voice recorder entry #6B – 8:39am, Saturday, July 12, 2017)

Now that I've completed my morning exercises and taken a bit of breakfast, it's time for another history lesson.

As I already noted in my opening segment – and I'll try not to repeat myself too much here – Hollywood came calling to the town of Harper's Cove in September of 1985. More specifically, Hollywood came to the Widow's Point Lighthouse.

Although town officials and a handful of local merchants were enthusiastic about the financial rewards Harper's Cove stood to gain from the production, the vast majority of the townspeople expressed extreme unease – and even anger – when they learned that the subject matter of the film so closely paralleled the lighthouse's tragic history. It was one thing to rent out the lighthouse for a motion picture production, but a horror film? And a ghost story at that? It felt morally wrong to the residents of Harper's Cove. It felt *dangerous*. A handful of women from the Harper's Cove Library Association even gathered and picketed outside the movie set, but they gave up after a week of particularly harsh weather drove them inside.

Rosemary's Spirit was budgeted at just over eight million dollars. The film starred Garrett Utley and Britney Longshire, both coming off modest hits for the United Artists studio. Popular daytime television actress, Lydia Pearl, appeared in a supporting role, and by many accounts, stole the movie with her inspired and daring performance.

The film's director, Henry Rothchild, was quoted as saying, "Lydia was such a lovely young woman and she turned in the performance of a lifetime. She showed up on set each day full of energy and wonderfully prepared, and I have no doubt that she would have gone on to amazing things. The whole thing is unimaginable and tragic."

Executive producer, Doug Sharretts, of *Gunsmoke* fame, added: "There were no signs of distress. I had breakfast with Lydia the day it happened. We sat outside and watched the sunlight sparkle across the ocean. She was enchanted. She loved it here. She was in fine spirits and excited to shoot her final scenes later that evening. And she was confident that she and Roger would work out their problems and be married. There were no signs. Nothing."

The rest of the cast and crew are on record with similar statements regarding Miss Pearl and the events of the night of November 3, 1985. Lydia was, by all accounts, in fine spirits, well liked and respected, and her death came as a shock to everyone involved in the film.

However, there was one dissenting voice and it belonged to Carlos Pena, *Rosemary's Spirit's* renowned director of photography. At the time of Lydia Pearl's death, Pena was one of the few members of the crew who refused to comment on record. Most people attributed this to Pena's reticent nature. He was that rare individual in Hollywood: a modest and private man in a very public business.

Fifteen years later, dying of lung cancer at his ranch in Mexico, it was a different story, as Pena told a reporter from *Variety*: "I've worked on over a hundred films and I've never witnessed anything like it. It still haunts me to this day.

"The rest of the cast and crew were on lunch break and I thought I was alone in the lighthouse. I was going over the next scene, pacing out camera shots and thinking about changing the angle on camera number two when I heard someone whispering from the level below me. I was surprised but I figured it was just one of the actors running their lines. After a few minutes, the whispering grew in volume and intensity, to the point where I couldn't concentrate any longer, so I went to investigate.

"Some of the crew had constructed a makeshift break room on the next level down. It was cramped quarters but there was enough room for a small refrigerator and a handful of uncomfortable chairs.

"I was surprised to find the room in total darkness when I reached the doorway. The lights had been on not ten minutes earlier when I'd passed it on my way up to the set. I figured once the person heard my footfalls, they would stop running lines and call out to me, but they didn't. The whispering continued unabated. It was a woman's voice, and now that I could make out the words she was saying, it chilled me. Whoever this was, hidden here in the darkness, she wasn't running lines; she was having a conversation – with herself.

"Uneasy, I reached inside the doorway and turned on the light, and I was shocked to see Lydia Pearl standing in the far corner facing the wall. The whispering continued despite my intrusion.

"I called out to her: 'Lydia? I'm sorry to interrupt.'

"She didn't respond. I walked closer, my heart beating faster in my chest.

"'Is everything okay?' I was almost upon her now.

"Again, there was no response. Just that frenzied whispering, almost a hissing, as though she were arguing with herself. She stood with a rigid posture, but with her arms dangling at her sides.

"Once I was close enough, being careful not to startle her, I softly called her name and reached out and placed a hand gently on her shoulder – and she whirled on me, a rattlesnake-quick hand lunging out to claw at my eyes. I back-stepped in shock, blocking her advance.

"Her face is what I best remember, even now in my dreams. It was twisted in rage. Spittle hanging from her drawn lips. Teeth bared. Her eyes were the worst. They were impossibly large and unlike any human eyes I had ever seen. They were feral and burning with unimaginable hatred. This woman I barely knew wanted to kill me, wanted to devour me.

"And then, as quickly as it had begun, it was over. Her face relaxed, arms lowered, and she drew back, blinking rapidly, as if awakening from a dream. Her eyes seemed to regain focus and she saw me standing there in front of her, quite a sight, I am sure. She sobbed, 'I'm...I'm sorry' and ran from the room, brushing against me as she fled. I remember her skin was ice cold where she had touched me.

"Later that evening, when news of her suicide reached me at my hotel, I was not surprised. I was sad, but not surprised.

"I've never spoken of this before and I never will again."

According to William McKay, the reporter from *Variety*, Carlos Pena had grasped his rosary in his hands and crossed himself numerous times while recounting this unsettling story. Six weeks later, he was dead.

(Voice recorder entry #7B – 11:44am, Saturday, July 12, 2017)

Hello there, again. I've spent the past hour or so scribbling in my notebook, thoughts and observations to look back upon once this experience is over. I've learned not to rely too heavily on memory. Memory is a tricky beast, as I have learned the hard way over the years. It's not to be trusted.

Lunch soon and then another history lesson, this one even more scandalous than the last.

(Voice recorder entry #8B – 11:49am, Saturday, July 12, 2017)

Did I mention that several times now I've heard the echo of foot-steps in this lonely place? Last night and twice again this morning. I'm fairly convinced that it's not my imagination, but if that is truly the case, then what is it I'm hearing? The Widow's Point Lighthouse, all these years later, still settling into the rocky earth below? The harsh Atlantic wind searching for entry and creeping its way inside these heavy stone walls? Hungry rats scavenging for food? Restless spirits?

(Voice recorder entry #9B – 1:01pm, Saturday, July 12, 2017)

Despite the highly publicized and controversial death of actress Lydia Pearl in the fall of 1985, the Widow's Point Lighthouse – save for a handful of NO TRESPASSING signs set about the perimeter – re-mained unguarded and largely accessible to the general public. It wasn't until almost three years later, during the late summer of 1988, that the razor-topped security fence was erected and local authorities began pa-trolling the area.

This is the reason why:

In the spring of 1988, fifteen-year-old Michael Risley had just finished his freshman year at Harper's Cove High School. Michael wasn't considered particularly popular or unpopular. In fact, he wasn't consid-ered much at all. Even in a school as small as Harper's Cove, he was largely invisible.

Because of this, no one knew of Michael Risley's fascination – his outright obsession – with the occult and the Widow's Point Light-house. No one knew that he had spent countless hours in the local library doing research and talking to the old-timers down at the docks about the turn-of-the-century legends regarding devil worship taking place in the woods surrounding the lighthouse.

And, because of this, no one knew that Michael Risley had spent much of his freshman year performing his own satanic rituals in those same woods just outside of the Widow's Point Lighthouse, sacrificing dozens of small animals, on several occasions even going so far as to drink their blood.

By the time July rolled around that summer, Michael was ready to graduate from small animals and move on to bigger things. On the night of a Thursday full moon, he snuck out of his house after bedtime, leaving a note for his parents on the foyer table, and met two younger kids – Tabitha Froehling, age 14, and Benjamin Lawrence, age 13 – at the end of his street. Earlier in the day, Michael had promised them beer and cigarettes and dared them to accompany him to the old lighthouse at midnight. Every small town has a haunted house and for the children of Harper's Point, it had always been – and always would be – the Widow's Point Lighthouse.

The three of them walked side-by-side down the middle of First Street, their shadows from the bright moonlight trailing behind them. They walked slowly and silently, backpacks slung across their shoulders. It was an idyllic scene, full of youthful promise and innocence.

Early the next morning, Michael Risley's mother read the note her son had left on the foyer table the night before. She managed to call out once to her husband before fainting to the hardwood floor. A frantic Mr. Risley bound down the stairs, carried his wife to the living room sofa, read the note grasped in her right hand, and then immediately called 911.

The police found Michael and the other two children exactly where the note had told them they would be. A break in the thick forest formed a natural, circular clearing. A fire pit ringed in small stones was still smoldering at the center of the clearing. Tabitha and Benjamin lay sprawled on their backs not far from the fire. Strange symbols, matching the symbols adorning many nearby trees, had been carved into their foreheads with a sharp knife. Both of their throats had been cut, their chests sliced open. Their hearts were missing. Deep, ragged bite marks covered their exposed legs.

Michael was discovered several hundred yards away – at the base of the Widow's Point Lighthouse – naked and incoherent. The officer in charge claimed in his written report that it was like looking at a "devil on earth." Michael had used the other children's blood to paint every inch of his body red. Then, he had consumed portions of both hearts.

According to the note he had left, Michael believed that once this final ritual was completed, he would be "taken in by the Dark Lord and spirited away to a better place."

Instead, at some point during the long and bloody night, Michael Risley's sanity had snapped, and the only place he was spirited away to was the mental hospital in nearby Coffman's Corner.

A week later, the security fence was in place.

(Voice recorder entry #10B – 3:15pm, Saturday, July 12, 2017)

On a whim, I took the video camera out onto the catwalk a short time ago and gave it another try. It's such a gorgeous afternoon, the sun high in a cloudless sky, the ocean, unusually calm for this time of year, sparkling like a crush of fine emeralds scattered across a tabletop. I spotted a pair of cruise ships steaming south on the horizon. Later, a parade of fishing vessels hauling the day's catch will journey past on their way home to port.

I filmed the entirety of this spectacle and tested the footage when I returned below. Alas, the screen remained blank.

(Voice recorder entry #11B – 4:56pm, Saturday, July 12, 2017)

You'll have to excuse my labored breathing, as you are kindly accompanying me to the bottom of the Widow's Point Lighthouse to re-trieve additional water supplies, traversing the same spiral staircase once climbed by killer and actress alike.

I can feel history here with each step I take. The atmosphere feels similar to a leisurely stroll through the grassy hills of Gettysburg, another haunted place where history and death lock arms and dance for all to see. A spectacle of names and dates flittering through your conscience while you construct a façade of mournful respect, all while secretly wishing to have borne witness to the ancient slaughter. A macabre thought, most certainly, but also an undeniable truth. Interstate rubberneckers don't clog traffic due to frivolous curiosity; rather they can't help themselves, hoping to be fortunate enough to see a splash of scarlet blood on the roadside or a glimpse of mangled flesh. After all, the scores of spectators that crowded into the ancient coliseums didn't come for the popcorn.

Navigating these endless stairs, I must admit I feel a closer kinship with Lydia Pearl and Joseph O'Leary than I ever have with any fallen sol-dier of the Civil War. Why is this the case? Perhaps it is simply the nature of time and urban legends...or perhaps it is just the nature of the Widow's Point Lighthouse. Ghosts surround me here.

(Voice recorder entry #12B – 5:10pm, Saturday, July 12, 2017)

I've just tested several bottles of water from the cooler and discov-ered something mildly alarming. The water has a salty tang to it. Subtle, but present nonetheless. The bottles were purchased from a grocery store just yesterday afternoon, and the water I consumed last night and earlier today suffered no such issue. Perhaps I'm a victim of my own overgrown imagination, or perhaps it's just an unexpected effect of the salty air here on the Nova Scotia coast. Regardless, I can't help but wonder and I can't help but tell you all about it. After all, my own voice is – *(chuckles)* and always has been – my greatest companion.

(Voice recorder entry #13B – 5:29pm, Saturday, July 12, 2017)

Ninety-one, ninety-two, ninety-three...

(Voice recorder entry #14B – 5:53pm, Saturday, July 12, 2017)

My goodness, I am winded. The journey down these twisting stairs felt endless, but the journey back up feels like forever-and-a-half, as my late father was wont to say. I tried counting the two-hundred-and-sixty-eight steps, as I did during my summit just yesterday, but I kept losing count. I swear to you I have climbed over five hundred stairs by now.

To add to my sense of displacement, I can hear the unmistakable rumblings of a storm approaching outside. Odd, as the skies were crystal clear just hours ago. I had been particularly meticulous about checking the local weather reports in the days leading up to this adventure. Each and every online report called for clear days and pleasant nights. Oh, well, no matter, a storm will just add to the mounting atmosphere.

(Voice recorder entry #15B – 6:01pm, Saturday, July 12, 2017)

Many of the historical volumes I read about the Widow's Point Lighthouse discussed the frequent storms that hit this particular section of the Nova Scotia coastline. More than one author claimed that during the most violent of these storms, you could actually feel the old stone lighthouse trembling on its foundation. I chalked this observation up to showmanship and hyperbole, but boy was I mistaken.

When I finally reached the lantern room after what felt like an eternity of climbing, I was stunned at the vision that greeted me outside. Heavy rain lashed the lighthouse windows. The once-crystal skies were now boiling with fast-moving, dark, roiling clouds. Jagged shards of lightning stabbed at the horizon. Angry whitecaps danced across the churning sea. The wind was howling and I could feel in the very bones of the lighthouse the surging waves crashing onto the rocky shoreline at the base of the cliffs.

I stared in awe – and yes, I admit, a sliver of encroaching fear. I have never witnessed the sea in such a state.

(Voice recorder entry #16B – 7:15pm, Saturday, July 12, 2017)

I've somehow managed to lose my flashlight. I carried it with me during my earlier journey down the staircase and I'm certain I brought it back with me upstairs. I clearly recall placing it next to my sleeping bag while I prepared dinner. But now it's gone. I've looked everywhere. Puzzling to say the least.

(Voice recorder entry #17B – 8:12pm, Saturday, July 12, 2017)

First my flashlight, and now I'm hearing things again. Twice in the past hour, I could've sworn I heard the faint strains of a child singing somewhere below me. Each time I moved to the doorway to listen, and each time the singing ceased. Perhaps the ghosts of Widow's Point and the storm are playing tricks on this old boy. Despite my initial sense of unease, I'm grateful for the experience. It will make a fine addition to my notes.

Still no sign of that blasted flashlight.

(Voice recorder entry #18B – 8:24pm, Saturday, July 12, 2017)

There! Can you hear it? A banging, like someone knocking on the floor right underneath me, and—

(Loud staccato rapping)

There it is again!

I'm not imagining it.

Can you hear it?

(Voice recorder entry #19B – 9:57pm, Saturday, July 12, 2017)

What a night it has been! First, the unexpected arrival of the storm and the disappearance of my flashlight. Then, the mysterious singing and knocking sounds. Perhaps most exciting of all, and I know precisely how trite this sounds, I now feel certain that someone is watching me. Several times I have sensed something...a *presence*...directly behind me. I have *felt* it. Yet each time I've turned to find nothing but shadows. I'm sure my colleagues would find great pleasure at my skittish behavior.

I've lectured and written ad nauseam about the psychic energy that is often trapped inside houses of haunted repute, especially those places where violent crimes have occurred. I now feel that energy here in the Widow's Point Lighthouse. And it's getting stronger.

It's not yet ten o'clock and I'm already tucked inside my sleeping bag, hoping for an early night of it. I can hardly see the floor in front of me. The lantern, although in fine working order last night, has proven a sad replacement for my flashlight, as the flame tends to extinguish within minutes of each lighting. Whether this is the result of a malicious gust or *geist*, I cannot say, but my temporary home certainly has a draft that I hadn't noticed before. And it's a chilly draft at that. I had been told that the summer heat would be retained in this old stone monolith, but it seems as if the ocean winds blow colder inside the lighthouse than outside.

Speaking of outside, the storm continues to rage. If anything, it's grown stronger as the night has progressed. Every few moments, lightning slashes the sky, illuminating the room around me with a startling brilliance before plunging it back into darkness. I can't help but wonder if—

(A long, silent beat followed by a beeping sound)

Well, what do you know, ladies and gentlemen, the video camera appears to have come back to life.

Video/audio footage #6A (10:06pm, Saturday, July 12, 2017)

As the video switches on, the screen is flooded with murky shadows. Only the time-code can be clearly seen. Then we hear a muted crash of thunder and a flash of lightning illuminates the lighthouse living quarters. A few seconds later, the lightning is gone and we are greeted again by mostly darkness.

"Initially, I dismissed what I was seeing as a trick of the lightning, but then I realized that the blinking red light at my feet was coming from the video camera. When I heard the beep of the battery, I immediately retrieved the camera and ran a series of quick tests. For whatever reason, it seems to be working fine now.

"I'm thinking perhaps I jarred something when I moved the camera after dinner or — JESUS, WHAT WAS THAT?!"

The video shifts and we hear heavy breathing growing more rapid by the moment. Then, the rustle of footsteps, moving cautiously at first, but gaining urgency. The echo of boots slapping pavement transitions to boots clanging against metal as Livingston ascends the stairs and ventures outside onto the lighthouse's catwalk.

We hear a door being yanked open and are overpowered by the cacophony of the storm. Wind howls. Rain lashes. Thunder roars. Skeletal fingers of lightning dance across the violent sea.

Livingston moves closer to the iron railing and points the camera at the ocean below. Enormous swells crash on the rocks below, sending sprays of whitewater high into the night. The camera zooms closer – and Livingston gasps.

"My God, do you see it?!" he yells, his voice swallowed by the wind. "Someone needs to help them!"

The screen goes blank.

Video/audio footage #7A (10:50pm, Saturday, July 12, 2017)

We see Thomas Livingston's haggard face staring back at us. His hair is wet and he's shivering. His bloodshot eyes dart nervously around the room. For the moment, the lantern is lit, bathing his skin in an orange glow.

He looks at the camera for maybe thirty seconds but doesn't say anything. We can see him searching for his words. Finally:

"I know what I heard. And I know what I saw."

He sounds as if he might break into tears.

"I heard it crashing upon the rocks."

He glances down at the ground, steels himself, then looks back at the camera and continues.

"It was a massive ship. At least two hundred feet long. And it broke into a thousand pieces. It was an awful sound. Dozens of men... thrashed and tossed upon the rocks...impaled on splintered planks...flailing and drowning in the waves. I can still hear their screams.

"I recorded all of it, I'm certain of that. I knew what I was witnessing wasn't possible, but I saw what I saw and I kept the camera rolling..."

A deep breath.

"But there's nothing there now. I checked the video after I returned inside and changed into dry clothes. I checked it a dozen times. There's nothing there."

He looks up at the camera and the brash showman we saw earlier is gone.

"You can hear the thunder and the crash of the waves. You can see the lightning flash and the ocean illuminated below...but there's no ship anywhere to be seen. No bodies. No screams."

Livingston rubs his eyes with his fists.

"I offer no explanation, ladies and gentlemen, because I have none."

Video/audio footage #8A (11:16pm, Saturday, July 12, 2017)

The video turns on and once again we see a shaky image of the churning ocean at the base of the cliffs. The rain has slowed, but the wind is still gusting and shards of lightning still decorate the sky.

"It's taken me the better part of an hour to summon the courage to come out here again."

The camera zooms in for a closer view. Waves crash onto an empty shoreline.

"The ship is gone."

The camera zooms back out.

"But I know what I saw."

After a moment, the camera lowers and we hear footsteps on the catwalk, and then a loud *clanging*.

"What the...?"

The camera shifts as Livingston bends down and steadies on the object he almost tripped over.

The missing flashlight.

"Jesus."

(Voice recorder entry #20B – 11:33pm, Saturday, July 12, 2017)

I must sleep now, if such a thing is possible in my current state. I've had enough adventure – or shall I say misadventure – for one day. Do you remember earlier when I said I was only here for the truth? Well, that was a fucking lie.

(Voice recorder entry #21B – 1:12am, Sunday, July 13, 2017)

(The sound of footsteps descending the stairway)

Sixty-eight, sixty-nine, seventy, seventy-one, seventy-two, seventy-three...

(Voice recorder entry #22B – 1:35am, Sunday, July 13, 2017)

Two-sixty-six, two-sixty-seven, two-sixty-eight.

(Shuffling of footsteps as Livingston reaches the bottom, turns around, and immediately starts climbing again)

One, two, three, four, five, six, seven, eight, nine, ten, eleven, twelve, thirteen...

(Voice recorder entry #23B – 2:09am, Sunday, July 13, 2017)

...two-hundred-and-ninety-nine, three-hundred, three-hundred-

and-one, three-hundred-and-two, three-hundred-and-three, three-hundred-and-four, three-hundred-and-five…

(Livingston's voice is monotone, deliberate, as if he has been hypnotized)

(Voice recorder entry #24B – 6:42am, Sunday, July 13, 2017)

The night was endless, a nightmare. If I slept at all, I don't remember. The hours passed in a fever dream. At one point, I heard someone crying, a woman, but was too frightened to get up and investigate. A short time later I thought I saw something moving in the doorway, the pale outline of a person, but it vanished when I fumbled with the lantern. It's so cold in here I can't stop shivering, even inside my sleeping bag. My entire body aches, and my feet are filthy and tattered, as if I've walked a great distance without shoes.

I need to eat and drink, but I'm too exhausted.

(Voice recorder entry #25B – 7:29am, Sunday, July 13, 2017)

It occurs to me now that someone might be playing a cruel and elaborate joke. Either that old bastard Parker or perhaps my bitch of an ex-wife. To what end, I haven't the slightest idea, but I don't know what else it could be.

All of the water bottles I brought up with me last night are empty. And I certainly didn't drink them. I was too shaken to even take a sip. And the crackers and the cheese I carried up, all stale. The apples and the one remaining pear, rotten to the core. I need to somehow summon the energy to walk downstairs to the cooler. My mouth is so dry I can barely spit. My stomach is growling.

(Voice recorder entry #26B – 8:17am, Sunday, July 13, 2017)

I've nearly reached the bottom, thank God. Just another couple dozen stairs.

(Labored breathing)

The video camera is once again malfunctioning. It was my intention to bring it with me to chronicle what I found below, but the camera wouldn't even turn on this morning. I tried several times to no avail, leaving me with this crummy voice recorder – sorry, Sony, and go fuck yourself while you're at it.

(A deep breath and the sound of heavy footsteps on the stairway ceases)

Thank God...after everything else that has occurred, I almost expected the cooler to be gone.

(Cooler lid is lifted. A rustling of ice as a plastic bottle is lifted out. The snap of the cap being loosened and a loud gulp of water being swallowed, then — a chorus of violent gagging and vomiting)

(Voice recorder entry #27B – 9:09am, Sunday, July 13, 2017)

All of the water is contaminated. Pure salt water. Every goddam bottle. The caps were all sealed tight. This isn't a joke. This isn't a prank. This is...something else.

All of the food has gone bad too. There are maggots in the lunchmeat. The fruit is rotten. The bread is brittle and spotted with mold.

I'm so tired. I feel like I'm losing my mind.

(Voice recorder entry #28B – 9:48am, Sunday, July 13, 2017)

I tried pounding on the front door, but no one came. Of course. The security gate is locked tight and won't be opened again until tomorrow morning when old man Parker arrives. Next, I tried prying the door open with a piece of scrap metal but it wouldn't budge. I'm considering bringing down my sleeping bag, lantern, and the rest of my supplies and holing up down here until tomorrow morning. It somehow feels safer here on ground level.

(A chortle of muffled laughter in the background)

Now that I've calmed down, I've given the situation a lot of thought. I can survive just fine until tomorrow morning without food and water. I've done it before.

(Another burst of laughter that Livingston obviously doesn't hear)

I just have to keep my wits about me.

(More laughter and then: 'I'm coming, darling. I'm coming.' The voice belongs to a man, deep in tenor and tinged with an Irish accent. A loud, wet cracking sound is followed by guttural cries. The man laughs again and there are several more wet cracking sounds. Livingston takes no notice)

Whether this is all somehow an intricate ruse designed to make a fool of me or truly the work of whatever spirits inhabit the lighthouse, I don't care anymore. I've already got what I came for. The videos and audiotapes I've made are pure gold. More than enough to seal another book deal. Toss in the other things I've witnessed and heard, and we most likely have a movie, as well. It's pay day, and just in time for me. Hell, I don't even have to embellish that much this time around. The only thing I truly wonder about is—

(Livingston gasps)

Get off of me! Get the fuck off of me!

(Frantic footsteps pounding their way up the stairs, finally slowing after a number of minutes. Heavy breathing)

Something grabbed me down there. I felt it on my shoulder... squeezing. Then I watched as a lank of my hair was pulled away from my head. But there was nothing there. My goddam hair was moving by itself.

(Footsteps pick up the pace again)

How in God's name have I not reached the top yet?

(More footsteps)

...one-hundred-and-seventeen, one-hundred-and-eighteen, one-hundred-and-nineteen...

(Voice recorder entry #29B – 10:27am, Sunday, July 13, 2017)

...two-hundred-and sixty-six, two-hundred-and sixty-seven, two-hundred-and-sixty-eight, two-hundred-and-sixty-nine, two-hundred-and-seventy...

Dear God, what is happening?

(Voice recorder entry #30B – time unknown, Sunday, July 13, 2017)

(Note: from this point forward, the voice recorder's time-code is corrupted for reasons unknown, displaying only 0:00 for the remainder of the recordings)

There are things occurring here clearly beyond my comprehension. Forget the hundreds of impossibly extra stairs I just climbed to reach the living quarters. Forget the fact that I witnessed an ancient fishing vessel crash upon the rocks below last night or watched my hair floating in mid-air right in front of my eyes this morning. Forget the cooler full of contaminated water and rotten food. None of that matters.

But the bloody fucking hammer with the initials J.O. carved into its polished wooden handle I just found laying atop my sleeping bag is another story entirely.

Get me the fuck out of here!

(Voice recorder entry #31B – time unknown, Sunday, July 13, 2017)

I'm sitting with my back against the wall. The lantern is aglow for now, and I can see the entire room and the doorway from this position. But I can't take my eyes off the bloody hammer.

All I have to do is make it until eight o'clock tomorrow morning. I would tell you what time it is now, but my motherfucking watch has stopped working.

(Voice recorder entry #32B – time unknown, Sunday, July 13, 2017)

How is this storm still raging? How is it possible? It's so dark outside it feels like the end of the world.

(Voice recorder entry #33B – time unknown, Sunday, July 13, 2017)

(Defeated whisper)

I came here for the money. Of course, I did. It's always been about the money.

(Voice recorder entry #34B – time unknown, Sunday, July 13, 2017)

Late last night and the night before, Tommyknockers, Tommy-knockers, knocking at the door. I want to go out, don't know if I can, 'cause I'm so afraid of the Tommyknocker man.

(Voice recorder entry #35B – time unknown, Sunday, July 13, 2017)

It shouldn't be night already. It can't be. It wasn't even ten in the morning when I was downstairs at the cooler. There's no way that much time has passed. It's not possible.

(Voice recorder entry #36B – time unknown, Sunday, July 13, 2017)

Get off of me! Stop touching me!

(Voice recorder entry #37B – time unknown, Sunday, July 13, 2017)

(Crying)

Someone...*something*...keeps touching my face. I can feel its breath on my neck.

(Voice recorder entry #38B – time unknown, Sunday, July 13, 2017)

(Sobbing)

Please just leave me alone...

(Voice recorder entry #39B – time unknown, Sunday, July 13, 2017)

Can you hear her singing? It's a little girl. She's getting closer.

(Voice recorder entry #40B – time unknown, Sunday, July 13, 2017)

Everything's gonna be okay. Everything's gonna be okay.

(Voice recorder entry #41B – time unknown, Sunday, July 13, 2017)

(The deep Irish voice heard earlier...
'Yes, love, it's done. Each one's nothing but a bloody carcass on a bed
sheet. Oh yes, darlin', very bloody.
'What's that? You want this one, too?')

(Voice recorder entry #42B – time unknown, Sunday, July 13, 2017)

This is a bad place. I can feel it whispering inside my head. It wants to show me something...something terrible.

(Voice recorder entry #43B – time unknown, Sunday, July 13, 2017)

(Screaming)

Oh my God, it hurts!

(Sobbing)

Somehow I dozed off and woke up with the most awful pain shooting through my leg. I rolled up my pants leg and found fucking teeth marks! Something bit me while I was sleeping! Oh Jesus, I have to stop the bleeding!

(Voice recorder entry #44B – time unknown, Sunday, July 13, 2017)

(Unintelligible)

(Voice recorder entry #45B – time unknown, Sunday, July 13, 2017)

Our father who art in heaven, hallowed be thy name, thy kingdom come, thy will be done...

(Voice recorder entry #46B – time unknown, Sunday, July 13, 2017)

(The following is spoken by Livingston in Hebrew, and has since been translated)

...for rebellion is like the sin of divination, and arrogance like the evil of idolatry. Because I have rejected the word of the Lord, he has rejected me as king.

We know that we are children of God, and that the whole world is under the control of The Evil One.

(Voice recorder entry #47B – time unknown, Sunday, July 13, 2017)

(Frantic footsteps)

I'm going out on the catwalk. It's my last hope.

(The sound of a door opening, then hard wind and rain)

I can't stop the bleeding in my leg. I can't stop the voices. They're getting closer.

(Thunder crashes)

The bloody hammer disappeared from atop my sleeping bag. I hear the echo of heavy footsteps on the stairway. That means he's coming for me now. Joseph O'Leary is still here. He never left. None of them did. If I can only make it until morning, I can—

* * *

OFFICIAL POLICE REPORT
FILE #173449-C-34
DATE: July 15, 2017
REPORTING OFFICER(S): Sgt. Carl Blevins; Sgt. Reginald Scales

At 8:47am on Monday, July 14, 2017, the Harper's Cove Police Department received a phone call from Mr. Ronald Parker, age eighty-one, reporting a missing person and summoning them to the Widow's Point Lighthouse.

Sgt. Scales and I arrived at the lighthouse grounds at approximately 8:59am. Mr. Parker greeted us at the security gate and directed us to park next to a red Ford pick-up and a gray Mercedes sedan.

Mr. Parker showed us identification and explained that the Mercedes belonged to a male in his mid-forties named Thomas Livingston. According to Mr. Parker, Mr. Livingston, a well-known author, had rented the lighthouse from Mr. Parker's company for the purpose of paranormal research. The dates of the agreement ran from Friday evening, July 11 to Monday morning, July 14. Mr. Parker was contracted to return to the Widow's Point Lighthouse at precisely 8am on Monday to unlock the front door and escort Mr. Livingston from the property.

Pursuant to this agreement, Mr. Parker claimed that he arrived on Monday morning at approximately 7:50am and waited inside his truck until 8am. At that time, he unlocked the front door and called out for Mr. Livingston. When there was no response, he returned to his truck for a flashlight and entered the lighthouse.

On the lower level, he found Mr. Livingston's cooler still mostly full of food and water. He also noticed a puddle of dried vomit nearby on the floor.

After repeatedly calling out to Mr. Livingston and receiving no response, Mr. Parker climbed the spiral staircase to the lighthouse's living quarters. There he found a blood-soaked sleeping bag, a video camera, a lantern, and several other items belonging to Mr. Livingston. He also noticed a series of strange symbols had been scrawled on the walls in what appeared to be blood.

Before returning to the lower level, Mr. Parker searched the catwalk for Mr. Livingston. He found no sign of him, save for a Sony tape recorder located on the metal walkway. Mr. Parker did not touch the recorder and immediately returned to his truck where he called authorities using his cellphone.

After Sgt. Scales and I finished interviewing Mr. Parker, we searched the lighthouse in tandem. Failing to locate Mr. Livingston, we proceeded to search his unlocked vehicle – where we discovered numerous prescription pill bottles, as well as a loaded handgun, all of which have been logged into Evidence – before searching the surrounding grounds and woods.

At 9:31am, I summoned the Crime Lab, and Sgt. Scales and I began establishing a perimeter.

As of today, thirty-one (31) items have been logged into Evidence, including the video camera and audio recorder. Additional analysis of the digital files found within the camera and dozens of audio files is underway.

Weather conditions remain sunny and clear, and additional searching of the lighthouse grounds is currently underway.

Sgt. Carl Blevins
Badge 3B71925

Messages

Mark Allan Gunnells

THE beach was deserted as David made his way across the sand.
Not surprising, considering that it was two in the morning, and David had come seeking solitude. He'd come to feel closer to Greg, and Greg had always said there was a special magic about the beach at night which it didn't possess in the light of the sun.

The powdery sand became wet and compacted as he neared the shore line, his bare feet sinking a little with each step. The water rushed up over his ankles, cool and soothing, dampening the cuffs of his pants. As he stared out at the dark, rolling raves, the lights of a few distant boats twinkling like earthbound stars, David thought that Greg had been right. There was magic here.

He sat down on the sand, letting the surf surge up around his legs, breathing in the salty tang of the air. To be honest, David had never much cared for the beach, preferring the mountains instead, but it had been one of Greg's favorite places in the world. So they'd compromised, spending half their vacations in the mountains and half at the beach.

When Greg had gotten sick last year, he'd wanted to see the ocean one last time, but the doctors had said traveling wasn't a good idea. Greg had pleaded, but David had sided with the doctors. A decision he'd regretted after Greg was gone. Which was why David had brought Greg's ashes to the beach and released them into the ocean.

Exactly a year ago.

Some people have a grave to visit, I have the Atlantic Ocean. Maybe it will become an annual pilgrimage for me.

David didn't know if he'd really come here every year; he hadn't even intended to come this year. Yet as the date of Greg's death approached, he found himself wanting to be close to his late husband. Since that wasn't possible, coming to the place where he'd laid his remains to rest seemed the next best thing.

Rest, David thought with a laugh. As he looked out at the constantly roiling waters, he thought there was nothing restful about the ocean. Which was somehow perfect. In life, Greg had been a boundless well of energy, always on the go, never satisfied with sitting still for too long a period of time. That was one of the worst parts of watching as the sickness progressed – it had stilled that which seemed incapable of being stilled.

"You'll never be still again," David said out loud, feeling like a fool. Of course, there was no one around to hear him.

Not even Greg.

This thought brought stinging tears to his eyes. His husband's death hadn't done anything to shake David's conviction that there was no God (or Zeus or Odin or L. Ron fucking Hubbard, his atheism applied to all religions and gods indiscriminately), but for the first time in his adult life it had made him *want* to believe. Made him wish he was a Mulder instead of a Scully. It would have been comforting to think that somewhere out there Greg still existed.

As the next wave rolled in over his lower extremities, David splashed his hand in the water then brought the salty brine up to his lips. If Greg still existed anywhere, it was here, in the sea where his ashes had been scattered.

Of course, David knew that was ridiculous, but life without Greg was ridiculous. Now he understood the pull of religion. The beliefs might be silly, but maybe only silly fictions could combat the painful realities of the world. If meaning couldn't be found, perhaps a fabrication of meaning could suffice. Maybe you could know something wasn't real and still get some kind of value from it.

As David contemplated these philosophical concerns while staring up at a sky too covered with tattered clouds to reveal any stars, another waved crashed over him and he felt something bump up against his crotch. He glanced down to find a dark green bottle nestled in the V of his legs, a crude cork stuck in the opening.

With a frown, he picked up the bottle. It was large, larger than the average wine bottle, with no label or any markings. The glass was opaque so that he couldn't see what, if anything, was inside. He held the bottle next to his ear and shook it. No sloshing of liquid, which meant the cork was securely jammed into the opening. He did hear a faint rattling, however, so it wasn't completely empty.

He grabbed the cork and yanked. At first the thing didn't budge, so he renewed his grip on the bottle with his left hand and strained himself until the cork popped out so suddenly that he nearly fell back onto the sand. He upended the bottle and let the contents fall out into his left palm.

Two items. A piece of yellowed paper, rolled up and tied with twine, and a stub of a pencil.

"Message in a bottle," he murmured to himself. "How Nicholas Sparks can you get?"

After plunking the bottle into the sand next to him, twisting it several times to anchor it deeply in the sand so that the tide wouldn't carry it back out, he broke the twin and began to unfurl the scrap of paper. The absurd thought popped into his mind, *What if it's a message from Greg?*

Ludicrous, he knew, but he still felt a rush of anticipation as he looked down at the words scrawled on the paper. The handwriting was sloppy, almost as if the author's hand had been shaking, printed in all caps. David read the note's three lines several times. It seemed an odd bit of poetry, but affecting for all its oddity.

"FROM MY VANTAGE THE WORLD ABOVE SEEMS LONELY AND FULL OF PAIN. I CAN WIPE ALL THAT AWAY. I MERELY NEED TO BE INVITED."

"Lonely and full of pain, that sums up my life," David said to the night. Since losing Greg, he'd gone through the motions of getting on with his life, but each day was a struggle. Each day was a chore. Each day was a void. And he realized his experience wasn't particularly unique. Everyone harbored some secret anguish, some hidden suffering. This knowledge, however, didn't unite the world but seemed to drive everyone further apart, into their own separate bubbles of grief and heartache. If only there was someone who could wipe all that away.

David turned the note over, and using his palm to bear down on, he wrote, "Come on up," pressing so hard with the dull pencil tip that he tore through the paper in several places. Then he popped the note back into the bottle, replaced the cork, and tossed it out into the waves. In the darkness, he lost sight of it almost as soon as it left his hand, but he heard the *splash* as the bottle hit the water.

He pushed himself up. From the waist down, he was drenched and caked with muddy sand. He stared out at the black ocean, doing its eternal dance, the sound of the waves like the universe shushing the world because there was no one to hear its collective cry for help.

As he started away from the water, imagining some angsty teenager writing that bit of cryptic poetry and putting in the bottle, the roar of the surf behind him increased. It sounded like thunder suddenly, a constant rumbling increasing in pitch.

David turned back slowly to see the water churning and thrashing, like a swimming pool during an earthquake. Not that he'd ever seen this in person, but in the movies he had. The waves began to crash onto the sand with greater force, moving further up the sand.

Tsunami, was the first thought to come to David's mind. Yet that was impossible, he'd never heard of a tsunami hitting the east coast of the United States.

There's a first time for everything. No one had ever heard of AIDS until the first time someone got infected.

David knew he should run, but he remained transfixed by the increasing violence of the sea. If it was in fact a tsunami, he doubted he could outrun it anyway.

As he watched, he realized that something seemed to be rising from the waters, several miles from shore. He couldn't make out specifics, but it was large, rising up toward the overhead clouds, the shape a mere darker silhouette against the darkness of the night. He thought he could make out the shape of a torso, a head, arms, and a strange three pronged fork-like instrument held even higher.

Trident, it's called a trident.

For a moment, David thought other forms were rising from the ocean around this thing, but then he realized these were waves, lifting higher than any he'd ever seen, perhaps hundreds of feet. The dark shape lowered its arms, and the waves began to advance toward the shore as if in a race to see which could reach land first.

His paralysis finally released him, and David turned to sprint back toward steps that would lead him back up to the parking lot where he'd left his car. Behind him, he heard the rumble of the approaching waves and realized his attempt to flee was probably futile, but still his legs pumped. In the nearby hotels, he saw lights coming on in windows as the tumult awakened vacationers who no doubt were pushing aside curtains to see what caused the noise. He imagined there would be screams and prayers.

Even in the blackness, David sensed an even deeper shadow falling over him, and a few feet from the wooden steps, he stumbled and fell face-first into the sand. As the pounding of the sea filled his ears and he felt the spray of the advancing waves, his last thought was, *I guess there is a god after all.*

Show Me Where the Waters Fill Your Grave

Todd Keisling

T HE rain's come again, and this time Jonathan is ready. He's spent weeks preparing for this moment, days and nights glued to the fancy thin television his son bought him last year for Christmas, endless hours watching the pretty young lady on the weather station. He's learned to tune out the commercials and advertisements. Though his body is withered and spent, Jonathan Crosby's mind is still sharp. He still has his wits, knows how to define right from wrong, and determine safety from danger. He's cognizant of his choices and fully aware of their repercussions.

So today, when the weather alert buzzes across the screen in a thick red band, bisecting the pretty girl talking about the non-stop rains in the northeast, Jonathan doesn't pay attention. He doesn't have to. He knows he's in danger. The promise of doom and rainfall is what he's been waiting for all summer long.

* * *

Last time the waters along the river rose high enough, he was still submerged in a different kind of mire. Glenda's passing had filled his head with the worst kind of depression, the sort that seeped down into the roots of the heart and stayed there. She'd been gone less than a week, and he'd spent the following days in a kind of stupor, wandering the rooms of their house, noting the lack of color, the absence of warmth. His joints sang together in a chorus of misery, a funerary ode to the moisture in the air.

The rains had started the day after they buried her and did not stop for a full week. Insult to injury, he supposed. When the world lost a soul like Glenda, he figured that shedding a few tears was to be expected. God knew he'd wept for days; why shouldn't the world? Her absence had left an aching void in his life, an open wound of the spirit that would never truly heal. A wound that was always at risk of being pried open by the most innocent of queries from friends and strangers.

"How are you today, Jon?" was the most common. Their neighbor, Sarah, was the most recent perpetrator of such an infraction. Of course she was only making idle chatter. Of course her heart was in the right place. But oh, the pain, how it seeped back into that wound, festering with a different kind of infection that would take weeks to cleanse. Sarah didn't know any better. She was half his age, with a family of four to tend to, and wouldn't learn the agony of losing a spouse for some years yet. Lying to her was one of the hardest things he'd done that day, next to getting out of bed and wandering outside for the mail.

Those early days, he kept to himself as much as possible, a heartbroken hermit locked away in a cave of perpetual melancholy. Although Glenda was entombed just a few miles down the road, their house had become her memorial, and he was its caretaker. He forced himself to pick up her routines, dusting the mantle and framed photos hung on the walls, feeding their pet guppies in the aquarium, and making the weekly grocery trip every Tuesday morning.

A few weeks after the funeral, Sarah's husband, Donald, invited Jonathan over for dinner and beers. Jonathan acquiesced, mainly to stem the tide of their incessant requests, and over the course of the evening proceeded to drink a number of Donald's brews. By the time the sun had set, Jonathan was two sheets to the wind, as Glenda would say, and confessed to Donald that he was just biding his time.

"For what?" Donald asked.

"For the rains," Jonathan slurred. "Ain't you ever heard that old saying?"

Donald shook his head and finished off his beer. He crinkled the can in his fist. "What sayin's that, Jon?"

"Sorry, Don. I forget you didn't grow up here." Jonathan sloshed the last gulp of beer in the can, made to take that last drink, and then thought better of it. "This whole area's in a floodplain. When I was just a boy, the gang down at Miller's Bar where my daddy used to while away his evenings, they'd always joke around with me 'n say that you know it's rainin' rough when your grandma comes to visit."

"That's kinda grim for a joke, ain't it?"

Jonathan shook his head. "Those were different times. We weren't as sensitive to things then. Anyways, the first time I heard it, I asked my daddy what it meant, and he told me that the flood of aught-nine caused all the coffins to rise. Took 'em weeks to round up and sort out all the caskets."

Donald uttered a low chuckle that gave way to a belch. He excused himself and frowned as he put the pieces together. "So when you say you're waitin' for the rains... Aw, shit, Jon, I'm sorry."

"Nah, no need for that, Don. It's just the beer talkin'."

But it wasn't. Jonathan thought it was, but when the rains came again, they made a liar out of him.

To tell the truth, Jonathan hadn't given much thought to that old joke in decades. Not until the storms that followed Glenda's funeral. He was standing on his back porch and watching the world fall down in thick white sheets when the warning buzzed across his TV. The steady drum of raindrops on the porch roof masked the harsh buzz, and Jonathan almost didn't hear it. When he turned back and looked through the window at the red band on the screen, he sighed and shook his head. After four days of rain, the weather station's announcement was obvious: water levels were rising.

He closed his eyes and listened to the rapid beat of rain overhead. *God's playing the drums again.* Glenda always said that. Now that she was gone, he'd grown conscious of the way her words haunted his lexicon. She was a part of him even in speech, living on as a linguistic phantom that could not be exorcised. Not that he wanted her to be. Painful though it was, Jonathan took comfort in knowing she was still there somewhere, living on in his words. He need only speak to bring her back to him, if only for a fleeting moment.

"God's playing drums again," he whispered. "Signalin' your arrival to His kingdom, darlin'. I hope you're having a hell of a party."

He wondered if that was true. Sure, he was raised in church, but in his adult years, he'd wandered off the path. All that fire and brimstone didn't suit him—there was enough of it on the nightly news—and besides, he'd rather enjoy his time instead of dwelling on his transgressions. He and Glenda saw eye to eye on that matter, so they'd lived their lives the best they could. Now, though, Jonathan's imagination ran wild with possibilities. Was she watching him from heaven? Was she really up there, sitting on a cloud and laughing at every little thing he did while he waited his turn to shuffle off this coil?

A slow, cold sensation slithered into his gut, carrying with it an alternate thought. *What if she isn't up there?* He wondered. *What if she isn't anywhere? What if she's just gone? What if…*

312

"Stop it," he told himself. The truth was, he had no way of knowing, and he was better off not dwelling on it. Easier said than done, maybe, but he didn't have much of a choice but to try.

He locked away those troubling thoughts and leaned forward against the porch railing, watching the churning waters of the river slowly surge and creep over their banks. Most folks would've found the rising waters to be cause for concern, but not Jonathan. He and Glenda had lived in their home for over thirty years before she passed, and not once in that time had the waters ever reached their foundation. The rising tide would break at the foot of his driveway, just like it had all the other years.

He watched until late evening when, in the failing light, he saw the river had crept high enough over the bank to kiss the edge of the road. By that point, the winds had picked up, slapping the branches from one of Glenda's dogwoods against the siding and reminding him that they needed trimming. He'd forgotten to do that this year, preoccupied with his wife's illness.

It'll keep until the storm passes, he thought, listening to the steady clap of limbs and pitter-patter of rain. *Maybe tomorrow. Couple days at most*. His vigil concluded, Jonathan turned away from the porch railing and retreated into his house.

Satisfied, his joints aching from the damp air, Jonathan curled up on the sofa and took his evening deluge of prescription pills. Cholesterol, arthritis (one for inflammation, one for pain), thyroid, and the latest to join an all-star cast: anxiety. He'd kept this last one a secret from Glenda in the final months of her life. She was already down on herself; he didn't want to burden her with his stress. "Just something to take the edge off," he'd told his doctor. "Until this ride is over."

The ride had ended, but Jonathan was still hanging on. He liked being leveled out. The pills made the nights a bit easier to bear.

He washed them down with a mug of cold coffee, lowered the volume on the TV, and wrapped one of Glenda's handmade blankets around him. He hadn't slept in their bed since she'd passed, couldn't bring himself to do so. Sleeping there seemed wrong somehow, as if the act might disturb some sacred oath he'd sealed with her in her passing. That if they could not lie there together in union, so shall the bed remain cold and empty, a monument to the time they spent together as husband and wife. And beneath that sense of marital duty, Jonathan supposed it just hurt too goddamn much.

Another weather update buzzed from the television, but he didn't bother reading it. Instead, he reclined on the sofa, closed his eyes, and listened to God play drums.

* * *

He waits at the bottom of the stairs, dressed in his Sunday best while reports of a perfect storm creep into the foyer. "Seek higher ground," they say. "If you need assistance—"

But Jonathan tunes out the meteorologist, focusing instead on his silver cufflinks. They're miniature books, a gift from Glenda on his thirtieth birthday.

"*Because you love reading,*" she'd said, "*and because you lost your old pair.*"

Jonathan traces his thumb across the smooth rectangle and smiles. The last time he wore them was at her funeral. The same as his suit, as a matter of fact, and for a moment, he wonders if his attire isn't appropriate for the occasion. After all, a three-piece suit and tie isn't practical when dealing with rising floodwaters, but he reminds himself that today is special. Concessions must be made in the face of extraordinary situations.

Elsewhere, the pretty weather lady says to expect another surge of rainfall by noon, with no signs of slowing down by nightfall.

He checks his watch.

Jonathan smiles. Not long now.

* * *

Three slow knocks woke him from his sleep. The first knock was loud enough to rouse him from his slumber—a troubled sleep of dark dreams filled with lily pads and koi fish and a cluster of small hands lurking beneath the surface. The second knock pulled him through the twilit veil of sleep into a world of consciousness.

Jonathan opened his eyes and stared at the ceiling. The room was filled with the bluish light of dawn, the sun just a promise beyond the horizon. Had he dreamed those two knocks? Could they have been the rain? He held his breath and waited, listening. The rain had stopped, the winds finally quieted, and the earth was still around him.

Just a dream, he thought, and closed his eyes.

The third knock came at last. Jonathan sat up, rubbed the sleep from his eyes, and squinted at his watch. Not even 5 A.M. Who the hell could it be at this hour?

He climbed to his feet, ignoring the fire in his joints and the urge to take his pills. They could wait. This stranger at the door, however, could not. Someone knocking on his door at this hour would have a good reason. They could be hurt. They might need help.

As he stumbled across the living room to the foyer, his mind raced with possibilities of who it might be or what might be wrong. He thought of his neighbors, Sarah and Donald and their two little ones. Had the waters risen too high in the night? His house's foundation sat at a slightly higher elevation, only by a few inches, but those inches could make all the difference in a flood.

Jonathan resisted the urge to peek out the window. Instead, he twisted the deadbolt and opened the door.

The floodwaters crested just beyond the edge of his driveway and were already receding, a dark oily border illuminated in the dawn by a pale streetlight overhead. The water, however, was not what held his attention.

The woman in his driveway wore a sapphire evening gown with jewels sewn into the trim. She shimmered when she moved, the jewels reflecting the light overhead, enhancing the curls of wet, silvery hair draped over her shoulders. The hem of her gown fell at an angle just below her knees, revealing pale legs that had danced the nights away in their younger days. Her bare feet slapped across the water as she approached his doorstep.

"I was wondering if you'd answer, love."

Jonathan's knees gave out, and he collapsed at the threshold. "Glenda…" Words failed him, their syllables like dry air through empty cornhusks. "Why…h-how…?"

Glenda Crosby tiptoed along the pavement of their driveway. A slow trickle of water followed behind her, an inky black umbilicus stretching back to the ebbing tide below the drive. The longer he watched, the less Jonathan could tell which direction the water flowed. The dark stream followed her footsteps, surging forward in time to her movement, his queen marching along a wet carpet of foam and errant leaves caught in the tumult of the night's storm.

She paused where the sidewalk met the driveway. The water stretched thin, barely more than a trickle at that distance. Her safety rope would let her go no farther; he would have to meet her halfway.

Jonathan remained on his knees, befuddled by what he was seeing, his eyes encased in tears. How was this possible? How could she be standing here when she was buried over in Morningside? Was this a dream? A phantom? Any possible answers were swept away in the maelstrom raging within his head, his heart.

"Don't weep, my darling."

Now that she was closer, he could hear the lilt in her voice, a gentle rise in pitch that might accompany a tickle in one's throat. The sound of talking when water's gone down the wrong pipe. His mind flashed with the image of a gutter spout clogged with twigs and acorns, and he cleared his own throat instinctively. His mouth filled with phlegm, but he resisted the urge to spit it out. Grimacing, he swallowed back the filth.

"Glenda," he said finally, bracing himself against the doorframe before climbing to his feet. His knees sang together in a chorus of damp agony. "This can't be. I watched the life go out of you. I watched them put you in the ground, for Christ's sake."

A smile spread across her damp, pale face. She held out her arms. "And yet here I am, my darling. Come to me."

He took one step across the threshold onto the sidewalk but couldn't bring himself to take another. *No,* he reminded himself, *everything is wrong about this. Glenda's dead and buried, Jon. She* can't *be here.*

She lowered her head and peered up at him. That look made his heart flutter. Her bedroom gaze. He'd teased her about it for years, when they were still young and virile. Even after their son grew up and moved out, she still gave him the stare from time to time. "*I'm yours,*" it told him. "*And you're mine.*"

Staring into her sapphire eyes, Jonathan felt compelled to join her. And why not? The one thing he'd desired most—to be with Glenda once again—had been granted to him. He'd won some sort of cosmic lottery, the recipient of a gifted miracle of nature. His wife, once deceased, now stood mere feet away from him, awaiting his embrace. How he'd longed for her, to hear her voice again, to hold her hand. All the nights he'd slept without her, even before her passing, raced back to him in that moment. Every night without her touch was another quiet reassurance from reality, a coarse blanket pulled over him that was too scratchy, too short to truly bring him any comfort. He feared those nights would define the rest of his life. One lonely evening of depression would bleed into the next, counting down to the day that he, too, would wither and fade away into the great big nothing beyond.

But now, somehow, beyond all hope and reason, here she was again. And she was waiting for him. Beckoning for him. Yearning.

"Come to me," she said. "Dance with me one last time."

And he wanted to. God, how he wanted to, his aching knees be damned. He took one step across the threshold, and then another.

Glenda turned away and gazed up at the side of their home. She smiled faintly. "You forgot to trim the dogwood again, love."

Jonathan choked back a humorless laugh. There was nothing funny about her statement; quite the contrary, her words all but confirmed that what he saw before him was truly happening. Only Glenda would give him grief about those damn branches. His heart climbed into his throat. "Is it really you?"

She looked back at him, reached out, and took his hand. Her skin was wet, cold, and touching her gave him goosebumps.

"Dance with me," she whispered, and leaned in to kiss him.

*   *   *

He's drifted off to sleep when Donald pounds on the door. The sound startles him so bad he bumps his head against the staircase banister. Dark, muted colors explode before his eyes as he clamors to regain his composure, pressing his hand against the back of his skull to dull the pain.

"Jon? You in there, old man?"

Old man. He hates when Donald calls him that, even if the name is apropos. Grimacing, with one hand clasped to his head, Jonathan staggers forward and opens the door. Donald peers up at him from beneath his poncho's hood. The rain's coming down so hard he can barely hear his neighbor's voice.

"Didn't you hear the emergency siren? The whole neighborhood's being evacuated. We gotta go." Donald pauses, confused by the old man's attire, and for a moment, there is a flash of understanding on his face. Jonathan can see the young man's epiphany through the downpour, tinged with a hint of sadness. *He thinks I've gone senile.*

"Yeah, I heard it," Jonathan says. "You get your family out of here. I'm staying. Go on."

He's about to close the door, but Donald holds out his hand to stop him, and for a moment, Jonathan sees red. He sees himself slamming the door in his neighbor's face. He wants to growl and shout and tell Donald to mind his business, but the anger is displaced in an instant as the shrill horn of Donald's SUV tears through the storm.

"Don't make me leave you here, Jon." Donald turns back and waves to his family in their vehicle. It's time to go. Past time, really. Jonathan can see the water is almost to the edge of his driveway. *Just like last time*, he thinks, and struggles to contain his smile.

"You aren't leaving me. This is my choice, Donald. Go take care of your family. It's your duty."

Jonathan makes to close the door, and this time Donald slams his palm against the barrier to stop him.

"She isn't coming back, Jon. Your duty is to keep living. So help me—"

Donald doesn't finish his sentence. He's stunned into silence by the barrel of Jonathan's revolver, held a mere six inches from his face. Jonathan keeps his head, maintaining an even tone and a poker face to match. He clears his throat, licks his lips, and speaks steadily: "I know what my duty is, young man. Now I'm giving you until the count of three to get the fuck off my doorstep. One. Two."

He doesn't get to three. Donald steps back with his hands held out, either in defeat or confusion, Jonathan will never know. He opens his mouth to speak but thinks better of it, offering Jonathan one more glance before turning away and sloshing back across the yard.

Jonathan watches long enough to see Donald climb into his SUV and drive his family to safety. He places the revolver—a gift from his daddy, many moons ago—back into his pocket, and reminds himself to load it. Glancing up at the dark clouds overhead and the sheets of rain pouring down from them, Jonathan smiles. Soon, now.

Soon, he can do his duty too.

* * *

Glenda led him down the driveway toward the waterline, her damp hand slick in his, their fingers entwined in a lover's knot.

"Dance with me," she said again, and this time he didn't protest. He was so lost in her eyes and her leaking smile that he didn't notice when she stepped onto the surface of the churning waves. Sickly yellow foam collected around the tops of her pale feet as she walked, and Jonathan had taken three steps with her before he realized that he, too, was suspended above the surface. *Another miracle*, he thought dreamily, but the act of walking on water was nowhere near as fantastic as Glenda's reappearance.

Somewhere in the back of his mind, Jonathan supposed this was a dream. This was the only way it all made sense. People didn't come back from the dead. Not since Jesus, by his count, had anyone truly come back from the dead. Glenda had been in the ground for six days at that point, twice as long as their savior, and he suspected that if they were to walk the waters all the way to her grave, they would find the headstone undisturbed.

Because this was a dream, he reasoned. Because this wasn't really happening.

Glenda pirouetted on the water, her soaked dress flapping behind her like a limp tail. She came to rest before him and laughed. Water trickled down from the corners of her mouth.

"Do you remember the steps? One-two-three?"

He placed his hand on the small of her back, and took her other hand in his. "I remember enough, I think."

Years ago, in the months leading up to their wedding, Jonathan took a series of dancing classes with Glenda. He was never a fan of dancing, had never had the rhythm for it, really, but Glenda insisted he learn the basics for their wedding. "I want to dance with my husband," she told him with her bedroom eyes, and how could he say no to that? He took those lessons and learned enough to get by, but he never did feel comfortable enough to say he enjoyed dancing. The night of their wedding, he stepped on her feet twice, but she just laughed at his embarrassment, slowly turning in time to Etta James singing 'At Last'.

"I can't fault you," she later said, after they'd made love in their hotel room. "I've seen you try to drive a stick shift. You're not much better at that, either."

She was right. Jonathan never did have much rhythm, but after her passing, he would've learned to tango if it meant being with her another day.

Later, Jonathan supposed the miracle of her resurrection wasn't the only miracle God handed out that day. For the first time since their wedding night, Jonathan danced again. He only stepped on her feet once, but he didn't care, and she didn't seem to mind. They had no audience in the dawn. There was only them and the flood, the detritus from the road and ditches, and a low breeze roiling the waters beyond the tree line.

She led him in the dance, the water spilling over the feet as they moved in counts of three. Jonathan tried not to question the logic of walking on water—after all, he was dancing upon the surface with his deceased wife. Instead, he tried to enjoy the moment and privilege to be with her once again, no matter how fleeting it was. If he was meant to wake from this dream soon, then he would enjoy it for as long as he could even if he knew the memories would haunt him for years to come. The worst dreams always did.

They danced along the surface, first across the road to the river and then along the shoreline. Glenda kept time for them both, humming a tune he didn't recognize. Every now and then, the air in her throat would catch, punctuating her song with a seeping gurgle of water and phlegm. Jonathan didn't mind the noise. He'd spent nearly a year listening to her hack up the remains of her lungs after the chemotherapy had done its damage. She was choked on the water, was all. Why wouldn't she be? Her grave was no doubt flooded.

A low fog creeped along the surface of the water, silhouetted against fragments of morning light poking through the canopy of gray clouds. Those thin sunbeams fell upon both of them, and in that moment, Jonathan saw the faint trickle of water dribbling from the corner of her lips, down the side of her cheek. When she leaned in close to him to put her chin on his shoulder, he glimpsed something else slipping out of her mouth: a black, viscous sludge.

Embalming fluid, maybe. He wasn't sure what else they pumped into her body at the mortuary. An assortment of chemicals for preservation, perhaps. Who was he to judge the finer intricacies of coming back to life?

But something about that thick, licorice blackness made a part of him grow cold. Glenda sensed his unease, pulling back long enough to look him in the eye.

"Is something wrong, my darling?"

"Nothing, dear." He looked away, already knowing that she knew better, but too ashamed to say anything on the contrary. "Hold on to me. Don't ever let go."

Glenda smiled, tightened her grip on him. "Never." She leaned in, put her chin on his shoulder once more, and he felt himself go ten degrees colder. The whole world around them had dropped in temperature. Jonathan peered out over the surface of the river at the rolling fog bank. Glenda was leading them right for it.

Later, after he'd collapsed on the doorstep of his home, Jonathan would recall that it was the fog that woke him from her spell and made him realize he wasn't dreaming. The cold moisture in the air made his knees scream. Until the drop in temperature, he hadn't noticed their stark agony; he'd been too lost in Glenda's emergence to think of much else. Now, though, the cold was what sobered him up, and he gasped at the sudden jolt of pain shooting down his legs.

He was about to ask if they could stop and sit for a spell when Glenda spoke: "We're almost there, my darling. Not far now."

"Where are we going?" he grimaced.

"To my grave. Where the waters are waiting."

The mere thought of that empty hole in the ground made him shiver. His whole body quaked, and she squeezed closer to him, yet her body offered no warmth. She was soaked through to the bone, her pruning skin like congealing fat on an old hunk of meat left out to spoil. In a warmer climate, Jonathan was certain that flies would've accompanied their dark, impossible dance across the surface of the flooded river.

"I… Glenda, honey, I need to rest a moment. My knees—you know how bad they get."

"Shhh," she said. "I'm so cold there in the deep, my darling. When the waters fill my grave, I get so cold. Won't you keep me warm?"

Her voice was almost apologetic, as if she could not help herself despite what came next.

Jonathan turned for the shore and tried to pull away from her grip but found he couldn't. Her pruned fingers clasped around him like handcuffs, and when he met her gaze again, her blue eyes did not greet him.

Black slime leaked from her sockets, mingling with a twin stream gushing out her nose. The skin around her face sagged, and for one horrifying moment, Jonathan realized that this thing was wearing his darling Glenda's face as a mask. He screamed, a hoarse cry for help that sounded too thin, too distant for anyone to hear.

The cold fog inched closer, threatening to envelop them. Jonathan pulled once more, resisting his late wife's grip.

"Keep us warm in the deep," the Glenda-thing gurgled at him. Flecks of that blackened ichor spotted his cheeks. Jonathan struggled to find his footing and brace himself against her, only to find that he had no footing to gain. He was slowly sinking into the depths of the river, the freezing waters thick, gelatinous, a sudden bog in the middle of a churning stream.

A sandbar, he thought. *Just get out of this mess, Jon. Just—*

He looked down. What he saw aged him by a decade, maybe more. His heart paused for a full beat before painfully chugging to catch up with itself.

Hands.

Dozens—no, hundreds of bloated hands reached up from the depths of the river, their fingers entwined with the tendrils of the looming fogbank. They clamored for him, gripping his shoes, pulling at his pant legs, dragging him down to the dark depths of the floodwaters inch by cold, agonizing inch.

He twisted around, back to the Glenda-thing to make a desperate plea for his life, and discovered that her form was collapsing into itself. Her face dripped like warm wax, slowly melting into a dark blob that sank into her torso. Within seconds she was nothing more than a puddle of the black ooze, oily and dispersing into the roiling waters before him.

"No," he cried as the hands slowly pulled him down. "No, Glenda, no!"

Jonathan struggled against them, fighting against the pain singing in his knees to lift one leg. Just one. Just enough to break free.

One-two-three, he thought, only he heard Glenda's voice in his head. *You remember how to count, don't you, darling? Keep the rhythm. There's nothing to it.*

He leaned forward, clenched his teeth, and flailed his arms into the water, pulling himself against the current. Still the hands pulled, yanking and pinching at him, pulling at his groin, his thighs, seeking any piece of him that could be held, gripped, and dragged down to them. For an instant, he speculated what might be at the other end of those bloated limbs, but the impossible things that stretched out from his imagination made him go numb. Instead, he focused his efforts on freeing himself and swimming to safety.

Jonathan slowly lifted one leg, crying out in pain as the tendons around his swollen knees flared and sang a tune. As he did, he pulled one arm toward him, then the other. He kicked his other leg, pushing off the cluster of hands beneath the surface. Still they gripped him, but less so, and slowly—*one-two-three, that's it darling, keep your rhythm*—moment by moment, Jonathan freed himself from their pull.

One of his shoes came off in their grip. A disappointed sigh breathed across the water's surface. The hands pulled his second shoe free from his foot, and he shot forward into the current. A cold wave slapped his face, stealing his breath for a precious second. *You're free, darling. Keep going. One-two-three.*

Jonathan swam. He swam harder and faster than he'd ever done before, his weak knees be damned, his old heart racing so hard he feared he might die of an attack right there in the river. *Wouldn't that be something*, he thought idly, *to drown after all this?*

But no such thing happened that day. Jonathan reached the shore, collapsing at the foot of his flooded driveway in time to watch the sun break through the overcast sky. The fog on the river had dispersed by then, and though the temperature had risen a few steady degrees, he found he could not keep warm. Out there on the water, he glimpsed a cluster of darkened, bloated hands for just a moment before their fingers slipped slowly beneath the waves.

Somewhere beneath the surface, he knew, Glenda was there. For the second time in his life, he'd lost his wife, and when the realization struck him, Jonathan Crosby turned away from the river and sobbed.

*   *   *

Jonathan waits at the foot of his stairs, ruminating on that bizarre morning after the flood four years ago. He runs his hand over the curves of the revolver. Every day since, he's watched the weather, waiting for the moment when the weather is right.

Every night since, he's suffered from dreams of drowning, of Glenda returning to drag him down to the cold stillness of her grave. He can't bring himself to visit her anymore. The last time he went to the cemetery was after the flood, to make sure she was still there and that her casket hadn't floated to the surface. It hadn't, of course. Deep down, he knew that thing that led him out to the water wasn't his wife, but the promise of her return—oh, it's too much to bear now. He prefers not to dwell on such things.

Instead, Jonathan passes his time watching the weather. He waits for a day just like today, when the rains will not let up. He waits for the conditions to be right. And when the sky opens up to let loose the furies of heaven, he remains steadfast in his resolve.

After he turns Donald away, the waters continue to rise, reaching record heights by mid-afternoon.

He doesn't know what she really was, or why he was chosen to be her prey. He wonders if maybe there's more to that story his daddy told him about the flood of aught-nine, but he will never know. Daddy's long gone, for decades now, and all that's left is speculation on Jonathan's part.

So Jonathan waits. He sits at the foot of his stairs and watches the floodwaters rise high enough to trickle under the doorway. He looks at the revolver in his hand, runs his thumb along the length of the barrel, and wonders if she really was Glenda. And if she was, can he do what he needs to do? Can he do his duty and put his wife to rest?

He waits, and the waters stream into his home.

He waits. There's a knock at the door. *One-two-three.*

He smiles.

The rain's come again, and this time Jonathan is ready.

Come Tomorrow

John Boden

"I F we'd had a dime for every year we got with our little Amy, we'd have a dollar. One measly dollar! That's what my little girl's time here would be...not enough for a fuckin' candy bar!"

His voice was almost sputtering-it came out in heaves.

Steve's face was boiled red, the sheen of tears from eyes to nose to chin gave him a high gloss. His eyes were nearly rolled over white like an attacking shark. The stern but soft presence of Mel's hand on his shoulder was the only thing keeping him from grabbing that doctor by the throat and squeezing until the man's eyes dulled.

"Mister Brody..."

The young man in the white coat paused as he carefully tried to sew together comforting words for this couple and having as much success as trying to carry water in a sieve.

The bigger man held up a hand, one finger pointed to the ceiling.

"You told us by the time the end came she'd be comfortable. You told us it would be peaceful: that she'd just go to sleep and not wake again or she'd be so weary she'd just close her eyes."

Steve's grimace of grief faltered into a deep sneer. It rose in the corner to show a glimpse of stained teeth.

"You were wrong!"

He sobbed and the roar filled the small room. The young doctor hung his head and Mel kept her hand on her husband's shoulder, the chain that held back the beast. Her tears flowed freely but quietly.

"You know what it was like? I mean, you fucking ought to, you stood right there. Right! Goddamn! There! You watched us hold our little girl's hands and try to calm her while she panicked. While she fought to breath. Fought to stay here. She *knew* what was coming and it terrified her. Her eyes darting! Her breath coming so fast. She knew and she tried to be calm but she was ten. Ten! How calm can a kid be when it's time to go?"

His rant was petering out. His strength bleeding from him like he was a gut shot deer. He looked at his shoes and then leveled a gaze at the doctor. His clean-shaven face looked scalded, his cheeks wet. Steve knew it wasn't the young man's fault. Wasn't anyone's really. Maybe God's. He drew a loud and deep breath and cried some more, spinning around and into the arms of his wife. They cocooned one another in their grief and the young doctor left them alone to do it.

*   *   *

Can you overdose on antacids?

Even his inner voice was rusted from disuse.

Steve's stomach was burning. It had been since Christmas. He closed his eyes and felt it-raw and paper cut scalding. He envisioned a lifetime of words he'd held back and swallowed. The verbal stillborn slowly digesting in thick belly fluids like dinosaurs in a tar pit. The sharp elbows of letters like M and L and V gouging and tearing tissues to remind him that words can be forever-even those never spoken. The only ghosts that cannot be exorcised. He looked at the pile of bills on the hall table. An offensive offering at the foot of the picture of his dear Mel. He slid them onto the floor and kicked them under the bookshelf. He palmed two more tablets and chewed them with aching teeth. Outside the sky stumbled and it began to rain.

*   *   *

It's only been two years, but every minute of every day of every single month of them has been itching with an aching. That longing to hear their voices bouncing off of the windows like trapped moths. To see their faces-smiling or, hell, I'd even take angry or crying, just to see them- would be the greatest gift of all. I'd relive a thousand fights with Melanie or fifty times as many fits with little Amy if it meant I got to hear them again. Why didn't you just take 'em both together somehow, Lord? Maybe Amy wouldn't have been so scared.

Steve flushed the toilet and looked at the haggard old man in the mirror. The man carved of old newsprint and stubble. More wrinkle than anything with welts for eyes that blew reddened kisses at him through his reflection.

I got Mel for almost a year and a half after Amy. Long enough to almost start to feel normal again. As normal as you can feel after you bury your daughter.

One is the loneliest number. It's barely a number at all. It's just a line.

*   *   *

Steve sat on the edge of the bed and looked at the closet door standing wide open like a mouth. The hanging shirts, the mounds of dirty pants and socks filling it, and his gaze settled on the fishing rod that leaned against the back wall.

Maybe that's just what I need to do...go sit by the water and not think. Just be and rest. Just occupy space.

He raked fingers through greasy hair and stood up. Bones crackled like a summer bonfire. He dressed and grabbed the pole from the closet. It had a thin coat of dust on it from the years it hibernated behind wedding dress shirts and funeral slacks. He hunkered and brushed away socks and underwear until he saw the orange plastic of the tackle box. He grabbed it gently like a treasure chest and opened it. Hooks and sinkers and jiggers and flies. Scissors and Band-Aids and extra spools of line. No frills. He almost smiled as he closed it and hefted it onto the bed. His mind swam back to the last time he had been fishing. Amy was all of four years old and patience was just a string of letters she couldn't pronounce.

Steve stepped into the boots at the foot of the bed and with his gear, left the house as empty as it was when he was in it.

*   *   *

The sun was barely up when Steve slowed the truck and parked in the loose stones at the end of the bridge. The NO PARKING sign that lived there had been knocked down by plows during the winter and lay beneath dirt and debris. Steve stepped over it without a thought and walked to where the railing began at the start of the bridge.

He managed to fold himself low enough to get beneath the side rail and scooched down the hill to the fallen pillar that edged the water. The cement was cold through the denim of his jeans. He popped the lid of the box and rummaged for a decent lure, gently pushing aside sinkers and rubber worms, but stopping when his fingers happened upon the hair tie. Hot pink and stretchy fabric. He gently held it to his face and inhaled. It held the faintest trace of Amy's scent- soap and strawberry shampoo. He even thought he could feel a strand of her pale hair on his upper lip. That lip raised into a smile as his eyes shed water.

"Let's go fishing, Little girl." He mumbled as he tied the pink elastic to the line about an inch above the hook. He knotted the sinker and worked a faux purple worm onto the barb. He leaned sideways to cast and watched the worm land in a pool out near the drop. He sat still and sang softly to himself. The smile stayed on his lips like a scar.

You'll never know dear....how much I love you...

He stopped singing when the line jerked and he heard the splashing.

*   *   *

The fish was small and its scales shone pink in the morning sun, even beneath the murk of the water. Steve reeled slowly and the fish barely fought him once it was out of the water. Its brilliance was dazzling-a prism of pinks and purples as the day's light met it. It reminded him of the pink sequins on Amy's school bag. He reached out with a shaking hand and gripped the fish, finding its flesh to be damp but not slippery. He squeezed slightly and popped the barb free of its pulsating lip. Its blue eyes never left his face. Steve stared and brought the fish closer to his nose, nearly touching it.

"Daddy"

A shiver scurried down his spine and he squeezed the fish a little tighter out of surprise. Its mouth opened wider and a wheezing sound escaped it. He tilted his ear closer to that gaping mouth and held the fish close again.

"Daddy"—croaking small voice-—*"Throw me back."*

Steve dropped the fish into the shallows at his feet and watched it swim away. A pink blur beneath the surface. It swam right to dark waters where it dropped deeper.

"You're off your nut, fella. That fish did not call you Daddy."

Unless it did and you knew that voice...

He looked at the line at his feet and realized the hair tie was no longer fastened to it. He hooked another worm and cast his line again. It sat, ignored, for nearly an hour before the sky grew dark as storm clouds began to appear. Steve packed up to leave before the sky broke open. He heard splashing out near the deep hole but he didn't look to see what it was.

*   *   *

Sleep that night was no more than a few troubled slats of tossing and turning with eyes closed but brain running full speed. When the sun worked its feeble fingers through the dirty blinds of his room, Steve groaned. He finally wrestled himself into a sitting position, and saw the pole against the dresser where he'd leaned it. He frowned and pulled on the same jeans he'd worn a day earlier and grabbed the pole.

He stopped in the room that was once his daughter's and from the dresser top, scooped another hair tie and a bead bracelet she had made in Bible school. He stowed them in his shirt pocket and headed for the door. He paused by the hall table and looked at the picture of Mel. He stared at that beautiful face he had kissed a thousand times and loved more than anything. He propped the pole against the bookshelf and pulled out the drawer in the table and removed the item he sought. He headed for the river.

*   *   *

The water was high and moving fast. The air felt heavy with humidity even after a night of storms. Steve closed the trunk of the car and slung his hip waders over his shoulder while he picked up the rod and tackle box. He maneuvered down the bank to his spot on the pillar. The water's edge was almost to the base of it and about a foot and a half higher that yesterday. Steve tied on an extra sinker and pulled the bright yellow tie from his pocket. He wrapped it around the hook and cast his line.

Within minutes there was a tug followed by another. Steve gave a quick yank and began reeling in his catch. The fish was similar to the previous day's-a bright yellow this time and the eyes were deep blue and enormous. He leaned to grip the fish and held it up to his face. The eyes were familiar to him. His breath hitched and he worked the hook free from the fish's lip.

"Daddy"

Steve held it and looked at the creature in his hand. It did not squirm but remained still, mouth opening and closing. Eyes never leaving his.

"Daddy"

"This cannot be happening?"

Steve knelt and held the fish to the water. It began to move frantically just before he released his grip. Before its mouth disappeared beneath the surface, he swore he heard it say *"I love you."*

* * *

He sat on the pillar and just stared at the water for the rest of the day. As the world turned and the sun moved, the shadows huddled in different spots on the water. The deep hole never got any light. The arms of the trees towering above it saw to that. Steve considered that he was losing his mind. That the last two years had eroded what sanity he had originally possessed. Losing Amy and then Mel had simply broken an already cracked windshield. He sat and watched the shadowed depths out near the middle of the river. His brow furrowed as he dug a hand into his pocket. He looked at the plastic strip laying across his palm. The white paper encased within it. The name **Melanie Brody** typed in simple font, followed by a patient number and then three letters he had hoped to never see again: D.O.A.

Steve picked up the fishing pole and tied the cut bracelet around the hook. He breathed deeply and looked at the fading sun as he cast the line. It landed with a plop out in the deep.

He sat and watched the sun slowly set and when the horizon appeared to be bleeding, a minute or two later, something took the bait.

*   *   *

Steve did not reel the line but instead leaned the pole against the concrete while he put on his wading boots. The line stayed taut as he began walking into the water. He slowed when he felt himself nearing the drop, felt his toes lose purchase on the soft ground beneath. He stopped and slowly began reeling.

It was dark under the canopy of branches and he caught a flash of something pale beneath the water. Something large. He felt flushed as he gripped the line with his left hand and slowly pulled toward him, leaning and pushing his right hand under the surface. He waved it back and forth under the water's muddy cowl and was about to pull back when he felt the hand grasp his.

Five cold fingers wrap themselves around his hand. He was not pulled—the hand just held his.

He traced his index finger over the holding hand and felt the band on the ring finger he had traced hundreds of times, both awake and in slumber. He laughed but it was a barking sound in the quiet dusk.

"Mel?" He croaked.

The hand pulled slightly and then released its grip on his. He heard a rush of water and a splash out in the darkness.

Steve stood there.

Cold water up to his waist in growing dark, he smiled while he cried.

*   *   *

Steve stood by the river and watched the sun stick its nose over

336

the mountain. He smelled the cool water rushing by. Breathed the odor of wet leaves and silt the river carried. He smiled and bent to pick up a stone. He picked up several more. He filled all of the pockets of his cargo pants with them. He slowly walked to the pillar and picked up the length of rope he'd placed there-one end tied to a cinderblock. He looped it around his neck and picked up the brick, cradling it like a newborn. He heard a splash out near the deep and smiled in that direction.

He took out his wallet and laid it on the pillar next to his tackle box and rod. He took furtive steps into the water and did not falter as he made his way to the shadows.

He had a reunion to get to.

A Night at the Lake with the Weird Girl

Ray Garton

I T was my first day at a new school and the weird girl plopped into the seat across from me at my otherwise unoccupied cafeteria table and said, "Hi. I'm Mina Narron. You're new."

I was too new to know that she was the weird girl at the time and wouldn't until she told me. That had been decreed long before my arrival by the students who decide that sort of thing: who's weird or fat or impoverished or ugly and needs to be isolated and belittled into submission. I had a lot of first days at new schools when I was growing up, and the one constant at every school I attended was that group of students, the school gods who live on the Mt. Olympus of beauty, popularity, and usually some wealth and privilege (although not *too* much or they would be in private schools), who pass judgment on everyone else and hand down their status and labels like divine decrees.

It would not have been hard to guess that Mina was the weird girl at Emberson Union High School in 1986 because she looked a little like an astronaut's wife in 1969.

She gave me a big smile when she greeted me, placing her tray in front of her. She began to eat immediately.

"Tuesday," she said, "My favorite day. Franks and beans day." She spoke between bouts of chewing and swallowing. "I love franks and beans, don't you? I don't know how anyone could not love franks and beans. They're worth all the farting. What's your name?"

"Tom."

"Just Tom?"

"Woolery."

"Like Chuck Woolery? On *Wheel of Fortune*?"

"Yeah."

"Cool. Oh, wait. Tom Woolery? That's like Tom *Foolery*."

I sighed. "Um, yeah. I get that. A lot."

"I promise I'll never call you that or say that horrible name again. Where are you from, Tom?"

"San Bernardino, California. And before that, Flagstaff, Arizona. And before that, Provo, Utah."

"You on the run from the law, or something?"

That made me laugh. "No, my dad's a...well, a salesman. But also an accountant. And a welder."

"Is *he* on the run from the law? Or does he just go where the jobs are?"

"Right the second time. I know it sounds like he's got a drinking problem, or something, but it's not that. He's a good guy, my dad. He just doesn't...he, um, he can't...he's just not a nine-to-five kind of guy, you know what I mean?"

She nodded emphatically. "I bet he's an artist."

"Yeah, he is. Kind of. How'd you know?"

340

"I don't think artists are made, I think they're born, and if you're born an artist, you'll never fit into the nine-to-five mold. What kind of art?"

"Well, I don't know if it's *art*, but he's very creative. He makes things with wrought iron. Lamps, tables, even couches. Sometimes he just makes weird, abstract pieces with it. He listens to audiobooks while he does it. All kinds of books on tape. I think he's seriously good with that stuff. He's good enough for people to commission things when they see his work. And I can tell he's happier when he's doing that than any other time of the day. He wanted to try it as a small business but Mom thought it was impractical and too risky, so he didn't. I think he should."

"The Scientologists would call your mother a suppressive person."

"Yeah, until they got to know her. Then they'd call her all kinds of things."

"Yep, artists just don't fit in, Tom. I know I won't. I don't fit in already. I'm the—" She lifted her hands and hooked four fingers into air quotes. "—'*weird girl*' around here. Have you noticed people looking over at this table a lot?"

I sat up straighter. "No. Are they?"

"Take a look around. Casually."

As my eyes slowly panned the cafeteria from left to right, I noticed people quickly looking away, people who had been staring at our table—not at Mina but at me—before I caught them.

"Part of it's because you're new," Mina said, "but mainly it's because you're sitting with me. They're wondering who's going to be the first to tell you that you shouldn't hang out with me."

"Oh, yeah. Them. I know them. Assholes."

"Yep, you've met. Anyway, I thought *I'd* be the first to tell you that you probably shouldn't hang out with me because I'm the weird girl."

I blinked several times. "What? Really? You don't want me to...

then why did you sit down with me?"

"It's not that I don't *want* you to, but *some*body was going to say it, and I wanted to be the first. I sat down with you because you're new and you were alone and I wanted to say hi. I'll go if you want."

"What? *No.* I'm glad you sat down. I hate the first day at a new school. Eating lunch alone."

"Do you have a car?"

"My dad lets me use his most of the time, evenings and week-ends. Why?"

"If you'd like, I can show you around town. Emberson looks dull and lifeless, but it's not so bad. It's not so *good*, but it's not so bad. We could go out to the lake and see the puppies."

"Puppies? Is that a euphemism?"

Her eyes widened slightly and she looked hurt. "A what?"

"You know, a euphemism. Something you say when you don't want to say exactly what you mean."

"Oh. No, no, it's not a euphemism. It's exactly what I mean. We'll go out to the lake and see the puppies." Another smile, even bigger this time. "You'll see. We'll have fun, I promise."

I already had no doubt of that. She was called the weird girl in part, I assumed, because of her look. Her bouffant hairstyle made her look like she was hiding a huge alien brain beneath it, and it ended in a coy little curl at the bottom. Pale lipstick, bright blue eyeshadow, and clothes to match. But I guessed it was also her personality. I could tell she was different. I looked forward to spending an evening with her. And seeing the puppies at the lake. Whatever the hell *that* meant.

* * *

There was tension at dinnertime that night. We still ate around the dinner table at that point, but only three or four times a week. They became more spread out as time went on. We would take our meals and scatter throughout the house. Mom hated it, but Dad, as usual, understood. "They're young," he would say. "They have trouble holding still." But that night, we were all around the table, and something was up, but we didn't know what or from which direction it was coming. We could have guessed that; tension usually came from Mom. Dad didn't get tense so much as distracted. It usually had something to do with Dad's work. Whatever it was that night, Mom and Dad were having another of their silent, air-thickening arguments.

"Hey, Dad," I said, "do you mind if I take the car tonight?"

"Where are you going?" he said. He always asked with genuine curiosity rather than the eye-rolling and suspicion Mom always slathered onto the very same words.

"A friend from school wants to show me around town."

He smiled. "A friend. Already? After your first day? Is it a girl?"

I looked down at my plate a moment as I blushed. "Yeah. Her name is Mina."

"Hey, there you go, getting things off to a good start. Sure, Robbie, you go right ahead."

"It's a school night," Mom said sternly. "Back by ten."

I nodded as I ate my meatloaf, but I don't think she saw me.

"Did you hear me? Ten o'clock on a school night."

"I will, Mom."

"And I'm telling you right now, young man—" She lowered her voice to a whisper, as if whispering across the dinner table would prevent my younger sister and brother, who were also seated at the table, from hearing her. "—I am not ready for grandchildren."

I blushed again as my twelve-year-old sister Fran dropped her fork onto her plate with a clatter and said, "Good *grief*, Mother, we're sitting right *here*."

My brother Eric, who was eight, giggled at his peas. He found peas funny. He said they were the funniest vegetable, and he always laughed when he saw them. He had nothing against them and happily ate them with butter and a little salt. But he found them hilarious.

"Well, there are some things you just don't say loudly at the dinner table," Mom said.

Dad smiled at her and added, "It would be nice if nothing were *ever* said loudly at the dinner table."

And with that, we returned our attention to our meals.

* * *

Mom drove a Buick station wagon in which to chauffeur us kids to our school functions, sporting events, and for family shopping trips when she wasn't working part time in a dental office. Dad would be driving his 1978 Chevette to his job at Four Star Accounting five days a week and sometimes on weekends during tax season, if his other accounting jobs were any indication. I thought it was an ugly car that looked older than its true age and it was always breaking down, but Dad loved it. Mom's station wagon, on the other hand, was pretty nice, with all the room of a limousine, and it ran faithfully without any problems, but she hated it. All my brother and sister and I cared about was that those vehicles could get us where we needed to go before were able to do it ourselves.

I was not allowed to drive the Buick, so I took Dad's midnight-blue Chevette to pick up Mina, although I thought the pick-up spot was odd. She had asked me to pick her up in front of our school.

I had said, "I don't mind coming to your house if you'll tell me where—"

"No, really. This would be better." She offered no explanation, but there was pleading in her eyes, so I had agreed.

I understood. Back in Arizona, I had a friend named P.J. We shared a lot of interests, spent most of our time together, and got along well. But he would never invite me to his place, and when I asked to visit, he always had reasons why I could not, just like he always had explanations for the bruises, cuts, and burns he often sported.

I understood. Some kids had good reason not to want their friends to visit them at home to see what life was *really* like in their families.

It was a balmy evening in early October and I found Mina standing by a lamp post in the school parking lot. As I slowly drove closer, I was struck by the figure she cut as she stood there leaning against that lamp post like a femme fatale in an old movie. Wearing tight jeans and a gray tank top with a long drapery of colorful necklaces hanging between her breasts and a big red bag slung over her shoulder, she gave me a playful little wave and smiled. I slowed to a stop as she pushed away from the post and headed toward me with a confident walk, almost a strut. Her 1969 'do had loosened and her hair looked looser, shaggier, had a little bounce to it as she moved. I rolled down the window on the passenger side and said, "Hop in," as she approached. The necklaces chattered quietly as they swayed over her breasts. She was not wearing a bra and the necklaces swinging back and forth over her breasts had made her nipples hard. They pressed against the material of the tank top

I was a sixteen-year-old heterosexual—that much I knew—with virtually no experience with girls beyond a little backseat groping and lip-locking on a couch or two at parties. It was difficult to form relationships when I knew we'd be moving out in a year or two or three. Dad's record for staying in one place, according to Mom, had been five years, but I never kept track. I never knew how long before we would be on our way to the next town, the next job. I was awkward with girls, with everyone, and it was hard for me to kick off even a friendly acquaintance. That evening with Mina was a defining point in my life in a couple of ways.

One of them was that, to this day, if I see a woman's erect nipples pressing against the material of her T-shirt or sweater or blouse or anything, it doesn't matter, I have to sit down immediately.

The other was that, in spite of everything that happened that night, it cemented in me a deep and abiding love of and desire for weird girls.

I knew Deepshadow Lake was nearby, but I did not know how near. After only fifteen minutes or so of following Mina's directions out of town and along a short, winding road through woods that the last faint glow of twilight could not penetrate, we were there.

"Turn left at the boat ramp sign," she said.

That took us down a short road that opened up into an empty rectangular parking lot with a few lampposts.

"Park over there by the boat ramp," Mina said, pointing.

I brought the car to a stop, put it in park, hit the parking break, and killed the engine, but I left the headlights on for a moment. The beams were swallowed up by the darkness that stretched out over the lake. A nearly-full moon was rising and it cast a shimmering bluish glow that sparkled on the lake in sliver-like flashes. Behind us was the glow of the four tall lights in the parking lot, and ahead the darkness of the lake.

"C'mon," she said, opening her door, "let's get out. The moon's bright tonight and I know a good spot."

We got out of the car, I locked it out of habit, and she led the way toward the lake. We walked a good distance along the edge of a bank that sloped sharply down to the water until we got to a flat spot of shore where there were some bushes and a single pine tree.

Mina led me between some of the shrubbery and around the tree to a grassy spot just above the rocky edge of the lake. We seemed utterly alone there, as if we were on our own island and cut off from the rest of the world. She reached into her bag and produced a folded-up blanket, which she spread out on the ground.

As we got down on the blanket, I said, "Why is it called Deepshadow Lake?"

She shrugged. "Deep and shadowy, I guess. It's a creepy name, isn't it? Like something from a scary movie?"

"It is." I looked out at the moonlight that glimmered in a broadening strip over the water.

"Listen to it," she whispered.

All we could see of the water was the reflected moonlight, but we could hear it gently lapping against the shore. Frogs croaked and crickets chirped. There were splashes now and then whenever a fish jumped near enough to hear. The air had a fishy smell to it that blended with the muddy, mossy odor of the lake shore.

"I guess it's kind of creepy at night. If you're not used to it. But if it was daytime, you'd see how pretty it is. Of course, some pretty strange things have happened here."

"Like what?"

"Oh, well, let's see, there was a family boating on the lake once. They were pulling a skier when their little boy fell into the water. Six years old, I think he was. They didn't notice at first and kept going really fast over the water. When the skier went down, they slowed the boat to a stop and turned around to pick up the skier. That's when they heard their boy crying for help and they realized he wasn't in the boat with them anymore. He cried 'Mommy! Daddy! Help!' over and over again, and his high voice traveled over the lake. They looked for him but couldn't tell where his voice was coming from and they couldn't see him, couldn't find him. They spotted him just as he went down the last time. Took a bunch of water into his lungs and drowned."

"That's horrible," I said, feeling a little sick for the family. "Not too creepy, but pretty horrible."

"Well, the creepy part is that people say you can hear him sometimes at night. The little boy, I mean. Somewhere out there in the water. 'Mommy! Daddy! Help!' Over and over."

That made my skin feel a little too tight and raised goosebumps across my shoulders and down my back. To be honest, I seriously considered suggesting that we leave immediately after hearing that little story. As I sat leaning backward, propped on my arms, my hands clutched the blanket hard and I told myself to stop being such a wuss. "Have *you* heard him?" I said.

"Me? No. But that's what people say. That you can hear him

sometimes at night." She stretched out beside me, propped up on one elbow. "Then there was this family that lived in a house on an island out in the middle of the lake. The parents, two kids, two dogs, and a cat. They disappeared."

"All of them? At the same time?"

She nodded. "The dinner table had been set, dinner had been cooked and was ready to serve. The TV was on. Their boat was docked there at the island and none of their things were missing. They were just... gone. Even the dogs and the cat. It's like they were sucked up into the sky and were never seen or heard from again."

"Did this really happen or is this just a story that local people tell?"

"No, it really happened. You can go to the library and look it up. It was in all the papers. It was a mystery that was never solved. Some people won't come near this lake at night. Some stay away altogether."

"You're saying it's a haunted lake?"

"I didn't say that. Did I?" She smiled up at me as she settled back onto both elbows with one knee up. "It's just a strange place, this lake. Strange things happen around it. It has, you know, a...a reputation."

I smiled down at her. "Like your reputation for being the weird girl?"

"Yeah, like that. What does that say about *you*, huh? Out at the lake after dark with the weird girl."

"Maybe I *like* weird girls," I said as I stretched out beside her, facing her on my elbow, our faces only a few inches apart.

She was still on her back, the necklaces draped to one side, her small breasts thrust forward by her position, hard nipples still pressed against the gray tank top.

"You've got good taste," she said, then reached out and grabbed the front of my shirt, pulled me to her and kissed me. "Mm, *and* you taste good. A bonus." She pulled me with her as she turned onto her back.

To the sounds of a screeching owl and a barking dog somewhere in the distance and the occasional gentle splash of a jumping fish, Mina and I ground our tongues and bodies together and writhed around on that blanket, her occasional moans rising above my frantic panting. We made out like I had never made out before and after a while, I began to feel a little panicky.

Would this lead to sex? Was it *supposed* to lead to sex? Did her behavior mean she was *expecting* sex? I was in unfamiliar territory and I was simultaneously hopeful and terrified that it would lead to even *more* unfamiliar territory, that our genitals would get involved and we would run the risk of procreation. My thoughts were not nearly that coherent, but they amounted to the same thing.

I had no idea how much time had passed when she pulled away suddenly and whispered, "Am I being too forward?"

"Yuh-you're asking that *now*?"

She laughed. "Yeah, I guess it's kind of a pointless question by now, huh? What with your boner pressed against me and all." That time I laughed with her. "I was just afraid I might be...I don't know, shocking you. Scaring you away."

"Do I look like I'm running away?"

"No."

"Not with this boner."

Her laugh was loud and skipped over the water like a stone.

"Hey," I said, "where are those puppies you mentioned?"

"The puppies. Well, the puppies show up when they're ready to show up."

"What does that mean?"

She smiled as she sat up, her hand still touching mine, and shrugged. "It means they show up when they're ready to show up."

I sat up beside her. In spite of her pleasant, relaxed expression, she seemed troubled. "Whose puppies are they?"

"That's another one of the lake's strange stories. Would you like me to tell it to you?"

"Yeah, I want to hear it."

She pointed at the dark lake. "Across the lake from this spot and just a little to the right over there is an old abandoned building. It's mostly swallowed up by the woods now, covered with vines and sprouting weeds all over the place. It used to be a kind of pound."

She leaned over and started kissing me again. I responded for a while before asking, "Pound? You mean for animals? Dogs and cats?"

"Yes."

"What do you mean it was a *kind* of pound?"

"Well," she said, pressing her lips to mine and whispering against them, "it wasn't official. It wasn't, like, the *county* pound."

After that, we spoke between kisses. Some pauses were longer than others.

"It was privately run?" I said.

"Uh-huh."

"That's not unusual."

"Well, this pound was run by one man. All the stray dogs and cats were...taken there to be adopted or, um, you know...euthanized. Not many were adopted, though...mostly because people didn't like going out there...to see the dogs because of the man who ran the place. Auggie Fennel." She pulled away slightly and looked into my eyes. "Ol' one-eyed Auggie Fennel. He was a real asshole." She said it with conviction, dragging out "real" and hitting the last word hard, then added, "He enjoyed his work."

If Fennel was a one-man dog pound, then he regularly euthanized dogs and cats. I believed her. He *had* to be an asshole to enjoy that kind of work.

"Why did he have only one eye?" I said.

"I don't know, but he wore a big black patch over his right eye. Nobody liked him, but he followed all the laws, paid his taxes like everybody else. No crime in being an asshole."

There was more kissing and it was delicious, they were kisses I felt all over my body. But my mind tenaciously clung to that name, Ol' One-Eyed Auggie Fennel, and it would not go away until I spoke up.

"What happened?"

She smiled, pulled back, and lifted the tank top over her head. I am pretty sure I gasped audibly, but not certain. The necklaces clacked and chattered and her breasts quivered as she dropped the tank top onto the blanket beside her.

"You mean with Auggie Fennel and the puppies?"

I nodded. It was the best I could do.

"You've been staring at my nipples a lot."

My face burst into flames.

"It *is* my nipples, right? Not just my tits?"

I tried to speak but it was an embarrassing jumble and I cut it off abruptly and nodded.

She grinned. "I thought so." Placing a hand gently to the back of my head, she lowered herself back onto the blanket and tugged me with her, then pulled my face down to her chest before continuing.

Her breasts were like pudding beneath flesh that was taut but supple, with nipples that felt like hardened silk against my tongue. And I was supposed to listen to her story?

"Auggie was up to all kinds of no good," she said as she stroked my hair, while I tried not to let myself be lost entirely in the heavenly-smelling softness of what I was doing. "For one thing, he wasn't giving this county, or any of the other counties he contracted to, what they were paying for, not really. His fee was supposed to cover the drugs use to humanely euthanize the animals, but he didn't buy any drugs. He killed most of the animals himself, by hand. He was supposed to incinerate the remains, but he never did. Nobody seemed to notice that there was never any smoke coming out of that chimney. Instead, he'd bag 'em up, take 'em out on the lake in his boat, weigh 'em down, and drop 'em in. Sometimes while they were still alive. And on top of all that, he was keeping more than just dogs and cats in that pound."

Horrible, all horrible. Somewhere deep inside, I reeled at how horrible it all was, I really did. But my lips and hands never left her breasts, and I did not stop kissing and sucking and squeezing, my breath coming hot and fast against her skin. Until that last part sank in. Then I slowed down.

"Nobody knew about any of it, though, until he drew attention to himself. A bunch of dogs got out, including a couple litters of puppies. The dogs got away and wandered around the lake, and they were found by a girl who lived not far away. Auggie caught up to them, though, and he found the girl. He decided to add her to his collection, so he took her *and* the dogs back to the pound. But she was the daughter of a city councilman, and when *she* disappeared people noticed, unlike all the others he'd taken, the runaways and homeless drifters. And that was the end of Auggie Fennel. If you want it to be, Tom."

I stopped then, froze up, and finally, with effort, pulled myself away from those beautiful breasts to rise up on my arms and ask what she meant, if *I* wanted it to be, but she was laughing. I saw the puppy licking her face. Then I saw all of the puppies, half a dozen of them, bouncing and yipping and rolling around us, and before I could stop myself I laughed.

"Aren't they adorable?" she said, rolling back forth, petting them, poking them with her fingers. As she rolled, her breasts shifted fluidly from side to side.

I breathed the words: "Yes, they are."

"I was talking about the puppies, not my tits." She giggled.

I nodded and chuckled and said, "Yeah, yeah, sure, they're adorable." I reached out to pet one of them when I was jerked backward violently by my hair and dragged away from Mina.

"Get the fuck away from my property," a wet voice growled as I was tossed aside.

I tumbled over the ground and stopped on the rocks, just before reaching the lake. Mina screamed as I scrambled to my feet and turned to see her draped over the left shoulder of a very large, lumpy man wearing a miner's helmet with a bright light on the front. He turned his head just enough to reveal the right side of his face and I saw the black patch over his eye. He lifted his right arm and I saw the pistol held at the end of it. The puppies scattered and he took aim at one and fired. There was a yelp as he turned and fired at another, then another.

"Goddamn you, stop it!" Mina screamed, writhing in the grip of his right arm as her upper body hung behind his shoulder. "Leave them alone!"

My mind stormed around a single thought that remained unmoving, like the calm eye at the center of a hurricane: stop him.

I hunkered down and groped in the dark for a rock large and heavy enough to do the job. When I found it, I pried it from the soft, damp earth and raised it above my head in both hands as I rushed up behind him. It connected to the back of his skull with a dull, moist crack that sent him lurching forward, then stumbling to the left. He dropped Mina.

The instant she hit the ground, she began to scurry away from him on all fours as I brought the rock down a second time on the back of his head.

Ol' One-Eyed Auggie Fennel toppled over with an ugly groan and hit the ground with a grunt.

Mina grabbed my left arm and jerked so hard that I dropped the rock and stumbled along with her as she pulled.

"Come on, let's go, let's go," she said breathlessly.

She pulled me back through the bushes and along the edge of the bank.

"You need to hide me and we need to get out of here," she said, panting for breath as we hurried.

"Hide you where?"

"Come on, come on."

When we reached the parking lot, she released my arm and broke into a run for the car. I could only run after her. She repeatedly slapped the trunk of the car as she turned to me.

"Hide me, hurry, hide me," she said, slapping the trunk.

"What? Where?"

She pounded her fist on the trunk lid, hissing, "In here!"

"But why—let's just get in the car and—"

"No, no, you don't understand, you need to *hide* me. Hurry, he's coming!"

I fumbled the keys out of my pocket and opened the trunk. She needed no help in climbing in and curling into a ball.

Looking up at me with wide, frightened eyes, she said, "Okay, okay, close it and drive, just get us out of here, Tom Woolery, and *fast!*"

I froze for a moment, uncertain of what to do. It made no sense to put her in the trunk, but she seemed determined and there was little I could do about it with Ol' One-Eyed Auggie Fennel on his way.

Bushes rustled some distance behind us. He would be in the parking lot any moment.

"Close it and get us out of here!" she said.

I closed the trunk and hurried to the driver's side, fumbling with my keys to unlock the door. I got in and, out of blind habit, took the time to fasten my seatbelt. I soon regretted not simply starting the car and taking off. As I turned the key in the ignition and the engine started, the entire car quaked with a great slamming sound.

He was on the car.

I slammed the pedal to the floor and the car lurched forward as I turned and sped out of the parking lot and back onto the road.

A loud banging sound made me jump. It came again and again. I looked in the rearview mirror and could see nothing until I drove beneath a streetlight just beyond the entrance to the parking lot. He was pounding on the rear window with something in his hand. It had to be the gun. He was hitting the glass with the butt of his gun. Or maybe it was a rock from the lake shore, maybe the rock I had used to hit him.

Mina's scream was muffled but unmistakable.

He shouted something, then shouted it again and again as he pounded on the window.

"Give me back my property!"

I jammed my foot on the brake pedal and the tires screamed over the pavement, but he did not fall off. Somehow, he clung to the car and kept shouting, kept pounding.

With the streetlight and the lights of the parking lot behind me, the car was surrounded by darkness. I went faster as my mind frantically groped for a solution.

I took the first curve of the twisty road fast and turned the wheel sharply, hoping to throw him off. It did not work. I took each curve after that as fast I could, jerking the wheel. The tires squealed around each bend, but the pounding continued.

My fear of Ol' One-Eyed Auggie Fennel was greater than my good sense, far too great to wonder how any of this possibly could add up to anything logical. That would come later.

I went even faster around the next corner. I'm not sure what happened. Suddenly the car was tumbling through darkness, rolling over and over. The seatbelt held me in my seat as glass broke and metal crunched sounds of impact exploded all around me. Then everything was gone.

* * *

"Where are my parents?" I asked the uniformed police officer as I fidgeted in my hospital bed.

"You'll see them soon."

"I'd like to see them now, please. I'm not hurt, I'm fine. Why can't I go?"

"They'll be releasing you soon. Whether or not they release you into my custody will depend on how you answer my questions." He pulled a chair over to the bed and sat down.

"To your cust—I don't under—what did I do?"

I had awakened about forty-five minutes ago to find myself in a curtained cubbyhole in what I assumed was a hospital emergency room. I remembered the accident immediately, and when the doctor examined me, I expected him to find injuries, sore spots, but I seemed to be unharmed except for a bandaged gash that sat atop a large lump on my forehead. The doctor answered none of my questions and hardly spoke to me at all. He left when he finished the exam and I was alone until the police officer arrived.

"Tell me about what happened last night," he said.

"Last night? How long have I been here?"

"You had to be pried out of the car, but you got lucky and came out in one whole piece. You were unconscious from that knock on the head when they brought you in and you slept through the night."

"How is Mina? Is she okay?"

His eyes narrowed beneath heavy brows as he leaned forward. He was an older guy with thick dark hair that showed streaks of silver and a hound-dog face that was drooping with fatigue and age. "Mina? Who's Mina?"

"She was in the trunk of my car. You got her out, right? How is she?"

"Why was she in the trunk?"

"She wanted me to hide her there before we left."

"Hide her from what?"

"From...well..." I suddenly felt hesitant to continue. "It's a long story."

"We've got time. Where did you find her?"

"*Find* her? I didn't *find* her anywhere, I met her at school. Today was—well, *yesterday* was my first day. I'm new in town. You probably know that by now. I don't know anybody and she sat down with me in the cafeteria and started to talk."

"Wait." He took a notebook from his pocket and opened it, removed a small pencil, and prepared to write. "You say you...you met her at school?" He jotted as I spoke.

"Yeah. At lunch. She introduced herself and we talked and decided to go out to the lake last night. So we went to Deepshadow Lake and she told me about all the weird things that have happened there. The little boy who drowned. She said people sometimes still hear him calling for help out on the lake. And about the family that disappeared from their home on an island somewhere in the middle of the lake. Is...is that all true?"

He nodded. "Yeah, it's a strange place, that lake. All kinds of stories about it. You know how people are. They love a good creepy story."

"Well, she told me about that stuff while we waited for the puppies."

"The puppies."

That was when I began to realize how crazy it all sounded. Puppies...Ol' One-Eyed Auggie Fennel...the whole thing. I took in a deep breath and let it out heavily, slowly, and said, "Look, it was her idea to go to the lake. She said there was an old animal pound out there that used to be run by a mean, one-eyed guy named Auggie Fennel. Is that right?"

Those bushy eyebrows huddled together as he nodded. "Yeah. Years ago."

"She said he used to...that he enjoyed killing the animals himself instead of euthanizing them with drugs and...she wanted to go see the puppies, and..." I lay my head back on the pillow and pressed the heels of my hands to my closed eyes. "I don't' know. Maybe that bump on my head..." I sat up and looked at him. "Have you talked to her? What did *she* say?"

He leaned back in the chair and folded his arms across his chest as he stared at me, studied me for a while. Then he stood and walked slowly around the bed.

"There was a pound out there," he said. "It's been abandoned for a long time. And it was run by a man named Auggie Fennel. A mean son of a bitch. But he up and disappeared one day. Just released the animals he had, packed up, and headed out without telling anybody where he was going, or even that he was leaving. He didn't have any friends or family and nobody liked him. Nobody knew where he went and nobody much cared."

He returned to the chair but did not sit down, only stood there and looked at me.

"But he's been gone for years. You've been in town less than a week. How did you know about Auggie Fennel?"

"Mina told me."

He nodded very slowly. "Mina told you."

"That's right."

"Last night."

"Yes. But she didn't say he left. She said he got in trouble. That he was...'up to all kinds of no good.' Her words. She said he'd been keeping more than just animals at the pound."

"Meaning what?"

"Well, girls, I guess. She said he snatched up a girl who was the daughter of some city councilman and that was the end of him. I figured she meant he'd been keeping...you know, kidnapping girls and keeping them out there. As sex slaves, or something. Isn't that what happened?"

He stood there and looked at me for a long time, just stared at me and chewed slowly on his lower lip. He stared at me for so long that I got scared. Then he lowered himself slowly back onto the chair.

"You say you met Mina in the cafeteria at your school?" he said.

"Yeah, that's right."

"I went to your school this morning and spoke with some of the students. They say they saw you sitting alone at a table in the cafeteria and, uh...talking to yourself."

I wondered briefly if I was dreaming. "Talking to my...what?"

"Tom, we found a mummified corpse in the trunk of the car you were driving."

At first, I thought he meant that Mina had been killed in the accident, but then the word "mummified" hit me over the head like a club.

"I...don't understand," I said.

"Neither do I, Tom, I really don't."

"What do you mean mum...*mummified*?"

He shrugged. "I don't know how many meanings that word has. I mean it was a mummified corpse. It was the corpse of a girl who died years ago. In fact, she's been identified. Her name was Mina Narron. She was the daughter of a city councilman, and she went missing sixteen years ago."

Goosebumps broke out all over my body and my eyes stung with tears.

"There was a big search. Just about everybody in town helped look for her. But obviously, she was never found. Later that same year, Auggie Fennel abandoned his pound and left town. It didn't seem significant then, but...it does now. Several girls went missing around that time. Teenagers, mostly druggies, hookers, that sort of thing. Nobody made the connection." He stood again and put his notebook and pencil back in his pocket. "I'm thinking we should take a good look around that pound. Maybe do some digging. Now that you've given us reason to."

Something Mina had said came back to me: *And that was the end of Auggie Fennel. If you want it to be, Tom.*

The police officer pulled the curtain aside as if he were going to leave, then turned back to me. "Your parents will be in to take you home. But I'll be in touch with more questions." He turned to go again.

"Wait." My voice sounded like sandpaper on wood. When he turned to me again, I said, "I...don't understand. You're not...I don't know...freaked out by this? Because...*I* am. I put a living girl in that trunk, a girl I met at school yesterday. She was the reason I went *out* to that place."

He nodded. "Yeah. Like I said. It's a strange place, that lake."

Then he left.

Alone

Taylor Grant

JESS was alone.

Unsettled, she scrutinized the beach for the third time since she'd arrived, squinting as windblown grains of sand stung her reddened cheeks.

This stretch of the coast was desolate during the winter, particularly late in the day, when darkness climbed the stairs of the sky and the sun began to disappear in the west.

Finally, Jess shrugged, concluding that aside from an occasional seabird flying overhead, she was alone.

She breathed in the moist, salty air and moved closer to the water's edge, listening to the eternal roar of the sea. She watched the fading sun glisten on the water and a gull soar across the face of a rolling wave.

This was the one place in the whole state of Virginia she felt a modicum of peace. Her father had brought her here a few times in the winters of her youth, when few others braved its icy touch.

During those memorable times, she and her dad walked together for what seemed like forever, the sounds of civilization swallowed by the pounding surf. Unlike most of the world, her dad had understood that her introverted nature wasn't a behavioral defect, but a misunderstood personality trait.

Jess was neither antisocial nor particularly shy, as many mistakenly defined an introvert. She simply preferred not to be in the spotlight, enjoyed listening more than speaking, sought meaningful conversation over small talk, and did her best work alone.

Jess's father related to this. "For people like us," he'd once said, "Solitude isn't a luxury, it's a necessity to recharge." He taught her that a deserted beach in the dead of winter was the perfect balm. And whenever they had walked in silence for long stretches of time it was never awkward, but an interval of mutual understanding.

She grinned at the thought. God, how she missed her father's gentle smile, bushy beard and understanding eyes.

Of course, she cared for her younger sister, Lily, and her mother too, as much as was possible with such a detached person. But the bond with her father had always been the deepest.

Jess gazed out at the cloud-flecked sky, flooded with the sunset's colors of fire red, lavender, and deep orange, its remarkable spell changing the way the world looked just for a moment.

Someone once said there was nothing so bittersweet as watching a beautiful sunset alone. At that moment, missing her father so deeply, she felt that to be true.

I understand, someone whispered.

Jess spun around to see who had spoken.

She looked in every direction, but there was only the rolling mass of the sea and grains of sand dancing across the surface of the shore.

She'd heard the voice clearly. There was no mistaking it. But the more she considered it, the words had seemed less like a voice and more like a thought.

Then she saw him.

She blinked several times before acknowledging he was truly there.

A man bobbed up and down amidst the waves, less than fifty feet from the shoreline. He stared at her through his scuba mask.

A diver surfacing? Out here?

Jess waved.

The diver didn't wave back.

She raised her hand to shield her eyes from the sun, and that's when she realized that it wasn't a man wearing a scuba mask.

It was something else entirely, and it watched her with bulbous, inhuman eyes.

* * *

The following afternoon, while sitting across from her sister Lily at the local *Coffee Shot*, Jess decided not to mention the strange aquatic being.

After all, she'd only had a glimpse before the figure disappeared into the black depths.

And let's face it, sister, you were probably seeing things.

That's what she kept telling herself, anyway.

"How's Tiger?" Lily asked, one of her perfectly manicured hands wrapped around a 32oz extra scalding, non-fat, decaf, caramel, soy Macchiato with a couple extra packets of Splenda.

Jess stared at Lily's royal blue crocodile skin handbag on the table. Clearly vintage. The bag's scaly surface reminded Jess of the sea creature's skin, which she thought she'd seen glistening for a moment in the fading light of the sun.

"Jess?" her sister said, with a slight edge to her voice. Lily never liked repeating herself. "How's Tiger doing?"

Jess did her best to ignore the table to their left, where three frat boys were gawking at her drop dead gorgeous sibling. It was something she had dealt with all her life.

"Oh, it's just a matter of time now," Jess finally replied.

Lily didn't even like cats, didn't seem to like animals in general. It was a perfunctory question to draw Jess back into their dying conversation.

Talks with Lily were generally one-sided, and Jess was used to them. But today it had been particularly hard to stay engaged.

"Maybe you should consider putting him down," Lily offered after a loud slurp. "You know, euthanize the poor little fella."

Jess stiffened at that, and her eyes flared.

Lily cleared her throat, her eyes apologetic. "What I mean is, you know, ease his suffering."

Jess didn't answer, instead she took a sip of green tea. She had been having suicidal thoughts for some time now, but her concern for Tiger had kept her from taking action. Who would take care of him? Even worse; would he think she'd abandoned him?

Jess couldn't bear the thought.

Mom had moved to Paris to live a fabulous life with her new investment banker boyfriend, Pete, and Jess felt lucky to get a postcard. Lily, on the other hand, could barely take care of herself, much less a dying cat. Her sister had always been oblivious to most things that didn't relate directly to her, and that included Jess's deteriorating mental health.

Unlike Lily, Jess had been devastated when their father had died from heart failure six months ago.

Their parents had divorced eight years ago. It was the same year Lily graduated high school and Jess from college. Soon after, their dad's health took a rapid decline.

Lily left for college and disappeared, while Jess dropped her career goals to become their dad's caregiver. For the next seven years she became her dad's full-time medical advocate, navigating the labyrinthine medical system, overseeing endless paperwork, doctor's appointments and weekly treatments.

She dealt with all of his meals, laundry, bills, and served as his counselor and sole emotional support. Yet Jess never regretted the decision. While the experience was an enormous stress at times, being of service had its intangible rewards. She and her father had only grown closer.

Not surprisingly, Lily hadn't offered to help once in those seven years. Jess didn't bother asking because that's not how things worked with Lily. She asked *you* for things. Everyone knew that.

Jess didn't resent her sister's self-centeredness; that would be as fruitless as resenting the sky for being blue. And yet, how she felt about Lily had changed due to a flippant but deeply painful comment made during a recent lunch.

It had been a typical coffee date and Lily had needed a shoulder to cry on. This time due to a breakup with yet another boyfriend from her seemingly limitless reservoir. In between wiping her mascara-smudged eyes, Lily said, "I know it sounds terrible, but it's a blessing you didn't get the looks of the family. Believe me, you're lucky men don't ask you out— they all lie and manipulate to get one thing."

Jess's heart had sunk like a wounded bird.

Her entire life had been one long reminder that her sister had won the genetic lottery and she had lost it. In every conceivable situation, Lily found herself in the spotlight, while Jess stood in a corner, completely invisible.

But what had always both surprised and impressed Jess about her younger sister, was that she'd never rubbed her beauty in Jess's face. Even when they were angry with each other growing up, Lily had never taken the low road.

That consideration had not been lost on Jess, and she had clung to it like a life raft during those times when she'd been drowning from her sister's self-absorption. They were both well aware of the chasm of attractiveness between them. But Lily had never acknowledged it so callously; she had never crossed the line so blatantly.

And that was why the comment had cut Jess deeply. Lily was many things, but she had never been mean-spirited.

It's a blessing you didn't get the looks of the family. You're lucky men don't ask you out.

The words had been sharper than knives, and they had hurt far worse than any teasing she'd endured through childhood.

And yet with mom in Paris, her father gone, and her beloved Tiger's inoperable cancer, Lily was just about all she had left. Sure, she would forgive her and move on eventually. But as she remembered once reading, you could throw a plate, watch it break, and say sorry. And while the act could be forgiven, the plate would still be broken.

"I appreciate what you're saying," Jess said after a long and uncomfortable silence. "But I'm torn between wanting to end Tiger's suffering...and not wanting to betray his trust by euthanizing him."

Lily dismissed the thought with a wave of her hand. " A cat wouldn't know th—"

"I would know," Jess said, cutting her off.

* * *

On her drive home, Jess couldn't shake the memory of the bizarre aquatic being she now jokingly referred to as 'Bob' in her mind.

It bobs in the water, get it folks? Ba dum bum. I got a million of 'em.

What had struck her the most were its eyes. They were multicolored, like the rainbow on the surface of an oily patch of water. But

368

there was something else in those eyes.

What was it?

Empathy.

It made no sense whatsoever.

But Goddamn if she didn't want to go back to the beach right then to see if she could find the creature.

Instead, she pulled onto her street and prepared herself for what was to come.

* * *

Jess's chest tightened at the thought of what faced her as she walked up the front steps to her apartment complex.

Tiger, her 14-year-old cat, would hear her come home and struggle like mad to greet her. There was a time when she looked forward to it every night.

But now his joints were a mess and every step an agonized effort. These days, it broke her heart to see him struggle and limp as he tried to meet her at the door.

She passed through the front gate to her complex and thought about the day she had found him while walking through the neighborhood. A tiny sound, almost imperceptible, had caught her attention.

If it hadn't been for the near total silence of the street at that moment, she never would have heard it. It took her a few moments to identify the direction of the mewling noise.

Then she glanced down and saw it, a tiny figure buried amidst the mud, trash and leaves of a rain gutter.

The emaciated kitten was barely alive but she spent the next two months nursing it back to health. He'd grown up to be the most affectionate cat imaginable. She gave him the obvious name of 'Tiger' due to his Bengal Tiger-like stripes, and he had become her one constant companion ever since.

Maybe Lily is right, Jess thought as she gingerly opened the front door. *I'm only prolonging the inevitable. Maybe the most loving thing to do is put an end to his suffering.*

As she glanced around her modestly decorated living room, she noticed that Tiger wasn't in his usual spot by the couch.

It didn't take long to find him.

He lay on his side on the tile kitchen floor, as emaciated now as when she'd found him all those years ago.

His glassy eyes were propped open by death.

Jess held it together until she touched his unmoving chest, felt the stiffness of his body and the coldness left behind.

And then the tears came.

*   *   *

Gloom crept through Jess's home like a poisonous mist the following day. When it became too much to bear, she drove to the beach to clear her head.

It was now three in the afternoon, and the fact that she hadn't slept the previous night had taken its toll. She dropped to the sand like a marionette cut loose from its strings.

Jess couldn't shake a mental loop of Tiger's eyes, as cold as the tile floor on which he'd died, and the image of his corpse being stuffed in a container by the disinterested pickup man from the Pet Crematorium.

Tomorrow she would go for a final viewing, before his body was subjected to 1800 degrees Fahrenheit and vaporized into dust and dried bones.

Jess had decided she would scatter those ashes into the ocean.

Maybe I'll follow you there, she thought.

She pulled up the collar of her double-breasted pea coat and stared out at the great expanse of the sea. Huge ice-floes of clouds sailed by in an ashen sky. Heavy. Bleak. Dispiriting. Just like her mood.

Could be worse, she thought. *I could be at work.*

Earlier, she'd texted her boss that she was taking a personal day, due to the death of a loved one.

Jess worked in the accounts payable department of a telecommunications company, and it was almost unheard of for her to take time off.

Maria, her supervisor, said it was fine, but didn't bother to offer any condolences. Briefly, Jess wondered if anyone would notice that she wasn't in the office.

Most likely not. She was as invisible there as she was everywhere else.

A whisper. *Not invisible. To me.*

Jess sat up and looked out toward the sea. It was that voice again. And like before, it wasn't a voice as much as a thought.

Had the strange aquatic being returned? God, she hoped so.

I hear you. Jess said in her mind. *Show yourself.*

She stood and moved closer to the ocean's edge, where the water's touch gnawed at the sand, writing sculpted secrets there.

Please, Jess thought.

Moments later, a reply: *I am. Here.*

Jess strained her eyes, scanning the waves for anything unusual or out of place.

A familiar head bobbed up and down in the water.

Bob, she thought.

* * *

Jess decided that Bob had the most expressive eyes she had ever seen.

In addition, this remarkable ocean being had the ability to

371

communicate between minds. *Telepathy.*

Upon communing, Jess soon learned that it had no name, no family, and no understanding of its own history. She did, however, ascertain that it was male.

Though slightly embarrassed to ask, Jess was delighted when it agreed to be called Bob.

Apparently abandoned, Bob had been left to fend for himself since as far back as he could remember. He believed he was the last of his kind, and he had swam in the depths of loneliness throughout his existence.

Jess knew what it was like to be a ghost gliding through the world, with no body and no shadow. Leaving no footprints. She knew how it felt to have the vice of loneliness on your heart, how it increased in pressure a little more each day. How it inexorably dimmed the light inside and replaced it with a darkness that overshadowed each moment.

Oh yes, Jess understood why this lonely creature had spent years using his unique abilities to read the minds of people like Jess. He'd wanted to learn how to communicate in human languages.

This was about connection. Any connection.

At first, Bob's ability to reach into Jess's mind was unsettling. But she quickly acclimated to it, and soon realized that it was far more advanced than typical verbal exchanges.

When she communicated with Bob, the feelings behind the words were also transferred between them.

It was...intimate, she thought.

Understandably, though a highly intelligent being, he had rudimentary English skills. But what he lacked in the nuances of spoken language, he more than made up for with his expressive eyes and psychic ability to convey feeling.

But perhaps the most notable thing about Bob was that he listened.

Intently.

For the first time in her life, Jess felt truly seen and heard.

And when she finally broke down and wept, her salt tears mixing with the briny sea, the creature wept with her.

*   *   *

Jess quit her job over the phone and spent the better part of the next four days at the beach, only leaving when the sun gave way to the evening's darkness and Bob would return to the ocean depths.

She spoke for hours and Bob listened. He was fascinated by everything about her. She told him everything she could about the surface world, as he seemed intent on understanding what it meant to be human.

When she brought Tiger's remains to the ocean's edge and poured his ashes across the surface of the water, Bob floated nearby, watching her silently with palpable compassion.

But on the fifth day, things took a dark turn. For Jess realized that whatever it was that she had with Bob would never go farther than these captured moments.

One day she would return to the beach and he would be gone.

The recognition of this was followed by familiar feelings of loneliness and despair; they never seemed farther than a single step in the wrong direction. And they always led to the same place, the same final destination.

As she expressed this, Bob swam closer. His rainbow-streaked eyes narrowed. And he listened.

Jess wondered how in the world she could explain these concepts to a being like Bob. How could she possibly make him understand why someone would choose not to live?

Tell more, Bob inquired.

Jess stared at her aquatic companion for several moments.

Where she would normally expect judgment, she saw only compassion. He truly wanted to understand. She could sense that. And so she tried.

No one ever really wants to die, she said in her mind. *They simply want to end the pain.*

Jess had been through all of this ad nauseum with her former therapist, Dr. Karen Burroughs. She had stopped therapy with her two weeks ago, because she had grown weary of a highly successful, beautiful, and happily married woman trying to convince her that she could possibly understand.

She imagined Karen's reaction if she returned for another session and tried to explain her relationship with Bob.

Well, Jess...I'm sure we can both agree that Bob is simply a figment of your imagination. The timing of his appearance is no accident. He came to you in your deepest despair, yes? He is merely symbolic of that.

No doubt delivered in her special brand of compassion and condescension.

No, Karen, Jess thought. Bob is real. So real that I could swim out and touch him even now. And, in fact, she wanted to.

As if in answer, Bob swam closer than ever before. She could see his throat expanding and contracting like a small balloon, his mosaic of scales glistening in the sun as sea water ran down his sinewy shoulders and chest.

Bob's eyes grew wide. *Tell more.*

So she did.

This dark place...it doesn't happen overnight. It's more complex than a single decision. It comes after a long internal battle, you see. It's the total collapse of your emotional reserves.

Bob's blinked as if he understood.

When you've lost your soul to a sea of emptiness and darkness, you feel like a terrible burden to the world. Beyond ending your own pain, you know it's unfair to make others—especially your loved ones—suffer along with you year after year. They don't deserve to be dragged down into your emotional abyss.

For a moment, Jess struggled to go on; the intense feelings hit her like a physical blow.

Bob remained silent. Still. Attentive.

She composed herself before continuing. *Some say that ending your life is selfish. Because of the collateral damage you leave behind. But that's bullshit. What's selfish is to expect anyone to suffer an intolerable reality... something that can only be understood by that person...simply to spare someone else from their own soul-searching.*

When Jess dared to meet Bob's eyes again, she saw more than empathy there.

She saw heartbreak.

Jess took an involuntary step back and examined the remarkable creature before her. In that horrifying moment, she realized that she'd dragged him into the very emotional abyss she'd just described.

Disgusted with herself, and not wanting him to see her this way, she turned and walked away.

I have to go, she said.

She had only taken five steps when she felt the gentle caress of something unseen.

She paused a moment, and then glanced back toward the sea.

Bob's arms were outstretched.

Welcoming.

Jess found herself moving towards the water, as if she were somehow observing this from outside herself, present but unable to control the outcome.

At first, she hardly noticed the ocean's icy grip as she waded past the first waves. All of her attention was focused on the eyes of the beautiful creature before her.

She freed herself from her waterlogged jacket, but her socks and shoes felt like lead weights, pulling at her with every wave that passed. She struggled to navigate through the slippery rocks and kelp churning in the surf.

Bob waited. Unblinking.

Salty water splashed over Jess, stinging her eyes. The frigid water began to numb her hands and feet, causing her breath to come in short, hard gasps.

When she finally waded close enough, Bob reached out and wrapped his cold, powerful arms around her.

She embraced him.

Soon she was underwater. Numbed.

She surrendered to it.

No more pain.

She glanced up at the last vestiges of sunlight reflected in the water.

There was a flash of monstrous teeth. The silhouette of a shark-like fin on Bob's back.

In that terrifying moment, Jess realized she'd made a grave mistake. There was a sharp clarity now that she couldn't see before. For the first time since she could remember, she wanted to live.

Oh God...please...let me live!

Her screams were absorbed into an indifferent sea as shreds of her flesh and entrails floated past her.

She struggled wildly to escape, desperate to reach the surface. Frantic for a second chance.

But it was too late

It was too late to do anything at all.

The Cerulean Tide

Somer Canon

MARTIN dug his toes deeper into the hot sand and sighed in contentment, relishing the salty breeze blowing in his face. He felt something strange against his partially buried toe and flipped whatever it was to the surface and grunted. It was a cigarette butt and he stomped it back under the sand with the heel of his foot. His wife, Linda, was next to him wearing a caftan and enormous hat despite the umbrella shading them both. She was listening to some ranting podcaster and he was doing his best to ignore it, instead taking in the lapping of the waves.

He pulled his binoculars out and looked at the massive gray ship on the horizon, a Navy ship from the nearby base in Norfolk. The presence was pure novelty and he secretly hoped that he could see it do tests miles out, but he had binoculars, not a telescope.

The ocean is so polluted, so destroyed by the human species that I wouldn't dare dip a toe into it, and I certainly wouldn't eat anything that previously lived in it! That's just asking for some crazy foodborne illness! I'm telling you, the next big disaster will be from those horribly abused waters, mark my words!

"For Christ's sake, Karen, will you turn that eco-warrior bullshit off?" Martin mumbled testily. He looked around self-consciously, wondering if anybody had overheard Linda's obnoxious podcast.

"You used to care about stuff like this," she said, punching at the flat face of her phone, silencing the nagging voice. "We need to be informed."

"I'm not against being informed, but we spent seven hours in the car driving here and dropped a cool grand paying for this vacation. A vacation *you* wanted to go on! So maybe, just maybe can you not blast that garbage so the other people fresh out of that so-called 'horribly abused water' don't hear it and think we're quacky? You think you can stop with that and enjoy this?"

Linda made a rude noise and pulled a book out of her beach bag. Martin glared at her a moment longer and decided that it was better that she chose not to engage. They fought too much at home and he wanted the vacation to be a nice reconnection for them. He lifted his binoculars again to watch the Navy ships.

He frowned. The ship was nowhere to be seen. True, it could have gone over the horizon, but not that fast. He moved his binoculars to the left and right and still, the massive ship was gone. Strange, but there must have been an explanation for it. Maybe he had glared at Linda for longer than he thought.

He reached into her beach bag and pulled out his own book, a biography of his favorite rock band from when he was a teenager, and settled in his chair. He watched lazily as a boat with a big sign in the back of it advertised a local crab shack. He loved the beach.

He must have dozed off, because he was startled awake by shouting all around him. It was coming from behind him on the boardwalk and all along the beach. Soon, the lifeguards started blowing their whistles in controlled bursts. Martin looked at Linda and saw her sitting up straight, looking alarmed.

"What's going on?" he asked.

"There's something out there. The water…it's not right."

Martin looked out to the ocean and stood up when he saw the band of bright blue creeping closer. It stood out in bright contrast to the greenish-gray color, the usual, normal color of the Atlantic. It was startling and beautiful. Like the Caribbean was creeping into northern waters.

There were still swimmers out in the water, obviously too far out to hear the lifeguard's warnings. Martin watched as they stopped and watched in interest as the bright blue band of water got closer to them. Some of them started swimming towards the blue while others stayed behind, wary of the drastic color change in the water.

"If that water were black or brown, they'd all be swimming away from it," Linda said at his side. "Look at them, they don't even know what's causing it and they're going right to it."

They watched in rapt anticipation. The first swimmer reached the bright blue water and immediately surfaced again, waving their arms wildly. Another swimmer close to them immediately turned and frantically started swimming away. Martin watched in horror as the swimmer in the blue water sank beneath the surface and did not come back up. The swimmer had been too far out, so if they had been screaming, the people on the beach would not have been able to hear, but the other swimmers heard and they were desperately making their way back to land.

Linda, a nurse for the past eighteen years, sprinted to the water's edge and waved the people out, waiting for those far-out swimmers to come in. Martin ran out with her and tried to stop a lifeguard, a young man with a deep tan, from going in after the people.

"I 'ave to 'elp dem!" the lifeguard screamed with a thick French accent. He ripped his arm away from Martin and splashed into the water.

"Jesus," Martin said, helplessly. He stood by his wife, curious and terrified, and watched as his quiet vacation suddenly and thoroughly went all to hell.

As the lifeguard swam towards the screaming swimmers, Martin watched as, one by one, the beautiful bright blue water caught up to them. With the swimmers closer to shore, their pained shrieks broke through the noise of the crashing waves, audible to all the petrified people on the beach. Many of the swimmers' heads went under that jewel-like swath of water and never resurfaced. The frantic splashing of the others became more so. Linda and other people on the beach were screaming reassurances to the swimmers, dancing away from the water lapping at their bare toes as they urged the people to land.

The first swimmer to make it to land was a young woman. She was the pale-faced picture of abject horror as she crawled from the waves, revealing that one of her legs below the knee was missing. Martin stayed in his place, his hands covering his gaping mouth, but Linda rushed to the girl and together with two men pulled her away from the water. Linda was talking to the people around her with confident authority, touching the girl's face and looking at the destroyed limb and Martin wondered at his wife. She was cool and collected, determined and working through a plan while he stood by in helpless horror, cowering before the grotesque image of the mutilated leg of that poor girl.

Unable to bear the gore any longer, Martin looked back out to the water and gasped when he saw that only two other swimmers had made it to shore. The rest were simply gone, including the lifeguard he had tried to stop. The others were lying on the sand, stunned and looking eaten up like the girl. A young boy was missing a foot and a middle-aged man, bleeding profusely and looking very much dead, was missing both of his legs mid-thigh.

Martin looked out at the lovely water and wondered what was eating away at the swimmers. Nobody was screaming anymore. Many of the others on the beach looked on in terrified quiet, and a few were on their cell phones relaying the happenings to the authorities.

There were many helicopters flying overhead, heading out to sea. Martin wondered what the water looked like from the sky. Could they see the people being dissolved in the cerulean wash? He rubbed his eyes and thought of the Norfolk Naval Station and of the ship that he'd seen on the horizon. If the water was destroying human bodies in a matter of seconds, what would it do to the watercraft?

Black jeeps were driving down the beach, depositing uniformed men and women carrying guns almost as scary as the water. They were ordering people away from the ocean, back and away from the gently lapping edge. The swimmers who had made it out of the water were gathered and put into the backs of the jeeps and driven away.

"Sir, you need to back away from the water," a uniformed young man said. Martin, feeling detached as if in a dream, looked at him and frowned at the man's extreme youth. He looked too young to shave and he was holding a large gun across his chest. When Martin made no move, the young man gently took Martin's arm and led him away and towards a group of people that had been herded to the base of the steps leading up to the boardwalk.

"Linda," Martin said, jerking back to the present. "Linda!"

"Martin," Linda called. She raised an arm and waved at him as she rushed to his side. Her gauzy white caftan was coated in swipes and splashes of bright red blood, her hands a Shakespearean spectacle. She went to his side and put her head on his shoulder, careful not to touch him with her soiled self.

"How is the girl?" he asked weakly.

"She's in shock, but not dead," Linda answered, sounding weary.

Martin breathed deeply, trying to center himself, and realized that the soothingly salty smell of the ocean was gone. There was no smell, no stink of rot, nor an expected smell of chemicals. Just the smell of the blood covering his wife and the sourness of his own sweat.

"Whatever it is, it doesn't have a smell," he said, feeling disassociated again.

Linda said something. He heard her voice, registered that she had spoken, but that was as deep as his understanding could take him at the moment. He was entranced by the rising waves of the lovely water, by the spray leaving the tops of those waves as they crested.

When the wind picked up, he actually closed his eyes and leaned into it out of habit, waiting for the salty kiss of the ocean spray to spritz his face. What he felt instead was an intense burning sensation. He swatted at his face in a panic, and felt his hands start to sting and burn as well.

"Ow. Ow, ah God! Linda, it burns! Linda!" He screamed, lifting his tee shirt to his face, wiping furiously at the bedeviled water eating through his skin. He opened his eyes and looked on in horror at the delicately pocked face of his wife. She was screaming, doing her best not to touch her face with her already bloodied hands.

The pain wiped any higher thought processes from his head. He lived in the pain, knew only that and the smell of his flesh being dissolved. He fell to the sand and pulled his shirt off over his head. He buried his face in the warm, soft fabric and said a prayer, begging for a break from the agony.

He heard Linda whimpering beside him and reached one of his still-stinging hands out to her. He touched her hair and felt comforted by her presence. Hands suddenly gripped him under the arms and pulled him to a standing position. He was being led up the stairs to the boardwalk, his face still buried in his tee shirt, a person close to his ear murmuring about getting to safety.

"I'm here, Martin," Linda was saying behind him, her voice thick with tears and pain. "I'm right here."

"I hear you," he replied. "I can hear you."

Martin was only mildly aware of anything happening outside of the outstanding pain that he was in. Hands were herding him, many voices around him were worriedly talking in low tones, and many others still were making noises through their own pain.

"Sit down here, sir," a voice said into his ear and he lowered himself into a hard chair.

"Linda?" he called out.

"I'm here, Martin," she answered. "Martin, can you look at me? Let me see your face."

Steeling himself, he lowered the soft fabric of the tee shirt. He forced his eyes open and saw that he was sitting at a small restaurant table with Linda across from him. She gasped and put her hands to her mouth.

"Oh God, Martin," she said through sobs.

He blinked, trying to get around the agony enough to see his wife's face. There were little red craters all over her face, all of them dripping with puss. He blinked again and leaned closer to Linda. Beneath her skin, he could see the delicate network of veins under her skin, normally blue or green, if visible at all, but now they were black, emanating from the sores and spreading up into her hairline and down her throat.

"What the…" he began. He reached a hand out to her, wanting to touch his better half as much to comfort himself as her. She didn't notice and kept her own hands on her face.

"Whatever it is, it's in our blood and it looks like it's spreading," she said. "I've never seen anything like this."

She turned and looked out of the window that overlooked the ocean. Martin marveled. The Atlantic always had its own mysterious beauty, a foggy brine reminiscent of primordial beginnings and ends. Now it was stunningly beautiful, something one would see in a tropical resort brochure. Bright blue water sparkled under the summer sun, looking full of the romantic promise clear water like that always seemed to hold. The only thing marring that serene beauty was the sky above, dark with various aircraft. Were they searching for something? Perhaps that ship that he'd seen earlier? Had the corrosive water damaged the hull? He had no way of knowing.

He reached out again and Linda put her hand in his. He closed his eyes, the pain getting to be too much and he listened to the voices around him.

"…it got to Dahlgren. It must be in the Potomac…"

"…you have to stay here, I can't allow you to leave…"

"…possibly terrorists…"

"…quarantine…"

"…extremely dangerous…"

"…multiple fatalities with more expected…"

He opened his eyes again and looked out at the cerulean water, the waves dashing at the soft sand. A tear trickled down his cheek and he squeezed Linda's hand. It was really beautiful.

Night Dive

F. Paul Wilson

WHAT is wrong? Silvio wondered as he cast his little net again.
He stood waist deep in the clear warm water near the
big coral head. He held his thin brown arms high and squinted into the glare of the morning sun as gentle Caribbean swells lapped
at his ribcage. Every morning for two years now, since he'd turned six,
Silvio had waded offshore to net bait fish for his grandfather. A simple
task. The shallows were alive with silversides, and one or two casts usually netted more than enough.

But not lately. Every day for the past week or so Silvio had found
fewer fish wriggling in the fine mesh, and needed more and more casts to
fill Granpa's bait bucket. Today was the worst—eleven casts and nothing.

Granpa too was having bad luck in the deeper waters around the
island. Usually he had no trouble bringing home enough snapper, bar-
jack, and grouper to keep everyone well fed, but lately his catches had

been falling off.

Silvio pulled on the string and hauled in his net for the twelfth time. It felt heavier. Success at last.

But when he lifted the net out of the water, instead of silversides he found a six-inch squirrel fish. He grinned. Never before had he caught anything this size in his little net. But his excitement faded as he took a closer look at the feebly flapping fish. The scales seemed to be sloughing from its red-and-white flanks, and its huge black eyes looked dull and blind. As he watched, it stretched its gills wide, then lay still.

Silvio lowered his net back into the water but the squirrel fish remained immobile. It looked dead. He reached into the net to examine it, but as he lifted the body it broke in half, releasing a sickening stink. Silvio cried out in shock and quickly washed off the putrid goo that coated his hand.

He was afraid now. Something was terribly wrong. Holding his net at arm's length, he splashed toward shore. He had to show Granpa. Granpa would know what to do. This was Granpa's island. He knew everything about the sandy land and the sea that enclosed it.

*   *   *

Michael Stover ascended along the mooring rope to a depth of about fifteen feet, then shut off his light and hung in the inky water. He waved his free arm back and forth in figure eights, watching bioluminescent plankton flash in its wake like a mini Fourth of July.

Cool.

He hadn't been deep—fifty feet, max—so he didn't need much of a safety stop. The water was warm and he was comfortable in his nylon bodysuit. He wished he could stay here all night, but the 300psi reading on his pressure gauge was a reality he couldn't ignore. Reluctantly he released the rope and followed his bubbles to the surface.

Time to face the music.

Cries of relief and concern greeted his arrival on the surface. He lowered his mask and blinked his eyes. A moonless night, with bright stars glittering above, and the bars and hotels glowing along Seven Mile beach far to his right. The voices came from the dive boat looming over him.

"Are you okay?"…"Need any help?"…"Thank God! We've been worried sick about you!"

"I'm fine," Stover said.

He shot a little more air into his BCD and stroked to the platform at the rear of the boat. He clung to the ladder as he removed his fins, then climbed aboard.

"Shit, man!"

Stover looked up and saw his assigned dive buddy—Lawson or Dawson or something like that—a bearded, balding, overweight talker. Like Stover he'd booked as a single and the dive master had paired them up.

"What happened? We hit bottom, you give me the O-K, we start toward the others, then a minute later I look around and you're gone!"

He and the half-dozen other divers on board were crowded around him now.

"I got lost," Stover said, seating himself on a side bench and sliding his tank into an empty slot. "I got disoriented down there in the dark. I didn't know where everyone—"

"Bullshit!" said another voice.

Stover saw the divemaster pushing through the semicircle.

Uh-oh. Here it comes.

His name was Jim—or was it Tim?—late twenties like Stover, blond, deeply tanned, with one of those thorny freeform tattoos encircling each of his considerable biceps. An affable dude on the trip out, but thoroughly pissed at the moment.

"Pardon?"

"You heard me," Jim-Tim said. "You weren't lost. Our lights were visible from a hundred-fifty feet down there."

"Then why didn't you see mine?"

"We should have…unless you were hiding behind a coral head. Anyway, if you were lost you would've surfaced and come back to the boat. But you never came up. What the fuck's your *problem*, man?"

Michael Stover's "problem" was that he preferred to dive alone, a preference that broke one of the sacred rules of the sport. No, he wasn't stupid—the buddy system made tons of safety sense—and no, he wasn't a loser loner—he sort of liked the crowded dive boats and the après-dive sharing of wonders seen below.

But *during* a dive…

Once he was under, Stover had his own priorities. First off, he loved the silence. Once below, all you heard was your own breath bubbling through the regulator. And tagging along with the silence was this wonderful sense of solitude. He loved to imagine he was the only person on the planet with a scuba rig, and that his were the first human eyes to gorge on the wonders of a Caribbean reef. But having a dive buddy—or worse, being part of an excursion group—shattered that illusion. Plus you had to go where someone else wanted to go.

So Stover tended to sneak off on his own as soon as he hit target depth.

In the world of scuba, this was sacrilege, anathema, the ultimate no-no. And Stover couldn't blame them, really: The divemaster descends with eight divers; a few minutes later he looks around and counts only seven. He raps on his tank with his knife handle, but no answering clang comes back. He goes back to the surface and no one on the boat has seen the missing diver. That's when his wetsuit tends to acquire a brown stain.

Thirty minutes later, when Stover surfaces, there's the all-too-brief joyous celebration, followed quickly by anger: Where the hell did you go? Don't you know better than…blah-blah-blah…yadda-yadda-yadda…

Was it worth it? He asked himself as the red-faced Jim-Tim rattled on.

Yeah. Especially on a night dive when you chance upon a coral head as spectacular as the one he'd found tonight. The colors alone are worth the grief. Water leaches the sunlight as it filters down from the surface, so even in the extraordinarily clear waters of the Caymans, you get down to a hundred feet and the brightest gobies and hydroids look faded. But at night, when you shine your torch from six inches away, the colors leap out at you. Tonight he'd found diamondback blennies among the anemones, and brilliant Christmas tree worms jutting from a brain coral formation, and he'd spent a good ten minutes watching two bright red hermit crabs battling over an empty shell.

But colors were only part of the story. Lots of things that stay hidden during the day come out when it's dark—octopus, squid, eels, snakes—and they're all *hungry*. The waters are alive with death. And Stover liked to participate in the feeding frenzy—not by eating, but by playing maestro with the eaters and the eaten.

Hold your flash still and the beam will fill with teeny wriggling filament worms. When the cone of light gets crowded, slowly lower the beam to a sea anemone and watch it gorge until it's so full it hauls in its tentacles and shuts down for the night.

Diving in the dark—the best, man.

But then the grief.

Stover remained properly contrite during the lecture until Jim-Tim finally ran out of steam, then he promised never to do it again. But Jim-Tim was still mad as he stomped to the helm to steer them back to George Town…where Jim-Tim would no doubt hit the bars and blow-off the rest of that steam.

And that was where Stover's real problems began. These divemasters all know each other, all hang out at the same bars. Jim-Tim starts talking about the asshole who almost gave him a heart attack tonight, and another says, Hey, I had a guy like that, and pretty soon they find out they're all talking about the same guy.

The result was like major deodorant failure. Worse. If scuba were the Catholic Church, Michael Stover was excommunicated. If scuba were Hinduism, he became a member of the untouchable caste. He could offer double and triple the going rate for a dive—something his trust fund allowed without a second thought—and exhaust his charm and Jason Patric looks on the female bookers, but the answer was the same all over: Dive with someone else, Michael Stover.

Stover was already blacklisted in Cozumel, Belize, and had been edging toward that status here in the Caymans. And he couldn't book a dive under a different name because the certified outfits wanted a look at your C-card. Once they saw his name, that was it. And as for the un-certified fly-by-night dive shops, that was like playing Russian roulette. Stover had tried one of those, but a test whiff from one of their tanks smelled like midpoint in the Lincoln Tunnel, and he'd canceled out.

He'd approached the Caymans with a game plan, starting on the smaller out islands—deep dives at the Blacktip Tunnels on Little Cayman, and Cemetery Wall on Cayman Brac—before moving here to the main island. He'd done only two Grand Cayman dives—hundred-footers at Twisted Sister on the south wall and Main Street on the north wall—and already word was out. But the dive shop he'd booked tonight apparently hadn't heard about him. After this run, though, his name would be mud all the way out to Rum Point.

Ah, well. He hadn't been to Bon Aire yet. And all of Micronesia waited.

*   *   *

Stover took his wetsuit off the hanger and checked for moisture: dry. Should be. He'd rinsed it out two days ago and hadn't had it on since. Just as he'd expected, the dive shops had shut him out. Time to move on.

Only when in transit did he miss having a buddy. Soloing in an airport or on a plane was a whole different breed of isolation from soloing on a reef. He loathed it. But he'd yet to find a sympatico companion—a diver rich enough to have unlimited free time but who'd go his own way once they were underwater.

Maybe someday.

A knock on the door. Stover glanced at his watch. He'd told the front desk to send the porter by at nine; only 8:30 now. He pulled open the door.

"Look, I'm not packed yet so—"

He stopped. This dude was no porter.

"You dey man who dive alone?" said an old black guy who looked like a cross between Nelson Mandela and Redd Foxx, dressed by Dumpsters 'R' Us. A featherstar of a man, bright eyes with black-hole centers set in sun-blasted furrows of brain-coral skin, a ghost of a beard clinging to his jaws like Spanish moss.

"Who wants to know?"

The old man thrust out a spidery hand. "I am Ernesto."

Stover shook it with no enthusiasm, then began to close the door. "Great. Look, I'm packing to leave, so if you'll—"

"Oh, you do not want to be packed so soon," he said with that melodic island cadence. "Not until you have had the chat with Ernesto."

"Really? And just what is it you want, Ernesto?"

Ernesto stepped across the threshold and closed the door behind him. Stover didn't see how he'd had enough room to manage that, but suddenly he was in. He wasn't afraid of the old man. Hardly enough muscle on those matchstick arms to break, well, a matchstick. But still... the guy had an urgency about him...

"It be not what Ernesto want. It be what dey man who dive alone want. Do he want to be diving dey Atalaya Wall?"

Stover widened his eyes. "The Atalaya Wall? Ooooh, neeeeat! And how about we swing by the Seven Gold Cities of Cibola along the way?"

"Ernesto not be following dis talk."

"Come on, old man. You don't really think I'm going to fall for that, do you? What do I look like?"

"You look like dey man who want to be diving dey Atalaya Wall."

"And next you'll tell me you can take me there."

A shrug. "Ernesto lives on Atalaya."

Stover stared at him. No guile in those bottomless eyes. Could it be…?

Naw. The Atalaya Wall was a Caribbean myth.

Facts: The Cayman Trench runs from the Yucatan basin, passing the Caymans and snaking between Jamaica and Cuba to end up somewhere in Haiti's backyard. Troughs along its course reach depths just this side of five miles, the deepest spots in the Carib.

The concentrations of sea life along the trench walls are as dense as anywhere in the world, and make the Caymans an international dive mecca. But is that enough? No way. The scubaheads have to conjure up a Shangri-La called Atalaya, a lost island perched on the edge of a four-mile trough with a vertical reef that's absofuckinlutely the best dive site in the world…if only someone could find it. Those who search for it come back defeated, or don't come back at all.

"Ernesto be taking you dere if you want."

Okay, Stover thought. I'll play along. "Yeah? Why me?"

"Only dey man who wishes to be alone in dey sea, to be one with dey reef, can see dey Atalaya Wall."

"And I'm that man?"

"Dat is what dey be telling Ernesto."

"Too bad you didn't come by sooner. I've got a flight to Tampa in a couple of hours."

"Oh," Ernesto said. "Okay den." He turned and reached for the doorknob. "Perhaps dat be a good thing."

What? No hard sell?

"Why do you say that?"

"Because dey Atalaya Wall be ruinin' you for aaaaall other places. Once you see it, you not want to be diving anywhere else."

Stover put a hand on the old man's bony shoulder. "Hold on a sec." I know I'm going to hate myself for this, he thought, but asked anyway. "How much you want to take me there?"

"Five hundred dollars."

"Five hundred!" The average two-tank dive ran fifty-sixty.

"Cayman dollars."

That added another twenty-five percent. "Ernesto, my man, I do believe you're a few fins short of a whole fish."

"Is a long trip, and Ernesto must be sailing all dey way himself."

"*Sail?*" This was bugfuck crazy.

But just crazy enough to be the real thing. What con artist would dream up this approach? And hell, the money was nothing. Why not go for it? He had no firm plans other than hanging out with the manatees in Florida while he planned his next dive trip. And even if this guy took him someplace other than Atalaya, he'd be diving alone, on a reef he could call his own, with no grief afterwards.

But what if Ernesto really did know the way to the Atalaya Wall?

The prospect became a thousand pounds of sand, engulfing him.

"All right. When do we leave?"

Ernesto's eyes all but disappeared in parchment furrows as he smiled. "As soon as come dey dark."

"A night dive, then?"

"A night *trip*. Ernesto only travel in dey dark…so dat others may not be following him."

"Gotcha."

Sneaking off in the night to dive. This was getting better every minute.

* * *

Stover huddled on a bench on the windward side of Ernesto's small ketch as it slid across the starlit water. He clutched the handle of the six-inch, saw-toothed diving knife in the pocket of his windbreaker. No moon overhead, land was a memory, and Ernesto had the tiller.

Alone at sea with a crazy old man.

Crazy, yeah. Little doubt on that score. Anyone who truly thought he knew the way to the Atalaya was probably missing a couple of hoses on his regulator. But dangerous? Stover didn't think so. But he couldn't be sure. Thus the knife.

So why am I here?

Just as crazy.

But not stupid.

It had occurred to him earlier, on his way to the docks, that the old guy might plan to rob him, kill him, then toss him overboard. He'd almost chickened out, but then flashed on a deal: the first hundred bucks up front, and the other four when they got back to George Town. Which made Stover more valuable alive than dead.

Yeah, you had to get up pretty early in the morning to keep Mike Stover in your wake.

Ernesto didn't seem to have a problem with the arrangement. And Stover had no problem with the air tanks Ernesto had brought along. Rented from Bob Soto's shop. Good stuff.

And the old coot was a damn good sailor. He had only the foresail up but they were making good time running west with the swells. Up and down, up and down…a primal rhythm…soothing…lulling…

*   *   *

"Wake up, diver man."

Dark…smelly…something wrapped around his face, around his body. Stover thrashed violently, fighting the encircling coils, and felt himself falling.

Sunlight seared his eyes as he hit a hard surface and rolled free. He blinked, looked around. Still on the ketch. Sitting on the deck. A dirty, threadbare blanket that might have been navy blue once—might have been *clean* once—lay coiled around his feet. He kicked it away. Christ, for a moment there—

"We are here, diver man." Ernesto stood over him, grinning.

"Where?"

He gestured over the gunwale. "Atalaya."

Stover scrambled to his feet. A hundred yards away lay a short white beach lined with coconut palms, Caribbean pines, and a cluster of corrugated metal shacks. He didn't know what he'd expected, but he'd pictured something a little more impressive than this oversized sandbar, the mirror image of a zillion other tiny Caribbean islands.

"That's it?"

"Atalaya not be looking like too much above dey water. Ah, but below…below she have many, many charms."

She'd better, Stover thought. He was feeling a bit cranky at the moment. His limbs were stiff, and his back felt like he'd been sleeping with an air tank strapped on all night.

He glanced around. The sail was down, tumbled around the boom like an old bed sheet, and the sun sat maybe ten degrees above the horizon in a pristine sky.

"How long've we been here?"

"Just arrived."

"What happened to my night dive?"

"First you do daylight dive. Atalaya must be seen in day to appreciate. And while you down, you choose where you wish to be night diving."

Made sense.

"And not to be worrying. You will dive in dey dark. Ernesto promises."

Stover climbed up onto the deck and stood by the foremast for a better look. To his right, the sandy bottom lay a dozen feet below, a pale, pale turquoise expanse running in a gentle slope from the beach to the boat, marred here and there by dark splotches of coral heads. But directly under the keel the aquamarine hue darkened abruptly to a deeper, almost cobalt blue that stretched to his left as far as he could see. The color line ran directly under the boat, from the fore horizon to the aft. The lip of the Cayman Trench, a sheer almost vertical drop, where units of depth switched from feet to miles.

The Atalaya Wall, he thought. *If this is really it…and if it's half as spectacular as the fables say…Christ, the stories I'll be able to tell.*

The aches and pains drained away. He hopped back down to the deck and unzipped his dive bag.

"Let's do it."

As Stover was attaching his regulator to the first tank, he spotted movement on the island: a skinny little boy, a stick figure drawn with magic marker, ran down to the waterline and waved.

"Who's that?"

"Dat be Silvio, Ernesto's grandboy."

"Yeah? Tell you what—I'll bring him back a nice fat conch for dinner."

Stover thought he saw Ernesto's eyes cloud for an instant before he turned away and stared at the water.

"Silvio like dey conch," the old man said softly.

Stover was suited up and ready to rock in less than ten minutes. He seated himself on the starboard gunwale, waved to Ernesto, then flopped backward into the water. He released some air from his BCD and let himself sink to within a couple of feet of the bottom. He started kicking, scanning the sand as he moved.

Where were the fish? Shallow open water and sandy bottoms had nowhere near the life of a coral head, but he was used to seeing *something*—a flounder, a ray, a snapper or two, a school of baitfish. He found nothing, not even in the boat's shadow, usually a favorite hang for barracuda and others.

Not an auspicious start, but he was sure all that would change once he reached the storied Atalaya Wall. And that lay just a dozen feet ahead.

Stover stayed low, kicking for speed. He imagined himself in a single-seater plane, flying low over the desert, coming to what looked like the end of the world and *zooming* over the edge. But instead of finding the corrugated walls of the Grand Canyon…

Nothing but blue emptiness, deepening steadily in hue ahead and below as the miles of water beneath him swallowed the light…he was floating above eternity…the closest thing to flying without wings, to spacewalking without a rocket.

Stover relished the solitude a moment, looking into the abyss… and feeling suddenly uneasy as he sensed it looking into him.

Shaking off the feeling, he did a one-eighty and kicked back toward the wall.

What the hell?

Where was the color? Where was the *life*? The hard coral looked bleached and dead, and the soft coral looked like it had been turned to stone—the fans stood rigid instead of undulating gracefully in the currents, and the sponges looked like terra cotta pottery.

Stover's mouth went dry. What was going on here? Had some asshole started using the trench as a toxic waste dump?

He bled a little more air from his vest and sank deeper, studying the wall. Except for the need to pop his ears, he had no sensation of sinking; rather, the wall seemed to be rising. But nothing changed: the coral was as dead down here as it had been on the rim. And not one damn fish.

This was getting scarier by the minute. Something heavy going down here, something bad in this water, and Stover wanted no part of it. He wanted out. Now.

A shadow passed over him.

Jesus!

Stover whirled and looked up, expecting a manta or some other— equally harmless, he hoped—pelagic, but saw nothing but water. Darker water. A cloud must have found the sun. Funny, he didn't remember seeing any when he'd started.

As he checked his depth—ninety-five feet—another shadow passed like a dark wing, and now the water was definitely darker, almost if it were sunset up there.

Stover's heart began to hammer. Something very wrong here, and getting wronger by the second. He kicked toward the surface at a faster speed than usually recommended, but he didn't care. He hadn't been down long enough to absorb enough nitrogen to trigger the bends. And fuck the safety stop for the same reason.

Get me out of here!

And then it grew even darker, so dark he could barely see the wall to his right.

Terrified now, Stover began kicking frantically, bringing his arms into play to increase his velocity toward the surface shimmering so faintly above.

Another flicker of shadow and now even the shimmer was gone.

Stover heard himself whimper in fright through his regulator as he stroked and kicked upward. No! This wasn't happening—*couldn't* be happening. The sun doesn't just go out. Even if a total eclipse was going on, there'd be *some* light up there.

He was getting winded. Jesus, he should have reached the surface by now. Still kicking, he found his instrument pack and held it before his mask. He could barely make out the luminescent dial on the depth gauge, but he swore it read 120 feet.

He blinked a couple of times and rechecked the gauge. No question: 120 feet.

Had to be some mistake. He'd been ninety-five feet down when he'd started for the surface.

His checked his pressure gauge: 2000psi—he'd started off at 3100. He was breathing too fast, chewing up his air supply. Had to relax. No panic. *Think.*

Use the BCD—it called itself a buoyancy control device for a reason. Let *it* do the work.

Stover popped a little air into the vest's bladder and felt himself start to rise. He calmed himself, controlled his breathing. He was going to be all right. Somewhere was a rational explanation for all this, but he'd wait till he was on the surface before worrying about it.

He held up his depth gauge again, and damn, he couldn't see the dial. The water seemed to be eating the light. He fumbled in his vest pocket and pulled out his flash. The meager glow barely lit the dial, but he almost lost his mouthpiece when he saw the numbers—150 feet.

No! Not possible!

Nitrogen narcosis. That had to be it. Too much nitrogen made you giddy, crazy. Divers hallucinated, tore off their masks and regulators and tried to breathe water. The rapture of the deep, they called it.

But Stover felt no rapture, only panic. He pointed his flash above him and watched the bubbles rise. He was following his bubbles, that meant he was rising…so how could his depth gauge be reading deeper.

Air—Christ, he was down to 1000psi.

His weight belt. He carried eight pounds of lead around his waist to compensate for the body's natural buoyancy.

Dump it!

He grabbed the quick release buckle, pulled it free, let it go…

…and felt it slide away to his right. To his *right!*

He reached out and caught it, and yes, that was the way it was tugging him…to the right…perpendicular to the path of his bubbles.

But how…?

Oh, God, help! He was down here alone in the impenetrable dark with no idea of where was up or where was down. Somebody please—!

A rush of turbulence spun him half way around and tugged the belt from his grasp. What was that? A wave surge? That meant he was near the surface.

Stover turned and started swimming in the opposite direction, away from his bubble trail, toward where all his senses told him was *down.* Had to try it. Nothing else made sense. What did he have to lose?

Everything. He sobbed through his regulator. Absolutely every-thing.

Another swirl of turbulence, stronger this time, and Stover knew no wave or subsurface current had caused that. Something was moving out there in the dark, something *big*…big as the wall itself maybe.

But what could be that big? Something from the floor of the trench? God knew what could sleep in those deeps.

He redoubled his swimming efforts—toward the surface, he prayed. All he knew was that he had to keep going, keep moving, had to reach the surface before his tank ran out. The surface—air, *light!* Waiting somewhere ahead.

Had to be…

Oh, please! *Please!*

*　*　*

Please, Silvio thought as he made his first cast into the sparkling water. Please guide the fish to me.

He watched the fine mesh sink beneath the gentle waves, then hauled it back toward him. His heart leaped at he pulled the net from the water and saw the squirming, fluttering mass of silversides flashing in the sun.

They're back! The fish have come back!

"Granpa!" he cried joyously as he splashed toward the beach.

Granpa had been so quiet since that diver man had disappeared yesterday. Almost sad. Silvio had heard other adults comforting him, saying he had done what must be done.

Silvio didn't understand. All he knew was that the water was alive again—he had proof right here. And he hoped that would make Granpa smile again.

The Abalone Thief

Matthew V. Brockmeyer

T HERE is no internet access or cell phone service in this tiny cabin where I sit typing—perched on a cliff high above the Pacific Ocean—but I write this blog in the hopes that it might find some new civilization long after mankind is gone. May this be a testament of one man finding faith and religion after doubting for so long.

I am not spiritual or superstitious. I am a man of science. A student. A marine biologist. I never had what one would call 'faith' in anything resembling religion. To me, it's all math, everything, the strange mutations of life simply an exponential progression of evolution. But I am changed now, and as I watch the sacramental fires burning brightly on the beach below, and feel the awakening of the ancients echoing in my sleep and dreams, I realize man's time is over. It is a new beginning for beings much greater and more powerful than our own, and so I offer up a poem—a sacrament, a narrative—to the events that unfolded before the great awakening.

Let me start at the beginning …

* * *

I was a doctoral student at the University of California Santa Cruz working on my PhD in marine biology. Mollusks were my specialty. Specifically Haliotoidea Haliotis rufescens, or as they are known by their common name: red abalone. Abalone are an edible type of sea snail, a marine mollusk, single shell gastropod found in coastal waters around the globe.

They are considered a delicacy, their flesh being comparable to calamari. Red abalone, the largest and most prized of the species, are found only on the west coast of North America. Red abalone are not endangered but because of overfishing and acidification of oceans they have become rather scarce; that is why, California put a ban on the commercial fishing of them in the 1990s. They can be harvested for personal use only north of San Francisco, April through November, with a hiatus in July, and with a limit of only three a day and a total of eighteen a year.

Since I was writing my doctoral thesis on Haliotis rufescens it was deemed that I should spend the summer in a tiny fishing village called Shelter Cove. There I would study, measure, count and map the abalone and also report any suspicious activities relating to abalone poachers to the California Department of Fish and Wildlife. So, when the school semester ended in June, I packed up all my gear (scuba set, books, slides, specimen jars, microscopes) and strapped my kayak to the roof of my trusty old Subaru outback and headed north up highway 101 for Shelter Cove.

* * *

Shelter Cove is a quiet little hamlet on the coast of Humboldt County. The sign as you enter declares it, "An Island in Time". There is only one long, winding road in, which climbs up to nearly 2,000 feet as it transcends the summit of the King Range mountains and, conversely, only that one twisting, dangerous, cliff strewn road out. To the south is nothing but inaccessible shoreline facing steep cliffs, dotted with pockets of tiny beaches where the surf smashes down on jagged rocks, and deep, dangerous tide pools. To the north it is relatively the same, only a thin, potholed, dirt road winding over the cliffs slightly to the east.

The area was nicknamed The Lost Coast for this reason. The brave surfed and kayaked, but the place had a notorious riptide. Once an entire troop of tired Boy Scouts resting on the beach were swooped up by a sleeper wave and sucked out to their deaths in the ocean's depths.

My lodgings consisted of a small cabin, nothing more than a shack perched high on a cliff face. To the right I could see the boat launch, and the caged-in area where fishermen gutted their catch; a small stretch of beach lay there, where locals would drive their pick-up trucks onto the sandy shore and drink beer and barbeque. To my left was another stretch of beach called Deadman's, separated from the boat landing by a jutting cliff, and only accessible by ocean; the surfers have to paddle on their boards around the cliff face to get there.

The only internet access in Shelter Cove was from satellite, and the university was too cheap to put one in this shack they supplied. I couldn't even get cell service to use my phone as a hotspot. So when I had to upload my data on the University's Science Lab website, I would have to travel a few miles to a coffee shop in the lobby of an old hotel that had Wi-Fi. I managed to get cell phone service there, but only in the parking lot at the top of a steep embankment.

My closest neighbors lived down a rutted dirt road: a young single mother named Cathy and her nine-year-old daughter Suzy.

On my first day, as I was unfastening my ocean kayak from the roof of my Outback, Suzy rode up to me on her pink Huffy bike, an inquisitive look on her round little face.

"Who are you?" she asked in that bluntly curious manner children from small towns often have.

"My name's Theodore."

She nodded as if she approved, her eyes wandering along my equipment.

"What's all this stuff?"

"This is my scuba gear, these are specimen jars, and in these boxes are microscopes. With a microscope you can see really small stuff."

"I know what a microscope is. The sixth graders use them at my school. Why do you have all this stuff?"

"Well, I'm a scientist and I'm here to study abalone."

"Abalone? Oh gross, my Uncle Bob tries to make me eat that stuff every 4ᵗʰ of July. I don't like seafood."

"You live in a fishing village and you don't like seafood?"

"No. I don't like anything slimy, stinky, slippery, wet, or gross." She nodded in that same authoritative manner and then rode off, leaving me standing there laughing.

After that day, whenever Suzy rode past on her bike, she would stop and talk.

Though she claimed to hate slimy stuff—*"Oh!" she'd squeal, "Get it away!" when I held up a baby squid for her inspection*—she soon fell prey to the wonders of nature I'd bring back from the ocean for her amusement: marveling over a sea urchin, laughing uproariously at the awkward antics of a huge Dungeness crab, her big brown eyes gleaming as she stroked a starfish. I showed her the tiny holes in the mantle of the abalone's thick domed shell, the respiratory apertures, and explained to her how the sea snail vented water through them with its gills. And she stared into the microscope at macro algae as I explained how the abalone fed on them with the small median teeth of the radula. As her enthusiasm began to grow, I sensed a future marine biologist in the making and grew to truly love her visits.

THE ABALONE THIEF

* * *

I quickly settled into a routine of waking early and taking my kayak out for a dive. Even though it was summer, the water was cold, averaging about fifty degrees, and I had to wear a full wetsuit with a hood and gloves. I would pull my hood over my head, pull down my half mask, put my regulator's mouthpiece to my lips, and slip into the murky water to explore the underwater rock formations with my flashlight, looking for the domed, brick red shells— underwater homes of the abalone who had suctioned themselves to the craggy surfaces. I would count and measure them and then return to my kayak to scrawl out my findings.

It was peaceful work, but it could be dangerous. Every year, dozens of abalone divers wash up dead on the shores, smashed against the rocks by a swell or sucked into dark ocean caves. In 2004, an abalone diver, who ironically worked for the Recreational Fishing Alliance and was on a federal fisher management panel, was attacked by a great white shark while diving—not too far south from here—off the coast of Mendocino. When his friends first saw the huge cloud of blood in the water, they thought it was some kind of sick joke. They were gravely mistaken. His mauled and ravaged body washed up on shore a day later.

In the evenings, I would type out my statistics on my laptop, such as average abalone depth and proximity to the shore. And in my free time, I would wander the desolate shoreline exploring tide pools while sipping local micro-brews and sampling some of the fine cannabis for which the hills to the east of us were famous. I'd gaze up a sky streaked in pink and purple as the sun sank into the ocean, watching pelicans beat their wings in unison as the high-pitched wails of young harbor seals echoed off the towering bluffs. I was as happy as I've ever been.

By my third week, I had charted the entire shoreline.

At the end of the first month, I had made enough inroads with the notoriously secretive locals to be invited to a party. It was a wild event, held on a sprawling manor that sat on a grassy hillside with the ocean

407

spread out below it. It was the last day of June—and there would be a month-long hiatus for abalone harvesting all of July—so the abalone divers threw a feast. There were abalone wontons, abalone salsa, two kinds of abalone ceviche, abalone sausage, but the most scrumptious was abalone wrapped in dates, goat cheese, and bacon, and then deep fried; all this, as well as the standard fare of salmon, halibut, cod, and oysters. Bottles of wine from nearby vineyards littered the tables and ruddy-faced fishermen gathered around kegs of beer. Even the sheriff was there, in full uniform, and when someone passed him a joint, he puffed it and passed it on like everyone else.

* * *

A week into July I noticed a massive amount of abalone missing off the point of Deadmans.

Abalone concentrate where current flow causes drift seaweed to accumulate. The point of Deadmans was one of those places. Because abalone expand a large amount of energy when moving, they tend to stay in one location. Last week the point of Deadmans had been littered with abalone; now, there wasn't a single one left.

I shone my flashlight along the submerged rocks: nothing. I reached my hand into a narrow crevice, felt around the deep fissure for the telltale feel of those thick shells, cautious and aware that a swell could suck me into the narrow space, crush my bones, wedge me in and trap me: nothing.

Even if there wasn't a moratorium on abalone fishing, an absence of this size was unprecedented. This had to have been some kind of large-scale poaching operation. In San Francisco, in Chinatown, dried abalone sold as an aphrodisiac for two-thousand dollars a pound, so a haul this big could easily net over half a million dollars.

I alerted the fish and game department first. Then, figuring the poachers would move down into Deadman's cove—after having exhausted the supply on the point—and that they would most likely come in the early twilight hours, I decided to stakeout the beach.

The only means to Deadman's cove was over the ocean, so I hauled my kayak out to the boat launch, slipped it into the dark water, and paddled out as waves lapped at the concrete pier. There was a full moon, and fog rolled in thick across the relatively calm water.

A few pick-up trucks were still parked on the beach, surfers relaxing on the shore and having a few beers after a day of riding the waves.

I kayaked past the beach and made my way around the towering point of Deadman's, carefully avoiding the crescent of jagged rocks that rose out of the black water and fog. Paddling into the small cove, I rode the surf onto the beach. I pulled my kayak across the black, pebbly sand to the cliff face and found a small cave, nothing more than a craggy wrinkle in the bluff. I tucked my kayak inside, camouflaging it with driftwood, dried seaweed, and a few handfuls of sand. And then I hiked down the beach and set up my small one-person tent behind a large, washed up tree stump.

I hunkered down for the night, staying awake for a good while, but then drifted off to a light slumber, determined to awaken as early as I could.

In the middle of the night, I awoke to a garbled noise. I assumed it was the yapping of sea lions, but as sleep left me, I realized it was singing or chanting. I poked my head out of my tent and found the entire beach draped in a thick shroud of fog. In the distance was a mass of orange flames flicking up into the night sky—a huge bonfire—and silhouetted around it appeared to be a circle of people.

Was I dreaming?

I focused on the fire and, yes, around it was a ring of people in black hooded cloaks. They held hands and slowly circled around the flames, chanting, the fog swirling around their feet. On the outside of the circle were others—also in dark cloaks—as still and rooted to the beach as dark trees, holding torches. They couldn't see me, hidden in the fog behind the massive log.

It was definitely strange, and I watched curiously, assuming it was a bunch of teenagers getting weird, or maybe a coven of old hippy wiccans getting their witch on; neither would be unheard of in these parts. I watched the strange ritual for over an hour till they were done. Then they responsibly put out their impressive fire, burying its smoldering remains in sand (which impressed me), and wandered into a ravine where a trail took them up the cliff side.

So there was a way to Deadman's cove besides the ocean, I thought, knowing I would have to scope out that trail: maybe the abalone thief had used it to get to the beach.

Since the strange cultists, or whatever they were, had not waded out into the ocean, or given any sign of abalone poaching, I paid them no real mind—*live and let live, right?*—thinking it was just a bunch of kooks getting weird. Humboldt County was a weird place, after all, and Southern Humboldt even weirder.

I waited all day for signs of poachers, but saw nothing.

When the sun set and the sky began to grow dark, I packed my tent and retrieved my kayak. I had been on the beach for over twenty-four hours and had seen no sign of the abalone thief. I pushed my kayak into the surf, jumped in, and paddled back around the point.

* * *

That night, even though I was exhausted from my little expedition, I was restless and unable to sleep, tossing and turning in bed, so I went outside onto the cliff edge to smoke a joint and drink a beer to calm my nerves. A slight breeze stirred the leaves of the manzanita and dune tansy that lined the cliff edge. The salty smell of the sea hung heavy in the air.

It was then I noticed another fire burning on Deadman's below, and again tiny silhouettes of circling acolytes. I could even make out the torch bearers encircling the group. They were back, the local weirdos, probably a bunch of Goth or metal kids who listened to too much Marilyn Manson. Or maybe it was the beer and pot doing their tricks.

I yawned, feeling exhaustion take over.

That night, I had the first of the dreams …

I was in the ocean, deep underwater beneath the waves, examining the abalone. I ran my finger over their hard outer shells, imagining their fimbriated head lobes, their columellar muscles. It was breeding time, and their respiratory apertures were venting eggs and sperm into the ocean's water column. I had no scuba gear. I didn't need it. It felt as if I had some sort of gills, for I could feel the salty water swooshing in and out of me as it churned, cold and green.

Full of fascination, I studied the formations of rock and shell. And then a hand—almost human—crept over the craggy shelf, covered in pale-green scales, the fingertips ending in black claws. The hand reached out and took hold of a *Haliotis rufescens's* blood-red shell, and slowly peeled it off the rock. The slime trail the sea snail used to locomote left a viscous, oozing stain.

I gazed in wonder as a humanoid head rose over the rocky ledge, having a face with the features of a fish: gills, small holes where the nose should be, and massive black, empty eyes.

I stared on as the creature put the abalone to its mouth and with fanged teeth pulled the sea snail slowly out of its shell, and began chomping on it, swallowing in quick, eager gulps. Then it extended a long, thin, black tongue, forked like that of a snake, and licked the empty shell clean.

So this is the abalone thief, I thought to myself, with the calm and calculating mind of a scientist, without any fear whatsoever.

Out in the murky distance of the ocean floor appeared more of these creatures, hundreds of them. Maybe thousands. An army of scaled sea creatures feeding on the abalone.

They were gaining sustenance to strengthen themselves, I realized in the dream. They were preparing, readying themselves for the coming of a being greater than that which has ever roamed the earth. They await-

411

ed a great awakening.

In a massive epiphany, I realized the importance of their mission, and that I was needed: *I must join them, lend my psychic support*, and then I realized what the cult on the beach had been doing around those fires, their goal. And then I looked down at my hands, and found that they, too, were webbed and covered in scales. *I'm one of them.*

I awoke bathed in sweat, shivering, unable to dislodge the strange dream.

Obviously, the bizarre dream was silly, and had no bearing on reality.

Sea creatures poaching the abalone?

But something within me felt different, very *un*scientific. For the first time in my life, I felt an inexplicable spirituality: a desire to worship a higher being, a higher power. I also felt very scared, though I couldn't say why.

The next day, I searched for the path that led to Deadman's. I realized that from my cabin I could walk along the cliff edge, between clumps of coyote bush and dune tansy, and down a hill and into a gully that eventually formed into a steep, rocky ravine. This ravine led to the trail, nothing more than a deer or elk path.

On an impulse, I decided to stake it out again that night, to watch for that strange group of individuals gathering on the sand—for curiosity sake, to see what they were up to. *Maybe I could question them about the abalone thief*, I thought, in case they had any good intel on boats or strangers coming or going from the beach.

That night, sure enough, as I crept down to the ravine, a fire burned on the beach below. I positioned myself off the trail and above the cove, close enough to see the beach fairly well with binoculars. They were holding hands around the fire again, slowly rotating, most likely chanting the strange mumbo-jumbo I had heard the previous night. I tried to make out their faces, to see if I recognized anyone, but their hoods obscured their faces in dark shadows.

I scanned the gathering with my binoculars and noticed something strange, a sort of commotion against the cliff wall. Two hooded men held a struggling figure by flailing arms. I focused my binoculars and my gut clenched, my mouth dry.

It was Suzy, draped in some kind of white shroud, kicking and struggling.

As I watched helplessly from above, four of those cloaked maniacs held the girl as she squirmed. They pulled her toward the fire as another, one wearing a robe of crimson red, raised what appeared to be a knife, for it glinted in the moonlight, long and pointed.

What should I do? I wondered. *What* could *I do?*

There had to be at least a dozen of them down there.

Then it all happened so quickly: the knife came down, and Suzy's little voice—which I had come to know so well—cried out in pain and then silenced; her white cloak falling off her limp form. The crimson one hacked into her chest and pulled out a dark object I could only assume was her heart and brought it to his mouth. He then passed it on to the next cloaked figure.

Little Suzy's pale, naked body crumpled on the sand.

I have to do something. I have to call the cops.

I spun around and clawed myself up the ravine, and as I did my foot slipped and I sent a shower of pebbles and dirt to the mist-covered gully below. I froze, my mouth dust-dry, my hands clinging to the rock face.

Did they notice?

With a pounding heart, I started back up the ravine, and once I got to the top—out of breath and huffing—I sprinted over the bluffs to my Subaru. Fumbling with the keys, I started the engine and sped down the road, squealed into the parking lot of the Inn of The Lost Coast, leapt out of my car, and with sweaty, shaky hands dialed 911 on my iPhone at the only place I could find service. I told the operator what had happened, where I was, and she transferred me to the Sheriff's station.

"Calm down," he said, "and explain to me again what happened."

"They killed her," I said, "and ate her heart."

"Who?"

"Suzy Anderson."

"Suzy Anderson," the Sheriff said with recognition, "who lives on the corner of Toth and Steel Head with her mother Cathy?"

"Yes, I'm sure it was her. On the beach at Deadman's."

"You're saying she's been murdered?"

"Yes, by a cult in hoods on the beach! Yes. *Fuck.* They ate her goddamn heart. Are you even listening to me?"

"Okay, you said your name's Ted?"

"Yes."

"Okay, just calm down. Now, listen, what I want is for you to go on home. I'll check up on this and stop by your place after I get it all sorted out."

"But they killed her!"

"You go on home and I'll see you there later. Got it?"

I couldn't believe how nonchalant the sheriff was being, but what could I do? And had I even given him my address? I must have.

"Well, okay," I said, and the line went silent.

I stared down at the black device in my hand, knowing if I left this one small spot of land it would be rendered useless. I would be cut off from the rest of the world, alone, but what could I do? He was the sheriff. Even if he was an overweight pot-head, I had no choice but to listen to him. So I drove back to my cabin and waited.

I looked out over the cliff face, but the fire no longer burned. I drank a beer, tried to go over my data, but I was too shaken up. My hands shook so bad that I couldn't even manage to type numbers on the laptop.

Suddenly there was a knock at the door, startling the living shit out of me. It shook me to the bone. Wishing I had hightailed it out of there earlier—driven down that long and winding road, the only way in or out, never to come back—I crept to the door and cautiously pulled the curtain back from the window.

The sheriff stood at my doorstep with Suzy's mother Cathy, and a little girl.

I tentatively opened the door.

"This the girl you saw murdered?" the sheriff immediately barked.

The girl was the same age and height, with similar hair, but definitely *not* Suzy.

"No. This isn't her. I said 'Suzy Anderson.'"

The little girl looked up at Suzy's mother. "What's he talking about, Mama?"

"This is Suzy Anderson," the sheriff grumbled. "And this is her mother. Known both of 'em my whole goddamn life. Now what the hell is going on around here?"

"No. It's not," I said. "That is *not* Suzy. I saw them kill her!"

Somebody had to fucking believe me. I gazed up to Suzy's mother, who looked at me like I was crazy, and she clutched the little girl.

"Momma, Ted is scaring me!"

"Okay, you two go wait in the car," the sheriff said, waving Suzy's mother and the little girl along. He then put one of his big, beefy hands on my shoulder and pushed me into the cabin.

He closed the door behind him.

"Listen, mister, you're scaring that little girl half to death, and you need to tell me what the fuck is going on." He spoke into my ear, his breath hot on my face. "You on drugs? Doing a little meth to stay up all night and do your research?" He gazed suspiciously around the room at the specimen jars full of bugs and mollusks, the beakers of seawater samples and glass slides. "Do I gotta go get a warrant from my old buddy Judge Johnson and come back here and search this place?"

"Am I on *drugs?*" I shouted. "*Me?* I saw you smoking a joint at that party!"

The sheriff put his hands on his hips and laughed deeply, shook his head and regarded me with a big shit-eating smile. "Hell, son, that's for my glaucoma. I've had medical marijuana for over fifteen years. Was one of the first in the cove to get it. Everyone knows that."

I felt dizzy, the room beginning to slowly rotate.

"You all right, son? You don't look so good."

"But the fire on the beach. Did you check out the fire?"

"Yeah, I went down there. Looks like a bunch of kids was having a party, left fucking beer cans everywhere. But they're gone now."

"You went down? How?"

"How do you think? I walked."

"You know about the secret trail?"

"Secret trail? Damn, you're a dumb one, ain't 'ya? That fucking trail ain't secret. Everybody knows about that fucking trail."

I staggered back.

The sheriff pulled out a chair and pushed me down heavily onto it.

"I saw it," I said. "I saw them kill her. Kill her and eat her heart."

"You didn't see nothing, son. Sometimes the light of the moon reflecting off the water, or the sound and rhythm of the ocean, they can play tricks on your mind. Trust me, I've seen many a good man go a little crazy out here. Shelter Cove is known to have its share of crazies, and they didn't all start out that way."

I sunk my face into my hands and shook my head.

"But, I … but, I …"

He put his big mitt of a hand on my back in a tender way, gave me a pat and said, "Tell you what, son. You get some rest. Sleep on it. I'll come back tomorrow afternoon and we'll talk again. We'll take a little walk down to that beach. I'd like a walk with a scientist guy like you. Maybe you can tell me what some of that weird looking shit in the tide pools is."

How I fell asleep that night, I don't know. It was as if I had been drugged. I drank half a beer and a great lethargy fell over me. I simply stumbled to the bed with my eyes heavy and was asleep before my head hit the pillow.

The final dream came to me that night, along with a great realization ...

I was in the ocean with all the other deep ones, the cool salty water swooshing in and out of our gills, the light of the moon sending out great shafts of pale light through the deep, murky water. Of course, we were harvesting abalone. We ate some for our own strength, brought back armfuls of others for The Great One who slept in the ocean depths. The dark lord was awakening, and would soon rise in a fury of black leathery wings and tentacles.

Somehow, lost in that communal dream state, it all made sense: how the blood of the innocent could open psychic doors for ancient gods, portals to worlds beyond us. How, far from an innocent victim, Suzy was a necessary tribute to the dawning of a new age. What an honor and privilege her life had been. How we are all but mites and ants to the elder gods who rule this universe and how we are put here to serve them in their wrath and fury.

This sudden knowledge of the coming days cracked something in my head, shattered my heart and soul, and left me open and vacuous to the void. And in that dream, I was drowning, my gills useless, struggling to live and breathe, lost, deep below the sea in the restless ocean currents. Somewhere within me, I knew I had two choices: go mad from the revelation and let the indescribable horror of it all engulf my soul and drown in the chaos of insanity, or accept the deadly light and go forth into the peace and safety of a new dark age.

The next day, the sheriff arrived at my house, as he said he would.

He brought with him a box, and I opened it to find a large, black, hooded cloak. I slipped the cloak over my head, pulled up the hood, and together we walked down to the beach to start the fire and await the arrival of the others.

In the Shadow of the Equine

Kenneth W. Cain

WHEN I first heard the old man rambling about the sordid details of human nature, I intended to ignore him. My son and I had come to this island to camp. Not to find ourselves annoyed by unwarranted sermons.

"God sent his only son to die for our sins," the preacher said.

As I quickly learned, the man was becoming difficult to ignore. Still, I tried to block out his rantings.

We had come here hoping to behold the island's main attraction: the wild horses that sometimes graced the hillside across the small channel that separated this island from the next. Along the shore of the neighboring island sat a detailed metal statue that depicted a stallion in full stride. If we did not see a single living equine, the statue would have to suffice as our glowing reminiscence. That and the ranting of some old man, his face riddled with the scars of someone who once committed the crimes he now so passionately spoke out against. A pinch of skin creased between the man's eyebrows, showing his contempt for mankind and the sins they perpetrated against his God daily.

As I scanned the campground, I identified a dozen sites. Some people made their camps close to the channel that separated us from the equine habitat, so they wouldn't miss the wild beasts should they appear. Others took to more remote locations, away from the water altogether, perhaps to avoid the old man. Thirty to forty people made up the entire population of the island tonight, and while it was possible some didn't care about the wild horses, I was certain none had expected the lecture we all now endured.

His testimony seemed to amuse my son, Parker. Before I knew it, I found myself alone by the fire. My son's disappearance brought me instant shame for having lost sight of him. Why I should be so shallow to disapprove of my flesh and blood being allured by the word of God, I do not know, but I regretted letting him venture off on his own. It wasn't until a fight broke out that I realized how much. Before I could reach my son's side, my remorse intolerable, I observed the actions unfolding before me.

The first words I heard came from a younger man, one who obviously no longer cared for the good preacher's feverish judgments. This man antagonized the elder pastor. Dissatisfied by the preacher's response to his agitation, the man assaulted the preacher, driving the old man back with a forcible blow. Arms wailing, the crowd caught the old man, aiding him back to his feet.

Although outmatched, the blow did nothing to keep the older man from lifting a condemning finger to the skies. "You raise your fists in the sight of God almighty?"

I searched the mounting crowd of campers for my son while the preacher continued to riddle off passage after passage from the Bible. My eyes went wide with panic, my heart throbbing within my chest, concerned my son might get caught up in something bad. Relief washed over me when Parker came into view. He stood closer to the ensuing scuffle than I would have preferred, but he appeared safe.

The younger man lunged forward, knocking the elder man down by the channel. Seconds later, the crowd collapsed upon the brawl, likely enthralled by the spectacle, perhaps even hoping the young stud would shut the preacher up for the night. Only concern filled me though, as I'd lost sight of my son once again. Then, out of nowhere, Parker's ball cap billowed into the air, drifting back down into the throng as the fight grew in intensity. From my vantage point, I could hear blows landing, flesh pounding flesh, the sound of skin being slapped. Uncertainty overcame me, my anxiety doubled. It lasted but a few seconds, then the tussle broke up in the oddest fashion, without a single bark or threat. No one had stepped in to intervene. It simply ended.

What did I care? My only concern was for my son.

I found Parker sitting in the sand, his hat snug upon his head. He just stared at the strange old man, seeing what I should have noticed right away, that this man was trouble. At least Parker wasn't crying. And he hadn't screamed once. Perhaps that was the sole reason for me ignoring the others, the "Oh, my Lord" and "What is that?" expressions they made quietly while I tended to Parker. When I finally saw what they had, an empty feeling ate away inside of me like the atrocious fury of a brush fire through a drought-ridden field. The elder man's pallid face reflected the trepidation struck in Parker's eyes. Despite the man's dark-pitted eyes, filled with shadows, a hint of sunlight illuminated him as dusk approached. I might not have noticed the difference if not for that.

His eyes appeared sunken and vacant. Black pools of still water that reminded me of the back canals under the light of the brightest moon. I believed, in his mind, the preacher was readying to unleash the full power of his tongue, detailing the exploits of his Lord upon his adversary by riddling off apropos scripture. But that wasn't the case at all.

Finally, I noticed the thing the preacher now wore upon his head and realized why everyone had quieted.

At first, I thought it a hat. Perhaps some religious token, maybe even a ball cap like Parker's. Upon closer inspection, I identified the dangling tentacles waving back and forth in front of his face like thick strands of hair. It was some sea creature, maybe a starfish or perhaps a tiny octopus. But neither image of those creatures fit what I saw. This creature didn't struggle for breath as any sea critter would do to exist out of water. And, what I once thought a separate entity clinging to the elder man's skull, I stood corrected; seeing the infernal damnation had somehow attached itself to the man.

Had I been able to pull myself away from this astounding visual, I might have seen the younger man suffering an equal fate. Instead, I burst through the crowd, shaking away my shock and dismay to help the old man. I took the preacher into my arms and tried to ease him to the sand. However, we never reached the ground. The man stiffened like a board, and, with defiance, stood before us. To my utter surprise, he spoke.

"Now you see. The failings of mankind have forced God's hand! He recruits me to do his bidding."

The preacher's tone sounded deeper than before, making him far more convincing. And when that creature upon his head moved, I shivered. The creature's two precarious glowing eyes found me with a dull-red gaze. They continued to scan the rest of the crowd before closing, as if praying for their souls.

"Listen to our brother." The younger man who only just moments earlier had attacked the preacher now stood by his side, lifting his arms in praise. "I have seen the error of my ways. Be with us. Join us under God's protection."

The elder man opened his arms to the hesitant crowd, and I backed away toward Parker. I wanted nothing more than to escape this madness. As I retreated, I swayed my hands behind me, searching for my boy. When my hand brushed against his arm, I could feel him on the move.

I seized Parker and wrapped my arms around him, keeping him from joining the others.

To me, it appeared Parker was in a trance, not only dazed by the scuffle but also by the creatures attached to these men. Being skeptical, I was not one to place my faith so blindly. I watched one of the elder man's friends—the clear majority of the campers despite what I originally thought—join him by the water. This woman bowed before him and allowed him to push her down on her knees.

"I'm with you, Abraham," she said, willingly.

Abraham bent and scooped up some still ocean water in his palms. The liquid appeared alive in his hands. I saw a creature writhing and twisting there, eager for a place upon the woman's crown. With great care, Abraham rested the creature on her head. Within seconds, it had attached itself there with an audible sucking noise. The woman barely twitched, then she was on her feet, her eyes opened wide. The creature seemed to sense this and did the same, glowering upon the crowd for the first time from this vantage point. Then its eyes closed, as if deep in thought, and she sidled up beside Abraham.

"I feel his kindness," she said. "He is upon me, part of me. Do not be afraid, brothers and sisters."

One by one, the people who had come to this place with the weathered old man took a knee before him. They allowed Abraham to fetch a sea creature and place it on their heads, as if knighting each of them into God's kingdom when he did. After each crowning, they took their place by his side and spoke of their conviction.

I lingered, my son in my arms, both unable to pull away. Terror-stricken, I felt rooted to this place in the sand. In the background, waves crashed upon the shoreline of the nearby island, sounding faint and distant. The statue leered down at us, and I saw it then as a thing of sacrilege upon this Earth: a glorious golden calf.

Shaking my head, I glanced again and returned the statue to its original form. I sighed with relief.

Beyond the statue, a single horse looked our way. This was the reason we'd come. Yet, as it graced us with its presence, we could not stop gawking at the oddities unfolding nearby.

A shiver of cool washed over me as I realized the sun had set. We were now in the darkness of the ancient stone lighthouse, which shrouded the campsite in its eerie shadow. If it weren't for the lighthouse's lantern no longer functioning, its entrance locked, I might have sought refuge there. But I had yet to move. I gazed out across the short span of water to the shore from which we had arrived earlier. A ferry had brought us to this island, and it wouldn't return until daybreak. I considered attempting to swim the distance, my son in tow, but I didn't dare brave the water for fear one of those horrid creatures might secure itself to my head.

I could see our vehicle from here, back on the mainland. My eyes lingered upon it longingly. I believed it futile to even try. More so, there was no use in staying here and continuing to observe these people, the way they received these monstrosities. Already, they had converted more than half the population of the island. More waited.

The younger man's wife and child joined them in line. It reminded me of communion, where believers awaited their pastor to offer the Body of Christ to their lips. Frightened by what I saw, I tugged Parker back to our campsite, trying to regain some bearing on reality. Even then, I struggled to think of a way off this landmass, taking turns looking off in the distance toward our vehicle and then over to the lonely island, inhabited only by horses and the statue. I longed for either destination but could reach neither without the necessity of confronting the dark waters from which the creatures arose. Who knew what else lurked within those depths?

Of the two options, the equine island was closer, but there appeared no means of reaching it without a boat. I let my eyes linger upon the lighthouse, seeing the small balcony atop the structure and wondered if we might be able to dive across the channel. It wasn't so wide as it was deep, to discourage the horses from crossing. I was doubtful we could avoid the water, but maybe we could get close enough to the shore that we could scramble to the sandy beach unscathed.

I paced about our campsite and left Parker staring off at the phenomenon escalating nearby. Right then, I worried my son had been traumatized by what he'd been a party to. At his age, it would have affected me greatly. I tried to refocus my thoughts on breaking into the lighthouse. Then I realized, and I dug through our gear for the battered hammer I'd used to anchor the tent to the ground. I tore through our supplies, throwing them aside until I found that essential tool.

Hammer in hand, I held it to the sky like some mad warrior on the battlefield. The worst part was the thought I might end up using it for that specific purpose, to hurt someone or worse, kill them. It would be no easy undertaking reaching the top of the tower, especially if the others tried to impede our progress. Would these deranged people expect me to watch as my loving child knelt before their master to have some demon placed upon his head? To stand by while they took my son hostage and brought him into the fold? Not on my watch.

I tucked the hammer into my belt. Pulling at my son's arm, the dazed boy came with some hesitancy. We fled to the lighthouse where I studied the lock on the door, glancing back now and then at the crowd in the distance. Of the few who had resisted, they were now being forced to their knees before Abraham. Their cries of pain and terror went unheard by previous converts. Abraham smiled from ear to ear, content with his work. He dipped his hands into the water and fetched one of the tentacled creatures. As they finished converting all but my son and I, they turned their attention to us with horrifying indignation. The strange creatures upon their heads awoke, a field of glowing red eyes blinking off and on, as if communicating with one another.

Frozen by this terrifying visual, I couldn't follow through with the task I had set out to accomplish. I had to force myself to break free of this mesmerizing sight before I could bring my hammer down upon the lock. The first two tries proved unsuccessful. I grew impatient, uncertain if we would escape. On my third try, I found a glimmer of hope. The lock began to separate.

From the corner of my eye, I saw them approaching and something else too. It startled me enough to draw my attention away from the door. Parker was walking toward these people.

"Parker?" I struck the lock, this time without looking. "Parker, get back here!"

They were close, so I needed to break free of the door. I lunged out and snatched Parker's wrist. He staggered back when I tugged, and I quickly led him back to the door, where I released him and struck the lock as hard as I could, finally freeing it from the latch. With the door open, we entered the darkness of the lighthouse and closed the door behind us. A single foot kept it from closing.

"What are you doing, brother?" an unfamiliar man asked.

An unseen female voice added, "Are you not one of us, brother?"

I brought the hammer down on the toe of my enemy. No cry of agony resulted from the blow. When I looked into this man's face, I glimpsed the creature on his head, horrified by that red glowing gaze. As if unhurt by the attack, the man continued his effort to pry his way inside. The beast's glowing eyes regarded me, tentacles slithering about its host's face, sustaining a position close to the bone of the man's skull. A sick sucking sound rose from under its rubbery body, as if it were draining this man of the fluids in and around his brain. The man's face already appeared gaunt, his eyes sunken and dark. I shook loose, turned and found Parker at the base of the stairs. His silhouette stood motionless in the sliver of light stealing its way down from above.

Twisting the hammer in my hand, this time I brought the claw down upon the intruder's foot. After some effort, I forced the foot free of the door and shut it against the man's knuckles. Two severed fingers dropped to the floor, but no shriek of pain came from the man.

In the dark, I worked to maneuver the hammer through the handle and braced the door shut. It wouldn't hold long, but it would have to do. As we ascended the stairway, I heard them clawing and banging at the door. I surged up the spiral staircase, dragging Parker behind me, who seemed to resist more and more with each step.

At the top of the lighthouse, I spotted the moon. It offered enough light to see around the room. I examined the old cobwebbed lantern, observed the small balcony that extended out over the channel and then the equine island across the way. From this vantage point, it seemed even less likely I could reach the island safely by diving; let alone while holding Parker. Then I saw something else, a thing so out of place and unusual, I couldn't imagine what it could be.

A wooden handle stuck up from the shadows. I approached it, thinking I might have uncovered some weapon to better defend myself. Yet, when I began to draw it free, I discovered its true purpose. The long, wooden pole stretched far into the base of the lighthouse. It came away easily, but only if I walked it out toward the balcony. Once there, I identified a rusted metallic foothold at the base of the lighthouse and thought it the place to slide one end of the pole into, to vault across.

I pulled Parker in close as the lower door burst open. They were at the stairs by the time I freed the pole. With Parker by my side, I struggled to maneuver the pole into the foothold, missing several times before sticking it. They were at the top of the stairs, a few pairs of those unusual glowing eyes finding me in the darkness. Panic seized me, and I moved fast. Holding Parker tight, I lowered my chin against the top of his hat. With one arm, I took the top of the pole and thrust myself outward, off-balance, but at least on a path to reach the island.

We landed with a crash. Our bodies flung apart, I hurried to position myself on my elbows, and it surprised me to see Parker already upright, his hat still upon his head.

"You okay?" I asked.

No response. The boy sat staring back at the lighthouse, watching those awful blinking red eyes. I helped him to his feet, and placed a loving hand upon his head, taking a deep breath as our eyes met those across

429

the channel together, and then each other. That was when I felt it move.

I yanked away his cap and saw its glowing eyes. A scream started somewhere deep inside me, trying to force its way out. When I finally got it out, it came without end.

Parker's gaunt, black pools peered back at me with a distinct emptiness.

The moon, so full and bright in the sky, beamed down on the statue of the horse, casting an uncanny shadow upon me. It was there in the equine's shadow that I promised myself I would not harm my child.

As Parker lowered me to my knees, readying to make me one of them, I whispered this promise over and over in my thoughts. I wanted to make it truth but knew it would never be.

Thicker Than Water

Paul Kane

MEETING the family, it was a big step: a watershed.

Was there any wonder Naomi was getting cold feet now? Was getting jittery, in spite of the fact it had been her who'd insisted they should make this trip? That it was about time, after almost eight months of seeing Gerry? Only now the day was here, she wasn't so sure. What if they didn't like her? What if they hated her, in point of fact? Thought she was no good for him? Couldn't stand the idea of her being with their Gerry? Couldn't stand the sight of her?

Calm down, Naomi told herself. *Look at the scenery and relax for Heaven's sake!* And it was beautiful, it had to be said: all greens and yellows, rolling by the passenger window of the car as they drove along idyllic country lanes. In a year which had seen one of the harshest winters this country could remember (followed by devastating floods in its wake), Spring had finally arrived – indeed, it was so late it was almost giving way to the summer months.

She always did this, Naomi reminded herself when she found she still couldn't settle. Built things up, imagined the worst case scenario. Whatever could go wrong, would. Claimed she wasn't a pessimist, but rather a realist (painfully aware of the irony that every single pessimist in history had said the same). Couldn't allow herself to think things might work out, that she might well be happy this time, because of all the crap she'd been through before. All the heartache…

The abandonment.

Naomi shook her head. No, not today. She wouldn't allow it. Those dark thoughts could just go away, like dark clouds chased away by the sun. No rain, no storms today… or at least she hoped not.

It wasn't something she was used to doing, if she was honest: hoping. Not anymore, not these days. Well, not until Gerry came along anyway. Hadn't started out that way, she'd been quite a hopeful child she thought, always looking to the future but enjoying the present. However, losing both parents in quick succession at an early age – one to a debilitating disease and the other to suicide, she was told – tended to shake your confidence in the world. Destabilise you. A series of orphanages and foster carers later (no real homes, no real families) and she was out there being battered by the cold, harsh reality of the world; always the quiet one at university, then at work. The outsider. Never getting into the madness that was around her: the nightclubs, the drink and drugs…the casual sex.

Naomi told herself it was because she was better than that, she had more respect for herself than to get into the whole 'one night stand' or 'try before you buy' thing. And there was an element of that involved; *of course* there was. Saving herself, they used to call it. But she was also scared. Scared of the consequences of letting go, of losing herself, of opening up – opening her *heart* – to someone.

There had been boys, naturally. Someone who looked like she did was bound to get hit on (a natural beauty, apparently), and there were some she'd genuinely liked – those she thought liked her back for who she was. But when it came right down to it, none of them had waited until she was ready to *be* with them; to give herself to them. And the few times she had been stupid enough to almost—

Let's just say she'd learned her lesson, but good. Life wasn't a fucking Disney movie. You put your trust in people, they invariably let you down, deserted you.

Until she'd found Gerry.

She looked across at him now, sitting there in the driving seat of his sporty silver BMW, shifting gears as they crested a hill, and Naomi couldn't help smiling. He'd been good for her, Gerry. Was perfect for her. Naomi's smile faded at the thought of that word. Nobody was perfect, let alone someone who might be interested in her…

Might be interested? He adores *you, you idiot!*

Still, nobody was perfect…but he was just so, so…perfect! She couldn't think of another word that adequately described him. The fine blond hair, which matched his eyebrows. Perfect cheekbones, pouting lips any male model would think themselves lucky to be blessed with, such penetrating eyes. And that body of his…

It had been the first thing she'd seen of him. Sleek and lean, yet well-muscled, he was the only thing Naomi had actually noticed as she'd walked out through the back doors of the hotel at the tail end of last summer; part of the holiday she'd promised herself and saved up for after another miserable few months.

In front of her was the pool she'd been intending to read and sunbathe beside – though she was hardly likely to get a tan when she was mostly covered by that sarong and floppy hat. But absolutely no swimming, she hated getting wet…or was it just the stripping off to a bathing suit? Anyway, when she looked up, she'd been expecting to see the usual gaggle of children messing about, the older folk splashing around as they did their lengths for exercise. But instead she'd seen *him*, Gerry, gliding through the water arm over arm, as fluid as the liquid he was immersed in; flesh glistening in the sunlight, making him look as oiled as those strippers she'd witnessed once at a colleague's bachelorette party. But as impressive as those guys had been, they had nothing on Gerry – as she soon saw when he reached the other end of the pool and climbed out.

Realising she was in the way of a couple who were also looking to find a recliner, she'd taken a step – a couple of steps – only to almost trip and stumble. Naomi had never been the most spatially aware of people, never been one to mind her surroundings, but distracted like this… *Get a grip!* Naomi had told herself. She'd continued on to a seat nearby, trying not to make those glimpses through her sunglasses so obvious. Stealing glances at Gerry (not that she'd known his name then), aware that many of the other ladies present were doing the same. A woman walked past him with breasts that looked like they'd been pumped up at a garage, barely contained in that minuscule bikini top, skin as tanned as leather. But, as she'd taken her seat, Naomi had been impressed and pleasantly surprised by the way he'd hardly noticed that bimbo – continuing to towel himself down after the dip. The woman had walked on by, looking back only once with a frown, clearly not used to being ignored.

Naomi had settled down with her book, looking up a few times to see what the man was doing – sighing when she saw him heading to the bar on the other side of the pool. Resigning herself to the fact that he was probably meeting someone: girlfriend, fiancée, wife. Which seemed to make sense when she saw him with two drinks, two green cocktails with fruit and straws sticking out of the top.

But as amazed as she'd been by his ignorance of the plastic woman, she was even more surprised when he walked over in her direction with those drinks. *Oh no,* she thought, *please don't be one of those cheesy chat-up guys! Don't ruin such a* perfect *fantasy for me, that inside you're something more. That beneath the surface you're—*

Then he'd walked right by her, just like the enhanced woman had done with him, and it had actually physically pained Naomi. She felt that loss so deeply. Worse than finding out he was a dick would be not knowing him at all. So, when he'd skirted around, doubling back and placing one of the cocktails on the table beside her, she let out another sigh – this time of relief. When they talked about this afterwards, Gerry would always say that he'd been aware of her as soon as she appeared – though she knew he couldn't have seen her, he'd been too busy swimming, head in and out of the water as his arms propelled him further away from her. But that was his story and he was sticking to it.

During that first conversation, after he'd asked politely if he could sit on the recliner next to her, she'd found him confident but not overly so. Charming, though not to the point of nausea. But most importantly, very easy to talk to – and an extremely good listener. He hadn't used any lines, hadn't overly flattered her, he'd simply been Gerry. And Gerry had been lovely.

In the time between their parting and the dinner date they'd arranged for later at a nearby five star restaurant, she'd wound herself up again, thinking of all the things that might be wrong with him. He was cheating on said girlfriend, fiancée, wife – had kids, a family he wasn't telling her about. He was a rapist, a multiple murderer with a string of convictions to his name… He worked in the seedy underbelly of the city, pimping out his women to slavering perverts and was going to get her hooked on heroin so she could be next!

All ridiculous, as she'd discovered later. Gerry worked in shipping, imports and exports, above board with legitimate offices, which he offered to show her around (proof enough, she thought to herself, that he had nothing to hide in this department). He negotiated deals, travelled a fair bit – and was also doing very well for himself, thanks (she saw just *how* well with that first piece of jewellery he gave her, a gold necklace – an unusual design, but she liked it). He hadn't needed to save up for the hotel, no siree! Not that any of this mattered to her, she'd never been impressed by wealth; it was simply a bonus that he might be a good provider.

She'd found out then that Gerry had been determined to do

well, help out his family who – in a reversal of his fortunes – hadn't been doing so well of late.

'Only *just* keeping their heads above water, in fact,' Gerry had told her sadly after finishing his salmon en orwar, staring down into his glass of Perrier as if to further illustrate his statement.

'Oh, I'm…I'm really sorry to hear that,' she'd told him, at the same time envious of this connection he had to them; something she had never really known. She sensed a closeness when he talked about them, his mom and pop, his older brother. His childhood, being taught to fish from the jetty off the side of their house – it sounded idyllic. But she also felt that sadness when he'd had to go out into the world to make ends meet, that he hadn't been able to stay closer to home. In the end, after much deliberation, they'd made his choice for him, insisting he went out there and did them proud.

'You must be happy that you're now in a position to help them out though, surely?' Naomi had said, starting her dessert of chocolate torte, and he'd nodded.

'Yeah, I guess…' But he'd shaken his head at that point and moved the conversation along, asking her more about herself; her life, her job, her hobbies. 'I want to know *everything* about you, Naomi Jackson.' His smile spoke of genuine interest. Nobody had ever wanted to know everything about her. Nobody had ever been that bothered. So she'd talked, figuring what did she have to lose?

Hope? She could lose the hope that was starting to build inside of her, the hope that had continued to build all this time. Since she'd found Gerry; since they'd found each other.

Girlfriend, fiancée…wife? (Family?)

The hope she still had as she sat in the car, travelling towards their destination. But all that could be dashed, everything they'd been through in the last few months could be undone if Gerry's folks didn't take to her. It might change everything, leave everything in ruins. She asked herself again, why had she insisted on this trip? Especially when

Gerry had been so uncertain himself.

Maybe she shouldn't have asked him what was wrong when he'd looked so down that day. But Naomi had to know, wanted to make sure it wasn't something she'd done or said. 'No, no… it's just that… Well, my folks have been in touch and… Naomi, I hadn't told them about you yet. I just wanted to keep you to myself a bit longer. Now they want to meet you.'

She'd be lying if she said she didn't feel hurt by the first bit, but figured she could sort of understand it. All this time together, just the two of them, had been wonderful – the best of her life.

'I didn't want to… Not till I was absolutely sure about you. About how I felt.'

'And?' she'd asked, biting her lip.

He'd looked at her blankly then, questioning.

'How *do* you feel?' she'd clarified.

'Oh…' He'd smiled then. 'That's easy. I worship you, Princess – you know that.' The use of his nickname made her melt inside (just like Disney), especially used in that context. 'You should do. I've never…well, I've never felt this way about anyone else.'

Anyone else, all the others she'd been instantly jealous of as soon as he'd told her. There had been girls before, were bound to have been, but Gerry promised never anything serious, they hadn't really meant anything to him. Not like this. Now he was with her exclusively – which made her happy. She didn't want to share him with anybody. And it had been his idea to wait, not rush her – though they'd come close a few times, *really* close; her closest yet – because, as Gerry said, they were about more than that.

Never felt this way about anyone else.

Now she just wanted to feel that connection to his family as well, that belonging. Wasn't too much to ask, was it? But, as Gerry had warned her, meeting them would definitely 'change things'. The next big step (girlfriend, fiancée…wife; giving her that family), which could go either way.

'It's just that they can be a bit set in their ways,' Gerry had informed her again only the other day. 'Old fashioned, holding on to the past.'

'Anybody would think you don't *want* me to meet them or something?' Naomi had said.

'It's not that, it's…' Gerry nodded. 'Hey, I'm sure they'll love you as much as I do. You're very special, you know.'

She'd beamed at that.

But here, now, those doubts – fuelled by Gerry's words – were resurfacing. Worst case scenarios: the mother thought she was a gold-digging whore; the father said they'd disown Gerry if he didn't tell her to get lost; the brother was a monster, was everything she hated in a guy–

No! She willed away the dark thoughts. Easier said than done, when the weather seemed to be turning against her as well. Clear, bright blue skies had now given way to a dull grey horizon with ink-blot clouds that looked like shadows. Even the pretty fields that she'd been staring at in a daze had become strange bog-like stretches of land. When had that happened?

"Enjoy your nap?" asked Gerry.

Naomi didn't even know she'd been asleep. She'd been worrying about what was going to happen when they arrived and then… Telling herself to relax, she'd obviously relaxed a little *too* much. Now she'd woken up and everything had taken on a strange dull cast, as if the film of her life had just switched from technicolour to black and white.

'How long was I…?'

'Not long. But it's actually not that far now,' Gerry informed her. She couldn't tell if he was pleased about that or not. She knew he was looking forward to seeing the brood again, but maybe under different circumstances? Maybe not with *her* in tow. Perhaps they were mad that he'd kept Naomi from them all this time? Moms in particular could be like that, couldn't they? Not that she'd know. Not that she'd ever really known her mom properly before she'd—

(Blood, water. The razor… How she always pictured it in her head.)

No, stop it. You're doing it again. Stop that right now!

The car carried on, and through the window now she could see the coastline – the angry sea running parallel to them. Rain suddenly started up, striking the windscreen and causing her to jump in her seat.

Battered by cold, hard reality.

'You okay?' asked Gerry, flicking on the wipers, and she gave a small tip of the head.

But she wasn't. Far from it. The downpour was making her even more anxious, doing little to calm her nerves. By the time they were driving down what Gerry called 'Federal Street', the rain had settled into a steady drizzle and it was almost dark – in spite of the fact it was only afternoon and the nights were supposed to be getting lighter by the day.

Dark clouds, dark thoughts…dark place.

Gerry was going to take her on a little guided tour first, he informed her. Naomi wondered if he was just putting off the crunch time, but that was okay – she wasn't in any rush to sink their relationship (she'd already decided in her head by now that this whole thing would be a washout). He pointed out landmarks such as the old churches that surrounded the New Church Green, the hall on her right where the townspeople used to hold gatherings, the old town square and what had once been the refinery, before they passed over the bridge which ran across the Manuxet River and he drew her attention to the lighthouse in the distance. When he spoke about his hometown, it was with such a sense of pride, of belonging, and Naomi wished that she could experience that as well. Because all she saw was a place that might well have been really nice once, but was now in a state of disrepair and ruin.

Everything in ruins…

Gerry was clearly seeing all of this through rose-tinted glasses; as if through the eyes of a child. And that smell! Naomi did her best not to crinkle up her nose, but the aroma was so strong. A distinctive stench of the ocean, of fish.

Touring round the town square, Gerry showed her the old fire station, the Gilman House hotel, a couple of stores and what had been his favourite restaurant when he'd lived here. 'Makes the best calamari in the northeast,' Gerry stated; he did so love his seafood. It looked like a bit of a dive to Naomi, but she said nothing.

Gerry's family lived down by the sea itself, she knew, and Naomi peered over when he pointed to exactly where. It looked like some of the worst houses were situated down there, their wood and brickwork plagued by rot. He hadn't been kidding when he said they were barely keeping their heads above water…in every respect. She couldn't help gaping across at him then.

'Your parents…live down *there?*'

'Ahuh,' he said simply.

She looked again, thinking maybe she was missing something – but she wasn't. If anything this closer scrutiny showed her that the problem was even more severe; some of the houses were tilting, as if they were about to simply fall into the waves and be swept away.

I know Gerry said they weren't doing so well, but this is ridiculous, thought Naomi. All that money he earned, how little of it must he have been sending back home for them to still be living in such squalor? In such a town as this?

A ghost town, for in all the time they'd been driving around, Naomi had yet to spot one person. Yes, it was raining and she didn't blame anyone for staying indoors in such poor weather, but that didn't explain why the buildings all looked deserted as well. There were no lights on, nothing. It was almost as if they wanted to purposefully give the impression here that nobody was home.

She was about to mention this to Gerry when he suddenly turned and said, 'I guess we'd better be heading off to see them then.'

Naomi nodded slowly, feeling her guts tying themselves into knots.

Gerry steered the BMW down a couple more streets, then parked it up by the side of the road, telling her they'd have to walk from there.

'You're kidding?' she said, looking up through the window. It was pouring and she hadn't thought to bring either a coat or an umbrella with her; it had been such lovely weather when they'd set off. Her summer dress would be drenched in seconds. But Gerry didn't appear to be thinking about that, probably more bothered about what his family would think of her – plus it wasn't his fault he couldn't get any closer. In any event, he was out of the car now, slamming the door, so she followed him.

Gerry had his head tilted back, eyes closed. He seemed to be relishing the water on his face, unlike her. She coughed and he finally noticed her, standing there soaking. 'Sorry,' he said and came round to escort her down the path.

She almost slipped once or twice, especially in those shoes she'd chosen for the occasion – nothing too flashy, but they did have heels. Naomi was grabbing on to Gerry for dear life by the time they arrived at the house: a ramshackle affair that looked like it was on its last legs, with slates missing from the roof. While off to the side was the small jetty Gerry had mentioned: uneven and held up by posts, it dipped and tilted and apparently led nowhere but *into* the sea itself.

Once again it looked like there was nobody at home.

Naomi got under the cover of the porch, but the rain still wasn't bothering Gerry. Her hair and make-up – which she'd taken so long over – would be pretty much ruined now; so much for first impressions. 'Oh Gerry, whatever are they going to think of me?'

'You look wonderful to me,' he replied. 'Perfect.'

Nobody was perfect, especially not her. She must look like a drowned dog.

'It's just a bit of water, they won't mind.'

Naomi stared at the battered door. 'I'm not so sure this is a good id—' she began, but it was already opening with a creak. Or maybe it was just finally collapsing, hanging there as it was on one hinge. The thought crossed her mind again that Gerry should be sending them more money, either that or relocating them completely. Getting them out of this god-forsaken hole.

'Let me go in first,' said Gerry, which she had no problem with at all. Then he was gone, swallowed up inside that darkness…

Dark place, dark house…

…and Naomi realised she was standing on the doorstep, what little there was of it, on her own.

Abandoned.

When she did peer inside she saw that there was a light coming from somewhere, flickering and casting shadows. The faint glow of a candle? Maybe there had been a power failure? Or it had been cut off for lack of payment? The putrid paintwork of the place was peeling, or perhaps it was just trying to flee the walls – she knew how it felt. The carpet she was treading on was damp and squishy, but there was little wonder as the rain was finding its way into the house from above. Perhaps that was what had caused the power to go off?

'H-Hello?' she called out, her eyes readjusting to the gloom.

Then she saw them, standing there in the hallway, Gerry next to a woman who was smaller than him, her outline dumpy. Mom-shaped. The dress she had on covered most of her body, made from a thick material. Her hair was tied up in a bun on top of her head, but various strands had leapt out and floated on the air – giving her a look of being submerged. Her smile was warm, though, welcoming. It was her who had the candle, stuck inside some kind of ornate holder.

'Over here,' Gerry said, unnecessarily.

Naomi continued to make her way inside, passing a set of what looked like the most rickety of stairs heading to an upper level.

'Mother, this is my…special friend. Miss Naomi Jackson.'

Naomi frowned. She'd been wondering how he would introduce her, when the time came. Is that what she was, then? His friend? You worshipped your *friends*, did you? She was savvy enough to know it was because of the old-fashioned thing, though, the being set in your ways. At least he'd called her special.

But still, *friend*?

The woman stepped forward, stooping, shambling almost in a way that made Naomi want to cover the distance between them to save her the trouble.

'Gerald's told us so much about yer,' said the woman, free hand out.

Naomi shook it tentatively. 'Really?'

'Oh yes.' Her strange accent made it sound like 'yersh'. Her eyes twinkled in the light from the candle as she looked Naomi up and down.

'I'm really sorry about… I must look such a mess,' she said to the woman.

'Naw, yer beautiful dear,' said Gerry's mother.

That made Naomi smile. 'I hate to ask this when I've only just arrived, but I don't suppose there's anywhere I can…you know, freshen up at all?'

'Course,' said the woman. 'Yer've had a long drive.' She pointed to the stairs. 'Just at the top there, oh and yer'd better take this.'

She handed Naomi the candle, which she took with a thanks. Then they went off, leaving her alone again, standing there staring up the stairs she'd have to negotiate. Naomi took her time, very nearly putting her foot through one slat, but eventually she reached the top. The bathroom was opposite, just as Gerry's mom had promised, so she carried the candle through and locked the door behind her.

Water was dripping on her from above, but ironically when she'd placed the candle down and out of its reach, she couldn't get any to come through the taps attached to the chipped sink. The pipes just rattled and gurgled. She sighed when she looked in the cracked mirror in front of her, it was like the Joker staring back. So she picked up a towel in an attempt to dry herself – only to realise that they were just as sopping as she was. Naomi could at least use it to wipe away the worst of the make up, she told herself.

As she was putting it back on the rail, she found herself gazing across at the old bath in the corner. Her mind went immediately to her own mother, as she pictured her in one very similar, water slopping over the edge as she held up the razor. Drawing it across veins, redness dripping into—

Blood, water. Water, blood.

She shook her head, snatching up the candle again and leaving as quickly as she could. The whole exercise had been a bit of a waste of time really, she looked almost as bad as when she arrived.

Naomi had one foot on the step to come down, when a big splash from the ceiling put out the candle, with no way to relight it. She swallowed, hard – left the candle and its holder on the stairs, as she figured she'd definitely need both hands now. By the time she was halfway down she was on the verge of tears. None of this was going right at all, and to make things worse she could hear raised voices coming from what had to be the lounge – where Gerry and his mom had retreated. She strained to listen, but couldn't tell what the argument was about; all she could make out were male voices – one of them Gerry's.

Though in her heart of hearts Naomi knew it had to be about her. Everything she feared was coming true.

When she reached the bottom and stepped off (a big step) her foot landed in a puddle of some kind. 'What the…' she managed. Instead of just damp, the carpet was now under at least a couple of inches of water.

Naomi swished through this…

Was there any wonder she was getting cold feet now?

…feeling her way around into the corridor again: aiming for the lounge. The arguing stopped when she reached the doorway and turned the corner. There were a couple more candles in this room, but these were no match for the murk inside. She could just about make out the shapes in there: Gerry with his mom again; and next to her was a seated figure, a man. Naomi squinted, thought that he had no legs at first, then realised he had a blanket over his knees. He was sitting next to a table which had one candle on it, so he was better illuminated than the others.

He was dressed in a suit that looked like it had seen its better days in the previous century – *early* in the previous century. The skin on his face was tight and shiny, as if it was about to rip at any moment, especially at the corners of his down-turned mouth – except for the flesh underneath his eyes, which hung in bags below two white, bulging orbs. He was virtually hairless, didn't even have eyebrows, but then, thought Naomi, what kind of hair could possibly grow on that head anyway.

Gerry's father, had to be.

'Come on in girly, don't be shy,' said the man, beckoning with a hand. He sounded like he'd been gargling with those words, before spitting them out. 'Let's have a look atch-yer!'

Gerry said nothing.

Naomi ventured in a little further, suddenly all too aware of how her dress was clinging to her, especially when the man's bulbous eyes lingered a little too long on her breasts. What started off as folding her arms across her chest soon turned into a hug she was giving herself, and not just because she was freezing.

'Ahh,' gurgled the man. 'Preddy you are.' He licked his lips; it made Naomi feel physically sick.

'Now, now, Benjamin,' said his wife. 'Stop that.'

No, stop it. You're doing it again. Stop that right now!

'Yer scaring the poor lass.'

'N-Not at all,' said Naomi, struggling to keep the hitch from her voice.

The woman picked something up from the table with a rattle and a clink. 'Would yer like a cup of tea, dear?' she asked Naomi, obviously deciding that the girl was going to get one regardless. 'I've just this minute made a pot.' Again she was shambling across the space, forcing

Naomi to meet her halfway, taking the chipped cup and saucer from her hands.

Naomi looked down at the tea. It was thick and gelatinous… and, though it was hard to tell, there looked to be a greenish tint to it. The woman was waiting there expectantly. Naomi grimaced, took a sip. It was cold – very cold – and tasted brackish, but she forced it down with another hard swallow. It almost came immediately back up when she saw how the remaining liquid had settled back in the base of the cup, like mud in a river.

'Somethin' to eat, p'haps?'

Naomi thought of the calamari back at the restaurant Gerry had talked about and held up a hand. 'Oh, no…no thank you. I'm really not—'

'So whet d'ya think of our little town then?' This from the father, who practically coughed out the last of his phlegmy question.

'Erm…it's…er…'

'Bin around since the seventeenth century, it has. A hugely successful seaport at one time or annuther.'

'It…' Naomi was struggling for something to say. 'Forgive me, but it seems to have fallen on…dark times of late.'

All three of them looked at her, almost in unison – and as if to silently say that they might never, ever forgive her.

'There's bin darker,' said Gerry's mother, pulling back to join her son and husband again, wading through the water.

The older folk splashing around…

'But we endure,' her husband added. 'We endure. Like as after that nasty business back in the '30s, the persecutions. Some hid, some escaped. But if it hadn't a bin for the War comin' along when it did… people forgettin'.' He shook his head. 'We survived those hardships anyway. What few of us were left, we endured.'

'Let's not terk about all that,' Gerry's mom cut in, trying to change the subject. 'Let's terk about yer two. All very excitin', I have t'say."

More than just a friend then, if it was exciting?

'I'm… That is, Gerry's…' Naomi began. 'You must be very proud of him, all he's achieved.'

'Aye,' said the mother, 'he's a good lad. Loyal, y'know?'

She nodded; Naomi knew that. Everything else aside, all this aside, she was well aware of that. 'Proud of how well he's done for himself out there, with his business and everything?'

The man in the chair laughed suddenly then, a sort of strange gurgling noise. 'For 'imself?'

'Father,' said Gerry. 'Please don't.'

'You think 'e did all that by 'imself.'

'Benjamin!' This was the mother again. 'Now's not the time nor the place.'

'I'm sorry, but I can't go on pretendin',' said the father. "im there thinkin' he could just keep her to 'imself like that.' He coughed that watery cough again.

Naomi was frowning once more. So they *were* mad about him keeping quiet? Had that been what the argument had been about?

'Thinkin' we'd be all right about the two of 'em!'

No, this was all about her not fitting in again, wasn't it? Just like uni, like work. About her being an outsider, not being accepted. For God's sake, if you couldn't even be accepted here, by these people… But how would Gerry feel about that, she could see the way he…worshipped this place. Had basically been forced to leave it so he could try and bail his folks out – the water rising, up to her calves now – but what did his dad mean when he said Gerry hadn't done it on his own?

Naomi was already going through what would happen now in her head. The long drive home in silence, promises to call her when they got back and then never seeing Gerry again. Her ringing and leaving messages on his phone, getting increasingly desperate. Alone, deserted.

No girlfriend, no fiancée, no wife…no *family*.

Taking the razor, following her mother's lead?

Blood, water…

She couldn't have been more wrong. Couldn't have thought up this worst case scenario in a million years.

'Neglectin' his duties, his responsibilities,' the father continued on with his rant. And Naomi found she couldn't bite her tongue any longer, no matter how things transpired.

'Gerry is the most caring, responsible man I've ever known!' she blurted out. 'I love him – and he loves me. Don't you?'

Gerry remained silent.

'*Caring?*' said his father. 'Did yer care about them other lasses yer brought back here, eh? About what happened to 'em?'

All the others, the ones she'd been so jealous of. So they'd been brought back here too? And what had happened with them, he'd dumped them when he got bored? Gerry had told her she was special, that's why she'd wanted his family's approval so much. But now she wasn't so sure, about him or them.

Life wasn't a fucking Disney movie. You put your trust in people, they invariably let you down.

Their relationship was sinking…

'Naomi, it isn't how you think,' said Gerry now, finally finding his voice. Making to move towards her, then stopping.

'Aye, you know the way it has to be, boy. I teld yer. You've known all along how this ends, yer were just kiddin' yerself.'

'Breedin' or sacrifice,' said Gerry sombrely, his tones starting to match his family's.

Pimping out his women… His mother thinking she was a gold-digging whore…

Rapist… multiple murderer…

Yer scaring the poor lass.

'*What?*' shouted Naomi, thinking she'd misheard.

'It's just like I taught 'im, just like fishin',' gargled the father.

'Cept young Gerald's the bait now. We sent him out there, funded him with what was left of the town's gold. He brought back what we needed.'

A good provider.

Naomi looked across at Gerry's mom now, and she nodded. 'It's true I'm afraid, dear.'

Town's gold… Naomi's hand went to her necklace and its symbol.

'Well, we couldn't send out his brother – lookin' the way he does. As natural as thet might be.' The father pointed behind her and Naomi turned, screamed when she saw what had risen up out of the water.

Never been one to mind her surroundings…

Devastating floods in its wake…

Blood, water…

So close she could do nothing *but* see him: the naked thing in front of her. He had the same bulging eyes as the father, but these were much more prominent in the middle of a face that could only be described as hideous, framed by fine, slicked back hair. Lumps and bumps covered the skin, while a set of flapping gills opened and closed on his neck. The mouth was much wider than any normal person's, framed by blubbery lips, and when the 'man' parted these he revealed row upon row of needle-like teeth.

Gerry's brother, the monster.

Natural-looking…

'Came on 'im powerfully quick, it did,' Gerry's pop continued. 'But it gits us all in the end.'

Naomi tried to run past the brother, had to save herself, but he grabbed her, spun her so she was facing the room again – then wrapped two strong arms around her, the webbed fingers gripping.

'Be careful!' shouted Gerry. 'Don't hurt her!'

'Yer still don't get it do you, she's not yours!' snapped Gerry's pop.

'Not *just* yours,' corrected Gerry's mother.

Didn't want to share her…

'Yer…' She pointed at Naomi. 'Yer belong to all o' us. And yet to none o' us. He wasn't lying when he said yer were special, y'know.'

'You're all insane!' shrieked Naomi. She was still asleep in the car, hadn't woken up – and this was all some crazy dream, some nightmare brought on by her fears. Or something in that horrible tea she'd been given? Maybe she'd been poisoned?

'Can't you feel it, child?' the woman asked her. (Inside you're something more… Beneath the surface you're…) 'It's how yer two found each other, it's why yer felt the way you did."

The connection? Was that what this crazy bitch was talking about?

Was aware *of her as soon as she'd appeared.*

Always the outsider…

'Yer blood, dear. It's in yer *blood!* Yer heritage is the same as Gerald's."

Her father's disease? ('Natural as that might be…') Her mother not being able to live with the consequences…?

Blood in the water…

Some hid, some escaped.

Escaped and carried on with their lives elsewhere, loving other people, having families, having children… She'd never known her grandparents, had barely known her parents, but what if—

The woman shambled back over again and held Naomi's necklace up to examine it. 'The symbol of The Order. He would be pleased… *He* will be pleased. The one yer have been saving y'self for all this time.'

'What… what the fuck are you talking about?'

'Yer know. Deep down yer know, child… Princess.'

Girlfriend, fiancée, wife… family.

Naomi fought against the knowledge, just as she fought against Gerry's brother, but the woman was right. About the blood, about her family. She'd always wanted one and now she'd got it, hadn't she? One who adored her, in fact. It just hadn't been what she'd expected. And she realised then, that she hadn't been abandoned after all.

'A fine catch,' burbled the father.

He'd done them proud…

She was perfect.

The older man's blanket was slipping from his lap and now Naomi could see the many tentacles he had for legs, writhing and sliding over each other. She almost screamed again.

'And thers much to do,' said the mother. 'A festival t'prepare for, an end of the dark times to look orward to.'

Dark times, dark clouds. Dark shadows… They had hung over this place for such a long time, and would continue to do so for many years to come. Nothing they ever did would change that, not even giving her to—

A big step… a watershed…

She suddenly felt very, very scared: of letting go, of losing herself, of opening up to—

She'd feel the loss so deeply…

Naomi tried to imagine what would happen to her, the worst case scenario, but nothing would come. It couldn't, it was beyond her imagination.

All she could see now in her mind's eye was the redness, so thick. Thicker than—

Water… The water *and* the blood.

The blood and…

The water.

Walking With the Ghosts of Pier 13

Brian James Freeman

On these hot summer days at the beginning of the New World, we're all walking with the dead.

The thought repeated in Jeremy's mind as he approached his destination, his tattered sandals smacking against the splintered boardwalk with every step.

It *was* a hot summer day. Sweltering, in fact. The sun filled the sky, bright and scorching, and the blinding light reflected off the sand like a field of broken glass. The wooden walkway formed the boundary between the beach and the town, and the planks were timeworn and weathered. Pieces of litter traveled on the breeze.

There weren't many people around—just a dirty bum here, a dirtier teenager there, along with a few elderly couples who probably had nowhere else they could go.

Most of the shops were closed, their heavy hurricane doors bolted shut. Normally the boardwalk and the beach and the small town of Penny Bay would be packed with people this time of year—couples on holiday, families with kids, retirees parked at Pat's House of Bingo, beautiful singles mixing and mingling on the sand all day before heading to the Bermuda Bar and Grill to party all night—but not today. Not now.

In the distance, Pier 13 floated on top of thick supports like a mirage. The summer microcosm stretched over the beach and the changing tides and the fingertips of the Atlantic Ocean. The wooden roller coaster at the end of the pier soared high above everything else, and although the ride's thirteen cars were racing along the track, there were no people strapped into the bright red seats. The padded safety bars only restrained the humid, sticky air.

Jeremy inhaled the salty sea breeze while the waves continued breaking and foaming and retreating as they had for millions of years. The water was blue and beautiful. The sky was clear, nearly perfect. This day might be the dictionary definition of summer perfection, yet there was barely anyone around.

Jeremy could easily recall what this place had been like years ago: the cascading noise of the crowd and the shopkeepers selling their wares, the drone of the small airplanes pulling advertising banners across the sky, the kids running and playing in the surf, the young couples holding hands, the scent of sunscreen and pizza, the soft-serve ice cream cones, and everything else that had made the beach his summer home as a child, when his family lived in New York City and spent the hottest days of the year relaxing here without a care in the world.

Everything real from those memories was gone, but their ghosts remained.

* * *

There was a wooden ticket booth at the entrance to Pier 13 with an old-fashioned painted sign displaying the various rates for the amusement park. Locked inside was a kid Jeremy's age, his attention fully occupied by the cell phone he probably wasn't supposed to have with him while working.

"One please," Jeremy said.

The kid jerked back in surprise and looked up from his phone. His skin was acne-scarred, his arms tanned. His red uniform hadn't been washed in days and the expression on his face was tired and bored and maybe a little scared, too.

"One ticket or one All-Day Pass?" the kid asked. A rusted metal fan blew humid air around the booth and a battered radio sat by the ordering window. From the radio came the voice of a solemn reporter reading something off the newswire. The kid added, "We don't got many rides running. Most everyone quit."

"Why are you still hanging on?"

The kid shrugged. There was a bead of sweat forming on the end of his pimpled nose, near the metal stud protruding from a self-piercing that looked infected. "Don't got nowhere else to go."

"Yeah, ain't that the truth. Just one ticket, please."

* * *

Jeremy roamed the pier, passing the empty game booths and the empty rides, with the sound of the ocean forever in the background. When he finally found another human being, it was an older woman dressed not in a park uniform but a grimy Sunday dress. She was running the merry-go-swings every three minutes on schedule. There were no riders.

The woman sat under the direct gaze of the summer sun even though there was a bent umbrella on the boards nearby. She looked wired and tired, but Jeremy approached her anyway.

"Nice day, isn't it?" Jeremy said. The woman twitched and recoiled as if she had been struck.

"Is that you, Ralph?" she called, her voice raw and aching, her eyes searching wildly, as if she were blind. She looked right past Jeremy twice before she focused on him, her gaze like red-rimmed razors. "Goddamn you, Ralph! Why'd you bring the kids today! Goddamn you, Ralph!"

Backing away, Jeremy kept his eyes locked on her until he could turn a corner, and then he continued to explore the park, certain he would never say another word to the half-human husks haunting this wounded place.

*   *   *

But soon Jeremy found a man of Middle Eastern descent selling funnel cakes, and again he couldn't help himself. He approached the food cart, feeling sorry for the man standing in the blazing sun, dressed in his neatly-pressed red uniform. He probably had a family to support and couldn't consider leaving this crappy job. Where else would he find work these days?

"I loved these as a kid," Jeremy said as his funnel cake was prepared. He smiled.

The man didn't reply and Jeremy could see the worry in his eyes. He probably did have a family. Maybe he was thinking about them, wondering if they'd be alive when he got home... or if he'd make it home alive. Those questions were on everyone's mind when they walked out their front door these days, so it was easy for Jeremy to imagine what the man might be thinking.

The man said nothing as he accepted Jeremy's payment and handed over the funnel cake. Jeremy thanked him and dropped his change into the plastic jar with the word TIPS written in blue marker on a piece of masking tape.

As Jeremy continued walking to the real destination he had in mind for his visit today, he took a bite of the funnel cake and grimaced. He had certainly loved them as a child, but the sweetness tasted overwhelming and almost bitter to him.

He dropped the rest of the sugary confection into a blue trash barrel. A flock of seagulls descended in a pack, squawking wildly at each other, tearing the funnel cake apart and then turning on each other, sending feathers and bloody beaks flying. Their caws and screams and squeals pierced the shimmering air.

They had grown dependent on humans for their food, but there had been slim pickings lately and that dependence was leading to madness.

*   *   *

When Jeremy reached the wooden roller coaster known as the Screamin' Demon, he stood and watched it run a few times. Thirteen empty cars, chasing each other in circles, always starting at the same place and ending where they had begun their journey. Jeremy could relate.

The mid-day sun baked the roller coaster's fading paint. The metal cars seemed to sizzle. The peak of the first hill was at the very end of the pier, hanging out over the ocean, and Jeremy thought it was the most beautiful view in the world.

He and his brother Jason had ridden this ride hundreds or maybe thousands of times when they were kids. They had loved the Screamin' Demon, embracing the fear and the thrill and the rush that hit you directly in the gut as you barreled down the first hill toward the ocean. The next turn of the tracks was just out of view, giving you the momentary sensation of certain doom when all you could see was the water. Then the cars whooshed to the left, back onto the pier and climbing the second hill.

The sign over the entrance to the ride's loading line was blackened and scarred. The railed walkway was twisted and burned. Heavy plywood covered a jagged hole in the wooden planks. Yet the Screamin' Demon was still open for business.

The red cars were painted with bright yellow flames and grinning skulls and they roared by on the tracks, the grinding of metal on metal louder than normal. There was no one around to make any other noise: no shrieking riders, no chatting parents waiting on their kids, no teenage park employees pushing carts filled with ice and bottles of soda shouting about how refreshing an ice-cold Coca-Cola would taste. There were simply the cars on the track and the ocean below and nothing else.

"You want to ride?"

The teenage girl running the Screamin' Demon sat on a three-legged stool under a tattered yellow umbrella that had been patched back together with duct tape. She sounded hesitant and lonely at the same time. She probably felt the need for human contact, Jeremy guessed, just like he did. She was pretty in a simple, girl-at-the-beach kind of way with her blonde hair tied up in a ponytail, her blue eyes, her tanned skin.

She added, "Just two tickets."

"Oh, I only have one. When I was a kid, it only cost one."

"That's fine," the girl said, whispering as if there were someone to overhear them. "I really don't care. I'm not coming back tomorrow."

"Quitting?"

"Why bother? My paycheck is probably gonna bounce."

"I haven't been on this pier in a long time."

"Since you were a kid, right?"

"Yeah, my brother and I loved this place."

"Well, I hate it. My boyfriend and I are running away tonight."

"Where you going?"

"Anywhere but this shitty town. Maybe north."

"That's what Jason and I said."

"You queer?"

"No, Jason was my brother."

"Where's he now?"

"Dead."

"Oh."

"He was here last month, waiting in line."

"Oh." She glanced at the twisted metal. "I'm sorry."

"Yeah," Jeremy said, handing the girl his only ticket. She ripped it in half as he moved to take his seat. "I didn't really think the park would be open, let alone with the coaster running."

"You heard the President, didn't you?"

"Go on living, right?"

"Like nothing has changed," the girl said. "Like there's nothing to fear."

"You scared?"

"Out of my mind."

*   *   *

At the top of the first hill, the roller coaster paused for just a second, allowing Jeremy to take in the full view.

The sparkling waves of the Atlantic had conquered the world from below his feet to the horizon a hundred miles in the distance where the ocean met the beautiful, clear sky. The dazzling rays of sunlight formed an elongated diamond of fire on the dancing water.

Jeremy's skin tingled in the heat even as the ocean wind whipped past him. He could hear the cries of the seagulls and the crashing of the waves against the supports under the pier. He inhaled the salty sea air, conjuring a million memories of summers long gone, awakening a million ghosts who still lived here, and only here, and only in the summer.

"I miss you, bro," Jeremy whispered, and then his stomach rushed into his throat as the roller coaster roared down the hill, the cars screaming along the tracks like the demons they were named after.

He laughed like a kid.

He laughed to release the pain.

He laughed because he had to laugh or his heart would explode in anger and sadness.

When the ride was over, he was crying, and the laughter had been lost to the waves.

*   *   *

"You okay?" the Screamin' Demon girl asked. "Oh man, you didn't knock your teeth on the safety bar or something, did you?"

"No, I'm all right," Jeremy said, removing his seat belt, pushing the safety bar up quickly so he could exit. He wiped away the tears with his hand.

"You're scared, too, aren't you?"

"Yeah, a little."

"We're probably safe, you know? I mean, they hit Disney in Florida the other day. They're kind of moving away from us. We might be safe."

"What did they do at Disney?"

"Man, don't you watch TV?"

"Not lately."

"Well, yeah, a bunch of them landed in a small plane and started shooting everyone with machine guns. Park security was useless. All of the news channels showed it live, too, from a local traffic helicopter. At least nine hundred people dead, lots of kids. The bastards were dressed in black masks and heavy jackets and when they were finally cornered by the Army, they blew themselves up."

"Makes the bombing here look like small potatoes, doesn't it?" Jeremy asked, considering the scarred sign, the twisted metal, and the plywood covering the hole in the pier.

This was where Jason died.

What had he been thinking right before the bomb went off? Had he been watching the ride following the tracks? The beautiful teenage girls in their bikinis? The seagulls swooping down for pieces of pretzels on the boards?

What had been going through his mind?

Jeremy thought about what it must have been like to be standing in line, enjoying the day even though you were packed in with hundreds of other sweaty summer revelers, waiting for your turn when...

Well, what happened next? It wouldn't be like the movies where the audience knows what's coming thanks to the music cues.

No, not at all like that.

There would be no warning.

If you were really close to the bomb, the force would shred your body instantly. You wouldn't hear or feel anything. One second you'd be alive and smiling or laughing or shading your eyes from the sun or wiping your brow or memorizing the curves of the hot chick in front of you in line, and the next second you'd be dead. You'd never have to worry about how your death would affect your family. You'd never have to think about the things you were going to miss or the things you would never get to do or see.

If you were a few yards away from the blast, maybe you'd hear the thunder a split second before the explosion ripped the life from your body, but there wouldn't be time for you to truly understand what was happening. A loud sound and then darkness. No pain, no thoughts.

But if you were a dozen yards away, you might be one of the unlucky ones who was wounded severely enough to bleed to death. You might hang on for minutes or hours, knowing you were doomed once the confusion settled. You'd be frightened and angry and you'd spend your last moments facing down every regret you ever had while wondering how the people you loved would take the news of your death. There would be a lot of pain and not all of it would be from the shrapnel that tore your flesh apart, severing your limbs or blinding you. Then, slowly, darkness and death.

"Small potatoes?" the girl finally said, studying Jeremy with fierce eyes. "Well, do you see all the reporters and cops? They're gone, right?

We're old news. No one cares about the people slaughtered here because there's already bigger and bloodier stories to report."

"I'm sorry. Did you know anyone who died?"

"A couple of employees. One of my best friends. I think he went instantly. Didn't feel nothing." A tear had trickled past the girl's nose. Jeremy stared at her for a moment, at the tear, at her blue eyes, and he wondered if her eyes were bluer than the sea. "At least I want to believe that. Probably isn't true. I miss him. Sometimes I feel like he's still here."

"Yeah, we're all walking with the dead now, I think," Jeremy said and turned away.

The girl called after him, but he didn't look back.

* * *

"Was it worth the trip?" the kid in the ticket booth asked as Jeremy exited Pier 13 and stepped onto the boardwalk.

"Huh?"

"Coming to see what they did."

"Yeah, I guess so. My bro is dead. Died here."

"I'm sorry." The kid with the pierced nose sounded sincere enough. "Don't worry, the Army will get the fuckers."

"Anything new on the news?" Jeremy nodded at the battered radio sitting in the booth where the fan continued to blow warm air around.

"Not really, just that the Prez is pretty sure this has something to do with the Middle East. Some new group of extremists with a crazy name. Makes sense to me. You'd have to be really fucked in the head like those desert-baked bastards to strap bombs to your chest and kill innocent people."

"Fucked in the head, or just really angry."

"Yeah, I guess. But angry about what? What could make someone so pissed they'd do this shit?"

"Maybe they don't think they'll be heard any other way. You never know what angry young men will do. It's a fucked-up world."

Before the kid in the ticket booth could respond, the radio crackled. He adjusted the tuning and turned up the volume.

An earnest reporter stated: "Earlier today, the Department of Homeland Security alerted police in eight major cities about possible threats to theaters. The threat is said to be credible, although no other details were provided and citizens are urged to not change their plans based on this report."

"This shit won't never end, will it?" the kid in the booth asked.

Jeremy shook his head. "No, I don't think so. Not for a long time."

"Where you going now?"

"New York City. I used to live there, with my brother and our parents. It's been a long time since I've been back."

"Just stay away from Broadway, man. You heard the news."

Jeremy didn't reply as he walked away, the boardwalk creaking under his steps. His face was coated in sweat. The sun was cooking him, burning him up, and the heat felt good.

He thought of Jason and the beach and the wooden roller coaster and the ocean and the summers of years past.

He thought about anger, and angry young men who feel they must go to extremes to achieve their goals.

He thought about Jason at Pier 13.

He thought about the explosion and the deaths and the future to come.

He thought about the last thing Jason had said to him the day he died: "On these hot summer days at the beginning of the New World, we're all walking with the dead. Love you, bro. Miss you."

Jeremy thought about all the people who might be attending a Broadway show this weekend, following the President's advice to go on living life like the world was just fine and dandy and not coming to an end all around them.

How could anyone look the other way so easily while the nation's body count rose so quickly?

How could anyone pretend everything hadn't changed forever?

How could they go on living their same old lives when so many people were already dead?

Jeremy walked and he remembered the people he had loved and lost. He remembered the ghosts haunting him, the ghosts he loved, the ghosts guiding him.

Some of those ghosts still lived on Pier 13, some only lived in his heart, but he could feel them everywhere he went.

He vowed to never forget his brother, no matter what happened.

Jeremy thought about anger and angry young men with a cause, and he walked with the ghosts, and he prepared himself for one last trip to New York.

About the Authors

Elizabeth Massie is an eighth generation Virginian, has been writing professionally since 1984. Most of her works are in the horror/suspense genre (Sineater, Hell Gate, Desper Hollow, Wire Mesh Mothers, Homeplace, Afraid, It, Watching, Naked on the Edge, and more), but she also writes mainstream fiction (Homegrown), media tie-ins (The Tudors, Versailles, Buffy the Vampire Slayer, Dark Shadows), educational materials for American history textbooks, and poetry (Night Benedictions). Her first novel, Sineater, and her novella "Stephen" have both won Bram Stoker Awards from the Horror Writers Association. Her Tudors novelization (Season 3) won the Scribe award. Her short fiction can be found in numerous anthologies and several years' best collections. She is currently working on Ameri-Scares (Crossroad Press) a 50 novel series of spooky books for middle grade readers (age 8-12), a series which is currently in development for television by Warner Horizon and LuckyChap. She also continues to work on new horror novels and short stories for adults. Check out her lead story in Freedom of Screech, edited by Craig Spector.

Justin M. Woodward is an author from Dothan, Alabama. He lives in Headland, Alabama with his wife and two small boys. He currently has three novels: The Variant (a sci/fi horror thriller), Candy (a noir crime/comedy/thriller) and Tamer Animals (a coming of age horror tale). He specializes in dark fiction grounded in reality with nods to Chuck Palahniuk, Robert Mccammon, and Richard Laymon. You can find out more on his website www.justinmwoodward.com and his Facebook group "Justin M. Woodward Fan Club" where he does frequent giveaways.

Tony Bertauski is a USA Today Bestselling author. He grew up in the Midwest where the land is flat and the corn is tall. The winters are bleak and cold. He hated winters. He always wanted to write. But writing was hard. And he wasn't very disciplined. The cold had nothing to do with that, but it didn't help. That changed in grad school. After several attempts at a proposal, his major advisor was losing money on red ink and advised him to figure it out. Somehow, he did. A few years later, Socket Greeny was born. It was a science fiction trilogy that was gritty and thoughtful. That was 2005. He has been practicing Zen since he was 23 years old. A daily meditator, he wants to instill something meaningful in his stories that appeals to a young adult crowd as well as adult. Think Hunger Games. He hadn't planned to write fiction, didn't even know if he had anymore stories in him after Socket Greeny. Turns out he did. www.bertauski.com

Gene O'Neill is best known as a multi-award nominated writer of science fiction, fantasy, and horror fiction. O'Neill's professional writing career began after completing the Clarion West Writers Workshop in 1979. Since that time, over 100 of his works have been published. His short story work has appeared in Cemetery Dance Magazine, Twilight Zone Magazine, The Magazine of Fantasy and Science Fiction, and many more. O'Neill has had many occupations besides writing including postal worker, contract specialist for AAFES, college basketball player, amateur boxer, United States Marine, right-of-way agent, and vice president of a small manufacturing plant. He also holds two degrees from California State University, Sacramento and University of Minnesota. He currently writes full-time and lives in the Napa Valley with his wife, Kay.

William F. Aicher is an independent author who primarily writes thrillers and what he describes as "philosophical fiction" who holds degrees in journalism and philosophy from the University of Wisconsin. A proponent of the value of creative work, he is also a champion of intellectual property rights. A Wisconsin native, he currently lives in northern Mississippi with his wife, three sons, and a pair of lazy cats.

Kevin J Kennedy is a horror author & editor from Scotland. He is the co-author of You Only Get One Shot & Screechers, and the publisher of several bestselling anthology series; Collected Horror Shorts, 100 Word Horrors & The Horror Collection, as well as the stand-alone anthology Carnival of Horror. His stories have been featured in many other notable books in the horror genre. He is an active member of the Horror Writers Association. He lives in a small town in Scotland, with his wife and his two little cats, Carlito and Ariel. Keep up to date with new releases or contact Kevin through his website: www.kevinjkennedy.co.uk

Mark Matthews is a graduate of the University of Michigan and a licensed professional counselor who has worked in behavioral health for over 20 years. He is the author of On the Lips of Children, All Smoke Rises, and Milk-Blood, as well as the editor of Garden of Fiends: Tales of Addiction Horror. Matthews has run 13 marathons, and has two running based books, The Jade Rabbit and Chasing the Dragon. He lives near Detroit with his wife and two daughters. Reach him at WickedRunPress@gmail.com

Lisa Morton is a screenwriter, author of non-fiction books, award-winning prose writer, and Halloween expert whose work was described by the American Library Association's READERS' ADVISORY GUIDE TO HORROR as "consistently dark, unsettling, and frightening". She began her career in Hollywood, co-writing the cult favorite MEET THE HOLLOWHEADS (on which she also served as Associate Producer), but soon made a successful transition into writing short works of horror. After appearing in dozens of anthologies and magazines, including THE MAMMOTH BOOK OF DRACULA, DARK DELICACIES, THE MUSEUM OF HORRORS, and CEMETERY DANCE Magazine, in 2010 her first novel, THE CASTLE OF LOS ANGELES, was published to critical acclaim, appearing on numerous "Best of the Year" lists. Her book THE HALLOWEEN ENCYCLOPEDIA (now in an expanded second edition) was described by REFERENCE & RESEARCH BOOK NEWS as "the most complete reference to the holiday available," and Lisa has been interviewed on The History Channel and in THE WALL STREET JOURNAL as a Halloween authority. She is a six-time winner of the Bram Stoker Award®, a recipient of the Black Quill Award, and winner of the 2012 Grand Prize from the Halloween Book Festival. A lifelong Californian, she lives in North Hills, California, and can be found online at www.lisamorton.com.

Neil Gaiman - I make things up and write them down. Which takes us from comics (like SANDMAN) to novels (like ANANSI BOYS and AMERICAN GODS) to short stories (some are collected in SMOKE AND MIRRORS) and to occasionally movies (like Dave McKean's MIRRORMASK or the NEVERWHERE TV series, or my own short film A SHORT FILM ABOUT JOHN BOLTON). In my spare time I read and sleep and eat and try to keep the blog at www.neilgaiman.com more or less up to date.

Andrew Lennon is the bestselling author of Every Twisted Thought and several other horror/thriller books. He has featured in various best-selling anthologies, and is successfully becoming a recognized name in horror and thriller writing. Andrew is a happily married man living in the North West of England with his wife Hazel & their children. Having always been a big horror fan, Andrew spent a lot of his time watching scary movies or playing scary games, but it wasn't until his mid-twenties that he developed a taste for reading. His wife, also being a big horror fan, had a very large Stephen King collection which Andrew began to consume. Once hooked into reading horror, he started to discover new authors like Thomas Ligotti & Ryan C Thomas. It was while reading work from these authors that he decided to try writing something himself and there came the idea for "A Life to Waste" He enjoys spending his time with his family and watching or reading new horror. For more information please go to www.andrewlennon.co.uk

John Skipp is a New York Times bestselling author, editor, film director, zombie godfather, compulsive collaborator, musical pornographer, black-humored optimist and all-around Renaissance mutant. His early novels from the 1980s and 90s pioneered the graphic, subversive, high-energy form known as splatterpunk. His anthology Book of the Dead was the beginning of modern post-Romero zombie literature. His work ranges from hardcore horror to whacked-out Bizarro to scathing social satire, all brought together with his trademark cinematic pace and intimate, unflinching, unmistakable voice. From young agitator to hilarious elder statesman, Skipp remains one of genre fiction's most colorful characters.

Jason Stokes is an author and artist living in the mountains of western North Carolina. When he's not at work in the studio he's raising a pair of indomitable Cornish Rex cats and travelling the world with his wife and best friend, Anna.

Chad Lutzke lives in Michigan with his wife and children. For over two decades, he has been a contributor to several different outlets in the independent music and film scene, offering articles, reviews, and artwork. He has written for Famous Monsters of Filmland, Rue Morgue, Cemetery Dance, and Scream magazine. He's had a few dozen stories published, and some of his books include: OF FOSTER HOMES & FLIES, WALLFLOWER, STIRRING THE SHEETS, SKULLFACE BOY, and OUT BEHIND THE BARN co-written with John Boden. Lutzke's work as been praised by authors Jack Ketchum, James Newman, Stephen Graham Jones and his own mother. He can be found lurking the internet at www.chadlutzke.com.

Hanson Oak - I am a writer who works across platforms. From film and television to novels and short stories, I want to tell tales and connect people through them. I've been writing my whole life and, though it has gotten darker over the years, I want my work to cross all genres because no good story is just one thing. In short, Hanson Oak is the manifestation of my decades of writing, experiences, travels, and dreams. I hope to connect with you and have you join me on the adventures I've completed and those I've yet to go on. In the end, that is the magic of writing and storytelling, the intangible link with the audience.

Stephen King is the author of more than fifty books, all of them worldwide bestsellers. His first crime thriller featuring Bill Hodges, MR MERCEDES, won the Edgar Award for best novel and was shortlisted for the CWA Gold Dagger Award. Both MR MERCEDES and END OF WATCH received the Goodreads Choice Award for the Best Mystery and Thriller of 2014 and 2016 respectively. King co-wrote the bestselling novel Sleeping Beauties with his son Owen King, and many of King's books have been turned into celebrated films and television series including The Shawshank Redemption, Gerald's Game and It. King was the recipient of America's prestigious 2014 National Medal of Arts and the

2003 National Book Foundation Medal for distinguished contribution to American Letters. In 2007 he also won the Grand Master Award from the Mystery Writers of America. He lives with his wife Tabitha King in Maine.

John R. Little is an award-winning author of suspense, dark fantasy, and horror. He currently lives in Ayr, a small town near Kitchener, Canada, and is always at work on his next book. John has published 20 books to date, and most of them are available here. He hopes you enjoy his work.

Kelli Owen is the author of more than a dozen books--her fiction spanning from thriller and psychological horror, to an occasional bloodbath, and the even rarer happy ending. She was an editor and reviewer for over a decade, and has attended countless writing conventions, participated on dozens of panels, and spoken at the CIA Headquarters in Langley, VA regarding both her writing and the field in general. Born and raised in Wisconsin, she now lives in Destination, Pennsylvania. For more information, please visit her website at kelliowen.com

John Palisano has had short fiction appear in many places. Check out: Dark Discoveries, Horror Library, Darkness On The Edge, Lovecraft eZine, Phobophobias, Terror Tales, Harvest Hill, Halloween Spirits, Chiral Mad, Midnight Walk, Halloween Tales, and many other publications. His non-fiction has appeared in FANGORIA and DARK DISCOVERIES, where he's interviewed folks like Robert Englund, director Rob Hall, and Corey Taylor from Slipknot. NERVES is now available as an Amazon exclusive. Print copies of the first edition are still available from third party sellers. DUST OF THE DEAD and GHOST HEART are novels originally published from Samhain Publishing. They will be available in updated versions soon! His work has been cited by the Bram Stoker Award® four times. "Available Light" was nominated for the Bram

Stoker Award® in 2013. "The Geminis" was nominated for the Bram Stoker Award® in 2014. "Splinterette" was nominated for the Bram Stoker Award® in 2015. "Happy Joe's Rest Stop" won the Bram Stoker Award® in 2016. John's had a colorful history. He began writing at an early age, with his first publications in college fanzines and newspapers at Emerson in Boston. He's worked for over a decade in Hollywood for people like Ridley Scott and Marcus Nispel. He's recently been working as a ghost-screenwriter and has seen much success with over two dozen short story sales and his novels and short fiction continue gaining critical and reader acclaim. You can visit him at: www.johnpalisano.com

Richard Chizmar is the author of Gwendy's Button Box (with Stephen King) and A Long December, which was nominated for numerous awards. His fiction has appeared in dozens of publications, including Ellery Queen's Mystery Magazine and multiple editions of The Year's 25 Finest Crime and Mystery Stories. He has won two World Fantasy awards, four International Horror Guild awards, and the HWA's Board of Trustee's award. Presented here is the original short story WIDOW'S POINT that he cowrote with his son **Billy Chizmar**.

Mark Allan Gunnells loves to tell stories. He has since he was a kid, penning one-page tales that were Twilight Zone knockoffs. He likes to think he has gotten a little better since then. He loves reader feedback, and above all he loves telling stories. He lives in Greer, SC, with his husband Craig A. Metcalf.

Todd Keisling is the author of A Life Transparent, The Liminal Man, and the critically-acclaimed novella, The Final Reconciliation. His most recent releases are The Smile Factory and the horror collection, Ugly Little Things: Collected Horrors, available now from Crystal Lake Publishing. He lives somewhere in the wilds of Pennsylvania with his family where he is at work on his next novel.

John Boden lives a stones throw from Three Mile Island with his wonderful wife and sons. A baker by day, he spends his off time writing, working on Shock Totem or watching M*A*S*H re-runs. He likes Diet Pepsi, cheeseburgers, heavy metal and sports ferocious sideburns. While his output as a writer is fairly sporadic, it has a bit of a reputation for being unique.

Ray Garton - Since I was eight years old, all I've wanted to be was a writer, and since 1984, I have been fortunate enough to spend my life writing full time. I've written over 60 books -- novels and novellas in the horror and suspense genres, collections of short stories, movie novelizations and TV tie-ins -- with more in the works. My readers have made it possible for me to indulge my love of writing and I get a tremendous amount of joy out of communicating with them, which I've been able to do on various social media outlets such as Facebook and Twitter. You can also visit my home on the internet at http://www.raygartononline.com. This is the place to find out what I've written, what I'm writing and where to get it. You can read my blog, keep up to date on new releases, take part in contests and read an occasional short story online.

Taylor Grant is a two-time Bram Stoker Award Nominated Author, professional screenwriter, and award-winning filmmaker. His work has been seen on network television, the big screen, the stage, the web, newspapers, comic books, national magazines, anthologies, and heard on the radio.

Somer Canon lives in Eastern PA with her husband, two sons, and five cats. Her preferred escape has always been reading and writing and horror has always been the hook that catches her attention best. Feel free to find her on social media and never fear, she's only scary when she's hungry!

F. Paul Wilson is an author, born in Jersey City, New Jersey. He writes novels and short stories primarily in the science fiction and horror genres. His debut novel was Healer (1976). Wilson is also a part-time practicing family physician. He made his first sales in 1970 to Analog and continued to write science fiction throughout the seventies. In 1981 he ventured into the horror genre with the international bestseller, The Keep, and helped define the field throughout the rest of the decade. In the 1990s he became a true genre hopper, moving from science fiction to horror to medical thrillers and branching into interactive scripting for Disney Interactive and other multimedia companies. He, along with Matthew J. Costello, created and scripted FTL Newsfeed which ran daily on the Sci-Fi Channel from 1992-1996.

Matthew V. Brockmeyer lives in an off-grid cabin, deep in the forest of Northern California, with his wife and two children. He enjoys howling at the moon and drenching his fangs in human blood. He is the author of the critically-acclaimed novel KIND NEPENTHE: A Savage Tale of Terror Set in the Heart of California's Marijuana Country. His short stories have been featured in numerous publications, both in print and online, including, among others, Infernal Ink Magazine, Not One of Us, Timeless Tales Magazine, Body Parts Magazine, Alephi, Pulp Metal Magazine, and the anthologies The Edge: Infinite Darkness, After the Happily Ever After, and One Hundred Voices. He's a regular contributor to Cultured Vultures, where he writes book reviews and interviews authors.

Kenneth W. Cain is the author of four novels, four short story collections, four novellas, and several children's books among his body of work. He is the editor for Crystal Lake Publishing's Tales From The Lake Volume 5 and When the Clock Strikes 13. The winner of the 2017 Silver Hammer Award, Cain is an Active member of the horror Writers Association, as well as a volunteer for the membership committee and chair of the Pennsylvania chapter. Cain resides in Chester County, Pennsylvania with his wife and two children. Website: http://kennethwcain.com

Paul Kane has been writing professionally for almost fifteen years. His genre journalism has appeared in such magazines as Fangoria, SFX and Rue Morgue, and his non-fiction books are the critically acclaimed The Hellraiser Films and Their Legacy and Voices in the Dark. His award-winning short fiction has appeared in magazines and anthologies on both sides of the Atlantic (as well as being broadcast on BBC Radio 2), and has been collected in Alone (In the Dark), Touching the Flame, FunnyBones, Peripheral Visions, Shadow Writer, The Butterfly Man and Other Stories, The Spaces Between and GHOSTS. His novella Signs of Life reached the shortlist of the British Fantasy Awards 2006, The Lazarus Condition was introduced by Mick Garris - creator of Masters of Horror - RED featured artwork from Dave (The Graveyard Book) McKean and Pain Cages was introduced by Stephen Volk (The Awakening). He currently lives in Derbyshire, UK, with his wife - the author Marie O'Regan - his family, and a black cat called Mina. You can find out more at his website www.shadow-writer.co.uk which has featured Guest Writers such as Neil Gaiman, Charlaine Harris, Dean Koontz, John Connolly and Guillermo del Toro.

Brian James Freeman is the author of Walking With Ghosts, The Painted Darkness, Blue November Storms, The Echo of Memory, The Halloween Children (with Norman Prentiss), Darkness Whispers (with Richard Chizmar), and four mini-collections of his short fiction. With Glenn Chadbourne, he's creating the "Friendly Little Monsters" series, which launched with The Zombie Who Cried Human. He is also the editor of Dark Screams (with Richard Chizmar), Detours, and Reading Stephen King.

Eugene Johnson is a Bram Stoker Award®-nominated author, editor, and columnist of horror, science fiction, fantasy, children's books, and supernatural thrillers. He has written in various genres, and created anthologies such as the Drive In Creature Feature with Charles Day, the Bram Stoker Award®-nominated non-fiction anthology Where Nightmares Come From: The Art Of Storytelling In The Horror Genre with Joe Mynhardt and more.

Gestalt Media is an independent publisher dedicated to finding and promoting original, quality content from indie creators that challenge the norms of the industry and experiment with new concepts. It is our goal to evolve media while honoring the integrity of storytelling in all its forms. Website: www.Gestalt-Media.com

Photography by:

Pete Federico - I play with light. That's what photography is to me. The art of manipulating light. What I like to tell people is that I capture things you forgot to look at the first time you saw it. I live in Virginia Beach which provides me with endless views of the Atlantic Ocean, Bays & Byways in and around Hampton Roads and the surrounding areas. I can be found on any given day waking at 3 A.M. to catch a sunrise or on a beach at 8 P.M. watch the sun setting. Drop me a line and let me know what you think. www.petefedsphotography.com

CPSIA information can be obtained
at www.ICGtesting.com
Printed in the USA
LVHW110639081019
633405LV00001B/38/P